Praise for
Mary Hollis Huddleston
and Asher Fogle Paul

"Put a ring on *Without a Hitch*—a sweet, Southern confection of a book about what it takes to orchestrate everyone else's happily-ever-after when your own heart has been broken. A sneak peek into the world of high-end wedding planning will keep you laughing as Lottie deconstructs the fairy tale and finds her authentic self."

—JODI PICOULT, #1 *NEW YORK TIMES* BESTSELLING AUTHOR
OF *WISH YOU WERE HERE* AND *THE BOOK OF TWO WAYS*

"*Without a Hitch* is a delightfully quirky novel that proves the age-old adage 'We plan. God laughs.' Filled with fascinating insights into the world of high-end wedding planning, you can't help but cheer for Lottie Jones as she learns that you can't script your life and that, sometimes, the best-laid plans are the ones you never make."

—EMILY GIFFIN, #1 *NEW YORK TIMES* BESTSELLING AUTHOR
OF *ALL WE EVER WANTED* AND *THE LIES THAT BIND*

"*Without a Hitch* is a must-read. It is absolutely fabulous. As someone who works in the wedding industry, I found this book's brevity, humor, and the glamorous over-the-top world of Southern weddings a true joy to read. This is the book you will be gifting to all your friends!"

—MINDY WEISS, BESTSE‌   OK

"*Without a Hitch* kept me laug‌   ‌ge!
Cancel your plans because you‌   ‌wn
once you start! I absolutely love‌

—LISA PATTON, BESTSELLING AUTHOR OF *RUSH*
AND *WHISTLIN' DIXIE IN A NOR'EASTER*

"Welcome to the wild and hilarious world of high-dollar wedding planning! In *Without a Hitch*, authors Huddleston and Paul have penned a tale that combines glamorous locales, dizzying hijinks, and ingenious fixes for wedding-day disasters with the all-too-familiar fears and longings of early adulthood. Pour a glass of something bubbly and get ready to laugh!"

—LAUREN DENTON, *USA TODAY* BESTSELLING
AUTHOR OF *THE HIDEAWAY*

"Lottie Jones, heroic wedding planner, is an endearing guide through the world of high-maintenance, no-holds-barred, crazy-rich Texas nuptials. Wrangling chickens, appeasing ghosts, and fending off paparazzi are only a few of the on-the-job challenges Lottie faces while trying to figure out her own next steps in love and life. This sweet, fun novel may lead to elopement—and leave you pining for a shot of Jose Cuervo and some good Tex-Mex."

—SUSAN COLL, AUTHOR OF *BOOKISH PEOPLE*

★ PIECE ★
of CAKE

PIECE of CAKE

A Novel

Mary Hollis Huddleston
and Asher Fogle Paul

HARPER MUSE

Library of Congress Cataloging-in-Publication Data

Names: Huddleston, Mary Hollis, author. | Paul, Asher Fogle, author.
Title: Piece of cake : a novel / Mary Hollis Huddleston and Asher Fogle Paul.
Description: [Nashville] : Harper Muse, [2023] | Summary: "After seeking a fresh start in the South, Claire is determined not to repeat the mistakes that brought her there--but when she's forced to share her new documentary series with a guy from New York, all bets are off in this hilarious romp"-- Provided by publisher.
Identifiers: LCCN 2023000504 (print) | LCCN 2023000505 (ebook) | ISBN 9780785258902 (paperback) | ISBN 9780785258919 (epub) | ISBN 9780785258926
Subjects: LCGFT: Romance fiction. | Humorous fiction. | Novels.
Classification: LCC PS3608.U3223 P54 2023 (print) | LCC PS3608.U3223 (ebook) | DDC 813/.6--dc23/eng/20230113
LC record available at https://lccn.loc.gov/2023000504
LC ebook record available at https://lccn.loc.gov/2023000505

Printed in the United States of America

23 24 25 26 27 LBC 5 4 3 2 1

To our children:
May you define yourself by your best moments, grow from
your worst, and always, always know that you are enough.

PROLOGUE

I was happy for them, really.

A white vintage A-line dress brushed just below her knees. Soft tendrils escaped her honey-colored bun, a grandmother's antique brooch the only accent. She clasped a loose pink bouquet in one hand, his hand in the other as they stood solemnly before the judge.

Lush, wild clusters of pink peonies and white hydrangeas interspersed with soft dusty miller lined the aisle of simple white folding chairs. Two larger arrangements in antique silver urns flanked the couple. A single cellist sat in the corner of the room. All simple, but stunningly elegant.

She couldn't stop smiling, and I realized I'd never seen her so at ease.

They quietly said vows they wrote themselves. Our small crowd watched in happy silence.

I tried not to shift too loudly, every movement echoing on

the cold marble tiles. Someone sniffled. The sound reverberated in the cavernous space. The groom's mother caught me staring and winked at me across the room.

This bride had sent me on quite a journey, forcing me to finally reckon with my past and my future. With my identity, even. It hadn't been easy, but I was grateful.

I had no right to be here, but here I was.

CHAPTER 1

SEVERAL MONTHS EARLIER

In front of me, matching fluorescent-pink shirts glowed in the hazy morning light of Broadway. Eight A.M., it seemed, was not too early for Tanya's Bride Tribe to hit the streets in a "pedal tavern," a self-propelled bar on bicycle wheels.

Only two more blocks. Almost there, I huffed, my red-soled heels keeping time with the truly terrible Shania Twain sing-along coming from the already buzzed bride-to-be.

Stay classy, Nashville.

Even with four-plus inches of pure fashion torturing my feet, I was quickly gaining on them. Though it was rush hour on a *Thursday* for Pete's sake, the Bride Tribe seemed disinclined to pull over to allow traffic to pass, making me temporarily grateful my cheap-ass job refused to pay for employee parking at the lot closest to the office. Nope, to save the extra $47.10 per employee annually, we'd been banished to Skippy's Park and Pay off a side alley close to the overpass, adding another seven blocks of walking to my already *wonderful* commute.

So here I was, walking faster than seven pink cowgirls on a bicycle built for booze during rush hour. But the women kept cycling down the street—ignoring, imbibing, and blocking traffic. Bachelorette bike rides could not be constrained by time or traffic laws.

Neon signs on honky-tonks named after country singers cast their own glares on us hapless passersby. It felt appropriate for a city on fire, metaphorically speaking. Nashville was booming before the pandemic, but it had blown up in the time since. People from all over the country flocked here. Whether for a weekend celebration or a fresh start with a lower cost of living, they kept on coming. Not for the first time, I was grateful I had moved before rent prices skyrocketed. My East Nashville studio apartment was only three miles from downtown, but sometimes those three miles felt like thirty.

My breath was visible in the dim February morning. *One more block*, I thought, pausing at the crosswalk while the bright little sign mocked me with its Do Not Cross. The neon hand, held up like a teenage Claire, almost screamed sass today—*Talk to the hand 'cause the face ain't listening.*

I could practically see my office from here. Putting on my game face, I smoothed my blonde strands in my phone's camera. Those wretched baby hairs that stuck out would be the eternal bane of my existence. I wiped a smudge of mascara from my brow bone. Now I was ready to sprint to my desk—if I ever made it there.

I would *not* be late to work. *Not today, Satan.*

Last night, my boss had sent a company-wide email with the helpful subject: "DO NOT MISS THURSDAY'S STAFF MEETING." The way magazine publishing was going, one could presume it was to announce more layoffs and budget cuts. I didn't want to give Michelle any reasons to include me in this next round of firings. Which was why I needed the traffic light to change. Like, now.

The universe seemed to understand and gifted me with a walk signal. Hiking my inexpensive canvas tote back on my shoulder, I took one step off the curb—today was going to be a good day, I could feel it!—and was knocked immediately back down to the curb, pain radiating through my hip bone, Shania ringing in my ears.

Dazed, I looked up at the grey morning sky, then slightly down to the shock of fluorescent pink. *Have I just been in a hit-and-run with a pedal tavern?*

"Oh my gosh!" a thick Minnesota accent screamed. "Don't ya know, I think we killed her!"

In that moment, I actually considered whether it was true. This surely was hell. Tanya, I presumed by her flower crown and veil, leaned over me off her bike/barstool, with her breakfast beer still in hand, to verify whether I was alive.

"I'm getting married!" she cheered as if that was an excuse to run someone over with a bar, before she and her "tribe" did their best Peloton impersonation and kicked off. Felt really right.

I slowly sat up, assuring the few locals on the street with me that I was okay and that yes, tourists were menaces. If the universe really did give signs, what did this one say? Something about how the bridal business was ready to run you over, I guess. The light changed again, and with it a massive pickup truck with a flatbed trailer towing a hot tub turned into the intersection. A banner hung on one side that read "Stan's Stag Do"—a nicely Anglophile and alliterative bachelor phrase for someone I imagined was not remotely British. As the truck veered in front of the tipsy women, the pedal tavern failed to brake yet again.

The scene seemed to unfold in slow motion into a beautiful mess. The women's vehicle careened keg-first into the side of the truck, which was still blocking the intersection. The bike frame bent, though the women seemed unhurt. Then I watched as the trailer wobbled and tipped just enough for a large quantity of murky hot tub water to splash over the side and douse two-thirds of the bridal party. Forget the coronavirus—these women would be leaving the city with a nasty fungal infection thanks to their baptism on Broadway.

As the murky water washed over my own precious Louboutins, I looked up into a flickering pink sign and prayed for the pavement to swallow me whole.

❧ ❧ ❧

A brutal thirty minutes later, I was finally perched at my desk and working on my first interview of the day. Through my earbuds, the harsh noises of downtown were washed away by the gentle sound of crashing waves. A breeze softly rustled palm fronds. My bare toes curled as if feeling the sand beneath them instead of the grungy carpet covering my office floor. Some exotic bird squawked. Loudly.

"Oh, sorry, Claire!" the woman yelled in my ear. "Jim dear, can you close the sliding door? I can't hear the phone. What was I saying? Yes, so our first dance was—"

I sighed and stopped listening to the call. My recorder would capture the relevant details, and Intern Lauren would dutifully transcribe them for me by Monday.

Unfortunately, I was not, of course, in an overwater bungalow near a lush shoreline and turquoise waves. But the subject of my interview was. Instead, I basked in the glow of my massive desktop monitor at the granny-chic offices of *Piece of Cake*, the South's oldest, most esteemed, and least profitable bridal magazine. Listening to the drone of a bride discussing the minutiae of her big day was my only distraction from the daily hustle that had become my life.

After hanging up, I leaned back into my desk chair. I'd made it to the office just in time to squeeze in my interview before the staff meeting. I eased my bare feet back into my drying high heels before limping to the coffee maker on the other side of our open-concept workspace. Thanks again for the bruised hip, Tanya.

We'd recently upgraded to a Keurig with a reservoir, which meant I no longer had to refill the water each time. Sometimes I thought longingly of the caffeine castle in the breakroom at my first (and only other) job back in Dallas at a wedding planning firm. But times were tough in publishing, so small improvements would have to do.

At *Piece of Cake*, gone were the days of merely offering

advice to the South's most sophisticated brides. Covering real-life events had become our bread and butter. We could sell ads to most of the vendors featured, and our website was full of registry resources, including helpful links to retailers. When readers clicked through and spent money, we got a percentage of the profits. *Synergy*, the business side called it. It all helped pad low subscription revenue and fund my pathetic salary.

I ran into Amaya, one of the other two assistant editors, in our tiny breakroom.

"How'd the interview go for your 'Tying the Yacht' piece?" Amaya quipped while adding sugar to her coffee.

"When Michelle assigned me weddings on boats, I envisioned sailing off into the sunset with a cocktail in hand on at least one boat. Instead, I just drowned in a sea of puns."

Amaya giggled. "I still can't believe you had to keep that ridiculous title."

"I refuse to add any more bad wordplay to this piece. If I'd been playing a drinking game based on the number of times people said 'love boat' to me when describing the wedding, pretty sure I'd have been washed away by tequila."

We both laughed. I liked Amaya, but I'd learned not to get too close to colleagues. You never knew when you'd be in competition for the same role or opportunity. It was lonely, but cleaner, this way. I was sticking to the rules outlined in my mental *Claire Sommers's Guide to Business*. I'd neglected to do so in the past and was still reaping the consequences.

"I see they're jazzing things up in here with flavored options," I said as I inserted my French vanilla K-Cup into the Keurig.

"Only the finest for the star assistant editors," she replied, examining a coconut crème cappuccino pod. Revolting, but you do you. "Tell me, where is the couple honeymooning? I assume you had to do the follow-up interview from your lowly hovel of a cubicle while they're lounging on some fabulous beach somewhere."

"Pretty much," I said. "They're in Barbados, and it physically hurt to overhear a waiter in the background offer them another round of mai tais."

"Ugh, I could really go for a vacation to the tropics right now," said Amaya, shaking her dark curls.

"Girl, me too," I replied.

"Well, I'd better get back to it. Deadlines, deadlines, deadlines," she said as she headed back toward her desk.

I thought longingly about a vacation. Over the last four years in Nashville, between a shuttered world and my shrunken bank account, I hadn't exactly had much opportunity for travel. Truthfully, I hadn't even gone out much to reacquaint myself with this ever-evolving city.

Back at my desk, I looked out the tiny office window down onto Seventh Avenue, just off Broadway, the honky-tonk capital of the United States. It was just shy of ten o'clock in the morning, but the downtown blocks were already bustling. Nearby, the bars' doors were open, the country music hopefuls were singing their hearts out, and the tourists were ready for a full day of partying. I was still recovering from my own narrow escape from the scene. I cringed thinking of Tanya's soaking-wet and now-sober crew.

Clearly, Nashville's hospitality industry was ablaze. A new hotel was opening just about every week, and with it came a new event space. This meant more weddings and corporate events coming to town, and the past couple of years had been some of the busiest for weddings in a generation. From speaking with both brides and local vendors, I knew every weekend and many weeknights were booked at the best venues in town.

The coronavirus shutdowns were a thing of the past. Weddings were back. And Nashville had come to party. *Great*, I thought. The hours in the magazine world pretty much sucked already, and we were going to be busier than ever. At least work would keep me preoccupied and help me forget how crappy the rest of my life was at the moment.

My phone vibrated on my desk, rattling me out of my thoughts. I answered while glancing at the time: 9:47 A.M. I could take Blake's call and then conveniently get off for my 10:00 A.M. meeting, if it came to that.

"Hi, Blake," I said, absently moving my mouse back and forth on the pad.

"Claire, you didn't answer my last few texts, so I just wanted to make sure you were okay."

"Sorry to worry you. I've been fine, just busy."

"Are you up for that music festival I mentioned on Friday? My buddy has a couple extra tickets."

Blake and I met on Bumble. I'd had a weak moment after opening a bottle of wine one night and decided to also crack open a dating app. Blake was finishing up his MBA at Vanderbilt. We'd enjoyed a handful of dates together, including one fairly romantic picnic at Centennial Park. But Blake was a man with a plan, and his plan didn't include staying in town.

"Blake, I've had a great time getting to know you, but I'm not sure this is leading anywhere."

"Why? I thought things were going well. I had an amazing time the other night."

"You're leaving Nashville after you graduate this summer. You're fantastic, really, but you should be free to pursue the life you want wherever you wind up and not worry about me." I thought the last part was a nice touch. *See, Mom, I can be diplomatic.*

My wall of self-preservation resolidified, the ice froze back intact. He put up a few half-hearted protestations, but by the time we hung up two minutes later, he'd only confirmed my suspicion that no one was worth the effort of maintaining a long-distance relationship.

Plus, a new boyfriend was a distraction I didn't need right now. I'd dated enough to know starting over with someone new could end up getting in the way of bigger goals. Better to nip it in the bud. Free from any romantic entanglement, I'd be able to focus all that extra time and emotion on my career. For once, I needed to follow my own rules and stick to the professional, not the personal. I'd throw myself even more into my job and try to succeed in at least one area of my life that was still somewhat in my control.

Time to dash. Our editor in chief, Michelle Zhang, had of course asked that everyone be in the office today for the biweekly staff meeting. Watercooler scuttlebutt was that they were announcing more cuts. As if the staff could get any leaner. We were all writing, editing, posting, and promoting our own content these days. I figured the next step was for me to go to the printer and typeset the magazine myself.

Piece of Cake had always been run by the same family, but rumor had it they were trying to sell to a larger publisher out of New York. If Janice in HR was to be believed, said publisher had a lot of ideas about our revenue streams. I had my own ideas, if anyone cared to ask. Not that I was involved in any decisions or held any power whatsoever, but I'd started following some big-industry Twitter accounts to stay up on the news. Figured it was better to be in the know if I was going to get pink-slipped sooner or later.

We're in trouble, I thought as I walked through the empty space toward the conference room. The vacant cubicles now used for "storage" made the office feel like a ghost town. But I had one advantage: boots-on-the-ground experience. I understood weddings—what went into them and what connected with people. And I had a lot of suggestions for how to bridge the fiscal gap.

One late night while waiting for my pages to close, I put some of my ideas together and compiled a deck about mini-documentaries. I'd gotten the idea while watching *Say Yes to the Dress* (while also wallowing in self-pity and self-soothing with a pint of Jeni's) a couple of months ago. I sent it to Michelle, who was notoriously behind on email. When I followed up, she said she would consider it, run it up the flagpole. So I'd waited. And watched more layoffs.

As I neared the conference room where I'd surely learn my fate, I steeled myself and thought back over the last four years.

Piece of Cake had been a haven for me after I'd practically run away to Nashville without a real plan and with barely enough in my personal savings account to secure an apartment and survive a few weeks while looking for a job. I hadn't been a total stranger to the city, and given its growth and surge of new residents, I figured I could do something in the event-related world, like working for a caterer or stationer. But when I saw the entry-level job posting at *Piece of Cake*, I actually felt excited about the idea of a wedding-based magazine—and one of my longtime favorites at that. The feeling had caught me off guard.

Sure, I wasn't fully qualified for the role and had to start at the bottom. I'd studied writing and been on the newspaper at Vanderbilt, which—coupled with my prior wedding planning experience in Dallas—was enough to get me an interview at *Piece of Cake*. I glazed over some details and fast-talked my way through the conversation with Janice in HR, who kindly passed me along for another round. I started out fact-checking stories. I hustled harder, worked longer hours, and generally went overboard to earn the attention of the top editors. I eagerly walked pages directly to their desks in attempts to get them to recognize my face among the rotation of freelancers. I spent seven months calling every fashion label, wedding planner, or bride mentioned in our pages to verify everything from name spellings to vendor contact information. It was mind-numbing, but someone had to do it. Or so I thought.

Fortunately, it paid off. I got promoted to assistant editor just before the entire fact-checking department was eliminated completely. Now writers were expected to confirm their own accuracy, and outsiders checked only the most controversial of stories (which, for a bridal magazine, meant none of them).

I never expected to enjoy doing something like this, but I'd fought tooth and nail to get a foot in the door here and was determined to stick it out. If holding on to my job meant begging Michelle to keep me as the last employee standing, I wasn't above it.

I'd resorted to drastic measures and gone to great lengths before, which led to some of my biggest mistakes. I was unrecognizable to myself afterward. Those choices still haunted me. I still wasn't sure I'd ever recovered. Hopefully, it wouldn't come to that again.

Taking one more deep breath at the end of the hallway, I walked through the door to the conference room. I'd be darned if I was going down this time without a fight.

CHAPTER 2

I took my seat at the long reclaimed-wood conference table in our cozy meeting room. Chintz fabric lined the walls. I crossed my feet at the ankles because I'm a *lady*, thank you. After my promotion, I'd moved up from having to stand in the corner and now felt very powerful, despite my chair being at the farthest possible spot from Michelle. Honestly, I probably got a seat because too many legacy editors with bloated salaries got laid off, but I wasn't complaining.

Sadly, today's team was a lean machine. I was the bottom rung of the full-time staff, along with Amaya. Our senior editor, Kevin, made sure our articles made sense. Alex and Liz covered beauty and fashion, respectively. Nancy was the copy editor, and she oversaw a couple of freelancers who came into the office when we were closing pages. We had a handful of Vanderbilt and Belmont interns, mostly for running samples and helping post social media content. Michelle was, of course, at the top. She only answered to the publisher, a shadowy name for the representative of the business side. And then there were people in advertising sales, who clearly had their work cut out for them now that subscriptions had taken a nosedive.

After welcoming everyone, Michelle cleared her throat and got right to it. "We're going to implement some important staff changes," she said. The communal cringe was palpable. I didn't look around the room but braced myself for the bad news.

As she continued, Michelle threw around a lot of phrases like *sponsored content, branded content, social media promotion, influencers, live streams, socially conscious, ethical consumerism,* etc. I think I zoned out during the jargon. But I got the gist. Our esteemed Southern belle was transitioning into a modern, digitally savvy woman. Michelle didn't have a very specific plan to save the old girl, it seemed. But somehow, we were going to make expensive Southern weddings appeal to Gen Z brides on the coasts. Easy-peasy.

"So to that end, I wanted to let you know about a thrilling new direction that I think is going to help us all." I perked up. This sounded promising.

"We'll be launching a documentary series that will include a select number of brides covered in our Real Weddings section. The plan is to sell to a partner like Discovery Plus, Netflix, or another streaming service. To run it, we have a true visionary. I am so excited about all the experience this person brings to our team. Such insight, creativity, and passion will be a huge asset as we take *Piece of Cake* into the future."

Was there a chance she'd actually read my deck and wanted

to give it a shot? (I *may* have sent it to her twice, just to be safe. The ol' casual-yet-desperate "bumping this in your inbox" routine.) I had hustled the last few years to finally get some reporting experience, and a docuseries was *my* brainchild. I knew it was a stretch, but maybe she'd gotten the publisher's approval or found a partner to coproduce it with us.

I gripped the arms of my chair. I started to sit taller and made sure my shoes were on securely so I could stand when she said my name. This was my moment, finally.

"Which is why I want you all to give a warm welcome to our new social media consultant, Dominic Gravino."

Seemingly out of nowhere, a lanky brown-haired man stepped into the room and slid into the empty seat next to her. Actually, he was a boy. That's what he looked like. An overgrown boy. Who the heck was this? Stealing my baby, my idea?

"Thank you, Michelle," he said with a crooked grin, running a hand through the floppy hair that had fallen across his dumb forehead. "It's an honor to be here joining the team, and I won't let you guys down."

I was fuming. Seeing red. I couldn't hear a word.

Michelle nodded and opened her mouth once more. "We're thrilled to have Dominic joining us all the way from New York, where he worked for the *Huffington Post*, as well as a couple other media start-ups. He also runs his own massively successful socials about weddings, known as 'The Brides' Man.' He's a born-and-bred New Yorker, and I've promised him a warm Southern welcome from y'all."

At this my ears perked. Now *that* was fascinating.

"And I am glad to share he will be partnering with our very own Claire Sommers on this project." She gestured to me and smiled as if I should be thrilled by this news.

Like hell he will, I thought. Instead, I smized back and waved a hand at Michelle in acknowledgment.

With my phone casually in my lap under the table, I fired up Instagram as she spoke. I typed in *Dominic Gravino*, and there it was: the Brides' Man. Prominently featuring his stupidly handsome face, if you liked green eyes and cleft chins like some daffy prince from early nineties Disney. The page had an annoying number of reels and TikToks, which not only made my eyes cross but also meant I couldn't watch in the meeting. I grudgingly could admit that some of the images looked lovely, and his follower count was in the high six figures. Sure, he could edit video. And he seemed to know his way around a wedding. But could he tell stories brides actually wanted to read? *I can't believe they gave the assignment to some Gen Z Yankee social media star. C'mon, Michelle, whatever happened to female solidarity?* I left his profile open to do a deep dive later at my desk.

I looked up from my phone to find Dominic staring at me, like he somehow knew I was already stalking him online. I started to blush like a child caught passing notes at school, then avoided further eye contact.

No way he knew what I was doing. He was probably just trying to intimidate me with his unfortunately handsome face and, in doing so, enact his master plan of taking over my job. I hadn't met many influencers at his level in person, but the few I had acted as if they were a superior breed. They seemed to think they were entitled to anything they wanted in life given their "status." And if Dominic was like the rest of them, he would be a thorn in my side for sure.

After the meeting ended, everyone dispersed. I watched Dominic walk down the hall with Janice in HR, presumably for boring onboarding stuff. This was my moment. Once Michelle was back in her office, I gave her a precise fifteen seconds at her desk before knocking.

"Come in," she said coolly.

I took a breath and stepped inside. If *Piece of Cake*'s décor was granny-chic, Michelle's space had elevated the aesthetic to elegant vintage. Toile curtains framed the bricked window facing downtown. A pair of recovered velvet French bergère chairs sat before an antique partners desk. She absently tapped a manicured nail on the aged leather as I approached.

"I wondered whether I'd hear from you," she said.

"Then you must know that I was, well, a little taken aback by that announcement." Michelle Zhang was known in the industry for being a straight shooter, so I attempted to meet her in kind. "I realize it isn't exactly revolutionary, but doing mini-documentaries on our brides and pitching them to sponsors was kind of my idea."

"It was, which is why I'm letting you stay on the project."

"But . . . ?"

"But you're an associate editor on our Real Weddings beat, Claire. Just last year, you were calling in samples and getting coffee. Do you have any video editing skills? Or on-the-ground wedding experience?"

I was faced with the increasingly familiar conundrum of whether to remind her about my prior career in Southern weddings, which had ended in disaster, or simply to let her think me inexperienced, which was a blow to my pride. Instead, I just mumbled, "I understand, I just—" But she cut me off before I could go on.

"Which is why I want you to partner with Dominic. He's got great video and editing chops, and he has a built-in, loyal audience. He's got enough charm oozing out of him to make women swoon over his socials. It's like watching a *Bachelor in Paradise* contestant talk about weddings. Women love that, especially coming from a handsome, young, *straight* man. That makes him a bit of a unicorn in this industry, and we're lucky to have him on the team."

Did her eyes just get all misty? Was she under this pest's spell? Suddenly I was riled up again.

"With all due respect, are you kidding me? He's some narcissistic influencer who is probably only out to promote his personal brand. I doubt he has ever read a physical magazine in his life. Plus, he's from *New York*. What does he know about the particular flavors, history, and nuances of the events we cover down here? I bet he—"

"Is this a bad time?" A smooth, deep voice chuckled behind me.

"Not at all," Michelle said with a Cheshire cat grin. "We were just discussing your new project. Dominic, this is the famous Claire I've been telling you so much about. Claire, meet Dominic."

I stood up from my chair, face basically into his chest. I hated having to look up at anyone. Especially someone I intended to metaphorically look down upon for the foreseeable future.

He extended a hand and gave me a rakish, crooked smile. "It's Dom. Nice to meet you, ma'am, as they say."

"Watch who you're calling *ma'am*." At twenty-nine, I probably had a year or two on him, but I was still at least a decade or so from *ma'am* status. "And lovely to meet you, too, I'm sure."

We sat down next to each other, the air between us tense. I could tell he was glaring at me again, and the hairs on the back of my neck stood up. The air was also weighted with the smell of the full black coffee in his hand, mixed with something woodsy and masculine. I started breathing through my mouth.

"This is great—saves me from having to email you both to set something up," she said. "Let's dive into how this is all going to work."

I looked around, not for the first time, at her walls. Impeccable modern art broken up by Ivy League diplomas and magazine covers. It was a real power move to display award-winning covers you created for other brands. But that was Michelle.

"The publisher has approved the budget for six episodes, due by July first. So you're looking at four months and change. Then we'll take those out to creative partners, TV networks, streamers, places like that, and try to sell it as an unscripted franchise."

"Sounds good," Dom said before I could. "I have a couple producer contacts, too, and a decent pulse on what they're looking for."

"I know. That's why I'm counting on you."

Suck-up, I thought.

Michelle went on. "And remember that we need *drama*, you two. These need to be glamorous and Southern, like all the weddings we cover. But if you can find a hook, lean in to that. We need an angle that sets us apart."

"That makes sense," I said, wheels turning.

"We'll do a soft launch for the series, let you two get your feet wet on a couple weddings while we find the right one to use as our main feature. There's a lot of corporate stuff going on, but I'll spare you the details. Just know that in addition to some lower-profile but stunning weddings, we'll need to find one massive, elaborate event with the perfect wealthy or high-profile couple to film so we can sell this thing."

"Brilliant," I said, jumping in. "It's like *Say Yes to the Dress* meets *Four Weddings* meets *Southern Charm*."

"Exactly. Such a nightmare, but people eat this stuff up. You've got the elevator pitch down. First up," she continued, "will be the Preston wedding in Murfreesboro."

"Oh, that's great," I replied. Wouldn't have been my first choice necessarily, given that the wedding was in Murfreesboro of all places. But since I'd already done some pre-coverage work on the event for the magazine, I had a leg up on Dom. "I've been emailing with the bride, who seems lovely. Potentially a little rough around the edges, but very sweet. Can't wait to meet her in person."

"I'm glad you've developed a rapport with the bride, Claire. The family seemed thrilled with the idea of any coverage of their wedding, so this is the perfect trial run for the series. They could be the ideal guinea pigs, if you will. Hopefully it will be quirky and over-the-top enough to keep viewers interested."

"Well, you can count on me to capture all the great moments and details—" Dom started to say.

"Me too," I said, cutting him off before he could toot his own horn. "The bride has already really warmed up to me, and over-the-top weddings are a specialty of mine." (I wasn't going to elaborate on this for Dom, but he needed to know I had expertise.) "So you can count on me to deliver as well."

"Good, good," Michelle said, taking off her glasses and rubbing the bridge of her perfect nose. "Now, I don't have to tell you, and frankly I shouldn't, that times are tough at the magazine. But they've given us one month after submission to sell this baby, or they pull the plug."

I wasn't following. "On the project?"

"On *us*." Her dark eyes were somber. "No more print magazine. We go all-digital, the way they did with *Southern Crafter* and *Belle Home* last year. That's what most media corporations are having to do. They'll probably keep two or three staffers and use freelancers and algorithms for content."

I shuddered despite myself.

"Yes, it's horrific. So please don't mention that part to the rest of the team. We don't want morale plummeting even further . . . But this has the potential to really save all our necks and change the direction of this company. No pressure." She fake-chuckled like a maniac.

No pressure was like *no worries* or *sorry to bother*. It *absolutely* meant we should feel pressure.

"Roger that, boss," Dom said.

Shut up, Dominic.

She practically ushered us out of her office, and Dom and I stood in the carpeted hallway lined with iconic covers from decades ago. After an awkward beat, I turned to go just as Dom said, "Hey, want to grab a coffee? Talk more about this first gig and get to know each other better? I'm getting the vibe that we started out on the wrong foot."

I paused. Looked him up and down and decided to play dumb. "No, I think we're good," I said. "We can go over the details of the wedding in the car on Saturday. I've got a very busy workday." I really didn't have that much to do at the moment, but Dom needed to think I played a critical role here at the magazine and had zero time to stroke his huge New York ego—or anything else for that matter.

As I wobbled back to my desk, determined to project strength in my heels, I reminded myself that Mom always said, *"If you can't say something nice . . ."* And I did not want to disappoint her any more than everything about my life already did.

CHAPTER 3

That night, I walked into the rear entrance of my apartment in East Nashville. When I moved back to town, I'd managed to find a cozy studio carved out of what was once a charming bungalow. Now there were three units in the building, but at least I had my own kitchen and separate entrance. I'd even landed the unit with a fireplace.

Not for the first time, I longingly remembered my high-rise apartment in Dallas with a pool and a doorman. Now, I considered days with consistent water pressure a win. *C'est la vie.*

I slipped off my shoes and padded into the kitchen. I opened the freezer and threw an Amy's organic dinner in the microwave. Then I grabbed the half-eaten bag of tortilla chips from the pantry and poured a small bowl of my favorite salsa, Joe T. Garcia's, which I kept in stock. More accurately, my younger sister, Lucille, kept me stocked by regularly sending it over from Texas.

Nashville had become my home for the second time. Though I attended college here almost a decade ago, I'd moved home to Dallas immediately after graduation. Then, three years later, I moved *back* to Nashville, tail between my legs.

At first, I'd relished nights like these. No commitments, no family obligations, no after-hours work. Just an entire evening to do with as I pleased. Now, I'd exhausted most offerings from the few streaming services still in my budget, and the nights stretched endlessly on. Meetup sports teams required costly dues, postgame drinks, and athletic ability I didn't have. I couldn't afford takeout I actually wanted to eat, and I'd never properly learned to cook. (Cooking wasn't exactly part of the Sommers daughter training, alas.) So I usually checked out romance novels and thrillers from the online library—the physical ones were too dirty, ew—and subscribed to every true-crime podcast that didn't have a paywall.

I wasn't exactly sure what it was that drew me in. Maybe it was because true crime offered a polar opposite to the wedding frivolity I was constantly surrounded by—brides by day and serial killers by night. Maybe it was in line with my admittedly cynical outlook on the world. Maybe it was simply an escape, though probably not the healthiest one for a single woman living in a ground-floor apartment. Either way, I needed more free hobbies other than self-flagellation and despair, and I chose murder.

Wow, something is wrong with me. Whatever, I thought as I searched for a clean fork, instead finding a pile of dirty forks in the sink. My relationships might be nonexistent, but I hadn't signed up to be pen pals with any convicted criminals, so it couldn't be that bad. At least not yet.

"And in the cold, dark winter night, he crept up to Beverly's kitchen window" came the typically soothing voice of my favorite podcast host. "Watching her as she cut vegetables and washed dishes as usual. Biding his time . . ." I looked up from the sink through my own window at the dark side yard and shuddered. I closed the sheer café curtain, as if that did much good. A dog might be a nice idea. Or some friends.

My college friends and I believed we'd stay in touch. Most of my crew scattered to the coasts or back home where they came from. A few took corporate jobs in Houston or Chicago; others headed to law school or teachers college. Or, of course, they got married, and that became their world. I'm sure I knew more people in town than I realized, but without being active on social media, it just seemed like too much effort to seek them out.

I wasn't that lonely, really. I liked my coworkers. Amaya and I got drinks once, which was plenty. And in an emergency, I could call my old roommate, Jill, who lived in Franklin with her family. Well, she might not make it to me quick enough for an actual life-or-death emergency, sure, but she'd be there in a pinch.

As the haunting podcast underscoring played, I carried my plate across the room and imagined how long help would take to arrive if I got attacked. Would I decompose before someone found my body? Surely Michelle would notice my absence, but it wouldn't hurt to have a few safeguards just in case.

I plopped on the couch to eat my sad dinner and check my email while safely immersing myself in Beverly's cold case.

> Claire,
>
> Good to meet you today. Really looking forward to our collaboration.
>
> > Best,
> > Dom

Not a name I was excited to see on my screen. I rolled my eyes and then stood up to pour myself a glass of Trader Joe's wine with my meal. Dom might have been brought in to help, but at least Michelle was giving my idea a shot. That was something to celebrate, even if I was celebrating alone. I finished my microwaved meal before replying to Dom's email. No need to look too eager and available.

> Dom,
>
> Nice meeting you too. Someone with your video expertise is important to making my idea a successful series for the company. Hopefully you'll enjoy Nashville during your brief time here.

Yes, I said *my idea*. And yes, I suggested he would only be in town briefly, but I couldn't help myself. He needed to know his place as soon as possible. But he responded way too fast.

Claire,

Well, if I know anything, it's how to capture a moment on camera. And hopefully by sharing my skills, I'll convince you that we're on the same team and can pull this off for the magazine together. I also hope we can explore Nashville while we work. I could use a good tour guide for my very, very brief stint. ;)

Geez, high road. Now I *really* didn't like him. Not wanting to poke him anymore and feeling somewhat stupid for what I'd said, I simply replied:

Sounds great. See you tomorrow.

Two minutes later:

Can't wait!

Ugh, his optimism. No one was naturally *that* positive. No one in the workplace had entirely pure motives. Especially not a New Yorker. He had to be playing me in hopes of eventually stealing all the credit from this project if it worked out in the end.

Thoughts of my former colleagues in Dallas entered my mind, unbidden. There, I'd been the new kid on the team, along with a few other recent graduates, almost all of us plucked straight from the same echelon of Dallas society as our clientele. No one expected that any of us would make a career of wedding planning or show any promise. Just biding our time until trust fund access or our own wedding days. Well, no one except Lottie.

I allowed myself to spare a rare moment for my former supervisor. Even as just a junior planner herself, Lottie Jones had taken me in, shown me the ropes, and encouraged me to pursue an actual career in events, not just a stopgap. I ignored the pang of regret.

I'd enjoyed wedding planning far more than I'd expected, especially since I'd come by it through pity and charity. In short, I'd been hired as a favor to my mother. Already an embarrassment, I wasn't running a business or crushing law school like my sisters. I wasn't expected to like it, let alone succeed.

Somewhere buried in my inbox was an unanswered email from that time. Parts of it, though, were burned in my mind: *I thought I knew you, and I guess I don't—but I don't think you know yourself either.*

The words still tormented me. I'd done something awful. In my efforts to succeed at all costs, I'd become someone I didn't recognize or know. What was so broken about me that I could do that? Could it be fixed? Could *I*?

But those were mistakes I vowed never to repeat. I rolled my neck and shoulders to loosen up muscles and shake off ghosts. My sisters and I were taught to perform, to be the best. Our competitive edge, as outlined in my mental business guide, came from doing our thing, working hard, and not getting wrapped up in the personal. Attachment was a recipe for losing that advantage, as I'd learned. Memory lane had just given me enough fright for one night, so I decided to forgo the podcast after all. I polished off my second glass of wine and headed to bed.

CHAPTER 4

I never realized that typing on an iPhone could have a sound. As someone who left her ringer off for years at a time, I'd believed a touch screen was silent. Turns out it did not, in fact, have to be—if said screen was operated by a total psychopath. I twitched at each *click*.

I clenched the wheel of my trusty old Range Rover on the highway to Murfreesboro as Dom lounged in the passenger seat, eyes on his phone. We'd met at the office this morning to save on gas for the long drive. Long legs crossed, he started to rest one on the dash, glanced up at me, and quickly put his foot back on the floor. I needed to drive this baby until the wheels fell off, and he wasn't about to make that day come any sooner.

"So, why Nashville, Dom? Not just our fair magazine, I imagine." I gritted my teeth and bravely attempted to be Southern and conversational and spare us both from his incessant tapping.

"Honestly, I had some friends from New York move down

here in the last few years. Thought it could be a fun place to try out for a while."

It must be nice to decide to move somewhere "just for fun" as opposed to moving because you were in exile. "Tell me about it. Seems like half of Brooklyn and all of Los Angeles relocated to Nashville. Well, here and Austin. Have you seen the 'Don't California my Tennessee' signs?"

"Classy. Hopefully the influx isn't all bad. But yeah, I wanted a change. I grew up in the same neighborhood in New York. Been there my whole life, aside from six months in San Diego. So when this contract opened up, I jumped on it."

Just what we all needed right now. Another coastal transplant to the heart of the South.

"Michelle mentioned you were a consultant?"

"Yeah, I'm only committed here for six months, through July, which sounds like enough time to wrap up this project too."

Noted. At least I wouldn't have to deal with him forever. "And then what? On to the next?"

"Something like that. I've always liked not being tied down to one job for too long. I get restless. It's fun to try out new ones."

"How are you liking Nashville so far?"

"I like it just fine. I've only been here since Tuesday, though, so ask me after I find a sublet and settle in."

"Where are you looking? Rents are pretty brutal these days."

"That's what I hear. But coming from New York . . ."

"I guess everywhere else is cheaper?"

"Unless you're in San Francisco. A buddy of mine just moved out there . . ."

He rambled on for another ten minutes about how crazy the real estate markets were in certain cities following the pandemic. Thankfully, I had a long-term lease. I used to think I'd own my own condo or small manse in Highland Park, Texas, by now, but with less access to resources than I once had, my studio was as good as I would get. As though he was reading my mind, he asked, "So where do you live?"

I told him about my apartment—a studio in a decent but not posh part of town. East Nashville was great, but it was definitely still transitioning—or gentrifying, depending on who you asked. One street would be newly built with chic restaurants, boutiques, and charming townhomes. But the next block housed a mix of renovated bungalows and some dilapidated homes with spare car parts strewn about front yards.

"I'm just grateful I moved back here before everything got crazy."

"You're not from here?"

"Nope, Dallas born and bred. I went to college here but was back in Dallas until the past few years. You must not be able to tell the difference between the accents."

"No, it all just sounds Southern to me . . . How do I sound to you?"

For a moment, all I could think about while I pointedly kept my eyes on the road was the lovely deep timbre of his voice, even with a slight northern scrape to some of his words. Instead, I said, "Like *Good Will Hunting*!"

He laughed. "That's the Brooklyn—not Boston—you hear. I grew up in Carroll Gardens, which is way different from

Manhattan—at least it used to be. Don't ever say *Bahwston* though. My mom always tried to teach me to sound less rough, but you can't take the Italian outta Brooklyn . . ." He made a hand gesture à la *The Godfather*.

I envisioned the tutors my sisters and I were subjected to— and I imagined them coaching some kid from Brooklyn on cotillions and couldn't contain my giggles. There's no way Dom would survive learning to foxtrot or to use a cocktail fork. Then again, those are just a few of the many "skills" forced upon me at an early age that I'd never once used in real life. Does anyone still foxtrot to big band music? Should've learned how to twerk or whatever was going around TikTok these days instead. I envisioned Dom twerking and felt my face turn red. *Focus, Claire.*

"You'll certainly stick out like a sore thumb," I said, "but not as much as you would've before the pandemic. Like I said, so many people are moving to the South now. It's always been diverse, but it's become a different kind of melting pot."

"Yeah, but I don't mind. I'm already a bit of an outsider being a straight, single guy who covers weddings for a living."

Though Michelle had mentioned that Dom was straight, I was still curious. Most men in this industry, especially ones with such Ken doll charm and raffish eyebrows, were . . . not. "So *why* are you covering weddings? You're not into the design or planning side, and you know all the women are taken, right?" I shut my mouth, embarrassed that I'd said my thoughts aloud.

"That's fair." He chuckled, a sound like summer rain on the roof. "It took awhile for my friends to understand what I was doing or why I was doing it, but I saw an opportunity and took it. No other guys were really in this market. I'm laughing all the way to the bank now."

"Must be nice," I quipped, imagining all the women out there who probably drooled over him interviewing famous cake bakers and florists online. Weddings and good-looking men: two things most women (and some men) love to follow. I hated that I'd admitted to myself yet again that he was attractive, but I wasn't blind.

"What? It's not like you're exactly struggling," he said. Guess I'd sounded more caustic than intended.

"Excuse me. How would you know?" I asked.

"I googled you, of course."

"You *what*?" I fought to keep my eyes on the road. "You've got to be kidding me."

"Oh, please," he said. "Like you haven't googled *me*."

"Don't flatter yourself, Mr. Influencer or whatever you are," I said, trying to keep my tone light. "I found out about you literally forty-eight hours ago. I haven't had much time for googling."

"You *did* start following me on Instagram," he said with a wide grin.

Wow, someone was very self-confident. Also, dang it.

I couldn't believe he noticed. He had a bazillion followers. How in the world did he notice my one meager follow? I was more irritated I got caught over anything else.

"Yes, but that's not at all the same as googling someone," I said with frustration I could no longer hide.

"When Michelle offered me the job, she told me I'd be working closely with you. I just wanted to know a little bit more about my future work-wife, Claire Sommers. You don't really have much of a social media presence, so I hit up Google," he said.

"Wow," I said, blushing despite myself at the word *wife*. Only work-related, of course. I wasn't very active on Instagram and basically nonexistent on Twitter or Facebook, but I still felt a bit offended by the whole meager social media presence bit.

"Sorry I don't post every detail online for people to see. I was raised to value privacy, so I just don't put that much out there related to my personal life. And it doesn't really seem to be an asset in my job either. No offense to what you do, of course," I muttered.

He laughed. "Of course not. No offense taken. And I definitely got that vibe when I googled you," he continued. "It appears you come from Dallas royalty, so I'd expect you'd want either total privacy or a huge following. That tends to be the case for those kinds of people."

"And just who are 'those kinds of people'?" I was now white-knuckling the steering wheel.

"Whoa, whoa, whoa." He raised his hands. "Don't get upset. I just mean that typically socialites, or at least the ones I've heard of in New York, either hide from the spotlight or chase it down and revel in it. I'm not judging either way."

"It sure sounds like you're judging," I said. "And I'm not a socialite . . . well, not anymore, at least."

"Okay, okay," he said. "Clearly I've struck a nerve, and there's no need for us to go into our first event together all bent out of shape. All I meant to say was that I didn't find too much about you online, which is impressive given the world we live in and how much is published these days. Looks like I'll just have to keep digging." Such was his poor attempt to lighten the mood.

"Or not," I replied, turning off the highway exit. We were still a few miles from the Preston family farm. Beads of sweat inconveniently formed on the backs of my knees, and I realized I was starting to panic. I came unglued at the thought of anyone digging up anything about the past few years. The last thing I needed was my new frenemy/work-husband, Dom, finding out about the mistakes I'd made in Dallas. The ones that led to this very moment, stuck with him in a Range Rover on the way to Murfreesboro.

"You don't want to talk about it. Got it." He shifted in the passenger seat. "We'll start small then. Claire the ex-socialite, name something you hate."

It was an interesting question to toss out there, so I decided to play along and help change the current mood.

"People who yell at waiters?" It was the first thing that came to mind.

He shook his head. "Too easy. I'd have to be a sociopath to disagree with you."

"Pets other than cats and dogs then."

"That's specific and discriminatory against people with allergies. The reptile community would be appalled." He clutched a strand of imaginary pearls.

"Their cages smell, and most of them don't *do* anything. You can't snuggle a bearded dragon, cool as they are. You can't teach tricks to anything in an aquarium. I stand by it."

"Ah, she's practical, I get it."

Or just lacking in human contact or affection, I thought. "Now you," I said.

"That's easy. Heights, people who name their cars, a dark restaurant where you can't see the menu, QR codes, acai bowls—"

"Wait, why? Those seem very . . . in your lane."

"I need to be able to chew something, of course. If I wanted soup, I would have gotten soup. Or a smoothie." He held up a hand. "I'm not done. Bow ties. I had a stylist as a guest on my socials, we did a whole TikTok tutorial on how to tie them, but I'm still no good. Fortunately, I almost never have to dress up."

"Now, I can tie bow ties. I'm practically an expert. My dad taught me when I was a kid, one night before he went to some gala with my mom." I thought of the countless groomsmen I had helped over the years. "I once did an entire wedding party, like an assembly line, including both fathers and every groomsman."

"You sure you want to phrase it that way?" he asked. I blushed. "*Anyway*, then you may be my official bow-tier if it comes to that. I'll need you. Oh, also, I hate toenail clippers." He fake-gagged.

"What? How, um, do you trim them then?"

"It's not the clippers themselves. My sisters used to do their nails on the couch while we'd watch movies. I don't mind hair in the drain or most bodily functions, but that clipping sound just gets me, as does not knowing where the trimmings went."

I shuddered. "Seriously? That sort of grooming was only and always relegated to the bathroom in our house. We just magically walked out of the bedroom looking armed and ready. I never even saw my mother so much as put on mascara in the rearview mirror."

"Well, my mother could put it on using the subway window—in motion—which should qualify her for some sort of award."

"She sounds like quite a legend."

"Oh, she is." He reached for the radio to turn off the third rendition of "Tennessee Whiskey" in the past thirty minutes. Thankfully, I was saved from our game of twenty questions by our arrival at the Preston family farm. I mean, *compound*.

When the assignment first came through my email, I thought surely I'd misread the location. Nothing I'd heard about the city of Murfreesboro was glamorous. Though it was a thriving city of about 130,000 residents located forty-five minutes from Nashville, its main claim to fame was Middle Tennessee State University, some hiking trails, and a major Civil War battlefield. There wasn't much else that I knew of going on in the city, except that as Nashville expanded, so did the outlying areas where people could live more affordably and still commute to work. The development business grew rapidly, which made for a lot of new money in the area. And the biggest subdivision developer in town was hosting his daughter's wedding in his newly built personal air hangar—a unique detail we shouldn't miss covering.

In this moment, I couldn't help but think of one of my all-time favorite movies (of course), *The Notebook*. In the words of Allie's mother: "This is gonna be a celebration the likes of which this town's never seen!" It was unlikely that a wedding of this size and caliber had ever taken place here. I could only imagine what the locals were thinking as word got out about this one.

Apparently owning a private jet no longer meant that you'd "made it." (I'd have to inform my parents' neighbors in Dallas.) Owning an entire hangar full of private planes and luxury vehicles was the new definition of extreme wealth. Seemed a bit overkill to me, given that you could only ride in one at a time, but if nothing else, it would make for a striking video to bring back to the magazine. This was going to be quite the transformation for our readers, or I guess they were viewers now.

Before I ever learned about the docuseries, I had requested "before" pictures of the hangar so that when I wrote about the wedding, our audience could see the full effect—from vast, open warehouse to fully decorated reception venue. We'd be able to use all of it as B-roll now for the video.

I was coming into the project prepped and ready to go. I wanted to stay one step ahead of Dom as much as possible. He needed to understand I was a professional. More important, Michelle needed to see I wouldn't be easily replaced—no matter how fab our shiny new vlogger, or whatever he was, was.

We arrived early to interview the bridal party and get additional B-roll before guests arrived. I parked behind a giant metal hangar with "Preston Properties" emblazoned on the side. Three beautiful jets were all lined up outside, making for quite the entrance. We started walking toward the stone Mediterranean-style villa, which we presumed to be the primary residence. Apparently you could bring Tuscany to Tennessee if you so desired and had enough money. Dom grabbed his gear from my trunk and loosely held in one hand a camera that cost more than my rent.

"Hold on one second," Dom said suddenly. "I need to story this quickly."

I stood there dumbfounded as he turned on this different persona, addressing his phone and the legions presumably waiting for his updates.

"I'm here at a wedding in Murfreesboro, Tennessee. This sleepy little town is hosting one heck of a party—at an airplane hangar—that I'll be sharing with you guys throughout today and tonight. I won't give everything away, but let's just say you'd better fasten your seat belts and make sure your tray tables are in their upright positions. This one's really going to blow your minds, so prepare for takeoff!"

I stared back at him with eyebrows raised. *Wow, he's really milking this thing.* At least ten sarcastic comments verged on spilling out of my open mouth. I had to clench my teeth to keep from asking whether Dom was the captain now or snarkily pointing out that nothing screamed romance like "an upright position" that was gonna "blow their minds." A serious gag.

Instead, I muttered, "Um, you done now?"

"Yeah, sorry, part of my deal with Michelle is that I can also include some snippets on my personal channel."

"Gotcha. Well, if you're finished playing the role of Maverick to the online wedding world, why don't you follow me and try to keep up? They paired us up for a reason. You bring the pizzazz or whatever, and I bring the authentic journalistic touch that will anchor this story," I said, nodding my head toward the front door of the villa.

"Yes, ma'am," he replied, saluting me and swinging his camera over his shoulder. "You bring the serious, and I'll bring the fun."

"I told you to drop the whole *ma'am* thing," I said, resuming my march toward the villa. "I can't be that much older than you, but it sounds like you're addressing my mom. And I take it back about the pizzazz. 'You bring the serious, and I'll bring the fun' basically means we're a mullet." I paused to face him. "You know, 'Business in the front, party in the back'?"

"Roger that," he said.

I gave up and kept walking.

"Listen, I'm thrilled that we're expanding my normal beat and making this story a potential pitch option for a TV series, but we can't forget to cover the basics too. I can't imagine they want any of this looking overly scripted or fake, so let's try to stick to the formula for the interviews and then see where things go."

"Totally get it," said Dom. "It's going to take two of us to make this sing, and I'm thrilled for you to take the lead."

I sighed, relieved he wasn't a total goober and could act normal when needed.

"I'm typically stuck behind a desk asking questions about wedding details on the phone, but this time we get to see it all go down in person. So keep an eye out for the way things are executed—because that's often where a lot of the good drama occurs. Usually at least one thing doesn't go precisely to plan or happen just how the bride envisioned it. I don't care how good your planning team is." *Something always goes wrong. And I should know.*

"Aye aye, captain."

"And for my own personal sanity, I'm going to need you to drop the airplane puns," I said. "At least where I can hear them."

"Yep, 10-4," he said, giving me a weird wink. I was pretty sure that wasn't airplane jargon, but since I wasn't going to tee him up for any more dad jokes, I just rolled my eyes and moved on.

We stood on the stone steps, the February air crisp around us.

The bride's father, Albert Preston, greeted us at the front door and led us inside the house.

"You're welcome to go anywhere you'd like on the property," he said as he chewed on the end of an unlit cigar. "We're pretty proud of our gal and have been preparing for this day for a long time. Well, her mother has, at least." He laughed.

"Your home is beautiful," I said. "And we can't thank you enough for allowing us to cover this special day for your family."

"Of course," he said. "I love this town, and it seems that everyone's just as excited about this wedding as we are. We're all like family here."

"I love that sentiment," I replied, and I meant it. Even in my work as a wedding planner, I seldom experienced a small-town wedding like what he described. And even if Murfreesboro wasn't that small, I completely understood what he meant, and it was heartwarming.

Dom and I followed Mr. Preston as he continued to tell us how excited he was for the press coverage and the exposure it would bring his business and the city. We ended up in a two-story great room where people were bustling about.

I looked around the space, listening to the groomsmen laughing down the hall and the caterers calling to one another in what I assumed was the kitchen. It still felt odd to be at a wedding that I wasn't working on. This new assignment certainly held plenty of responsibility, but the pressure was different from ensuring the wedding went off without a hitch. I was good at that. Or I had been. Some good that did me, in the end.

One of two Nashville-based wedding planners in charge of the festivities was seated next to the mother of the bride, who wore a blue robe and donned a full set of curlers in her hair. In front of them was splayed a massive piece of poster board with round tables drawn all over it. The two women were moving around tiny Post-it notes with a guest's name written on each one. *The dreaded seating chart.* I remembered the days of having to help clients move people around at the last minute because a guest got ill, divorced, or even died right before the wedding. Seating charts could be nightmarish, and I felt bad that Mrs. Preston was still making adjustments the day of her daughter's wedding. However, it did present the perfect opportunity to grab quotes from the wedding planner and the mother of the bride since they were stationary at the moment. But first, the FOB.

I looked at Dom and motioned for him to turn on his camera.

"Mr. Preston, before we start interviewing the others, we'd love to officially hear from you. What are you most looking forward to about today?" I asked.

"You mean, besides the fact that now Nate is responsible for covering Jacqueline's credit card bills and I'm off the hook?" He laughed.

Dom gave me the side-eye and a smirk.

"Oh, I'm just kidding, of course," he said, walking over to the most incredible built-in bar I'd ever seen in a private residence—and I'd certainly seen some doozies. The bar and entire back wall of shelves were made of backlit onyx and edged in antique copper. The floating shelves were stocked with countless bottles of bourbon that probably cost enough to demand their own insurance policy. Mr. Preston poured himself a glass and then offered drinks, which we politely declined.

He set down his chewed-up cigar and took a sip of the brown liquid. "Jacqueline is my baby girl, and she's been looking forward to this day for a long time. We all love Nate, and he'll be a great addition to the family. I'm just thrilled we finished the hangar in time to host her reception here."

"Wow," I said. "So you built the entire structure just for their reception?"

"Well, Jacqueline always wanted a wedding at home, and I've always wanted a hangar for my planes, so this was the perfect reason to pull the trigger and make us both happy."

"We can't wait to see it," I replied.

"I'll do just about anything for my girl," he said, taking another sip. "Now, if you'll excuse me, it's almost time for me to put on my penguin suit."

"Thank you so much for your time, Mr. Preston," I said. "We're thrilled to be here and to participate in such a special day."

"Anytime," he replied with a tip of his glass. Then he headed off to some other wing of the estate.

We did a quick circuit around the house, interviewing the wedding planner, Mrs. Preston, and even a few groomsmen. For the most part, the responses were pretty standard. *"We are so happy for the bride," "Today is a real fairy tale," "Bro is gonna choke on his vows."* Standard fare, but with a couple of special moments.

Thankfully, we got a bit of flavor from the groom, whose answer to "How did you two meet?" really hit home the fairy-tale narrative.

The gist was that he'd tried every single dating app in the history of the world to no avail. (I unfortunately related way too much to that part of the story.) He moved back to his hometown of Murfreesboro a few years after college and, quote, *"Didn't realize that my high school best friend Cliff's little sister had gotten hot in her twenties."* How sweet. He insisted that Cliff set them up, and after meeting Jacqueline at a local bar one Thanksgiving, sparks flew. The rest was history, as they say.

I turned to go, head-motioning for Dom to follow me out.

"Yeesh, are they always that . . . um, eloquent?"

No fewer than four similar grooms from my planning days immediately came to mind. But Dom didn't need that info. "In the past, I've just had to interview them over the phone, so it was certainly easier to ignore any eccentricities."

We climbed the circular rear staircase. As I looked back to talk to him, my foot missed the narrow pie-shaped step.

I slipped on the marble and barely missed nailing my knee

on the edge of the step when he grabbed me. "Thank you," I finally got out. Very aware of his arm across my stomach and his other hand covering mine.

"Don't mention it. You okay?"

"I'm perfectly fine. Thanks again. Now, we were going . . ." He quickly obliged and released me. I was fairly certain my irritation was at his invasion of my personal space and *not* the withdrawal of his very solid arm.

We continued climbing, carefully, up to the bridal suite. I always loved brides who got ready in their adolescent bedrooms.

Jacqueline's room was less juvenile than usual. It was a mix of rustic Restoration Hardware furniture and layered ruffled bedding. Two signed posters of Harry Styles and a framed portrait of a show horse were the only concessions to individualism in the space. Mrs. Preston had apparently remodeled the entire home prior to the wedding. A new house *and* a new hangar. Some parents will stop at nothing and spare no expense to create the perfect atmosphere for their offspring's big day.

I walked over to Jacqueline, who sat at her vanity getting her makeup done. When she reached a stopping point, she turned to face me, and I nodded at Dom to turn on the camera. "You look radiant, Jacqueline. The loveliest bride I've ever seen!" I couldn't help myself. Old wedding planner habits. I heard my former boss's voice in my head reminding his team to always say that. Every bride *should* feel that way, true or not.

She thanked me, fidgeting, before suddenly asking, "Hey, instead of talking in here, how about the three of us sneak out back for a cig break? I need a smoke."

"Um . . . sure? We can take you out the back stairs if that works for you. Here, let me help you with your train."

She grabbed her cigarettes and lighter, and we followed her back down the treacherous rear stairs, through a butler's pantry, and into the side yard. Were we supposed to film her while she smoked? Dom's eyes held the question. He arched one irritatingly lush dark brow at me. Mine had been overwaxed in the early aughts in a concession to "taming" them and never recovered.

I shrugged my shoulders as if to say, *"If she doesn't care, why should we?"* I was positive her parents would die if this ended up on a TV show, but they all signed the consent forms and knew what we were doing. I hoped this would make for the kind of drama Michelle wanted.

He raised the camera, and I began.

"So tell me about your gown. It's gorgeous."

She contentedly smoothed a few duchesse silk bustles with the hand not holding the cigarette. "I found this at Vera Wang in New York, although they made some design alterations for me."

"Oh, what did you have done?" I asked, thinking she'd come back with a long description of lace detailing and necklines. Brides love to talk about beadwork and trains, and the number of seed pearls sewn into the bodice that were repurposed from a vintage 1970s gown worn by the cousin of their aunt.

"You know, just some minor things." She paused to place her cigarette between her perfectly painted rosy lips and inhaled. "Mostly I wanted to be able to really get down. Like movement was big for me. I didn't want to be some stiff cake topper. I needed the flexibility *and* the look."

"That's smart," Dom chimed in. "I take it you aren't doing a second party dress then?"

Shooting him a glare—weren't cameramen supposed to be seen and not heard?—I interjected, "And how *did* you decide whether to change out of it and into something else for your reception and departure? That seems to be quite the trend these days."

"Well, I thought about it, but my fiancé wants me to keep my wedding dress on so we can have sex in it." Jacqueline nonchalantly took another drag.

"Oh, well, um . . . okay . . ."

"Weddings are about compromise, you know?" She shrugged. "My bridesmaids threw me a really cute lingerie shower, too, but this was the only real thing Nate asked for. So, yeah, flexibility!"

Dom valiantly held the camera steady, trying desperately not to laugh.

Right—movement, flexibility. Good Lord.

I almost jumped out of my skin when I heard a low voice over my shoulder. "Yeah, I told Jackie to keep it on so I can deflower her in it. I have always wanted to do that!"

The groom had popped out from behind a long row of Italian cypress trees that I'm sure were a nightmare to keep alive in Middle Tennessee. Dom turned the camera to both of them now as Nate reached for a cigarette from Jacqueline's pack and started smoking with his bride-to-be. At least we knew for sure that they had one thing in common.

They stood, heads together, and stared at Nate's phone, whispering in between puffs. Le sigh.

This was definitely the most unique "first look" for a couple I'd ever witnessed. If Michelle wanted drama, all Dom and I needed to do was stick around for the wedding planner discovering this was how the bride and groom had first seen each other on their wedding day. Not at the end of an aisle or under a beautiful archway dripping in roses. No, Jacqueline and Nate were dressed in all their finery while hiding behind a bush, playing their daily Wordle, and smoking cigarettes as two reporters filmed it all.

"Wow, that's so sweet of you guys. Love that you're waiting. So beautiful these days, especially with, um . . ." My voice sure sounded unnaturally shrill.

At this point, tears were coming from the corners of Dom's crinkled eyes. I gave him my death stare.

"Well," I recovered, "we couldn't be more thrilled for you both and wish you all the happiness today. We're going to take some B-roll in the event space but can't wait to see your ceremony. Best wishes!"

We turned and made our escape to the front of the house. "In any other world, I'd tell you to burn that recording," I muttered. "But I guess we'll be keeping it since Michelle's looking for 'unique moments,' and that certainly qualified. I hope ash didn't fall onto her dress. She's lucky she didn't catch fire with all that hairspray in her hair."

Dom beelined for the grey stone wall as we turned the corner. He leaned his head back and exhaled through pursed full lips, laughing hysterically. Dom might be both awfully cute and awfully inconvenient, I was beginning to realize.

"I hope you enjoyed that, sir. You're gonna need to do better at maintaining your poker face in this job."

"I have no idea how you do it." He shook his head. "I'm mostly used to dealing with vendors and brides beforehand. I haven't been on the inside of day-of antics."

"If you'd seen half the things I've seen at weddings, your composure would be ironclad too." *Or if you had a mother like mine.*

"We've got a minute. Give me one example."

"Once I was at a wedding and the bride was obsessed with chickens. Like, kept them as pets—"

"Is that part of the evolution of your pet bias?" he interrupted.

"One hundred percent," I continued. "But things didn't get super creepy until she wanted to go dance in her attic with her deceased father's ghost before the ceremony."

"No way."

"Yes way. Fortunately, I didn't have to go up there, but my boss did and said it was the most bizarre thing she'd ever seen. An old record player and this middle-aged woman dancing by herself in a dusty attic. I couldn't look her in the eyes the rest of the ceremony, and I even had to help her pee twice."

"Hold on. Why the heck would you have to do that?"

Crud. There it was. *Smooth, Claire.* "Before this job, I worked on the planning side."

He looked at me as if the pieces were clicking. "So that's why you know so much."

"Or I'm just good at my job. But let's get going. We need to take video of the décor before the guests start arriving."

Thankfully he didn't ask any more about my former job. Probably because he was dumbfounded by what we saw next. The airplane hangar had been completely transformed for the event. The space was divided into two areas—for ceremony and reception—which helped it feel less vast.

On the ceremony side, the wide hangar doors were rolled back so the view of the Tennessee hills served as the backdrop. Even if temperatures dropped later in the day, there were enough heating units pumping in warm air to keep the chill out. And if that wasn't enough, every other white Philippe Starck Louis chair was draped with a white fur throw for guests to use.

The pièce de résistance was the aisle and spot where the couple would say their vows. The aisle itself was made of white plexiglass, and above it were draped lush, dimensional bouquets of white flowers with silver and blue accents. At a glance, it looked like fluffy clouds in a blue sky. The planners had managed to rig up other mirrors at angles to reflect the afternoon sky outside of the hangar. It would look like Jacqueline was walking on clouds to meet her groom. My internal wedding planner gave a silent slow clap. Bravo.

Dom and I had a half hour before the guests would begin arriving. I scanned the notes on my phone to ensure we'd hit everything on our to-do list thus far. You never knew at what point the bride and groom might become too emotional, too intoxicated, or too busy to chat, and we needed more quotes from them, sans cigarettes.

"Hey! Claire! C'mere!" I turned my head, scanning for where Dom had scampered off to. I found him just outside the main doors hanging on to the side of a vintage Cessna. A "Just Married" sticker had been custom-printed in script and plastered to the side.

What was that overgrown child up to? I walked over. "Should you be doing that?"

"Yes! It's so cool inside. Go take a look." I could only imagine that the cockpit was filled with gears and buttons and controls, but with a sigh, I indulged him.

I stood up on the outside step and stuck my head inside the cockpit. "This must be their getaway vehicle, which is the *only* reason that justifies you clowning around right now and not getting additional B-roll for ceremony coverage . . . Oh my! Dom, what?!"

He had jumped down, shoved my backside up and in—a harassment suit waiting to happen, that guy—and clambered into the chair next to me. He grinned boyishly as he gripped the controls.

"At least film the inside of the plane," I muttered. "Like, can you *try* to be somewhat professional?"

Dom pretended not to hear me and, like an overgrown kid, abruptly turned and scrambled toward the back of the plane—no mean feat considering how much he contorted his long legs to fit. "Come on!" he yelled. With another loud sigh, I did.

He lounged across a beautiful banquette and gestured for me to take the swivel chair opposite. The interior had been gorgeously redone, I noted. Comfortable and not fussy. No oligarch vibes here. An ice bucket and pair of flutes stood ready for chilled champagne and the happy couple.

Dom evidently noticed me evaluating the upholstery. "Your family flies private, huh?"

"Stereotyping is going to get you in trouble, and you hardly know anything about me."

He had the decency to look at least partly ashamed. But I could tell he was also picking at me. "Well, I'd like to. I mean, it wouldn't be the worst thing for us to become friends during this project. Beats hating each other," he said, smiling.

Before I could stammer that I had a rule about befriending colleagues, he continued, "Why worry about carbon emissions when planes like this exist?" He stretched his arms across the length of the banquette and leaned his head back. His biceps pulled against the fabric of his button-down shirt, it was impossible not to note.

I laughed. Then sobered. Then semi-lied. I mean, he wasn't wrong, but he also wasn't right. "Yes, we used to. I mean, my parents still do. But it's coach for me these days. I'm just trying to go it on my own. Pay my own bills, stand on my own two feet, you know?"

"But . . . why? I'm all for independence, but are you just trying to prove a point to your parents? From the little I did read about you—and yes, I'll admit again I googled you—you're basically part of a Dallas dynasty. It's hard to believe someone would give all that up to try to make it on their own."

"My parents have actually always been the types who wanted us to succeed on our own. Both of my sisters are really driven."

"No doubt." He winked. "And then there's you. Claire the writer?"

"Claire the still-figuring-it-out, more like." I tried to keep the bitterness out of my voice. I didn't need to give Dom any more ammunition against me. Sometimes the past was better left in the past, even if what happens in Dallas doesn't actually stay there. "Enough about me. How did you get into this whole influencer thing? Does a person just set out to make videos of themselves all day?"

He laughed. "You're asking because you want to get into it?"

"My gosh, never. I would be horrible at it. I can barely stand listening to my own voice on a tape recorder when I transcribe interviews. I would absolutely die watching myself on camera. Call it friendly professional curiosity."

"Fair enough. You know, practically my whole family still lives in Brooklyn, other than a couple cousins in Long Island. But two of my favorite cousins got married the same summer, between my junior and senior year at Fordham. Because I was in the city and we're close, I tagged along on all their bridal stuff that spring. They wanted an impartial male opinion, and I wanted to see what all the fuss was about. My uncle's a very successful attorney, so their weddings were both really nice and a bit over-the-top. We hit all the major spots—I don't have to tell a girl like you."

"There you go again. You'd better cut out that 'girl like you' stuff or you're going to need a parachute when I throw you out of this plane."

"No need to push the Eject button on my seat just yet." The corners of his eyes crinkled when he smiled. "All I mean is that you've probably been to those types of places. I never had, and it was incredibly awkward. But it was also fascinating. So I started taking videos just for fun, and then we started putting some on Instagram. My older sister had the idea to film the Kleinfeld sample sale, back when brides still lined up on the sidewalk overnight to get a spot. That was the video that really blew up. You know how it goes. Then you get an audience."

"Of course, naturally." No idea, but I was trying to be polite. I'd also probably never known a bride whose dress was from a sample sale, if I really thought about it.

"I kind of reverse engineered it after that. Started a blog and eventually a TikTok account about a regular guy's perspective on women and their weddings. More snarky and real talk than professional—like, 'These are my uninformed male pet peeves.' Some of it made fun of bro-ish, straight white guys and the things we think about weddings, but some of it was genuine advice. For whatever reason, it worked."

"Your stuff is pretty smart, I'll give you that. But making it as an influencer sounds a bit like striking oil or winning the lottery."

"Yeah, it's a mix of hard work and good luck. Either way, it's helped me pay off most of my student loans while living with my mom the past few years. Entry-level salaries, even in digital media companies, are nothing to write home about. But like everybody, I needed a change of scenery."

"We could all use something different after the last couple years."

"Nashville certainly seemed as different from New York as possible."

"There you go again with assumptions. What's so wrong with it being different? You're really on a roll here, buddy." My Southern apologist antennae had perked up. We could rag on our own hometowns and regions, but outsiders shouldn't even start. This was a universal truth.

"Easy there. Just that it's so much . . . slower. Sleepy, almost. It's cute."

I thought of the bustle and noise of downtown and felt he couldn't be more wrong. I said as much.

"Yeah, but you have to admit it's still basically a midsize city. A nice one, but—forget about comparing it to New York or LA. It's adorable that you guys think you're even in the same conversation as San Francisco or Chicago."

Wow. With that attitude, good thing this guy never planned to stay down here long.

"Some people happen to prefer 'midsize' cities, as you so charmingly put it," I drawled. "We have all the amenities, culture, and access, without the congestion or real estate prices of bigger urban areas."

"I'd say your traffic and real estate prices are both starting to get competitive, but I hear you. Not trying to ruffle your feathers. Sorry."

Slightly mollified, I nodded. For a guy who was supposedly übersmooth with his words on camera, he sure had a knack for putting his foot in his mouth with me. But I didn't have the energy to engage with him anymore. Let him think what he wanted. He'd be gone at the end of this project anyway.

He continued. "And regardless, we've both come here to try

something new, build a life on our own, away from family support . . . Nashville has offered us both that."

"That's true. And if I'm correct, guests are arriving just about any minute now, so we should get back to work or there won't be a project for either of us to build."

He climbed back into the cockpit and jumped down. Then he turned around and extended a hand to help me descend. I would have refused on principle, but I didn't want to fall in my wedges or flash him in my dress. His hand was strong in mine as I reached the ground, facing him. I looked up. Something I couldn't place briefly flitted across his green eyes. They were almost gold at the center. He released my hand and said, "After you."

I led the way back toward the reception setup. The entire ceiling of the main space was draped in billowy white fabric, except for the area over the shiny white dance floor. That space was covered in mirrored panels and what looked like thousands of white origami birds hanging at various levels. It was the perfect nod to an aviation theme without going overboard. I'd seen a similar installation at the downtown Dallas Neiman Marcus years ago, but it was executed in butterflies. I almost shed a tear thinking about the last time I'd been in Neiman's to shop. Who knew whether I'd ever step foot in that beautiful flagship again?

I also wondered which poor souls had to fold all those origami birds. They had surely suffered countless paper cuts from the task. I didn't know the planners at all, but they clearly knew *not* to use a mirrored dance floor and chose to install the mirrors above the dance floor instead. My former boss had learned the hard way that a mirrored floor reflects *everything*. Great for voyeurs. Not so great for guests in short dresses.

Dom captured every last detail of the room, from the ceiling installation to the mirrored bars and lush, white floral trees—yes, *trees*—that were the centerpieces on every table. Plush white velvet lounge furniture flanked the dance floor, and white panels with mirror inserts were built as faux walls around the entire room. Gone was the industrial warehouse. In a space that size, it was go big or go home. The planners had gone big and nailed it.

It wasn't long before we took our place at the back of the ceremony and recorded the main event. If I'd been a crier—Sommers women, as a rule, don't shed many tears—the sight of Jacqueline walking the aisle with her dad would have gotten me. She looked truly lovely, and her big-talking father was practically bawling.

The ceremony wrapped, and everyone moved over to the reception space to celebrate. After eating a handful of hors d'oeuvres behind the catering area, Dom resumed filming, and we managed to cover all the major moments from the first dances to the cake cutting with ease.

"So far, so good," I said to Dom as the twelve-piece band took the stage to get the dance party started. "Things have been pretty uneventful, which is impressive at a wedding of this scale."

"What do you mean?" he asked, almost shouting at me now that the band was in full swing.

"Usually something goes wrong at every wedding," I shouted back. "It's just a matter of how big that something is."

"Oh really? Well, it looks like you might've spoken too soon," he yelled, motioning to the corner of the dance floor nearest the stage. "What's Mr. Preston messing with up there? Is he standing on a ladder?"

I rose on my tiptoes to see what Dom was referring to.

"It looks like a confetti cannon," I said. "Maybe he's trying to set it off, though usually that's done from a remote."

As though my words were the trigger, suddenly there was a massive *bang* and an enormous burst of gold-foil confetti exploded out of the cannon, completely covering Mr. Preston from head to toe. What didn't directly hit him was spewed over the nearby guests and created a golden glassy surface over most of the dance floor.

Dom and I gave each other a quick look, then speed-walked to that side of the room for a better view, aka to record it all.

Mr. Preston was bent over, coughing up confetti, when we arrived. The guests on the dance floor were slipping on the foil pieces and falling all over one another. At least two groomsmen landed in the splits, and poor Mrs. Preston could barely stand up as she tried to wipe the confetti off her husband.

"Why in the world would they use something like that on the dance floor?" Dom stage-whispered while filming every second of the mayhem.

"I've seen them in action before, and when they work properly, they're supposed to gently spray small amounts over time above people's heads while they dance. Like snow softly falling. Clearly there was a major malfunction, as that was way more of an explosion than a gentle mist."

"Clearly," Dom said, holding back a laugh.

His camera was now pointed at the wedding planners armed

with brooms as they frantically tried to sweep off the dance floor. It was quite the scene given that the band never once stopped their Beyoncé medley during all this. The wedding planners were getting sandwiched in between half the people who were sliding around trying to flee and half the people still trying to dance despite the confetti catastrophe.

I motioned to Dom to pan over to the bride and groom, who each had an arm around the bride's grandmother, who was probably on the verge of breaking a hip, as they escorted her off the dance floor. We both went over to lend a hand.

"I told Daddy I didn't want that darn thing," yelled Jacqueline to Nate as they helped her grandmother into a nearby chair. "He just can't help himself with all his toys. Planes, four-wheelers, and now confetti cannons."

"Well, thankfully that's the only thing that blew up today," Nate replied.

Jacqueline gave Nate a glare, and then he grabbed her and pulled her in for a kiss. She started giggling and grabbed his hand.

"Well, looks like he got what he deserved. He'll be pulling confetti out of his ears for weeks," she said as she led Nate back toward the dance floor.

"What a mess," I said to Dom once the couple headed off.

"Literally and figuratively," he replied.

"Very funny," I said. "I feel like I jinxed them with what I said earlier. Let's take a break once you're done here and catch our breath before the departure."

"Sounds good to me, boss," he replied with a wink. *Ew.*

Before either of us realized it, it was time to get ready for the departure. We got a few more questions with the couple as they readied with their planner to make their final exit.

"I'm just so glad Mama won all that money in Tunica and then hid it in her boot for us to use for the wedding," Jacqueline gushed. "Dad was very generous with our budget, but it was Mama's savvy gambling that made all the extra details possible. And aside from an overload of confetti, wasn't it a total *dream*?!"

"This couple is the gift that keeps on giving," mumbled Dom.

"This has been the best day of my life. Now—time to get you outta that dress." Nate winked at Jacqueline. I shuddered.

"That's our cue to leave," I said jokingly (but not really).

Dom filmed a final shot of the happy couple climbing into the Cessna—piloted by a professional, fortunately—to go ruin Jacqueline's wedding dress. I wondered how it was I still managed to know more about strangers than I ever should. It wasn't just the wedding planners who couples overshared with.

Barely two minutes later, a massive semitruck pulled into the gravel drive, startling the guests still lingering under the stars and drunkenly blowing their tiny bubble wands. Sparklers or pyrotechnics of any kind were forbidden given the amount of jet fuel on the property.

The valet drivers promptly started steering cars onto the two levels of the trailer. I thought for sure people would question what was happening, but everyone acted like this was perfectly normal behavior. Thankfully one of the wedding planners appeared beside me and explained.

She said that when everyone had RSVPed, they included their home address or nearby hotel. The flatbed would deposit their vehicle overnight so it would be waiting for them tomorrow. I'd been to parties that offered shuttle buses from nearby hotels, but this was next-level.

And why go for a bus when you could afford to arrange a fleet of rainbow Hummers to chauffeur guests to their various residences? Where did one even find that many Hummers in one place and in so many bright colors? They had the resources, and it saved everyone from small-town tuxedo mugshots. Dom was having the time of his life capturing it all on film.

The organization of this operation was truly a thing of beauty. I inwardly gave the wedding coordinator another round of applause.

"Wow, you just can't make this stuff up, can you?" Dom said as we walked back to my car, ready to head home.

"Oh, Dom, you have no idea."

CHAPTER 5

Most of the car ride home was silent. I shut down Dom's attempts at trying to ask me more personal questions by turning up the radio to a nineties country station. This was the music that took me back to Dallas traffic—the music that never failed to make me feel at home. My parents, proper as they both were, shared a deep, unapologetic love for George Strait, Alan Jackson, and Garth Brooks.

Dom and I could work well together professionally. We proved that today. But I wasn't interested in spilling my guts or really getting to know him. Who knew if we'd actually pull off saving the entire magazine from being shuttered, but as much as I didn't want to acknowledge it, that was my mission here. Not to make a new friend. Especially not a Yankee one who couldn't help but offend me in every possible way.

I dropped Dom off at his buddy's apartment, a cozy bungalow

in Germantown, and made it back home. I tossed my beat-up Chanel bag on the hook by the door and scrambled to answer my vibrating phone. I hadn't turned on my ringer in at least two years, much to my family's annoyance. I knew I'd missed two calls from my sister during the reception and drive, but she followed up before I had the chance to even text her back.

"Hiya, Lucy." My little sister was the kind of person who FaceTimed anytime she called, even if it was just to catch up. She was about the only person allowed such an invasion. I never, *ever* wanted to see my older sister Evelyn's smug, unblemished face for the duration of a conversation. But for Lucille, sure.

Without fanfare, she squealed and thrust her left hand in the frame. "Claire Bear! Look!"

The largest Asscher-cut stone I'd ever seen took up the entire screen. A bed of tiny diamonds and a lovely pair of amethysts glittered around it as Lucy waved her hand frantically. "Collins proposed!" As if I hadn't picked up on that yet.

Lucille had met Collins in law school at the University of Texas at Austin. Nearly three years later, she was now less than one semester shy of graduation—and I had made next to zero progress on my own life. *This is just peachy*, I thought to myself. But I mustered my elder sister enthusiasm. "Oh my *gosh*! Congratulations! Wow, I'm so happy for you! What a wonderful surprise!"

She took that as her cue to give me the entire story. I could see Evelyn, bump finally starting to show, and her husband, Ford, in the background. Clearly, I was the only family member who didn't know to prep for the engagement. I felt a momentary twinge that no one thought to ask whether I would or could fly in for it. I guessed they assumed it wasn't in the budget. Accurate. And that explanation stung less than thinking I wasn't wanted.

Truly, Lucy was one of my favorite people, which was not a hard contest when faced with our eldest sister and our parents as alternatives.

She paused her gushing and looked me straight in the eyes. "How did the first event for your documentary go?"

Lucy was studying corporate law, so she had the financial acumen *and* common sense to run numbers and do businessy stuff. So of course I had floated my documentary idea past her before sending it to Michelle. Like any true kid sister, she told me it was brilliant—but Sommers women don't blow smoke. It's not in our nature. She would have saved me from myself if it had been a bad idea.

I told her about the wedding today and how I was forced to partner with Dom, some New Yorker social media interloper, on a project that was fully my idea.

"That bites. Need me to write up some sort of threatening note in legalese?"

"Nah, but I appreciate the offer. I'll let you know if the situation escalates."

"Okay, please, please do. You know I'm here for you."

"I do, and you know I am, too, always. Especially with this wedding! I know a thing or two about the process, so let me know what you need me to do."

"Of course. Mom is, you might guess, already raring to go with her spreadsheets and appropriately vetted vendor list."

"I can only imagine."

Our mother popped her smooth, lean face into the frame. Those blue eyes we'd all inherited sparked with practically predatory excitement. "Claire, dear! Isn't it the most delightful news?"

"Yes, Mom, it's incredible," I gushed sufficiently for her.

"We're all so proud of your sister," Mom went on. "She'll be getting her JD and heading on a honeymoon at the same time." Mom had that subtle skill, honed over the years, of comparing us without blatantly insulting me. "Well, we'll let you go. I'm sure you have plans tomorrow."

If you count The Great British Bake Off, *then yes*, big *plans, Mom.* I yelled one more "Congrats!" to Lucy as they signed off.

I slipped on my favorite set of Madewell sweats, lit a Le Labo candle I got for Christmas, and curled up on the sofa. The rose-pink velvet was soft under my hand as I absently stroked it. We'd all known this day was coming. And I was as genuinely happy for Lucy as I was unsurprised that she was getting married before me. Aside from a couple of relationships when I was at Vanderbilt—who could forget soccer player Gabe the Babe?—I hadn't dated much.

I met Gabe at a mixer. Our relationship was lovely, easy, fun. But he was also from Dallas and knew too much about my family. He had too many preconceived notions about what being a Sommers meant. I'm not saying he didn't genuinely want to be with me. I believe he did. But he also wanted another perfect, driven, entrepreneur-socialite. Frankly, he wanted someone like Evelyn. That was not ever going to be me. I knew he'd figure that out sooner or later, so I ended it after almost a year. He was disappointed, but he eventually got engaged to one of the Bass cousins, so I imagined he recovered just fine.

And Nashville guys were proving to be pretty meh so far. For the next couple of guys I dated, I tried to channel Evelyn: be the strongest, most ambitious version of myself. One broke up with me because he said I spent too much time at work. (Good thing he wasn't around during the Dallas years. Magazine hours had *nothing* on wedding planning schedules.) The other met a nice girl at church Bible study and said that God put her, and presumably not me, in his heart. Well, I wasn't here to fight divine inspiration.

I was really good for the first few dates, but there always seemed to be something wrong with them that gave me a reason to bail. I wasn't lonely, per se, but I had enough self-awareness to know that I wanted more than a solo studio apartment in East Nashville for too long.

◊ ◊ ◊

On Monday, I was writing up a story on alternative wedding desserts for our upcoming April issue—titled "Pie Do"—while Dom did a first pass at the footage from Jacqueline's wedding. Although his cubicle was two rows over from mine, having someone other than just Amaya and me in the otherwise empty coworking space helped it feel less depressing.

I imagined what it would have been like to work here in *Piece of Cake*'s heyday, with bright, talented writers and editors bustling about the halls. We ran the only photos of Tim and Faith's surprise ceremony; we even covered Johnny and June's vow renewal. Rumor was we had the exclusive deal on Elvis's second wedding before he died. Bottom line was that the magazine had once been thriving, a destination for the wealthiest and most famous couples in the region. It would be a long, improbable road to restore the brand to her former glory. I sighed.

I submitted my draft to Kevin and started mindlessly scanning my favorite websites. For story ideas, of course. But after a few minutes, I pulled out my phone to do something productive: find a date for Lucy's wedding. It wasn't like the wedding was tomorrow, but who knew how long it would take to find a suitable candidate. No time like the present to start the search.

Bumble was not exactly a place I enjoyed spending my time, but I'd be lying if I said I didn't scroll through the endless sea of male faces almost every night in bed while simultaneously watching reruns of *Grey's Anatomy*. But the news of Lucy's engagement meant it was time to reactivate and give it some actual effort. He didn't have to be "Mr. Right," but he needed to be "Mr. Right Now"—or at the very least "Mr. Just in Time for Lucy's Wedding so I Don't Seem like a Loser." I wasn't one to need a date to everything, but I certainly wanted to avoid all the questions I knew I'd face if I attended the wedding alone. So back to Bumble it was.

I couldn't believe I ever thought the dating scene in Dallas was rough. It had nothing on Nashville. The issue wasn't a lack of single, straight men. There were plenty of them around, from what I could tell. The issue was that none of them seemed to want a serious relationship. They were here to have fun or get famous.

You had the guys just out of college, who moved to Nashville to start their careers in a city full of bars, barbecue, and bachelorette parties. A serious relationship was the last thing on their minds. You had the single men of all ages, hoping to make it as a country music singer or musician with no time for distractions from their "true calling." You had the traditional Southern "gentlemen," who, like their fathers, grew up in the Deep South, inherited more money than they'd ever need, played golf every day, drank bourbon starting at noon, and were basically mini versions of, well, my own dad. And last but not least, you had the cultured Paul Bunyans of East Nashville—a growing population of Brooklyn transplants and wannabes. These bearded gents had mullets, worked in coffee shops or restaurants selling overpriced organic food, attended all the festivals, and cared more about their dogs than they ever would a girlfriend. I wasn't exactly sure who my "type" of guy was, but it didn't seem to be any of the above.

Even though the dating odds were stacked against me, I decided to give it another shot.

"Working hard or hardly working?" a voice chirped over my shoulder.

I quickly threw my phone to the side of my desk, which was anything but discreet.

"Oh, hey, Amaya," I said, wondering how long she'd been standing behind me.

"You'd better open that app back up right now, Claire," she said as she handed me my discarded phone. "I'm thrilled to see you taking a minute for yourself, and I absolutely love hearing about all the weirdos people come across on the dating apps. It's better than reality TV."

"Well, I'm glad my love life, or lack thereof, can provide some entertainment." I pressed the phone screen against my chest. "Not all of us held on to our adorable college sweethearts like you did. And I'll let you observe, but don't you dare tell anyone what I'm doing or that I'm messing around on Bumble at work."

"Oh, please. All you do is work, work, work, and we're at a wedding magazine, after all. This is basically research, isn't it?" She winked.

"Good point," I said. "But still."

"Mum's the word." Amaya made a lip-zip motion with her hand.

I opened the app back up and allowed her to watch.

"Okay, so I've been messaging with a few guys on here who don't look like total sickos, but to be honest, I let a lot of my matches expire. I saved some of their profiles, but I tend to let things go stale. So even if I do swipe over, I don't do anything after that, and the guys move on."

"Well, that's going to get you nowhere fast," Amaya said as she eyed all the guys I was scrolling through. "Sounds like you need to get serious and do a better job following up—especially with one who looks like *that*."

Her eyes went wide, and she pointed to one of the guys who'd superswiped me in the past twenty-four hours and was awaiting a return swipe. It wasn't obvious at first, but the face that Amaya was now hovering over was none other than stupid Dominic.

"You've *got* to be kidding me." I swatted Amaya's hand away from my phone. "Don't you dare get any closer, Amaya. It's *Dom*, and this has to be some ridiculous joke. Either that or he's trying to get under my skin."

"I'm sure this is his comical attempt to break the tension between you two. I bet he found your profile and thought you'd find it funny," Amaya said. "Besides, you have to admit he's a fox."

I nearly choked on my own breath. "Well, I don't find it funny at all," I said. "It's embarrassing and weirding me out. That's a hard swipe left."

"You're not even going to see what he says?" Amaya scoffed, once again reaching for my phone.

"Um, no. And you aren't either," I replied, guarding the screen. "Look, here's a real option for you to fawn over."

I quickly found some old messages between me and a guy named Trey. "Don't pull any funny business, and I'll let you see," I said as I reluctantly handed her the phone.

"Well, he's no Dom," she said after reviewing some of our online conversation. "But I do see a lot of potential here. I approve. May I do the honors?"

"Go ahead," I said, rolling my eyes, glad at least someone was enjoying the dating app.

Amaya sent Trey a new message, and just like that, I had myself a date.

CHAPTER 6

My getting-back-in-the-saddle date would take place the following Friday night with "Trey from Charleston." Trey and I had been chatting casually for a while, before I took a Bumble break, and I liked a lot about him (at least on paper). After Amaya had sent her casual "Hi again!" from my account, he had replied within minutes and set up a dinner. It was time to take things off the app and into the real world.

My only real hesitation was that he was from Charleston, which also had a reputation for being a city full of single Southern men who never wanted to settle down. But Trey lived in Nashville now and worked for a healthcare start-up company. He was in his early thirties, which also seemed promising, and he had that Southern swoop hair thing going on that was annoyingly attractive to me for some reason. Oh, and he didn't wear pants tighter than mine. Another plus.

We agreed to meet at a bar in Midtown before heading out

for a meal at a location of his choosing. Of course, I requested that we meet somewhere very public for our first date, just to be sure I wasn't murdered (too much true crime in my life), and I was optimistic when he suggested one of my favorite spots. It had to be a good sign, right?

I pulled out an oldie-but-goody dress for the occasion—one that was effortlessly chic, but not too dressy, as I wasn't exactly sure where we'd be going for dinner after drinks.

I decided to head out a bit early, as I always wanted a minute to compose myself upon arrival. And getting a jump start on a cocktail never hurt to calm my nerves.

I gave myself one last glance in the rearview mirror. The freckles across my nose never faded, no matter what skin cream my mom gave me for Christmas. Those, combined with our fair coloring, gave me a look occasionally referred to as "cute." It used to bother me, but now as I crept closer to thirty, I was finally beginning to see the upside.

Feeling pretty good about my appearance, I took some deep breaths, walked inside, and ordered my go-to Ranch Water cocktail from the bartender at the Patterson House. I loved that this place was a bit hard to find and the lighting was ideal for first-date meetings. "Nothing makes a gal look better than candlelight"—one of the many tips bestowed upon me while I worked at the wedding planning firm in Dallas. Inside my dress, I also had a trusty panty liner in place under each armpit to make sure no sweat stains marred this warmer-than-usual late winter evening. I thought again about my former supervisor, Lottie. This trick was her go-to move. I wondered what she was doing right now and whether we'd ever be able to reconcile after everything that happened. Thankfully, before I really started spiraling about the past, Trey appeared.

"Well, well, well," said a rather sexy rasp over my left shoulder. "Am I finally meeting the elusive Claire in person?" He pulled back the barstool next to me.

I stood up and gave him a quick hug as I said hello, and I had to perch on my tiptoes to reach him. Trey smelled divine, and darn if he didn't look even better in person than he did in his photos.

He ran a hand through his sandy hair and smiled at me with a glint in his brown eyes. My stomach fluttered. I took another deep breath, reminding myself to play it cool even though I was now nervous—a feeling that was simultaneously off-putting and enjoyable.

"Sorry for ghosting you," I said. "Work's been crazy, but I'm glad we're finally able to get together."

"I almost gave up on you," he replied while motioning to the bartender to order a drink. "But I figured you'd come back around eventually. Either that or you wanted to let enough time go by to ensure I wasn't a stalker or murderer." He laughed.

"Well, that, too, of course," I said. "This whole online dating business isn't for the faint of heart."

"Tell me about it," he said after ordering a beer on tap. "I held out those first few years after college, thinking I'd never get on one of the dating sites, but here I am. It's the necessary evil of our generation, I guess."

"Totally agree." I took a sip of my drink. We just might have more in common than I thought.

"If nothing else, you can chalk this up to a free meal with a new friend," he said.

"At the very least," I replied with a smile, raising my glass to cheers his.

We spent the next hour chatting about our jobs, places we explored in Nashville, and a bit about our pasts. I skipped over the time I spent in Dallas and focused more on my time in college and then the past three or four years. Apparently, we were both looking for fresh starts in Nashville when we moved here.

Trey had only been here for about a year, but he said he was really enjoying his experience thus far. Of course he was. I had to suppress my cynical self from making a comment about how Nashville must've been heaven on earth for him. He had a high-paying job in a city full of bachelorette parties. But instead, I kept sipping my drink and nodding politely. He really was nice. I willed myself to give getting to know him a real shot.

After we finished our drinks, Trey asked if I was ready to head to dinner.

"Since I'm still relatively new to the city," he said, "I thought we could go somewhere I've been dying to try out but haven't had the chance to visit yet."

"Well, I'm embarrassed to say I haven't explored Nashville's restaurant scene much myself, so most places are new to me. Is it close by?"

Though I was reasonably comfortable with Trey at this point, I hoped we'd be able to walk wherever we were going for dinner. I wasn't about to get into a car alone with him.

He laughed. "Yes, it's actually around the corner, so we can walk out in the open air. I try to keep things easy and serial killer-free."

I laughed. Was I that transparent? This guy was good. And I was actually having a nice time with him. Clearly, I should've put myself out there more often.

We walked about two blocks to find ourselves in a line of people standing outside a white clapboard building. Below the restaurant's name, Fletcher's Feisty Fowl, a large red sign proclaimed: "Hotter than Yo' Mama's Chicken."

"Don't worry, I hear the line moves really fast," he said.

"Oh, I'm not worried about the line," I said, smiling at him. "I'm worried about the insanely hot chicken. You know this place has sent people to the hospital." I laughed.

"Absolutely. That's why we're here. I *love* spicy food. But they do have regular fried chicken, too, that's supposed to be amazing."

"This is very brave of you to attempt on a first date," I said as we inched forward in the line. "You'll definitely get bonus points for that."

"Oh, my goal was always to impress you by eating chicken so hot my tongue melts off," he said, laughing. "It's basically the modern-day version of showing you how tough I can be. Next time, we'll do CrossFit or I'll smash a beer can on my head."

"It's going to be very impressive, I'm sure."

The thirty minutes it took for us to move through the line and find a table inside flew by. So far, this date was a ten out of ten.

I also appreciated the casual setting of his restaurant choice. I'd been on dates in the past that felt awkward just because the restaurant was super fussy and quiet. This place was the exact opposite. It was packed with families and couples laughing and enjoying their food, and I felt no pressure to fill a silence. There were also a few people sweating and chugging beverages in what looked like an attempt to cool off their mouths. It was quite the scene.

We looked over the menus for a minute before the waitress took our orders. I went with the very safe option of chicken tenders and fries with "no heat," while Trey requested wings with Shut the Cluck Up sauce that came with a "burn warning," whatever that was. I waited for the waitress to try to talk him out of it, but she clearly didn't give a "cluck" about what patrons decided to order. "Eat at your own risk" was this place's motto, and she wasn't going to waste any time outside of taking down our order and moving on to the next.

"You sure you want to jump straight to the hottest option?" I asked. "Isn't this your first time here?"

"Yes," he said, "but I've eaten hot chicken at a few places like this in town, and so far, nothing's even made me sweat. I grew up eating the hottest sauces I could find on Southern food, so it takes a lot for me to think something's too spicy."

I appreciated his confidence. We both grabbed a beer from the bucket he'd also ordered and talked about Trey's favorite restaurants in Charleston, a city known for its cuisine.

"I think one of the big draws to Nashville besides my job is the food scene. So many of the places I loved to eat back home have opened up a location here. I'll have to take you to Husk next time," he said. "That place has the best brussels sprouts."

Next time. Trey was already thinking about our next date, which was a very good sign. If nothing else, I was thankful I still knew how to go on a date with someone. I sipped my beer, thinking this guy really had potential.

Ten minutes later the waitress was back with our baskets of food, some wet wipes, and a glass of milk.

"I won't need the milk," Trey told her.

"I'll leave it here just in case," she said. "Don't worry, we don't charge for it." She then turned and headed off to the next table.

Instead of trying in vain to talk people out of ordering their insanely hot sauce, she came prepared to deal with the aftermath. Smart lady.

I took a bite of my chicken, which was delicious, and tried not to act too interested in watching Trey eat his. After all, this place supposedly served the hottest chicken in the South. The kind that even seasoned hot-chicken connoisseurs couldn't handle more than a few bites of.

He took his first bite from one of the wings, then set it back down as he chewed.

"Not bad," he said. "It's actually really good."

"Wow," I replied. "Color me impressed."

I continued to eat my delicious and mild tenders as Trey ate two drumsticks at an alarming rate. Within seconds of him setting down the second piece, beads of sweat appeared on his brow. He started blinking. A lot.

"You okay?" I couldn't help smiling.

"Yeah," he said, taking a gulp of water. "It's definitely got some kick to it." He took another gulp.

His smile long gone, he was turning red. Sweat droplets started running down his face.

"Whew, it's definitely hotter than I expected," he said in a low voice, dabbing his hands with the wet wipe. "I just might not be able to astound you with my chicken-eating skills after all." He finally reached for the milk.

"Oh, don't worry about that," I said. "I can't believe you even took one bite. I can smell the sauce from here, and it's making my eyes water. Are you sure you're okay?"

"Yeah, I just need a minute," he gasped. He breathed heavily in and out of his mouth. Then he wiped his forehead with his napkin and continued to drink the entire glass of milk.

"Take your time," I said. "Do you want me to grab the waitress to bring you another glass of milk?"

"No, no . . . Actually, yeah, that would be great," Trey whispered.

The sweat was now pouring off his reddening face. He looked like he was doing everything humanly possible to hold back tears.

"I'm just going to hit the restroom really quickly." He stood up and almost ran across the restaurant before I could reply.

About twenty minutes went by, and Trey *still* hadn't returned. I decided to text him to check in on things but received no reply. What in the heck was I supposed to do? I'd finished my chicken and was sitting alone, drinking what was left of my beer, when our waitress appeared again.

"First date?" she asked.

"Yes, how'd you know?"

"Unfortunately, this happens about once a week."

My eyes widened. "*What* happens?"

"Some guy comes in here with a cute girl and thinks he can impress her by eating our special sauce. But he clearly can't handle it, and inevitably he ends up camped out in our restroom waiting on a clean pair of pants," she said way too casually.

"I'm sorry. *What?*" I hoped I'd misheard her.

"Yeah, I don't care what people say they can handle. That stuff is dangerous if you don't have the palate or the stomach for it," she said. "I used to try to warn people, but no one would listen. I'm not a betting woman, but if I was, I'd put down some serious cash that he's texted a friend from the bathroom to bring him a change of clothes. Then he'll make a run for it if he hasn't already. My guess is he'll be too mortified to ever talk to you again."

"You can't be serious."

"Serious as a heart attack," she said. "Which hopefully isn't what's happening to him in the bathroom right now. That's actually happened here too."

"That's horrible," I replied, now wide-eyed *and* confused.

"Listen, don't say anything, but dinner's on us," she said in a low voice. "You clearly weren't expecting your night to end like this, so don't worry about the bill."

"Does anyone *ever* expect their dinner to end like this?"

"No, but that's life for ya," she said. "Sometimes it's a home run and sometimes you crap your pants."

Is this really happening? I thought to myself as I opened up Bumble.

"Oh my gosh, you're right," I said to the waitress, who was now clearing our table. "He's already unmatched me. This is crazy."

"It happens," she said. "But there's plenty of fish in the sea, darlin'. Just make sure they don't order the cluck sauce next time."

"Don't worry, I will." I stood up and pulled out a twenty-dollar bill to give her. "Thanks for dinner, I guess."

I thought about waiting around a little longer or even knocking on the restroom door, but that felt super weird. So I gave up and walked back outside the restaurant, where there was still a long line of people waiting to get in. What the cluck was happening to my life?

CHAPTER 7

The Tennessee hills rolled outside my window the next morning. I wound through roads that were unpaved or seldom traveled only a decade ago. Franklin used to be a sleepy town. Mostly rural, the "neighborhoods" were acreage where country and Christian singers spread out on major tracts of land. But in the past dozen years, the area boomed with the rest of Nashville. Subdivisions sprang up for families of commuters. Now it resembled a hilly version of Plano or many of the other sprawling cities surrounding Dallas.

For once, traffic wasn't terrible in Franklin's historic downtown. It was early enough on a Saturday that the brunch crowd wasn't fully out. Otherwise, I'd never have found a parking spot. Frothy Monkey was one of my favorite places to post up in my East Nashville neighborhood, and the Franklin one was equally adorable.

I climbed the brick steps of the converted Craftsman, pushed open the door, and inhaled deeply. Long before I ever developed a taste for coffee, the smell was one of my favorites. Mom never drank the stuff, instead surviving on willpower and Diet Coke, but Dad always did. It would forever remind me of early mornings in the kitchen at home. He'd eat a bowl of Raisin Bran cereal, drink the better part of a pot of coffee, and read the *New York Times*. I'd sit on a counter stool and read the comics with my bowl of Cap'n Crunch while he pointed out stories that would impact the global markets. I'd seldom felt so respected or included in his grown-up world. Alas.

My friend Jill waved from our favorite corner table. Her brown ringlets bobbed as she sat back down to read the specials. I squeezed in next to her, gave her a quick hug, and pulled up an online menu.

The warm, wooden space immediately felt homey. I ordered my usual French toast and an iced latte. A double, to recover from yesterday.

The waiter was cute in the typical Nashville way: scruffy beard, flannel shirt, worn-in boots, slightly unruly hair. He set the latte down in front of me. "Here you go, ma'am."

Every time that happened, I could feel the collagen in my face wither and crack just a little more.

We grabbed brunch one Saturday every month or so when I wasn't working. Jill had two young kids, so it was usually all she could commit to, and I understood. The dormitory potluck gods paired us freshman year, and we'd managed to not kill each other and even remain friends. When she married her high school boyfriend, Chip, during our junior year, I thought she was insane and that I'd never see her again. But she managed to graduate on time and stay involved in my life. And I hadn't really made any other friends since I moved back. Nada. So I forgave her for occasionally bailing on brunch for baby emergencies—and willingly drove to Franklin. Today she was all ears and ready for another mimosa.

It took her a few minutes to regain her composure after I recounted my "hot chicken date" from the night before. I knew she often felt like she was listening to a reality TV show with all the stories I told from work and my online dating disasters. But once she'd stopped laughing, I brought up the real news I wanted to tell her about: Lucy's engagement.

"I'm really happy for Lucy. Truly. Overjoyed, even. Not to make this about me, but for a moment, can we? Could there just be one thing that I get to do first or better than my sisters?"

"What do you mean?" Jill asked sympathetically. "I know they're both a bit aggressively accomplished, but you're also very different people."

"It's just one more way that she's living up to expectations or leaving me behind. No matter what I do, no matter how much I excel, they always one-up me. It's never enough. I've eaten Evelyn's dust since I learned to crawl, but Lucille has always been the darling baby. I'm proud of her, and so are our parents, but she's almost got a law degree and a brilliant, kind fiancé to match. And I have . . ." I shrugged my shoulders in defeat.

"Gotta tell you, the fiancé or husband isn't the be-all and end-all. Chip and I are good and happy—I don't mean anything by that. But it's also not a guarantee that the rest of your life will be rosy. Or even that you've ticked all the boxes on personal goals. Quite the opposite, in fact."

"I know. It's also that, well, it's a *wedding*. In Dallas. Even if my old company doesn't plan the event, I'm sure I'll know some of the vendors. My name is mud there."

"Oh." The final piece clicked for her.

Jill was my only friend in Nashville—or anywhere, really—who knew the details of my departure from Dallas. "That's pretty rough on top of everything. But you'll just have to get through it as best you can. It's Lucy's big day, and you can cheer for her like the amazing big sister I know you are."

"Thanks for the pep talk, Mom."

"Ha, don't mention it. I've been practicing with Reeve, who is at a particularly challenging stage."

"Gosh, I love that girl. She's a firecracker."

"Reminds me of someone I know." Jill smiled at me. "Next time, I'll sacrifice the kid-free time and you can come over to see them."

"I'd like that a lot."

"The last few years have been good for you, C. I've watched you come a long way. Now, you still can be a little flaky or a little ruthless, depending on the day. But I still love you, and you're not bouncing around all the time like you did in college."

She was right. Dropping classes I didn't think I'd ace, dropping potential boyfriends like bad habits. I was usually either throwing in the towel or going down in flames.

"You're all or nothing," she continued. "You win, you quit before you can fail, or you find a reason why something won't work. You switched majors more than anyone I knew. You did most group projects single-handedly."

"I mean, I just wanted to make sure everything was done correctly. I was being nice."

"Sure . . . You dropped out of student government entirely instead of getting elected to a position you didn't want. You even tried to manipulate the intramural system so your volleyball team stood the best chance of winning. Want me to go on?"

"No, I get it. And I maintain that our coed team should have been in that division all along." I sniffed.

"But you've stuck with this magazine, even as it's gotten bleak. College Claire would have bailed at the first sign of lay-offs."

"College Claire had other options to fall back on!" I recalled just how expansive my safety net had been with a pang.

"Be that as it may, I'm proud of you. Now, tell me about how working with this Brides' Man guy is going. I love his stuff. All the other moms in Reeve's class follow him."

"Why? Aren't they all married already?"

"Of course, but it's suburban mom catnip. Hot guy talks about weddings and shows us pretty details. Lots of wedding advice still makes for good hostessing tips. And did I mention he's funny? And hot? I might be married, but I'm not dead. Need I go on?"

"No, I get it. And it sounds like you've already done your research on him."

"No, I have an overactive fantasy life and need to know *from you* whether he lives up to it in person. The hookup line after school is long, and we moms have got to come prepared to chat about something."

I cracked up. "I still don't understand why Nashvillians call it 'hookup' instead of 'carpool' or 'pickup' like the rest of the world. And it's especially unsettling in the context of *children*, but that's beside the point. Listen, he's certainly charming and slick. But he's also got this goofy side and a weird sense of humor." I recalled his imaginary game in the airplane and lack of composure at the wedding. "He hasn't ever done planning or worked with brides, but he knows his stuff. He guesstimated the cost of our first bride's wedding dress—and even bet me five dollars he was right."

"Definitely a goofball."

"Yes, but he's also so annoying." I needed to keep my head in the game. He'd stolen my role on this documentary and was getting credit for my idea. We could work together but shouldn't be friends. The magazine wasn't handing out promotions these days—or bonuses, for that matter. It was every person for him- or herself.

We caught up about a few more friends from college and the new boutique in downtown Franklin. Then Jill dashed home to relieve Chip before his softball game.

❧ ❧ ❧

I used the following week at work to get ahead of things, as I was scheduled to leave for Collins and Lucy's engagement party in Dallas on Friday. Apparently, Mom planned their party prior to

Collins even popping the question so that it could take place the following weekend.

This meant I'd be traveling to Dallas on short notice. I had a few vacation days saved up thanks to a lack of both funds and plans to go anywhere, and Michelle was happy to approve all PTO as long as I turned in any pending assignments before I left. Not the vacation I'd hoped for, but I didn't want to miss Lucy's party.

And eventually, I'd have to go back home. The pandemic had given me ample excuse not to travel, so I'd kept my distance, aside from a few days at Christmases. Lucy's wedding was as good a reason as any to go home and start rebuilding bridges.

"What am I going to do here while you're gone?" I heard Dom creepily ask over my shoulder as I checked my flight status online.

I really needed to be more aware of people standing behind me.

"Not sure you'll survive without me?" I asked, turning my chair around to face him.

"Probably not, but I'll do my best," he said. "There's some hot chicken festival this weekend that sounds promising. We don't get many weekends off from this docuseries, so I thought I'd go try it out."

Not hot chicken again. I'd literally just recovered from that disaster.

"Well, be careful," I said. "That stuff can be deadly. I thought I liked spicy food, but some of the hot chicken in this town will take the skin off the roof of your mouth. And I've heard it can have . . . other adverse effects."

"Like what?" he asked.

"Just trust me," I said. "I know from experience, thankfully not firsthand, but close enough. Start out with mild, *maybe* medium sauce, and see how it goes. Don't even think about trying the hottest option. Not sure how well an influencer does when they're unable to speak or sweating to death on camera."

"That might make a good live stream." He pinched the cleft on his chin while pretending to mull it over.

"Just come prepared to sweat—and bring milk."

And possibly a change of pants, my friend.

"Good to know. I'll start slow and work my way up," he said, changing the subject. "Are you excited to go home and see your friends and family for the weekend?"

"Yes and no. I told you, it's complicated. But yeah, I guess so," I replied.

"No family's perfect," he said. "I mean, look at the people we've been interviewing. And, of course, the Gravinos have our own set of problems. Italians are hotheaded people, after all."

"Hot chicken for hot Italians," I fired back.

"Are you calling me hot?" Dom smirked.

Zoinks.

"Don't flatter yourself," I said as I turned quickly back around. "You know what I mean."

"Yeah, *okay*," he said sarcastically. "Well, be safe, try to have a good time, and I'll catch you on Monday. Maybe when you're back you can explain why you rejected me on Bumble."

I could feel the color drain from my face.

"Oh, that," I said, annoyed he even mentioned it. "I just get on there every now and then for fun, but I'm not seriously dating anyone on there. And you're ridiculous for trying to—"

"Slow down there, partner." He held out his hand and laughed. "I was just trying to get you to loosen up a bit and see if I could lure you into drinks together. I'm still waiting for you to give me the official tour of the city, and when your profile popped up after I changed my location, I had to swipe right. I'd never do something as horrific to you as swipe left." He flashed that annoyingly charming grin of his.

"Well, clearly I have no problem swiping left on you, and for the sake of a healthy work relationship, I suggest you just send me a proper email or text next time you really want to book a Claire Sommers Tour. My Bumble account is off-limits, and now you're going to have to earn that drink," I said, trying to beat him at his own game.

"Fair enough. We can see about that when you're back," he said, strutting off like he owned the place. Curse the confidence of this man.

I hit Send on my last email for the week and started prepping mentally for my return home. It got a little easier each time, but a pit of anxiety and dread still opened up in my stomach every time I packed my bags for Dallas. I used to feel like I belonged, even if I wasn't the toast of the town, and now I tiptoed around, trying to blend into the background. I needed to prove myself to everybody again, show them I wasn't a failure, that I could succeed along with the rest of my family.

Coming back felt like holding up a mirror, one I studiously avoided most of the time, one that forced me into facing myself and my missteps. I knew I'd probably never be able to truly go home until I was able to stare down my past self, unflinchingly. In the meantime, though, I'd just pack a carry-on full of trepidation and regret—and try not to miss my flight.

CHAPTER 8

My Uber pulled up to the imposing facade of our parents' French château in Preston Hollow. We'd grown up here, but somehow, as I got bigger, the house seemed to grow as well. *More intimidating and imposing with age*, I mused, unbuckling.

As a child, I had no concept of the rarity of having several thousand square feet of nooks and crannies to play hide-and-go-seek in. I briefly considered my miniscule closet back in Nashville and sighed. The stone facade loomed overhead as I grabbed my carry-on from the trunk and rattled it across driveway cobblestones.

I hadn't been home in months, and it was honestly the last place I wanted to be. But I wanted to support Lucy. Thus, I went.

Before I could reach the front door, it swung open. Lucy barreled out, enthusiastic as ever. "Claire! Claire!" She wrapped me in a hug. Her strawberry-blonde hair smelled, as always, of Dior. I smiled as I pulled away.

"Let me see it!" She giddily obliged, extending her left hand so I could gawk in person. "Lucy, it's magnificent. So unique."

"Thank you! These are Gran's amethysts, and here on the side are his mother's diamonds." I gazed a minute longer, then hauled my bag up the steps.

We stepped inside the marbled entry. Atop the double staircase, our mother looked down on me, pausing a moment. She smiled and descended.

"Darling, how was your flight? I can only imagine how positively horrific DFW can be. I haven't flown out of there in *years*."

Not all of us have access to a jet, Mother. "Well, American runs a direct that's super inexpensive last-minute. And it wasn't too bad."

She visibly cringed before pasting on a smile. "We're just grateful you made it." Mom motioned for me to leave the bag in the corner so Carmen, their housekeeper, could carry it to my bedroom. I dutifully followed her to the family room while Lucy resumed her gushing.

Ah, my mother. Eleanor Hendricks Sommers. The kind of woman who held an actual position at our family business, all while chairing multiple charity events each season and serving on as many nonprofit foundations' boards as possible. The kind of woman who never perspired in August in Texas and would die before owning orthopedic footwear. The kind of woman who could be gracious and loving, sure, but was more often terrifying.

I settled into my favorite tufted chaise while Lucy curled into the sofa, still chattering. Mom headed toward the kitchen, presumably to order a midafternoon cocktail from the staff, while

Lucy filled me in on all the details. Collins had proposed in the backyard next to the lotus pond, Lucy's favorite place in the world. As a child, she could often be found there gazing at the reflective water or catching tadpoles, much to Mom's chagrin. "He'd asked Daddy, you know, and I am still shocked he managed to keep it a secret for weeks."

"Yeah, I can imagine that the only thing harder for Dad to do than keep a secret will be to give his baby away in marriage."

"Hey! That's not fair. I mean, I *am* the favorite." It was our longtime joke, but it was also rather true.

"It's not exactly a tough contest," I said without thinking.

"Hey, don't talk about my big sisters that way . . . But if it helps, you've always been *my* favorite," Lucy whispered conspiratorially.

"Ha, thanks for trying to cheer me up and salvage the shreds of my dignity."

"No, I mean it." She took a deep breath and turned to face me fully. "This wasn't exactly how I'd envisioned asking you, but would you be my maid of honor, Claire?"

"Aw, Luce. Are you serious?" I felt my throat constricting with unexpected emotion. I tamped it down to squeak out the words. "I'd be honored, of course, but why me? Evelyn is so much more . . ."

"More what?"

"More the kind of person who knows how to be a maid or matron of honor."

"Oh, please," replied Lucy. "She's wound up tighter than a tick. Between you and me, maybe starting her own family will finally make her happy and she'll relax for once. Her uptight vibe is not what I'm looking for. But you—you've always been adventurous."

"That sounds like a polite way of saying 'inconsistent,'" I quipped, feeling calmer and back to myself. "Are you sure you want to give me that kind of responsibility? What if I blow it? I don't think Evelyn has ever really messed anything up—not even something small."

"Of the three of us, you've always been the one who was most able to do her own thing. I admire how you've gone off, started over away from all this."

"I think a lot of what you're seeing isn't succeeding. It's called self-preservation."

"Maybe, but I've always respected you, sis. You're the one in all my favorite childhood memories. You're the one I choose to call. You're the one I want standing up there next to me. Evie will be there too, of course, but you're certainly the one I want planning my bachelorette party. Hands down."

"Oh, that is *for sure*." I guffawed, grateful for the lighter tone. "I would be honored to stand by you, Lucy. Thank you for always being there for me. I'm supposed to be the one who's there for you, and I can't wait to get the chance. I won't let you down."

Lucy got up and squeezed next to me on the chaise. We gave each other a giant hug, and I found myself getting surprisingly misty again. What was wrong with me? I *never* cried.

"Okay, enough of all that," I said, shaking my head and pulling myself together. "This weekend is all about *you*. So what's the latest on planning? I realize that's the most annoying thing—you get engaged and people instantly start asking when and where it is."

"Actually . . ." She turned to face me. "We're doing it here. In June."

"Wow, that's really quick! You sure?"

"Yes, I've always wanted to get married here, you know. Plus, there was no way I'd get Evelyn on a plane in her condition." She rolled her eyes. "Once the baby arrives, we all know it's going to be all about her 24/7, so we have to squeeze in my little ol' wedding before her due date. And with so many vendors still booked for a year or two out, it just made sense."

The postpandemic boom was no longer so intense, but it was still tough to plan a party of any size these days, let alone a wedding.

"You're not pregnant, are you?"

"No! I'll leave that to Evelyn. Just excited. And I'm tired of waiting for the perfect time. I'm already twenty-six. Let's do this."

"And after Evelyn's massive wedding, everybody has gone through the drill once, so that makes it easier too."

She flashed one of her winning grins. "Exactly. It won't be tough to pull together in a few months."

As ever, I knew that everyone from our family to the florist would move heaven and earth to make what Lucy wanted a reality.

Like summoning Voldemort, we heard Evelyn's voice echoing through the house.

"We're back here, Evie!" Lucy said cheerily.

Her heels clicked across the cool marble as she stuck her head in. "Hi, Luce. Claire, good to see you. Are you wearing that tonight?"

"I just landed, geez." One of my nicer sweatshirts, it was at least a lululemon—but Evie clearly had *thoughts*.

"I didn't know! Just wanted to make sure you were, um . . . comfortable."

"Right. On that note, I'm going to get ready. I'll see you guys in a few." I gave Lucy another squeeze, then walked past Evelyn without so much as a side hug. We always managed to start off on the wrong foot.

We were the Sommers Sisters. Insert any number of "Summer Girls" jokes here. But the truth was, the Dallas society pages loved to track our adolescence and early adulthood, odd as that may sound. We were a powerful trio, led by Evelyn, the shark. Evelyn had gone to Ole Miss (like Mom) after Hockaday. Instead of simply staying with the family business, she ventured into commercial real estate and now owned three restaurants and a boutique hotel in the metroplex. She and Ford were expecting their first baby, and yet she still managed to run the businesses and walk in four-inch heels. She was a one-woman machine. It was like she understood the Sommers family assignment—and then went for extra credit. I was always merely trying not to fail.

I'd long ago accepted that people—well, most people—weren't going to like me. So I preferred being admired or respected, even feared. I never needed many friends. I wasn't usually outright mean or cutthroat like Evelyn. But in the past, I had to admit I'd been more like her than sweet Lucy. Which is probably why Evelyn and I had never been too close. Everything came so easily to Evelyn. And to Lucy, who was successful—and well-liked. Evie didn't seem to care. The first couple of times I tried as a child to do the same activity as her, I wasn't as good (mostly due to our ages, of course). But then I figured I'd go find my own thing to be good at. But instead of finding it, I just bounced from thing to thing, job to job, city to city.

I trudged up the stairs to my childhood bedroom. Most of my personal knickknacks had been taken down and boxed up so that the room could double as a space for guests. But the furniture and faded wallpaper remained from when fourteen-year-old Claire picked them.

The home I grew up in was something you might expect to find in an F. Scott Fitzgerald novel. Domed ceilings with ornate moldings, inlaid marble floors, and more powder rooms than people. It was a small palace. Mom loved French architecture and décor and would take trips overseas to find unique antiques. There were two exterior swimming pools, a tennis court, a pavilion, plus a rose garden, Italian stepped stone fountains, and grounds galore. A branch of the Trinity River flowed near stone-covered walking paths, swaths of carefully tended grass in green spaces waving nearby.

The estate might feel like a museum to some, but I didn't think of it like that as a child. To me, it was just home. Lucy and I would roller-skate through the main living rooms while our nanny raced after us, chastising us about scratched oak floors. Evelyn just watched from the landing, but at least she never told on us. We'd have hour-long pillow fights under our canopy beds and build forts out of silk pillows and damask duvet coverlets. But our parents didn't care. I didn't realize it then, but looking back now, as posh as they were, they still wanted us to feel comfortable in our own home—provided we didn't scuff the furniture or behave like ruffians in public. I loved them for that.

Like Tennessee, Texas continued to be a magnet for people from all over the country. Especially wealthy ones hoping to avoid income tax without having to live in Florida full-time. We'd been in the state for three generations and watched the number of billionaires jump to include the likes of Elon Musk and Stanley Kroenke. Sure, we weren't quite the Basses, the Perots, or the Waltons, but my parents certainly ran in their set.

I understood why, with all the attention, my parents worked so hard to control the narrative about our family. When the Bush girls (whom we *adored*) made the news for some poor behavior at UT, Evelyn was just about to start high school. Mom took notes. Public misbehavior was out of the question. She wouldn't stand for any embarrassment. Until I came along, I guess.

Starting in adolescence, I started to feel the magnifying lens. Cotillion, deb balls, bar and bat mitzvahs at the Adolphus Hotel. The outside world and its expectations started to encroach on our personal space. (As if we didn't already have enough expectations coming from inside the family.) It became more difficult for me to deal with not getting what I wanted, what I worked for, what we were taught to value: approval, success, pride, wealth, social standing. I'd gone to great lengths for them and come up short. I still wasn't sure how to navigate back from that.

After freshening up in my childhood bathroom—which was the size of my entire Nashville apartment—I put on an old Missoni dress and a pair of YSL heels, then braced myself for intense family time. Hopefully Evie would approve of my glam-up. I wanted to fly as under the radar as possible while in town. I was going to nail the supportive older-sister role and then get the heck back to Nashville.

❦ ❦ ❦

I rode with my mother and her driver over to the event. Dad would be coming straight from the office and meeting us all at the venue. The car ride was short and silent. Seeing Mom made me think of my late gran. She created the Sommers woman mold. She and her husband started the concrete business all those years ago, and we were now all (well, I used to be) enjoying the fruits of their labor.

I couldn't take not knowing any longer. I finally mustered the strength to ask. "Mom . . . who's planning the wedding?"

She glanced at me, surprise evident on her face. A rare hint of . . . not sympathy but something almost gentle. *Almost.* "Oh, sweetie, I thought you would just assume Cedric was doing it. He did Evelyn's wedding. He did all your deb and graduation events, our thirtieth anniversary party, and my sixtieth. Of course he'll do Lucille's wedding."

"Of. Course." I gritted my teeth.

Cedric Montclair Celebrations, run by the eponymous Cedric, was the best event planning company in town—as well as my former employer. Known for inventive florals, impeccable designs, and precise planning, the company was one of the biggest in the South and acquiring clients around the country and the world. It was my first job out of school, thanks to Cedric's close relationship with my mother. And, in short, it hadn't ended well for me.

When everything blew up with Cedric—that is, when I blew up everything with his company—a "morality clause" was triggered in my trust. My parents cut me off from their support too. I'd be forty years old now before I could even petition for access to that money again—and even then it was pending trustee approval. I didn't really understand how all that worked, just that I didn't get it now or possibly ever. I know, I know, poor little rich girl. But as much as the whole situation sucked, I was proud of myself for showing I could make it on my own. It felt good, even. I just hoped I wouldn't be looking for another job if my project with Dom didn't work out. The pay wasn't great, but I really enjoyed what I did, and I'd stayed with it longer than anything else in my life. I wasn't ready to move on yet.

As we turned into the familiar circular drive, I was snapped back into the present.

"Come now. Cedric and I have discussed the matter, and it shouldn't be a problem," she said, all back to business. "Your attendance, I mean. He knows you're my daughter, of course, but if you could just stay out of his way and mostly out of sight, it should be fine."

I didn't have any room to quibble with her take, but I did love that in this moment her concern was for Cedric's comfort and emotional needs.

"I'm happy to do my part, but it might be a bit hard to stay *out of sight* as the maid of honor." I sounded a bit snarkier than I meant to.

"Well, yes," Mom said, not really addressing my point.

"Believe it or not, I'm not back to do anything other than show support for Lucy and the family." The car continued down the drive, nearing the Hotel Crescent Court. "I'll do my best not to humiliate anyone on this visit—or in the future, for that matter."

"Oh, Claire," Mom said. "You know we don't think that."

But I was out of the car and heading toward the entrance to the club before she could say anything else. I was rattled and needed to compose myself. Tonight was about Lucille, and the last thing I wanted right now was to draw additional attention to myself.

The engagement party was held at the Crescent Club. Our parents had been longtime members of the private club, located on the seventeenth floor.

I took a deep breath as I stepped into the expansive lobby. So many event-related memories were made here too. I looked around quickly to make sure there weren't any unwanted familiar faces before heading to the elevator. All clear.

Mom took her time catching up with me, and we took the elevator to the wood-paneled room framed by angled windows. Outside, the Dallas skyline glittered.

In classic Cedric fashion, no detail was overlooked, even for a "simple" engagement party. He had set the stage for the tone and scheme of Lucy's entire wedding suite of events. As usual, he'd nailed it. Every last detail looked and felt like something she would have handpicked. And as someone who'd voluntarily shared a room with her for years, I should know. Small children feel a bit lost in an eleven-bedroom house, so we often opted for slumber parties.

The décor was the perfect contrast to the club's existing dark wood walls and coffered ceilings. Cedric's team used accents of gold to tie in with the space, but lightened things up with oodles of ivory and blush flowers. They highlighted the massive arched window overlooking the twinkling lights of downtown by flanking it with two equally massive blooming dogwood trees. Where he found blooming dogwoods this time of year in Dallas was a mystery, but that was all part of his magic. Dining tables were draped in champagne-colored velvet linen, and atop every table was an ivory urn overflowing with blush antique garden roses. They reminded me of the roses that grew in our garden at home, which was certainly on purpose. Twinkling candles in glass sleeves covered every surface, and next to the bar stood a sparkling tower of champagne glasses. The enchanting space was truly fit for our family's little princess.

Thankfully, Cedric and his top planners had already left the venue, and Evelyn was kind enough to let me know as much when we arrived. Maybe impending motherhood was making her soft. Still, I relaxed a bit, knowing I wouldn't run into any of the ghosts from my wedding planning past tonight.

My guess was that there were at least a hundred people here, which felt quite large for an engagement party. Though, given the size of Evelyn's wedding, this was just par for the course. Lucy's guest count for her own wedding would be similar. Nothing like a casual celebration for your closest five hundred friends. I knew almost everyone at the party, except for Collins's set, and I managed to chitchat my way through most of the evening without any real discomfort.

Evelyn appeared next to me, drink in hand. "How are you holding up?"

"Oh, well, hello to you too," I said. "Are you ready to be friends now?"

"Don't be dramatic," she replied. "You know I'm your friend. I'm your big sister. I'm just coming over to check on you and see if you're having a good time. It's nice to have you home."

"I'd ask if you were drunk, but I know that's a mocktail," I said, giving her a smile. "Did Lucy put you up to this?"

"Absolutely not." She paused. "Well, maybe. But I'd have done it anyway. With Lucy's wedding on the horizon and the first grandchild coming soon, it's time we all put the past behind us and enjoy all the celebrating ahead of us." She rubbed her belly.

"That's all I want, Evie," I said in a tone that I hoped she felt was genuine. "I hate all the tension these past few years. I know I have a lot of things to work out, but your support would mean the world to me. We all know you basically run the show around here."

With Evelyn, flattery got me everywhere.

"Well, that's sweet, Claire," she said, still stroking her bump. What was it with pregnant women and touching their own bellies? "I've got your back—as long as you stay in line." She flashed a maniacal grin.

There she is. Supportive, but with a catch. I'd take what I could get.

"Are you ready for your speech tonight?" She sipped her pink drink.

"I'm sorry, what?" I asked, stunned.

"You're the maid of honor," she said with a hint of an edge. "The best man is going to say something, and we all think you should too."

"Who is 'we all'? And it would've been nice to know about this before right this moment," I said.

"I thought Lucy told you. But don't worry. You're a professional writer now, so this will be a breeze."

"First, no, Lucy did not tell me. Second, while I appreciate that you consider me a professional writer, that still doesn't make me feel confident about standing in front of everyone and giving a toast."

"Ugh, do you just want me to do it?" asked Evie.

I knew full well this was an empty offer, but she'd get credit for it anyway.

"No, just give me a minute to compose myself and think of something to say. I'll figure it out," I said.

"Well, at least you look great," she replied.

"I'm sorry, was that another compliment for me coming from those perfect lips of yours?"

"Don't push it, Claire," she said. "We're doing well tonight. No need to get snarky now."

Mom must have told her what I'd said in the car. I honestly didn't care. What I said was true. I didn't want to be invisible anymore. I didn't want to stand out either—just be a normal presence in the family again. Was that too much to ask?

"Fair enough," I said. "I'm going to grab a glass of champagne and get ready for my impromptu toast. Say a prayer for me, Evelyn."

I hated to admit it, but Dom immediately came to mind as I headed to the bar to order some liquid courage. He was annoying most of the time, but I bet he excelled at speeches and one-liners. His quick wit would've come in handy tonight.

Begrudgingly, I pulled out my phone and sent him a quick text.

Need a quick favor if you're free.

He replied almost immediately. Well, hey there. What's up? Ask away.

At my sister's engagement party, and apparently I'm supposed to say something brief to everyone since I'm officially the MOH. Any good jokes or tips you could pass along? What would "The Brides' Man" suggest?

Before he could reply I added:

And don't let this go to your head. I'm only asking because I'm in a bit of a pinch.

A moment later: Haha. Don't worry. I promise not to hold this over your head. I may make you buy me a drink, but then we can call it even.

You've got a deal.

He fired back: Okay then. Keep it short and simple. Don't try to be funny by telling any inside jokes. No one cares. And don't self-deprecate. That also falls flat on an audience. Speak from the heart and say how you feel about her. You can't go wrong with being sincere.

Thanks, Dom. I think I can manage that.

I shoved my phone back in my bag. With champagne glass in hand, I found Mom, who informed me that toasts would start in half an hour. At least I had a little time to pull some thoughts together. I'd given a toast at Evelyn's rehearsal dinner, but Lucy did it with me, and we'd practiced it for weeks. There was no way we could stumble through anything at Evelyn's wedding and live to tell about it, so we had to be prepared. And as a planner, I'd witnessed plenty of examples of what *not* to say at the mic. This was a different story. This was just an engagement party, so I'd keep things short and sweet like Dom said. For once, I was thrilled to have him around to lean on for advice.

I hadn't always been the family black sheep, but I had a long history of being the outlier. No matter how hard I tried, and I sure gave it my all, I was never quite the pleaser.

They used to say Evelyn came out of the womb organized. She probably had a full head of blonde hair, and even then, not a strand was out of place. One family story purported that she used to organize and coordinate her hair bows and pacifier ribbons as a toddler, and the only fits she threw were when someone tried to make her leave the house mismatched. By that age, I was doing well to have my shoes on the right feet.

And Lucille, a classic baby of the family, came out cooing and charming the pants off everyone who knew her. She couldn't leave the grocery store or go practically anywhere without strangers giving her gifts, from suckers to stuffies to knick-knacks. My mom started keeping a bin in the car to throw things in, and once it got full, she'd take it to Goodwill.

I was always smartest in my class but never especially popular, a decent athlete but never quite the all-star. It felt like every area of our lives was a competition, and we needed to be winners—whatever that meant. I put pressure on myself to try to find the greatest friends, boyfriends, college, and career, but always came up short. Evie and Lucy were always "winning" in life, and when I couldn't be the best at something, I'd start to spiral. A person can only come up short so many times before they stop trying entirely. It's pure self-preservation.

Regardless, my sisters had found their well-suited, successful careers and picture-perfect partners. And I, well, was trying to work my way out of the hole I'd dug. Trying to stay afloat financially. Trying to save my job and my colleagues. Trying to someday find love.

But tonight was about my sister. And genuinely celebrating her happiness.

I felt my phone vibrate and pulled it out to see one additional text from Dom:

Take a deep breath and remember to speak from the
heart. You're a great writer, and from what I've seen,
you've got great people skills too. You've got this.

It was hard to loathe someone so positive and supportive. I
gave his message the blue thumbs-up, then put my phone back
in my clutch.

Clink-clink-clink! Dad firmly struck the side of his cocktail
glass with the end of a spoon, signaling to everyone he was
about to speak. Mom stood by his side as—to no surprise—he
gushed about their precious baby girl and how thrilled he and
Eleanor were to welcome Collins into the family. I wondered
how it made Evelyn feel when Dad wiped away a tear on his
cheek, given that he wasn't even misty-eyed at her wedding
events. Come to think of it, he did walk pretty fast down the
aisle and shouted an emphatic "I do!" when the minister asked
who was giving Evelyn away. I choked back a chuckle at the
memory.

He wrapped things up by giving Lucille, who was also crying,
a massive hug. I needed to remember to bring extra handker-
chiefs with me to the wedding if the waterworks were already
starting. Dad gave me a wink and a hug as he passed me the
microphone and stood back with Mom. Maybe a wedding was
just what this family needed to bring us all back together. I took
a deep breath, took a sip of champagne, then began.

"Hi there, everyone. For those who don't know me, my name
is Claire, and I'm one of Lucy's big sisters and the maid of honor.

Well, I'm probably the maid of *dis*honor, but tonight's not about me," I said, hoping for a polite giggle or two.

Nope. The room was silent, and my palms started sweating profusely.

Okay, Dom was right. Clearly self-deprecation wasn't the way to start things off, even though at least half these people must know about my salty past.

"Anyway, I've had the privilege of knowing Lucy since the day she was born, and I couldn't be happier for my baby sister and her fiancé. Lucy's my best friend, and I've never seen anyone make her as happy as Collins does."

Finally, a few warm smiles broke out.

"If anyone deserves to find love, it's Lucy. I have no doubt this will be an epic union, and knowing my mom, an epic wedding as well," I said. A few laughs peppered the room.

Okay, wrap things up on a high note, Claire.

"Collins," I said, now looking toward him, "Lucy is a true ray of sunshine, and the fact that you get to enjoy the warmth of her glow for the rest of your life makes you the luckiest man on earth."

Collins smiled and tipped his glass toward me. Lucy was beaming.

"So now, everyone, raise your glasses, and let's toast to the happy couple. To Lucille and Collins!"

"To Lucille and Collins!" everyone shouted.

Lucy ran over and threw her arms around me.

"Thank you so much for that, sis," she whispered in my ear.

"Anything for you, Lucy. I really am so happy for you."

The best man was up next, and his toast consisted of him ragging on Collins and making a fool of himself, which was fine by me. I was thrilled to be out of the spotlight for the time being.

I ducked into the ladies' restroom to send Dom a thank-you text. I had to give the Yankee some serious credit. I'd basically acted like an ice princess toward him since he'd arrived in Nashville. It wasn't his fault I had to share my assignment for the magazine. In fact, there was no way I'd realistically ever be able to pull off the documentary pitch without his help. I still wasn't going to tell him that, but I could, at the very least, thank him for his advice.

> Hey, thanks again for your help tonight. I took your advice, and the speech went smoothly. I'm sorry if I've been super stressed lately. It's just dumb family stuff and clearly there's a lot going on at work. Anyway, I appreciate it.

Perfect. No need for more details, just clearing the air a bit and thawing some of my intentionally icy demeanor. *Wow*, I thought. *Lucy's sheer happiness and positive vibes must really be rubbing off on me.*

He texted back:

> Of course! Happy to help my favorite work-wife anytime. Hope you had a blast and received a standing ovation for your toast. I'll hold you to that drink. ;)

I almost typed "Looking forward to it," but decided instead on *Sounds good! See you at work* with a slew of dumb emojis like a plane, a silly face, and high-five hands. For a moment I wondered how I managed to write for a living when I could barely handle a text conversation.

CHAPTER 9

We spent Saturday and half of Sunday poring over Lucy's Pinterest board of ideas, lounging by our parents' pool, and thumbing back issues of *Piece of Cake*, *Brides*, and *Martha Stewart Weddings*. It had taken my move a little farther north to understand how bizarre it was to swim outdoors in March. Yet another "typical" part of my upbringing to add to the list, but I wasn't going to complain about the much-needed vitamin D.

And after a late-night flight back to Nashville on Sunday, there was no way I could make it through Monday morning on one cup of coffee. I dragged myself into the breakroom for a 10:00 A.M. round two only to find our copy editor, Nancy, cornering Kevin, my senior editor, and HR Janice.

In past generations, *Piece of Cake* had boasted a massive staff of award-winning journalists. We poached writers from places like *Southern Living*, *Martha Stewart Living*, and even *Vogue*. Our offices were a destination for writers who wanted a satisfying journalism career but a nice, somewhat affordable place to raise a family. (At least, that's how Kevin described it to me at a depressing going-away party after the last round of layoffs.) While that was far away from my current life stage, I was beginning to see the appeal.

The trio before me looked like the last ones standing after an apocalypse. They'd managed to survive, despite it all.

Nancy had been at the magazine for about twenty years. Her husband was a teacher, so they always relied on her income as well. But she was the kind of woman who had no significant aspirations to move on or up. She had reached the highest level she likely would and would continue to work at *Piece of Cake* until another wave of layoffs wiped her out. That, or until she retired to their long-held condo off 30A. Whichever came first.

"You should try it," Nancy said. "I started listing our house on VRBO sometimes, whenever we're down at the condo. Just for a little extra, you know." Her salt-and-pepper bob swayed as she nodded.

I casually put in my coffee pod, not wanting to interrupt their conversation. Over time, I'd sussed out the dynamics of the staff. A lovable bunch of misfits and quirky people, the kind who want to work at a regional magazine. It was not New York or LA glossies, but it was also not quite like covering breaking news at the local paper. Somewhere in between the grit and the glamour, it drew a specific type of person.

"I bet you can make a killing," Kevin said enthusiastically. "I've read about people buying up houses and just running real estate empires on Airbnb. It's why the cost of living keeps going up." To note, Kevin and his husband had flipped their longtime home in Richland–West End recently, so he was a bit of an expert on the market.

"Maybe, but it's just helped us out while Jason's been in college. Anyway, I only rent to people who seem responsible. Like families who are here for a football game since we're pretty close to Vanderbilt. Once it was to people having surgery at the children's hospital. Or here for a funeral. No one's throwing a kegger after a funeral, I don't think."

"Unless they're my in-laws!" Janice chimed in.

"Thank you, Janice. Other than that, I mean . . . Anyway, this emergency room nurse messaged me asking about some dates, and I had a couple days off, so we planned a long weekend in Florida. I thought to myself, *She saves people's lives. I bet she will be safe and responsible.*"

"Well, what happened?" Kevin was getting antsy.

"So we've had the same pool guy for ten years. If you ever need a pool guy, I can give you his name. Levi is the best in the business. We had this leak a few years back and couldn't figure out where the water was going—"

"Nancy!" Kevin was clearly getting annoyed. "I need to get back to my desk. We've got a couple sections closing this afternoon."

"Yes, sorry. Levi came by on Friday afternoon like he usually does. He walked in the back gate, and do you know what he saw?"

He shook his head. "I can only imagine. Please."

"Forty women in nurse costumes around the pool. And not like scrubs. The *sexy* nurse Halloween stuff you see. Turns out it was a bachelorette party, and all the 'nurses' were drinking from red Solo cups and plastic martini glasses. Thank the good Lord they didn't have glass on the pool deck."

"My goodness." Now Kevin was back in. Janice leaned forward in anticipation.

"But the best part, you'll never guess." She continued at the look from Kevin. "They thought Levi was a stripper."

"My word," Janice said.

Kevin positively cackled.

At this point, I gave up any pretense of slowly pouring creamer into my coffee and leaned against the counter. None of them noticed nor seemed bothered by my presence.

"Levi took the long pole he uses and walked to the deck. He told me the nurse with a veil was close to the gate, so he tried to be polite and said, 'I assume you're the bride?' And 'Don't mind me, I'm just going to clean up the place. It's gotten pretty dirty this week.' Which is something he'd usually say but was probably the wrong thing this time."

"Go on." Kevin was pushing this closing, clearly.

"The dear man is pretty handsome, if I do say so myself, and stays fit carrying all his gear. Those arms! But he tried to start skimming the pool and they practically attacked him. A horde of skanky nurses surrounding this poor man, pulling at his coveralls and shrieking, 'Take it off!' He kept protesting, but I guess they thought it was part of the act. Finally, one of them got a little too frisky and reached for his belt buckle. So he jumped right in the pool."

Janice was, at this point, snorting. I looked outside to make sure no one else could hear, but the designers were in a conference room going over layouts.

Nancy continued. "Unfortunately, a couple drunk nurses jumped in too. What a mess. I'm afraid Levi may never come back. Plus, it's going to really wreck our savings plan if I can't list the house anymore."

"I think there are, um, laws about that sort of behavior," I piped up. "Have you filed anything with VRBO?"

Janice, who knew a thing or two about sexual harassment laws, gathered herself enough to chime in, and I left them to it. Kevin was wiping away tears of mirth.

I now had a couple of ideas about what *not* to do for Lucy's bachelorette. The image of that poor pool man filled my mind as I made my way back to my desk. Before I could make it, I was jolted from my reverie.

"Claire!" Michelle flagged me down, moving faster down the hallway than anyone in four-inch Louboutins deserved to. Her dark hair swished and then whipped obediently back into place with each step. "Why didn't you say something?" She held out her massive new iPhone for me to look. My eyes struggled to focus on the screen. "I just saw this *stunning* engagement party featured on *Guest of a Guest* and didn't realize it was your sister until I saw your picture. How positively wonderful that must be for your family."

"Why yes, definitely. It's great. We're all so thrilled." I sounded like a robot, but Michelle possessed the emotional perception of an android herself.

"When is the wedding?" She pursed her lips.

"It's in June. In Dallas. But I probably won't need to take off much time for it! It shouldn't conflict with any of our closing dates. I know we'll be working on the September issue by then. You know you can count on me."

Shut up, Claire. Close your big mouth. Whatever business expert said to always say just what you're asked and not offer more clearly never met me. Needed to review my *Claire Sommers's Guide to Business.* I was certain that Evelyn never suffered from verbal diarrhea. How nice for her.

She nodded and said, "See you at two," over her shoulder.

I sat down in one of the midcentury conference room chairs promptly at two. Dom sauntered in three minutes late, but for once Michelle seemed not to care. The guy got away with everything.

We already had the footage from Jacqueline's wedding pulled up on the projector screen to review it together. As the scenes of the wedding scrolled by, I admired Dom's eye for detail again. The editing was seamless, and it told the story of their day beautifully. He really was a stellar videographer, especially for doing it all himself on his laptop. But when I realized he left in the deflowering comment, I winced and immediately turned to Michelle, trying to read her face.

"Michelle," I started, "we can cut that out. I know it's off-color and inappropriate."

He quickly contradicted me. "I thought it added some *fun* color in an event that lacked it."

"And *I* think it will make clients not trust our judgment."

"Listen, bro said it. We just captured it."

We were volleying back and forth when Michelle cleared her throat. "I'm fine leaving it. Dom's right; these events need drama. Now, let's watch the rest."

We sat in silence for three more minutes, and then the dummy credits rolled. "That's great," she said. "Good job, you two. I think you're going to work well as a team."

"Thanks so much," Dom and I said simultaneously. We stopped at her exasperated look.

"We've got Claire's friend Daphne's wedding at Blackberry Farm on deck for next month, so we're probably only looking for a couple others. Claire, what else is on your slate? Needs to be local, since we still haven't gotten much budget approved."

We'd received some decent submissions from our social media channels and event planner contacts in the area. "I have an event at the zoo, which is always fun. And a country singer, Dixon Jackson, is getting remarried on his estate in Brentwood in a few weeks."

"Those are some solid contenders for midseason. Please put them in an email to me and copy Dom. Good news is, we may only need one or two more. I wanted to let you know I've homed in on the perfect event for the finale of our series pitch. I just got off the phone with the regional director, who is at one of the best planning firms I've ever worked with or covered. As long as the bride gives her approval, we're in." She looked directly at me, eyes gleaming.

"Think Dallas, summertime, a blown-out backyard event for one of the wealthiest families in the area." I got a sinking feeling in my stomach. My mouth involuntarily opened. She held up a hand at my expression. "Yes, it's Claire's sister Lucille's wedding!"

I was in shock, though I managed to squeak out, "Michelle, isn't that a conflict of interest?"

"Not if we're transparent about your involvement. We're not curing cancer or doing investigative journalism here. We're covering parties for nice, rich people."

"I'm just not sure I'm comfortable—"

"It's not your wedding, Claire."

Thanks, I am fully aware.

"It will be perfect," she went on. "We'll have great access as I assume you're in the bridal party. The June timing is ideal for our September issue cover, and our publisher jumped at the chance to cover a nonlocal wedding without having to pay a lot of travel expenses."

I was running out of excuses. "But I'll have a lot of wedding duties to attend to as maid of honor."

"That's why I'm sending Dom to accompany you. I imagine you don't have a plus-one yet?"

Did she lurk around the breakroom just sniffing out dirt on my dating life?

"No, not yet," I mumbled.

"*Perfect.* Then it's all settled. You know we have a lot riding on this and need it in by deadline." She pushed back her chair and flounced out of the room.

Dom was being uncharacteristically quiet in his chair. I finally turned to look at him. "We're going to have a lot of rules if you come to my sister's wedding. I don't know what they are yet, but *I'm* in charge."

"Of course, boss. I wouldn't have it any other way."

"Why are you being so compliant? This is a switch."

"It's your sister's wedding. That's a big deal. I'd never try to mess that up. You tell me what to do and when, and I'll do it."

I wasn't sure how to handle a nonpushy version of him. "Thank you."

We went back to our respective desks. I understood that the stakes were high. We needed to make a big splash with this project regardless of how I felt about it in the moment.

This New Yorker was only going to be here for a season. Hopefully he'd help me save this place that I'd come to genuinely like, with her scrappy staff and musty ideas. It made me sad to see the way that *Piece of Cake* continued to shrink and become a veritable shell of herself. The old girl needed something to bring her back to her former glory, and fast. I didn't have to understand Dom. I didn't even have to like him. But we could team up and do this.

I didn't love the idea of including Lucy's wedding in our series, and I was shocked that Mom approved the coverage. It was a risk, allowing the world to see behind the "Sommers curtain," and I knew better than anyone that my parents always wanted control of the narrative. Then again, sometimes allowing the press direct access could be better than trying to keep them out. Giving the right people permission at least ensured no one would go rogue. I was sure my mother negotiated that she be given final approval of the piece before anything went public.

I admired the fact that Michelle was moving forward with our fall editorial calendar like the "end" wasn't looming over us. Her optimism that the docuseries would provide the lifeline we needed seemed a bit delusional, yet inspiring. Yes, she was using my family as clickbait, but I had to hand it to her—she was fighting to save this place.

Still uncertain about the *Piece of Cake* feature and my willingness to sacrifice my baby sister's wedding on the altar, I decided to look for other potential weddings to cover. I stared at my screen, going through old files and wedding announcements for inspiration. I was scrambling.

Finally, I had an idea.

Virginia "Ginny" MacDougal, of the railroad-turned-shipping-empire MacDougals, had gotten engaged to Ravi Chowdhury, a renowned orthopedic surgeon for the Titans and Predators, in 2019. Their April 2020 ceremony had been rescheduled to December, then to summer 2021, and then they finally eloped that fall. They'd planned a larger reception once things opened up again, but then discovered they were pregnant.

Now, all this time later, they were finally doing it. Some might say it was unnecessary, but Ginny had dreamed of a wedding and was not about to miss the moment to celebrate with everyone. All the celebrations rolled into one—engagement, wedding, baby shower, you name it. She was marking it now. Making up for lost time.

I'd interviewed her that February, what seemed like lifetimes ago, and the magazine had been all set to cover the event prepandemic. We'd stayed in touch, and she let me know that they were finally holding a massive reception in April. Also attending would be their one-year-old daughter. There was a lot to celebrate—and a lot of pent-up energy (and budget) directed toward this long-awaited party. They were planning a blowout at Cheekwood Estate and Gardens with one of the biggest coordinators on the East Coast. It would be perfect—and, I hoped, a big enough event that we could scrap our plan to cover Lucy's wedding. I'd have enough to deal with that day as it was.

I dashed to Michelle's office. She was not on a call, fortunately, so I rapped softly on the open door. "Can I come in?"

"Yes, I've got a moment. What's up?" Michelle was a machine. She was always busy and bore the weight of our publication on her narrow shoulders. She could have gone back to any number of successful brands, but she was committed to us. And she somehow also felt the occasional responsibility to mentor or share insight with the junior members of the staff. She didn't consistently read my emails, but she'd usually hear me out. She respected when you had the guts to come talk to her. I took my shot.

"I found a wedding for us: Virginia MacDougal. Well, now it's Virginia Chowdhury."

"I didn't know she was still having a wedding. Remind me?" Michelle mused.

I filled her in on the evolution of Virginia's wedding plan. "Cut to now. Lots to celebrate. Lots of money. Lots of athletes. Her parents are big philanthropists and on the boards of a bunch of charities here. It's sure to be a massive party at Cheekwood."

"I'm listening." Michelle twirled a stray dark lock and looked out her window at the rain.

I took a deep breath. "Picture this: an English garden setting, a statuesque redhead bride, handsome surgeon husband, the couple's adorable baby—born *in* wedlock, to boot!—rolled down the aisle in a wicker wagon, roses in peak bloom, and every socialite in town."

"Could we get access, and will the planner work with us?"

"I don't know Sophie Bloom personally, but she has a reputation for being very collaborative. She often works with local vendors, so I don't see why not."

"If you can convince her, then let's do it. This could fill our open slot nicely . . . Well done, Claire."

I took that rare compliment and fled from her office, taking the win with an inward fist-pump.

CHAPTER 10

After my successful chat with Michelle, I went back to doing my usual job of, you know, writing multiple sections of the magazine.

Truth be told, I was learning a lot, but it could get pretty lonely in the office, especially when working later into the evening. Sounds echoed too loudly and gave me the creeps. Even if I wasn't looking to befriend any of my coworkers, it would have been nice to have people fill the vacant cubicles in the bullpen area of the office. And no, Dom didn't count.

I was scanning through old issues of the magazine that I kept filed neatly on my desk. I had a single framed family photo of all of us at Evelyn's wedding. Felt appropriate and inspiring, given the subject matter. It was also one of the last big celebrations we had as a family before I left Dallas.

For now, this docuseries was the ladder before me to climb. All I could do was tackle it one rung at a time. I was optimistic that if this project was a success, I'd get promoted and might feel like I was really getting somewhere in my professional life.

My dad had a Steve Jobs quote on a sign in his office for years: "My job is not to be easy on people. My job is to make them better." It pretty much summed up both his professional and parenting styles, and it had been driven into his girls from the first. We were to respond to setbacks with improvement. We were taught to compete with those around us, to fight for every success. And part of gaining an advantage was seeking out people who would help make us better or push us along.

I winced recalling the people at Cedric's firm who had attempted to pour into me. I'd shrugged off their help, assuming I didn't need it. Lottie in particular had taken me under her wing, and I'd rejected her in no uncertain terms. My ruthlessness had been appalling, in hindsight.

Also appalling was what came after. I opened my personal email to a saved folder. I'd kept the message marked unread, pretending to myself that I (a) hadn't fully read the contents, and (b) intended to send a response one day. I took a deep breath.

Hi Claire,

I've been thinking a lot about what you said when you left. I still can't wrap my mind around what you did. As you can imagine, we're all baffled, disappointed. Personally, I'm furious. And Cedric has been raging. As you may have seen, however, the unwanted press has ironically helped our reputation and the clients'. So we'll be fine.

But I'm not writing to tell you how angry I am with

you—true as it may be. More so, I am sad. Sad about what happened. Sad at how things ended. And honestly, sad for you.

I did believe we were becoming friends. I do believe you could have succeeded here. The woman I worked with was responsible, funny, creative, talented, and even kind. There are people in this office I would expect this sort of betrayal from, but it wasn't you.

I thought I knew you, and I guess I don't—but I don't think you know yourself either.

I genuinely hope you figure out what version of Claire you want to be as you take on whatever comes next. Good luck.

Lottie

I never replied.

At this point, I wasn't sure what to say or how to address it before Lucy's wedding. A hate letter would have been easier to brush off. Instead, I felt haunted and, frankly, called out.

I didn't have it in me to fix it today, but in the name of moving forward—and figuring out an improved version of Claire—I could create better professional relationships in my current job. That felt controllable. I doubted that Michelle would be inviting me for deskside chats over espresso shots anytime soon, but she wasn't the only one with valuable experience still standing.

I stood abruptly, strode resolutely, and knocked on the glass wall of Kevin's office. "Can I come in?"

He looked up from his screen at me, surprised. "Yes, Claire! Let me just finish sending this email. Please sit down."

I sat in the proffered upholstered chair and recalled the luxe lounge furniture of Cedric's office in Dallas. The décor was night and day: Cedric Montclair Celebrations' slick offices were like walking into a red and gilt jewel box. *Piece of Cake* was a threadbare attempt at country chic. An odd mishmash of utilitarian office furniture with chintz floral wallpapers.

I looked at Kevin's desk, not for the first time noting the contrast here too. Cedric never allowed us to have personal items on our desks, too sentimental and cluttered for his taste. Michelle, for all her faults, wanted us to feel at home here—presumably so we'd work longer hours. Kevin had a couple of framed pictures of him and Dean with their twins. He also displayed a couple of framed cover stories, like our first gay wedding and the time he interviewed Carrie Underwood about her marriage.

"What are you still doing here? Shouldn't you be out on the town with friends right about now?" He turned away from his computer and smiled.

"Funny, as if I have any friends."

"I thought you had some from college. You went to Vandy, right?" He was always so kind.

"Yes, but most are either married or have moved away. And to be honest, a big night out isn't really in the budget these days."

Kevin turned to face me fully. "I know what you mean. We did well on our house, but Dean's mom was just diagnosed with dementia, so she's going to be moving into our new place with us. Things are pretty tight."

I got a chill, imagining what he would do if the magazine folded. I couldn't think about that. Dom and I needed to make this the best project possible. We could do it. *I* could do it.

"I'm so sorry to hear that, Kevin. That's a lot to deal with."

"It is, but it comes with getting older," he said. "Most of us end up having to look out for our parents at some point in time. This just came a little sooner than we expected."

I could not fathom a world where my own parents didn't have a retirement fund established, a ten-point plan outlined for their medical care, and a hand-selected beachfront community ready to enjoy during the years before their eventual physical decline. Evelyn undoubtedly had been entrusted with the specifics already. But once again, I was reminded how atypical my upbringing was—and how much I'd taken for granted.

"Enough of that. How can I help you?" Kevin said, kindly breaking my reverie.

"I'd love some advice," I started. This was uncharted territory for me. My inner Sommers girl was throwing a hissy fit. I told her to shut up and continued. "I want to do well here, to keep becoming a better writer and editor. What else should I be doing to succeed?"

"Claire, you work harder than anyone. Right now, that's all you can keep doing. That and keep an eye out for any job openings at other magazines if things don't pan out with the company and you want to stay in the industry," he said.

"I hate we have to think that way right now, but I get it. Better to be prepared. That is, unless Dom and I can manage to pull a rabbit out of a top hat," I said.

"Let's hope that fella's got some magic up his sleeves. I know you do."

"Thanks, Kevin," I replied, blushing a bit. "One more thing though: How did you know you wanted this? Why did you stay here? Did you ever want to try out New York or even Birmingham, with all the big Southern magazines?"

"When I started, I set out to be at *Martha Stewart*, long may she reign." We both mock-bowed and touched our foreheads in homage. "But I love Nashville. My life is here. It's where I met Dean and built a family. And I also love our work. When you find something you're good at, that you love, the benchmark changes. It no longer matters so much if you're 'the best.' Are you happy? Challenged? Fulfilled? Having fun? Creating a life you're proud of? I realized all that mattered more to me than any fancy title on a masthead. But that was probably way more than you wanted to know. Sorry."

"No, it's helpful. This is just so opposite of what was drilled into me growing up. Being the best was the entire point. Nothing else mattered as much."

"And how has that worked out for you?" Kevin was a skilled interviewer, I noted, and an even better friend.

"Honestly, not great. Nothing's quite good enough, it seems. Despite what I do, how hard I work, it all goes sideways or fails to measure up."

He looked at me with such warmth in his brown eyes. "Is that why you left Dallas? I imagine the last few years haven't been easy for you."

"What do you mean?" I replied. There was a pit in my stomach. I felt like I'd been playing cards with only part of the deck.

"I've been at this magazine a long time, so I've got a lot of friends in the industry all over the country," he said. "Southern weddings are a bit of a niche, and people talk."

I sat there speechless, felt the color draining out of my face.

"Don't panic," he said with an easy laugh. "I did hear a little something about your time as a wedding planner, but I have no interest in telling anyone about it. It's your story to tell." He reached over the desk to pat my hand.

I sat there, wondering what to say when I was able to find my voice again. How could I salvage this situation?

"I don't know all the details, but I got the gist of it," he continued. "I assumed you needed a fresh start after that, which is why you're here. There are always two sides."

I took a deep breath. Maybe it was better to come clean.

"That's extremely kind of you, Kevin. But the truth is, the only side to my story is that I was in the wrong. I basically sabotaged one of Cedric's weddings."

"Oh, Claire, honey. I find that hard to believe. Why would you do something like that?"

It all tumbled out. "I wanted a promotion that didn't seem to be coming to me . . . and I just snapped." I could hear my mother's voice back then, casually mentioning that she'd heard about Cedric opening an Atlanta office—and how I'd be such a great fit for it. Unless I wanted to be an assistant forever, of course.

I shook it off and continued. "I called an old friend from my student newspaper days who worked at a paparazzi agency, and I sold a tip about one of Cedric's biggest celebrity weddings. Nowadays I could use the money, but I certainly didn't need it then. Then to make matters worse, I intentionally let my boss,

Lottie, take the blame for what I did. That is, until I got caught."
I paused, but just long enough to catch my breath and jump back
in before he could respond. His face was hard to read.

"In trying to succeed at all costs, I became someone I didn't
know. I deserved to be fired and basically exiled from Dallas.
My parents cut me off too. No matter how much I want to, I
can't undo what I did. I can only be better. I *will* only be better," I
said. The burden of my confession weighed heavy. I still couldn't
tell him what, exactly, drove me to the point that I would do
absolutely anything, in this case sell out someone I liked and
respected, to pave what I thought was a path to success.

I finally stopped rambling and waited for Kevin to speak.

"Hmm," he said. I was still holding my breath. I thought for
sure he'd ask me to leave his office. Then he'd tell Michelle everything, and that would be that. Another career path cut short
before it ever really began.

"Listen," said Kevin after a beat. "We all make mistakes or
bad choices. Not necessarily to that extent, but still, no one's
perfect. Sure, there are consequences, as I tell my kids. Sounds
like you've still got a lot to process. But your poor choice doesn't
have to define you for the rest of your life. It doesn't have to hold
you back."

I finally exhaled. Tears were welling in my eyes. Kevin held
out a box of tissues from behind his desk. What was wrong
with me?

"I . . . I don't even know what to say," I said quietly. "As you
can imagine, I don't exactly tell most people what happened. I
can't thank you enough for being so nice about it all."

"Well, like I said, if my kids ever did something they regretted, I'd want them to have a second chance. You should have that too. My lips are sealed," he said, smiling.

"Thank you so much, Kevin," I said, still sniffling. "This isn't why I came in here today, but I'm really glad we talked."

He laughed. "I'm sure it wasn't, but keep your chin up. Your experience as a wedding planner, even if it was short-lived, works to your advantage with the stories you're writing. Michelle plays it cool, but she thinks you're doing a great job too."

"Please stop saying such nice things or I'm going to start crying again," I said, letting out a small laugh myself. My sisters and I were taught to be tough as nails, iron women all three, not showing weakness. But his genuine open-mindedness was disarming and unexpected. It was like my body could not compute and was leaking. I'd have been annoyed with myself had I not also felt so relieved.

"My door's always open." He smiled. "Let me know if you ever want to talk more about everything. And I hope it doesn't come to this, but if you end up looking for another job in publishing, come talk to me. Like I said, I've got a lot of friends still in the business, and I can write you a recommendation letter if need be."

This man was a literal angel. He even knew about my past and was still willing to go to bat for me. I couldn't fathom hurting Kevin or the rest of this team the way I'd done in the past. I felt ill just thinking about it.

"Just keep up the good work, but also don't hole up in here all the time. It's great that you're dedicated to your job, but you need to enjoy being young and single. Before you know it, you'll be stuck at home watching *Bubble Guppies* and eating your kids' leftover chicken nuggets for dinner."

We both laughed.

"Great advice, Kevin," I said. "I don't have much to offer you in return, but if you ever need a babysitter, I'd be happy to watch your twins."

"That's very kind of you to offer, Claire. I'll be sure to take you up on it."

"Have a great night," I said, leaving his office.

I grabbed my bags, turned off my desk lamp, and felt the weight I'd carried around the past few years lift ever so slightly. I still had a lot to prove to everyone I used to work with, to my family, and to myself, for that matter, but it was good to know at least one person—well, two, if I counted Lucy—had faith in me.

My mind immediately went to Cedric and Lottie, the people I'd damaged the most. Still didn't mean I intended to grovel or have our reunion/showdown at my sister's wedding. And certainly not anywhere near Dom. If I were them, I'd never want to see or speak to me again. Hopefully, Michelle would be happy with another featured event in its place.

❧ ❧ ❧

Ginny's spring wedding promised to provide plenty of fodder for a great episode—maybe even enough for the September issue of the magazine and our biggest documentary episode. All the postponements and rebookings due to the pandemic were relatable, timely, and dramatic. Perfect for our needs.

I drove myself to Cheekwood so I wouldn't be alone with Dom in the car again. I just knew he'd ask me about Dallas, and I was hoping to gloss over the whole thing with him. I technically owed him a drink after he helped with the speech, but I needed to be focused for today and finish my list of interview points.

Fortunately, he'd been scarce around the office lately. In between weddings and editing, he was presumably working on "content" for the magazine's channels as well as his own. Our engagement numbers were creeping up, which hopefully would translate to subscribers or at least advertisers. He was just a coworker—a temporary one—and I needed to concentrate. I needed this documentary to succeed and the magazine to stay afloat. I was running out of backup plans—and money too. Even after my pseudonormal weekend home for Claire's engagement party, my financial situation remained the same—that is, without any outside help. I still needed to stand on my own two feet and prove to practically everyone I loved that I was not only surviving but thriving as Claire 2.0—if only I could figure out who that was.

I'd somehow convinced Sophie Bloom's assistant to let us video the event. It's one thing to interview couples after their wedding using still images, but filming it was another story. Planners could be hesitant about "behind-the-scenes" video, given that we might capture things as they went wrong. I knew these mishaps were often never even witnessed by the clients. Wedding planners, at least the good ones, took care of any issues while no one was looking. That was just part of the job. If we were filming an event in action, we might reveal more than the planner was bargaining for, including chain-smoking brides and confetti malfunctions. Thankfully, Sophie's team was swayed. Maybe Sophie was hoping for good press coverage for herself, so she was willing to take the risk.

However, we had strict instructions to be neither seen nor heard, which was fine by me. We'd interview the couple shortly before their first look, which did feel absurd considering they'd not only already gotten married but also created a child. But I didn't make the rules. Unfortunately.

My Range Rover climbed the winding hill to the top of the Cheekwood estate. Dom had made it already, I noted. He was sitting behind the wheel of his car, probably posting something on his Instagram.

I wondered how he did it. Some influencers I followed seem to just love the affirmation. They posted about fashion or travel or their cute kids with all the right filters, and people ate it up. It was a daily ego stroke. Dom seemed more like the ones who viewed it as a business, whether it was a platform for serious information or entertainment. His attitude was somehow different. Less about the self and more about the audience.

He was so different in person than on camera—less carefully curated and charming, more goofy and sincere. Those unguarded moments with him were certainly making it easier to like him, even though he was still a total interloper.

Either way, it looked like a lot of work on top of having a day job. Not for the first time, I was grateful to have only 289 followers, all of whom I'd befriended before moving back to Nashville and who followed me before I went private and stopped posting entirely.

Dom noticed me staring through the car window, and I was jolted from my thoughts. I half smiled and got out of the car.

"Hi," he said. "You look really nice."

"Hey. Thanks, I didn't want to stick out at this one." As a matter of fact, I'd worn one of my favorites, a black McQueen dress from college with puffed sleeves and a short cut that flattered my runner's legs. Not that it was for his benefit.

Dom had on his classic button-down, this time in a pale-blue gingham that looked both crisp and soft, topped with a brown tweed blazer and well-cut brown slacks. His hair seemed less messy than usual, and it was the first time he looked like what I imagined a gentleman from Milan would. Very *Italian*. Sexy. No, not sexy but elegant and European. I wondered what his mother looked like. In my mind, she was the Brooklyn Sophia Loren.

"You don't look half bad yourself," I added. "Keep trying, and you might actually look like you belong in the South."

He laughed. "Y'all ready to head inside?"

"Oh, yeesh." I smiled while shaking my head. "I said you looked Southern, but there's no way you'll ever *sound* Southern. No matter how many times you try, yet butcher, our slang."

"Fair enough," he replied. "I'll just stick to the gingham for now."

We walked up the front stairs of the beautiful stone facade, a former mansion now turned museum.

The Cheek family, who once owned the property, had made

their fortune in the coffee business. The family had gifted the massive mansion and sprawling estate to the city a few generations ago. One of Nashville's crown jewels, it included numerous gardens to explore, art sculpture trails, an interactive children's garden, and rotating art exhibits throughout the year—both inside the museum and throughout the property. Not only was it a hot spot for visitors, but it also served as one of the prettiest backdrops in town for weddings and special events. The biggest parties always took place on the Swan Lawn behind the mansion in some sort of tent.

Dom stopped midway to take a panning video of the entire setting. I had to admit, it made lovely content. And his stupid face didn't hurt either. If you were into that sort of thing. I did my best to stay out of the background while he charmed his followers with detailed descriptions of the surroundings.

"Sorry, thanks for waiting." He turned to me. As we walked up the side steps to the Wisteria Arbor, I broke the silence. I was grateful I'd worn block heels—a rule for outdoor events I learned during my planning days. Stilettos were truly impossible on uneven surfaces like stone and grass.

"I still don't get how you can do that. I would be so awkward as an influencer."

He laughed. "You get used to it, but I bet you'd do great on camera. You're poised and beautiful. You'd be a natural."

I tucked the compliment away for later. The air smelled like wisteria and dusk. "Be that as it may, I feel this is never going to be a career path for me. Don't get me wrong, I love writing and covering weddings, but going fully digital or being the face of some blog? I'd never succeed. I'm just not sure I could put myself out there like that."

"Well, that's up to you, but my bet is you'd be a huge success. You're composed and well-spoken, albeit a little uptight—"

"Um, excuse me?"

"Apologies. I meant *seldom rattled*."

"Sure you did. Well, I have my old job to thank for that."

"That's the wedding planning you mentioned?" Dom snapped a picture of the front of the mansion while we spoke.

"Yes, and the situations we found ourselves in. The chicken-bride story was just a warm-up. I could blow your mind."

"I don't doubt that." He looked at me for a beat. I flushed. "You'll have to enlighten me sometime."

He helped me up the slippery stone steps to the house.

"By the way," he said as I gripped his firm forearm, "you know 'influencers' are people who wear cute clothes or buy pretty stuff for their houses, right? I guess that's technically still what I am, but now we're called 'content creators.'" He made air quotes with his free hand so I'd know he was only partially serious.

"Sure, so what does that mean?" I asked, letting go of his arm.

"We try to produce content people want to watch. In my case it's videos and guides for brides. This is a little inside baseball, but that also means—in terms of projects like our docuseries—a freelancer would typically work for hire, and the magazine would own all their interviews and other work. But since I create things on my own, all the video we shoot is mine . . . and technically yours, I guess?"

"Why would it be mine? Other than the fact that I've done as much work as you, of course."

"This whole thing was your idea, right? You could make a case that you originated the project. Yes, we've done the whole thing under the magazine's umbrella and access, because no one is buying 'The Brides' Man and Claire's Documentary' just yet. But I imagine that when they do sell this project, we will get a cut of that. It's about the only way they've afforded to bring me on. I get a percentage, which has kept my hourly rates down."

I whistled low. "Must be nice to be so powerful."

"Not powerful, just popular." He flashed that dimple again as we walked inside the grand entrance foyer.

Because of the extensive collection of antiques, none of the wedding events would be inside the actual mansion. But we had a moment to explore and appreciate the artwork before moving to the back garden.

We wandered into the library. A plaque relayed how the Cheeks amassed a collection of more than two thousand books. Wood paneling glowed with the patina of age. Leather-bound volumes lined built-in shelves. Even my parents' library couldn't compare.

Dom came up next to me, facing the time-worn wooden rails of old volumes. I could smell his clean cedar amid the room's dusty leather. "What's your favorite book?" he asked.

"Growing up in a house of sisters, it was hard not to love *Little Women*." I gazed longingly and gestured at the Cheeks' clothbound volume before me.

"That's certainly one I'm familiar with," he said.

I looked up at him, surprised. "Really? Did you have to read it in detention or something?"

"Nah, they played audiobooks during my stint in Sing Sing." He grinned. Curse that dimple. "Honestly, we used the neighborhood library a lot, but this was one of the books my sister actually owned a copy of."

"Oh really?"

"Storage space and money were just tight. Some of us grew up in Brooklyn railroad apartments and not Dallas palaces." Before I could protest, he winked. "But I did end up reading a lot because of the library. I'm sure that's why I still love reading to this day. It was the perfect way to escape and live out all the adventures I wanted to but couldn't afford when I was younger."

"Well, we had all the money in the world, and I still wanted to escape my life at times and live vicariously through the stories I read," I said.

"I get it," he replied. "I joke around with you, but I know money doesn't equate to happiness. And from the little you've told me about yourself, it sounds like there's a lot of pressure growing up in a family like yours. I'd want to check out every book I could get my hands on to escape into a world where someone wasn't monitoring my every move."

"My thoughts exactly." We stood, looking at each other a moment.

"Best movie adaptation?" he asked, gesturing to *Little Women*.

"Winona Ryder and Christian Bale, obviously. Susan Sarandon is Marmee goals."

"But Greta Gerwig's is good too. It's smart and empowering and even a little sexy." He paused. "What?" he asked, regarding my befuddled look. "I studied film in college."

"Ah, it's all making sense now . . . I still never pictured you as a reader."

"You mean, because in New York City public schools you don't learn to read until eighth grade? Not all of us had a classics tutor in preschool. I had a lot of catching up to do."

"Not what I meant at all and you know it! I just never imagined an influencer to have such a literary background."

"Just because I'm a hustler and use my filming experience to make a decent living doesn't mean I want to be glued to a screen all the time. Hence my sense of adventure, brilliant literary insights, and need to explore pretty much every new place I land."

"Hence your being pretty easily distracted." I nudged his shoulder with mine as we turned to leave the room, ignoring the electric jolt at the contact.

As we made our way through the house, we turned the corner and saw someone I never expected to see anywhere in Nashville. It was like I'd summoned her with our conversation. She managed to find her voice first. "Claire? Is that you?"

My former coworker looked a little leaner, and her dress was better quality than when I knew her. Her brow looked less pinched than the last time I saw her, which was under admittedly very stressful circumstances. She tucked a dark-blonde strand behind her ear, and I noticed an antique engagement band glittering on her ring finger. Looked like multiple areas of her life were going pretty well.

"Hi, Lottie. It's . . . nice to see you." My heart was thudding in my ears, and my tongue felt dry and stuck to the roof of my mouth. Gone was the ironclad composure Dom had just been complimenting. Her words echoed in my head. I found myself wanting to alternately grovel at her feet and act as if I had absolutely nothing to feel bad for—as if this interaction was strictly business. As I visibly deliberated, Dom coughed softly to jar me back to the present.

"This is Dom, my colleague," I said, recovering. "Dom, this is Lottie. She and I, um, used to work together too."

"Nice to meet you." He extended a hand. She took it, looking between the two of us.

"What are you doing here?" she asked, puzzled.

"We're covering Ginny's wedding for *Piece of Cake*." No need to give her more information than necessary.

"Oh, I see. Never heard from you, so I didn't know where you ended up." Was that disdain in her tone? Probably.

"Yes, I've been here a few years." Time to move the focus off me. "I didn't expect to see you here either. Aren't you in Atlanta? Running Cedric's new office?"

"Yes, still there. But Sophie is one of the planners Cedric partners with a lot, as you may remember. I came up to help with the design and execution of the ceremony and reception." Lottie looked at her watch.

"Is Cedric here?" I fought the urge to look about nervously.

"No, he's back in Dallas." Lottie glanced at her watch again.

"Well, I'm sure you have a lot to do. We'll be around tonight, so we'll probably see you."

"Try to stay out of the way, please," she couldn't resist adding.

"Of course." What did she think I was, an idiot? It wasn't uncalled for. But it still stung.

"What was that all about?" Dom said as we continued to the back.

"We just . . . parted on not-great terms."

"I gathered that."

"It's a long story." I debated what to tell him. I appreciated that he didn't know anything about me, my past, or my family, other than a few Google hits. His perspective wasn't wholly uninfluenced, but nevertheless seemed to be based mostly on me. *Just* me. So I decided to keep it simple. "I got let go, I guess you could say. It just wasn't a great fit for either party."

There, that was the truth. Sort of.

"I find that surprising. Who wouldn't want you to be a part of their team? You're Claire Sommers, whip-smart workaholic and soon-to-be heroine of our company."

"Well, thank you. I hope I've learned a lot since then." That was *also* true. I was killing it in the honesty department.

I did hope I'd become a better employee and less self-destructive. I was excelling here in a way I hadn't in Dallas, I thought. I worked hard to baby-step my way up our corporate ladder and had done it all without stepping on anyone else. Sure, I wasn't quite certain what kind of person that made me. And these past few years hadn't been easy, but I hadn't quit or gotten laid off. Yet. Pitifully small victories for a Sommers, but still. Anyway, I wasn't about to unload all that onto Dominic right now.

Thankfully, our walking conversation was halted by the sight of the massive tent, if the word *massive* did it justice. The structure occupied the entire lawn behind the mansion, and they had even moved the large concrete swan statue out of the way for this one. Now that I knew who was involved, I could see Cedric Montclair Celebrations' handiwork all over this event. The clear tent looked like a solarium, with powder-coated structural bars crisscrossing the clear plastic that looked just like glass. Lush ferns and green leafy trees were nestled among live rosebushes and peonies, all in metallic pots that glittered in the twinkling lights. Antique Parisian floral buckets held thousands of sprays of white flowers. The ceiling was draped with garlands of smilax greenery, wrapped in lights and interspersed with lavish white blooms. White antique lanterns hung above the long tables. It was a wonderland befitting the garden setting.

"This is going to knock people's socks off," Dom said, moving his camera around to capture every last detail.

"'Knock people's socks off'? Don't make me call you a 'goober.' If you say 'whoopsie daisy' next, I'm going to stage a vocabulary intervention," I said, thinking he sounded the slightest bit cute. "But it really is stunning." As Dom moved about the tent, I followed him and reviewed my checklist of things to film. "Cedric is a master of design, and people spend whatever it takes to work with him. He books out years in advance."

"Wow. He obviously has a reputation, and I follow him on Instagram, but I've never seen one of his weddings in person. It must have been quite the experience working for him," he said.

"That's putting it mildly," I replied.

"I can only imagine how epic your sister's wedding will be."

"Me too," I said with a sigh. "Okay, let's head down the hill and start our interviews with the bridal party."

We were given a golf cart to shuttle ourselves around the property since everyone was spread out until the ceremony started. We met up with the bride and her side of the wedding party in Botanic Hall near the front entrance. Dom had the idea of pulling Ginny outside in front of a nearby floral trellis to conduct her interview, so he had a pretty backdrop to work with. His eye for detail and cinematography continued to impress.

Listening to Ginny recount all the changes and work-arounds she and her now-husband had to deal with as a result of the pandemic was almost painful. Obviously, far more tragic events happened during that time, but I really felt for all the couples who had to cancel or postpone their weddings.

"What made it even more difficult was the fact that Ravi was a doctor in a pandemic. He was working crazy hours and was beyond exhausted most of the time. Wedding plans were the least of our worries. The whole process of getting married went from being a pleasure to a pain." Ginny pushed back a stray hair that had escaped her French twist updo.

"So why still go through with a wedding after getting legally married and even having a baby?" I asked.

"Like everybody else, so much of our lives changed these last few years. I didn't want to just give up on my dream of having a big wedding because it got hard," she said. "We put it on the back burner out of necessity. It was the right thing to do, but we also wanted a chance to finally celebrate all the life that had happened, the good stuff, in the meantime.

"Sure, it wasn't the perfect planning process," she continued, smoothing the fabric of her gown, "but once we felt like things were stable enough to confirm a new date, and Ravi's work hours got better, we decided to go for it. Plus, we wanted Sissy, our daughter, to be able to look at pictures of her parents' wedding one day."

"Well, from what Dom and I saw touring your reception site earlier, it's going to be an unforgettable event," I said. "Thanks so much for talking with us, Ginny. We'll let you go so you can finish getting ready, and we'll try to grab a few more comments from you later in the night. Congratulations again!"

Dom closed up his camera, and we headed back to our cart. "I'm happy for them that they went ahead with their big day," he said. "It really sucked for anyone trying to throw a wedding the past couple of years."

"Tell me about it," I said. "We were getting pretty desperate for fresh content at the magazine, and if I heard the term *microwedding* one more time, I was going to lose it."

"Speaking of micro, why don't we find out where they're keeping that baby of theirs and shoot some footage of her too?" Dom steered our little cart toward the catering tents to grab a quick snack.

"And while we're at it, how about adding in a puppy?" I quipped back. "I've been meaning to tell you that's what your channel is really missing: more babies and puppies. Just be careful you don't overload on the cuteness factor and cause women to faint when they watch."

"You're saying I need *more* cuteness factor?"

I couldn't look him in the eyes. "Not that I've been watching, but I imagine a baby goat or small rabbit wouldn't hurt."

"Michelle *is* always pushing to increase viewership. Tiny animals—and handsome men—will definitely do that," he said, laughing.

I rolled my eyes. "Let's not totally sell out just yet," I said. "Although, speaking of really cute, it just so happens we're about to interview Nashville's own Dr. McDreamy."

❧ ❧ ❧

We soon pulled our cart up to the designated spot for the grooms-men, and after our interview with the very dashing groom, we indeed managed to grab footage of Sissy toddling around the children's garden with her nanny. Dom was right. She was pre-cious, and our audience was going to eat her up.

We grabbed yet another snack and decided to swing by the closed Frist Learning Center for a quick break before the ceremony started in just over an hour. As I sat in the courtyard enjoying my pimento cheese sandwich and fruit tea, I watched one of Sophie's assistant planners bring Ginny around the cor-ner to take some pictures. There was a beautiful stone pavilion, and the assistant was draping Ginny's dress down the staircase for the full bridal portrait effect.

However, once the photographer finished getting his shots, Ginny started walking back down the stairs without stopping to pick up her train. Even from where I was seated with Dom across the way, we could hear the tear as Ginny's train got stuck between the rocks. The assistant planner had been staring at her phone like an idiot instead of noticing what was happening. What in the world was she doing? I could see the look on Ginny's face as she tried to survey the damage done behind her. Without hesitating, I stood up and rushed over.

"Don't panic," I said as I picked up the back of Ginny's train. "It's not too bad."

But it was bad. There was a massive, obvious tear on the lower third of the dress. No need for Ginny to know. She couldn't fully see the back without a mirror. The assistant's eyes were wide, and I could tell she was panicking.

"Listen," I said softly but firmly to the assistant. "I assume you have an emergency kit on you."

She nodded and started fumbling with the fanny pack around her waist. Most wedding planners carried around what they referred to as an "emergency kit"—a collection of random items that could come in handy should something go wrong. At Cedric's, ours were filled with Band-Aids, dress tape, tissues, breath mints, aspirin, Valium, lighters, Tide pens, bobby pins, mini sewing kits, and most important, safety pins. And during that time, I'd basically become MacGyver with a safety pin.

I shooed off the photographer and told him to meet us at the ceremony site and that we'd be just fine. The assistant looked at me carefully for a minute and then officially asked for my help.

"This is only my second wedding to work on with Sophie, and I don't want to blow it," she whispered.

"It's okay," I said. "I used to be a planner, and I'm happy to help. Radio Sophie and tell her we're helping Ginny with a quick dress issue but that you have it under control. We will get her back to the ceremony site in just a few."

"Thank you so much." She did as she was told.

"Okay," I said after she hung up. "I'm going to need every single safety pin in that bag of yours."

Dom had made his way over and was hovering near us. I was dismayed to see him subtly filming the proceedings.

"No need to capture any of this on camera," I said to him in my calmest voice while giving him a look that could've killed. Yes, this would've made for great content—but I wasn't ready to be on this side of the action.

"Just in case," he said. "Trust me."

I shook my head, angrily yet silently, like Tinker Bell telling off Peter Pan. He clicked off the camera after a moment and stepped toward where I squatted. He bent down and whispered, breath warm against my ear. "Don't worry, it won't show up if you don't want it to, but this is the sort of drama Michelle wants. We need it. And if this works out as beautifully as it seems it will, then you're a hero and the story is better for it."

I turned my head quickly and misjudged his proximity. We practically bumped noses. My retort died on my lips. As I looked up at him, breath heaving *only* from the effort of squatting too long, a safety pin in my hand jabbed my finger. "Ouch!" I said.

"Everything okay back there?" Ginny asked hesitantly.

"All good, just admiring Claire's handiwork," Dom said, straightening. He started chatting casually with Ginny to distract her from looking over her shoulder and worrying. I'd have to thank him for his help later—or not. I had an arsenal of compliments I was now withholding from this guy.

"Okay, Ginny," I said, my hands moving a million miles an hour. "I'm going to use some of the bustle loops already sewn in the back of your dress to pull the fabric together so the tear isn't noticeable at all. Is it okay with you if we lose some of the length of your train?" I asked her this fully knowing she didn't have another option, but typically it worked best to let a bride think she had options even if she didn't.

"Sure," she replied. "Whatever you think is best." Then she tried to turn around to see what I was doing.

Dom moved to chime in again. "Here, Ginny, why don't I show you some of the footage I got earlier in the day of Sissy toddling around in her little dress. She was adorable."

He sure did know how to charm. I was thankful Ginny had a distraction, and Dom was our only hope since I needed both of Sophie's assistant's hands to help hold up the dress while I worked.

"Okay," I said after about five long minutes spent with my head underneath Ginny's bustle. "I think that should do it."

I fluffed out the back and surveyed my work.

"That looks amazing," said the assistant. "How in the world did you do that?"

"Well, this isn't the first bustle I've had to fix," I replied. "When I worked as a planner, we had all kinds of issues with brides' trains. The ties broke all the time and we'd have to get crafty. This was trickier since it was a tear, but thankfully I had enough extra fabric to work with."

"Bravo." Dom stood next to us. "I'm impressed."

"Yes, I have a plethora of useless skills that I seldom get to employ these days." I chuckled. "Glad they can still come in handy."

"You saved the day, Claire." Ginny gave me a massive hug. "I thought for sure today would be the easy part, given everything else we've been through already. Guess not." She laughed.

"Don't worry," I said, picking up her train. There was no way I was going to let her walk over to the ceremony without my help now. "Something goes wrong at every wedding. It's just a matter of how big or small it is. This was your mishap, and it's taken care of, so it should be smooth sailing from here on out."

"Let's hope so," Ginny said. "Thankfully, anything outside a pandemic seems miniscule now."

"Very true," I replied. "Now let's get you over to the ceremony."

Sophie's assistant radioed in that the bride was ready, and in the nick of time. The three of us walked with Ginny over to the Wills Perennial Garden. Sophie's assistant offered to take over holding up the back of Ginny's dress, but I didn't want to take any chances. I suggested she hold the bouquet and let me tend to the dress.

Dom turned his camera back on and captured every beautiful moment of the ceremony, including one of the bridesmaids pulling Sissy down the aisle in a wicker wagon adorned with garlands and ribbon. Not a dry eye was left after the couple recited their own vows while Ravi held their daughter in his arms. It was perfect.

As everyone moved to the reception for dinner and dancing, I realized I'd forgotten all about Lottie for a moment. She was tasked with overseeing the décor installation, and we hadn't been back around the tent again. But I thought for sure our paths would cross at some point. This wasn't the best place to talk to her as we were both on the job, but I didn't know the next time I'd see her in person—hopefully not at Lucy's wedding.

I also didn't know exactly what I'd say if I got the chance. I still didn't have any real explanation for my actions, or for myself, aside from some misguided sense of competition and entitlement.

I was lost in thought when Dom elbowed me to pay attention as the couple was introduced into the tent by the band. Everyone cheered, and I managed to clear my mind and refocus on our task at hand. The hours seemed to fly by.

"You've got some mad skills with that dress, Tex," Dom said as we circled the perimeter of the tent. Guests were still eating, but no one needs video of people with food in their mouths—so instead we took some time to shoot details of the exterior décor.

"Thanks," I said.

"You didn't miss a beat and made her feel relaxed while you saved the day. That other planner was totally useless," he said.

"You can't be too hard on her," I said. "It's a lot to handle at times, and the stress can really get to you." Clearly, I knew this from personal experience. "She's new and will learn. Or she won't, and then she'll have to find another job." I laughed. "Wedding planning definitely isn't for everyone."

"Is that what happened with you?"

"Not exactly," I replied. But before I could go on, we turned the corner and yet again came face-to-face with Lottie. Had her ears been burning? Her timing was epic.

"Oh, hi again, Lottie." I swallowed hard. "It looks amazing in here."

"It does, doesn't it? Cedric never lets a bride down, that's for sure," she said. I'm sure she wanted to add "unlike you," but mercifully refrained.

"Would you be willing to answer a few questions for our docuseries?" Dom asked.

I froze for a second. I wished I'd thought to tell him she was off-limits for an interview.

"No thanks," said Lottie. "I don't trust the media. I'm sure you understand why, Claire."

I wanted to vomit.

"Oh, it's totally fine. We're good. Dom, let's go get some detail footage of the cake before they cut it," I said in a tone that I hoped indicated we needed to move on, *now.*

"Yes, why don't you go do that," Lottie called. "And try not to knock it over while you're at it."

I grabbed Dom's arm and pulled him in the direction of the loggia, where the cake had been set up in the center of the space.

"She definitely does not like you," Dom said, raising his brows.

I was mortified.

"No, no, she doesn't," I said, still recovering. "I really don't want to get into it tonight. Let's just finish up and get out of here, okay?"

I could tell he wanted to press for more information, but he was kind enough to let it go for now. I wouldn't be able to dodge telling him the whole truth forever. Certainly not if I kept running into old coworkers. No matter how far away I was from Dallas, my past could always catch up with me.

CHAPTER 11

Seeing Lottie threw me for a loop. Sunday, I moped around my apartment. Being unexpectedly confronted with my past failures, one of my absolute worst, was even more uncomfortable than I'd imagined. Did it bother me that I'd attempted to get ahead and it spectacularly imploded? Or was I having a genuine pang of remorse that I hurt people who were kind to me in the process? Was I a monster? I tried not to dwell too much on it, but it was difficult not to death-spiral.

That afternoon, scrolling Instagram as a distraction, I watched Dom's latest story. Screw the fact that he could see I was watching. He already knew I followed him.

Last week, he'd somehow found time to interview the hottest new baker in town, whose pressed-flower cookies had recently won some reality competition. He must have been going out on his lunch breaks and the rare weekend we weren't covering a wedding.

Regardless, he was systematically going through most of the top local wedding vendors—interviewing them, reviewing their strengths and weaknesses for his audience. His blog held more in-depth information, but these posts were a massive help to brides, I imagined.

I looked at his highlights, which were beautifully organized according to themes and neighborhoods in NYC, along with a few additional cities like Nashville and Los Angeles. I had to give him credit—again. He really had compiled some amazing resources for brides trying to do it on their own. He was like a straight, single guy wedding planner who came into your home—all for free.

Sure, he got paid by sponsors, but it was a lot of work to provide for brides who were never going to be your client. Not for the first time, I wondered what his endgame was. It sure wasn't bridal magazines in Nashville.

Like he said himself, he was a hustler. He saw an opportunity and took it. And not how I saw an opportunity and took it when I threw Lottie and the team under the proverbial bus in Dallas. His intentions continued to seem honorable. He saw a hole in the wedding market and worked his way up as an influencer with expertise in that space. To my knowledge, he did so without putting other people down along the way.

I'd dismissed what he did as amateurish and self-centered, but as it turned out, he was a real asset to brides. He made money while also helping clients and vendors in the wedding industry either find what they were looking for or advertise their services.

I'd had my own chance, too, in Dallas, and I'd managed to

blow it up for myself before I'd even seen how far I could go. Was that what I didn't like about Dom? Did I resent him for succeeding and making it all look so easy to obtain?

Even at *Piece of Cake*, I worked hard, but I'd be lying if I said I hadn't fought to prove my worth in comparison to other departments. That was the only way I learned to play the game.

If I'd wanted a distraction, I probably shouldn't have been deep-diving on a coworker's wedding planning feed. Still, I mulled over my thoughts the rest of Sunday afternoon, and by Monday morning I was a jumbled mental mess. I didn't know how I felt about much at the moment—Dom, my family, my job. It was a lot to process. But one thing I did know for certain was that I wasn't going to mess up this opportunity with *Piece of Cake*. At least, that was my plan.

◊ ◊ ◊

With the influx of weddings taking place in Nashville came a surge of new venue options for couples looking to tie the knot and host their reception. And with limited space available in hotels and buildings in the city, entrepreneurs took the opportunity to open new and "unique" spaces nearby to attract clients.

I'd recently heard about a refurbished fire tower in a forest just outside the city that was marketing itself as a site to host a ceremony "in the clouds." I could think of at least ten significant reasons why it was a horrible idea to recite one's vows at the top of an old fire tower. But I was sure it booked out a year in advance like every other spot in town, given how desperate brides were to secure a location.

Over the weekend, Michelle got wind that the *Tennessee Belle* was about to reopen and operate exclusively as a wedding venue. This massive paddleboat/showboat cruised the Cumberland River with a large dining room and theater for performances. It ran for decades to and from the Gaylord Opryland Resort, until a kitchen fire knocked it out of commission for the past few years. But now that the city was booming with new tourists looking for Nashville experiences, the boat was given a second life and updated décor.

So come Monday morning, Dom and I were tasked with checking it out. Lucky us. I had hoped that my "Tying the Yacht" article would be my last journalistic experience with love boats, but apparently not.

And to make matters even worse, they'd only opened to prospective clients. No media previews. So Michelle wanted us to go "undercover" as an engaged couple checking it out as a potential option for our wedding. There was no talking her out of it. Once she had an idea, she was like a dog with a bone.

"This will be such a fun story to write. I can only imagine the drama that could ensue on that paddleboat."

"But, Michelle—"

She waved me off and kept going. "Remember, we still have to fill the actual print magazine, and this will make for a great read. My senior prom took place on a dinner cruise, and it was tragic. Everyone was fighting, I hated my date, and there was nowhere to escape to for hours unless I wanted to swim to shore. I actually considered that halfway through the event," she mused.

So this was helping her work out her teenage trauma?

"Sounds like we're in for quite the trip," Dom added.

"But don't worry. This is a shorter cruise for couples who are interested in booking it for their wedding. It's like a venue tour, but on the water. I can't wait for you to report back." She clapped her hands once. "Now off you go! Bon voyage!"

And with that, we were destined for Nashville's newest "love boat." Thankfully the cruise was only two hours long, and they always served cocktails at these kinds of events. I could take one for the team.

"Please tell me I don't look like the type of bride who would choose to get married on a showboat," I said to Dom as we drove the half hour from our office to the Gaylord Opryland Resort.

He laughed. "Well, I'm not sure exactly what somebody who wants to get married on a massive paddleboat looks like. But I bet it's not a Dallas debutante."

"Here you go again," I said. "I'm not a debutante."

"Yeah, *okay*." He smirked. "Did you have a deb ball?"

"Well, yes, but that's not the point," I said. "I'm as far from a Dallas debutante right now as ever."

"Don't be mad," he said. "I'm trying to compliment you, but I'm clearly botching it."

"You think?" I replied, rolling my eyes at him. Just then we reached the Opryland complex, where the *Tennessee Belle* was docked.

"Wow!" he interrupted. "This place is huge!"

"What? Oh yeah. It's basically a country-lover's compound. The Gaylord used to be the Opryland Hotel, and before that it was a theme park. It's changed a lot over the years, and now it's one of the biggest hotels in the region." We wound through the massive parking lot to reach the river.

"Next venue tour?"

"Sure, I'd be down for it. As long as we can ride the little boats that wind through it and drink trash can punch."

"This sounds like so many of my dreams coming true."

"Oh, a guy like you would have a blast."

"But speaking of dreams, back to what I was saying. I just meant that someone like you would probably want to get married somewhere a bit more romantic. Like a swanky, old downtown hotel ballroom or a chic mountaintop lodge in Jackson Hole. I'm right, aren't I?" he asked with an unfortunately handsome smirk.

He had me there. Both of those locations were at the top of my list. My strictly hypothetical list, of course. But I'd never admit that. Instead, I turned the conversation back on him.

"What would *your* dream venue be?" I asked. "You seem to cover so many options on your blog, I'd love to know what you'd choose. And please tell me it's not the fire tower."

"I'm not fond of heights, in addition to the fact that it's just weird. I don't know if I could pick just one spot right now. I guess it depends on who I marry and what she wants. Sounds cheesy, but I like the idea of finding a place that would be special to both of us. And, like you, I'm not sold on the idea of rollin' down the river with my bride-to-be. So that probably means no showboats for me."

We laughed, but I also couldn't ignore his comment about choosing a place that was special to him and his future wife. It was inconveniently romantic.

"Welp, anyway, I can't wait to check out *our* potential venue today!" I gave him my broadest fake grin and batted my eyelashes.

To prepare for the tour, we spent a few more minutes going over our story as a fake couple. We needed to make sure we gave the same answers when asked questions about how we met, how we got engaged, and what we wanted for our wedding.

I wasn't as nervous about the details as much as I was about pretending to be in love with Dom. My acting skills were pretty solid. Heck, I'd faked it before in plenty of situations. From faking it through bad dates to convincing colleagues like Lottie I never wanted her job, from making up new toasts for each of the twelve deb balls I attended one season to spending holidays at Gran's house, I'd gone through life giving people whatever impression was most helpful. But I found myself not wanting to give Dom the wrong idea.

And he was my friend now, right? I could admit that to myself. I knew I was setting myself up for disappointment because he was inevitably leaving town, but I couldn't help but like the guy. As a person.

I found myself concerned for his feelings, a new development for me. Though I probably should have been concerned about my own. *C'mon now, don't go so soft, Sommers.*

Dom certainly wasn't helping the situation by being so nice

and charming all the time. Not to mention he was good-looking, and we seemed to have a natural chemistry together. But he was also a performer. He could just be trying to win me over until his assignment here was done. I'd certainly done the same. That was always in the back of my mind. The last thing he needed was for his colleague to hinder his job and long-term goals. It was so hard to tell what was real with him and what was for the camera. Why did this all have to be so complicated? And now we were about to pretend to be an actual couple on the verge of getting married. I guess I'd just live moment by moment for now, or at least for the next two hours on a love boat.

As we walked up to the platform where the boat was docked, Dom took my hand.

"Ready to pretend like you actually like me?" he said, giving me a wink.

CHAPTER 12

barely heard him, given that my heart was pounding so loudly I thought it might explode. This was pathetic.

"What? Oh, ha," I said as I willed myself to stop thinking about his strong grip on my hand. "I *do* like you, Dom. You know, like in the way you *like* your brother, but also in the way you hate him," I lied through my teeth.

What was I even talking about? He'd touched me, and I'd come completely unglued. This was shaping up to be less like *The Love Boat* and more like the *Titanic*.

He laughed and squeezed my hand, which was kind, given that I was acting like a total buffoon.

"Sorry, I'm just nervous about making 'us' seem believable."

"Well, don't worry," he said, giving me a sexy smile. "I'm very convincing when I need to be."

At least now I was thinking about my knees buckling and not my hand wrapped around his. If I thought he had charm before, this was a whole other level. It was oozing out of every one of his perfect pores now. *Pull yourself together, Claire.*

Once we walked up the gangway, a waitress greeted us and offered glasses of champagne, which we happily accepted. A few other couples were signed up for the event, so we were ushered onto the boat for a group tour while the staff prepared to launch.

On first glance, it looked like they'd done a decent job of renovating. The exterior of the all-white boat with giant red paddles in the back was polished and looked like the original ship I'd seen in pictures. However, as soon as we stepped onto the main deck from the gangway, it felt as thought we'd entered a floating Vegas casino. We were greeted by a man dressed in full Elvis garb, including white bell-bottoms and a cape—both completely bedazzled in red crystals.

"Well hello there, lovebirds," the man said in his best impersonation of an Elvis voice, complete with an arched upper lip. "Welcome to our floating chapel of love."

"You've *got* to be kidding me," I whispered to Dom.

"This job just gets better and better," Dom replied, taking an information packet from Elvis.

"Please head on inside the reception space where your hunka hunka burnin' love tour will begin momentarily," Elvis said.

"This has to be a joke," I said as Dom held the door open for us to go inside. "I mean, Elvis isn't even originally from Nashville. He's from Memphis."

"I don't think they thought too much about making this an accurate experience of a paddleboat or of Elvis. I mean, look at these." Dom gestured with a laugh as we walked through a pair of massive cherry-red heart-shaped doors. "Clearly, they're selling a very specific, stereotyped vision here."

I was having a hard time paying attention to Dom as I took in all my surroundings. The interior event space was covered in gold-gilded panels and the carpet was a deep-burgundy color. Large crystal chandeliers hung throughout the room, and it all felt like a sad attempt at creating a Versailles ballroom on the river.

"Do you think the ghost of Huckleberry Finn was replaced by Elvis's?" Dom whispered in my ear.

Without turning, I breathed back, "Elvis more likely booted out the ghost of Kenny Rogers, since this place was built in the 1980s."

He squeezed my shoulders and said in a voice of mock dismay, "What? We're not on an *authentic* paddleboat? I demand a refund. On my free tour."

"Alas! You'd promised me we could exchange vows on the same boards that shipped cotton downriver, but we'll have to settle for Las Vegas, circa 1970 . . . Michelle is going to die when she hears about this."

The tour took about half an hour, and Dom held my hand the whole time. It was hard to imagine anything could distract me from all the fringe and other ghastly décor, but my mind was on our intertwined hands. I attempted to be chill but could tell my palm was sweating.

Afterward, we were led to the back of the boat, where there was a space for cocktails before or after a wedding ceremony. It was the one place on the entire ship that wasn't adorned with velvet or sequins, and the fresh air felt amazing. Tables were set out, and a trio of musicians played lively classical music in the corner. We were invited to enjoy the appetizers and order another round of drinks while we traveled down the Cumberland on our showboat.

"Shall I fetch my beautiful bride-to-be another glass of champagne?" Dom asked.

"Yes, but only if you promise not to be gone for long," I said in my most cloying voice. "I simply hate it when I'm not with you!"

"Oh, shnookums, don't worry. I'll be back in a flash," he replied, squeezing my hand before letting go.

It took everything I had not to laugh aloud. Dom headed in the direction of the built-in bar, and I turned to stare over the railing. The landscape was surprisingly pretty, and the water didn't look dingy at all. I'd never spent any time on the Cumberland River, but clearly my preconceived ideas about it were dead wrong. Many of my preconceived notions seemed to be wrong these days. I needed to get out of my head and try to relax.

The water glistened as the boat glided through it, and I could see why couples might enjoy spending their evening aboard the *Belle*. That is, until I remembered what the interior looked like. A shame they leaned too heavily on whatever theme was happening inside, as the view from the decks was stunning. I could only imagine how romantic this setting would be at night, especially if we were far enough away from the city center to see stars.

"If I didn't know better, it looks like you might actually be a 'love boat' fan after all," Dom quipped as he handed me a fresh glass of champagne.

"Well, this whole area is amazing." I took a sip while motioning to the exterior deck space. "It's the whole burlesque casino vibe inside the actual ceremony space that makes me hesitate." I laughed. "And then there's the whole issue of entrapment."

"Entrapment?"

"Well, you'd have to be very careful with your guest list, since once you're on the boat, there's no getting off for four hours. I imagine that could make for some serious drama if a guest or bridesmaid got drunk or a fight between family members broke out," I said. "I've witnessed a lot of shenanigans, and I can't imagine what would happen if any of them took place on a boat. Being held captive would add an extra level of craziness to any situation."

"Very true," said Dom. "But I wouldn't mind being stuck on a boat with you. Even one that looks like an Elvis explosion." Bits of white blossoms from trees on the riverbank were floating in the early spring air like snowflakes. He gently brushed off one that had settled on my shoulder, his fingers tracing down the top of my arm.

I could feel the blood rush up to my cheeks. *Wow, that was very forward*, I thought. Before I could respond, I turned and saw two of the other couples approaching us. Maybe it was for their benefit?

"Hello!" An older woman with bleached-blonde hair teased as high as Dolly Parton's waved out a hand in greeting. "So how did you two cute young people meet?"

"Oh, we met at Margaritaville downtown," Dom responded without missing a beat.

"How fun for y'all," the woman replied. "I just love that place! Us old folks had to meet each other through Match.com since we're too elderly to find true love in bars anymore." She popped the olive from her martini in her mouth. I was a bit envious of the cocktail as I sipped my responsible midafternoon champagne.

We all introduced ourselves and naturally moved into a small circle so everyone could chat. I'd hoped we could avoid having to mingle with the other couples, but thankfully we'd prepared for this moment.

"Martha and I here are best friends and we're both working on our second marriages, which is why the idea of a 'wedding cruise' seems so fun." Pam, the Dolly Parton look-alike, gestured to her friend and partner.

"Whatever Pam wants is what Pam gets," said Bob, her equally middle-aged fiancé. He sipped a beer and wore a white linen Havana shirt. "Happy wife, happy life." He nudged Dom in the arm as he chuckled.

"That's what I hear," said Dom, taking a sip of his champagne and giving me an exaggerated wink. He clearly relished every minute of our charade. The guy loved making me uncomfortable.

"After that night we met at Margaritaville, we walked down to the river and sat in the grass near the amphitheater. That's where we had our first kiss, so the Cumberland has a special place in our hearts." He pulled me in next to him and gave me a squeeze.

That definitely wasn't a detail we'd gone over, but it was a clever touch for sure. I grinned blankly and nodded.

"And that's why we want to get married here on the *Tennessee Belle*," Dom finished.

I couldn't keep from blushing yet again.

"My goodness, look at how adorable you cuties are," said Pam. "I remember being young and in love. Didn't work out so well for me the first time, but you two look great together. Cheers to young love!" She raised her glass.

"Cheers!" said everyone else, bringing their glasses in to clink together.

"Now give that gal of yours a kiss," said Bob.

My heart stopped. *Oh. No.*

"Come on now," added Pam. "Don't be shy. We're all on this love boat together."

And with that Pam and Bob gave each other a kiss, and Martha and Tom followed suit. My guess was that whatever Pam did in life, Martha did too. Right down to leaving her first husband and finding a second.

"Well?" Dom stared down at me, a challenge. "Lay one on me, babe." He was grinning like the Cheshire cat.

Was this really going to happen? Right here? Right now?

Apparently, yes. Before I had time to think another second about it, Dom leaned down and kissed me.

His full lips were softer than I expected. He kept them closed like a gentleman since we were pretending, after all. The kiss wasn't long, but it lingered more than a peck.

But for a moment, something shifted. Like a jolt. His lips pressed firmer, and it was all I could do to keep from grabbing the front of his shirt. He tasted like cherry ChapStick and mint gum. My own traitorous lips started to part despite myself, and I pulled away.

I was dizzy. I couldn't look him in the face, so I stared at Pam's bejeweled tote bag instead. After a moment, he put an arm around my shoulders.

"Y'all are just precious," said Pam. "I hope you have a long and wonderful life together."

"Thanks so much," I said once I was able to speak. My cheeks must have been red as a fire hydrant.

Dom just stood there grinning like a fool.

They walked away with a wave, and he lowered his arm. Dom and I both spoke at once.

"I'm sorry," he began, "I didn't mean to—"

"Listen, that can't—" I jumped in.

"I should tell you—" he started again.

I started speaking again before he could finish. "I know that was just for show, but I don't want you to get any ideas about me either. Obviously, this"—I motioned between us—"isn't happening. It couldn't. But we probably shouldn't do that again. Let's keep it professional."

"Of course, I agree," he said quickly. "We just went along with the, um, moment."

"Good, glad that's settled. We have a lot at stake right now. I wouldn't want you to get the wrong impression or get distracted."

"Yes, you either."

I doubted Dom had any real feelings for me other than friendship. He was so good at turning it on for others, and his performance today was Oscar-worthy, I thought with a flutter.

We circled back to the front where the two older couples were stationed with fresh drinks. We chatted for a while longer before the boat pulled back up at the dock, then an employee handed us a sparkling tote bag that contained a massive packet of information about the venue as we stepped off the boat.

"Y'all take care now, you hear?" Pam shouted to us as they walked away.

"And don't forget," added Bob, "marriage is a relationship in which one person is always right and the other always needs more whiskey!"

Pam gave him a fake punch in the arm, and Bob squeezed her backside in return.

"Well, that was certainly interesting," Dom said once we got into the car.

"Um, yeah. You *really* sold our engagement. What was that you told Martha about my snoring?"

"Oh, come on. You didn't exactly seem to mind." He smiled rakishly. "And I thought the snoring was a convincing touch."

I died a little inside. Time to redirect.

"Well, I'm just glad that's behind us." I hoped I sounded like I meant it.

Acting like a fake couple had been more enjoyable than expected, complications aside. I was clearly lonelier than I'd been willing to admit to myself until now.

"I'm actually kinda bummed it's over," replied Dom as he turned up a song on the radio. "That was pretty fun. I hope you had at least a little fun too."

"Oh, I did," I said. "Sorry. I just meant that I'm glad to get back to work on the docuseries. In fact, why don't we grab a quick bite to eat before going back to work? It's the least I can do since you'll be paying for our showboat wedding."

His laugh rang out. "Oh really? I'm paying for our wedding on the *Belle*?"

"You bet you are. It's the twenty-first century, and couples split the bill a lot these days."

"Oh, I see." He smirked. "Well then, I'm picking out a fancy spot for us to eat tonight so I get my, I mean *your*, money's worth."

"Perfect," I replied. "As long as it's not someplace with hot chicken. I still have traumatic memories from a previous experience with that stuff."

"I'm going to need to hear that story over dinner," he said.

"Maybe," I said, grinning. We seemed to be back to our normal friendly banter. And we even managed to avoid talking about the kiss. Things were looking up.

"No hot chicken it is," Dom said. "After all: happy wife, happy life."

CHAPTER 13

I spent the next two weeks actively trying not to think about the kiss that transpired on our maiden voyage on the *Tennessee Belle*. Thankfully Dom was kind enough never to mention it again, so I did the same. I wondered whether he thought about it as much as I did though. Maybe it was because I hadn't been kissed in a while, but I just couldn't shake that moment from memory. When I spoke with Dom in person, it took everything I had not to stare at his lips the whole time he was talking. I'm sure he thought I was crazy for focusing so intently on his eyebrows.

Fortunately, the big Friday of Lucy's bachelorette weekend came quickly. And with it, more than ample distraction.

A giant embroidered Minnie Pearl grinned down at me as I leaned on the walnut counter in the lobby of the Graduate Hotel. Lucy had arrived—along with six of her nearest and dearest.

As the maid of honor, I was the hostess, and thankfully Lucy and I overlapped friends so they weren't all total strangers. Evelyn kept saying she was "near crowning" even though she had almost two months to go in her pregnancy. Thus, she wasn't going to risk a trip to Nashville for a "weekend of debauchery," according to her texts. To be honest, Lucy and I were somewhat relieved she was sitting, or rather waddling, this one out. Nothing kills a vibe at a bar like a very pregnant woman with permanent RBF.

Most of Lucy's friends had enjoyed their own bachelorette parties in Hawaii, Vegas, or New Orleans, but in a concession to my budget, we were bringing the party to Nashville. It helped that I already lived in the new bachelorette capital of the country, so no one was complaining.

Thanks to our parents, Lucille had stayed at some of the top hotels in the world. But for this trip, she wanted somewhere fun, girly, and located near the honky-tonks. Naturally, I chose the Graduate. Every detail of the hotel embraced maximalism—the idea that "more is more and less is a bore." (I could still hear those words in Cedric's voice.) The lobby was a visual feast as everything from the tables to the ceiling was covered in patterned wallpaper or country music kitsch. Artwork featuring Dolly Parton and other country heroines adorned each wall, including above each bed.

Looking around the lobby, I'd never been in a room with such high fringe-to-person ratio. Every woman had on fringed cowboy boots, miniskirt, or leather jacket—or all of the above. As a Texan, I prided myself on not typically wearing such inauthentic items. However, it was Lucy's weekend, and we were going all out. We had rhinestone-monogrammed denim jackets for each girl, along with pink-felt cowgirl hats with white fringe trim. And that was just the start.

Thankfully Evelyn wanted to pitch in for the weekend, which really meant she picked up the bulk of the tab. It paid to have a guilt-ridden sister with a hefty salary and total access to her trust fund. In addition to the festivities I planned for the weekend, we could also splurge on the gift bag that everyone received upon check-in.

The concierge handed me my massive monogrammed straw bag. I'd packed them myself at home this week but appreciated the formality. I glanced inside to make sure the goodies were all accounted for: pink silk sleep masks with matching Sleeper feather-trimmed pajamas, pearl-trimmed koozies with "Last Fling before the Ring" printed on them, a whole host of gourmet chocolates, various snacks, and a vanilla-scented Voluspa candle. I also threw in the traditional bachelorette party necessities like Advil and a face mask that could be chilled to reduce puffiness.

I carried my gift bag up to Lucy's suite, where I'd already checked in a few hours earlier. Lucy specifically requested that I refrain from adding in any "male genitalia items" (she actually said that instead of the actual word *penis*), which really took the wind out of my sails. But she was so darn modest, I kind of saw it coming. That was the baby of the family for you. Meanwhile, at Evelyn's bachelorette party, there wasn't an item *not* in the shape of a penis. Evie may have been uptight and overbearing, but the girl could party like the best of them.

"Clairrrrre!" Lucy squealed as I walked in the door. "It's so fun!"

"*Oof,*" was all I could squeak out as she gave me a massive hug.

Decorating her megasuite hadn't taken long given that phalluses were forbidden. Massive balloon garlands in various shades of pink and oversized balloons with "Future Mrs." printed on them would have to do. The pièce de résistance, though, was a rented floral wall made entirely of pink roses, so she'd have the perfect backdrop to take as many selfies as she wanted. After all, how would everyone know it was Lucy's big bachelorette weekend if she didn't post it all over Instagram?

I truly hated social media sometimes. Thankfully, we all made a pact not to post anything from the weekend that could be considered controversial. Mom and Dad were still überprivate, and I'd already embarrassed them enough for all time.

The whole crew was meeting in the suite for a catered dinner before heading out. We played the classic game of "guess what your fiancé said," where Lucy had to guess answers to questions that I'd emailed Collins several weeks prior. She guessed every single one correctly, including the one about his favorite childhood stuffed animal. They were so adorable together and well-suited that it was kind of nauseating.

"Okay, time to change things up and head downtown. Lucy, I know you don't want any 'male genitalia' at this party." I paused so her friends could boo. "So I have respected your wishes, and now you must respect mine. The only rules tonight are as follows: First, you must wear these at all times." I handed her a white satin sash with "Future Mrs." spelled out in rhinestones and a cowgirl hat with a crown on it. "And second, you must keep 'Collins' with you everywhere you go."

I had managed to find a male blow-up doll that I dressed in

the frattiest outfit I could find to mimic Collins. This included a polo shirt, some khaki pants, and a visor (all in a boy's size so they fit the doll like a glove). I had to have at least a little fun with Lucy this weekend.

Everyone squealed. He was a huge hit. Lucy giggled and said, "I accept! So handsome!"

After dessert, and with blow-up Collins in tow, we headed for the elevator. Lucy hooked her arm through mine and sighed contentedly. "Claire Bear, I'm so happy right now. I've got all my best girls here, and I can't believe I'm getting married in a few weeks."

"Me neither! Still shocked you guys are pulling it off this fast."

"Well, you know Cedric. I mean, of course you do. Sorry." She looked up at me with a brief grimace. "But you know they've got quite an operation."

"It's okay, sis. And you're right, he's the best. Who is working on your event?"

"Well, I've mostly been speaking with Mary Ellen and some junior members of the team. Lottie has done some planning calls, too, from Atlanta. She's handling flowers while Abigail is on maternity leave."

"Oh, that's wonderful news about Abigail! I didn't realize." Maybe staying off social media had some downsides. I still wished them all well, even if they would always hate me. It wasn't unmerited.

"Yeah, I'm loving the designs they've come up with so far. I can show you when we're back at the hotel and I have my computer."

"I'd love that." I could tell Lucy had been wanting to share the details and wasn't sure whether she could.

Downstairs, a party bus waited to take us down to Broadway. After my pedal cab accident, I refused to ride in any sort of outdoor alcohol situation. Fortunately, Lucy agreed.

The interior of our Sprinter van was furnished with luxe leather seats and neon track lighting that changed along with the music. It also held a full bar with dangerously breakable glassware.

Lucy's high school best friend, Allison, and I had decorated the interior with more streamers and balloons. Not a penis piñata in sight. There was also a glitter railing that presumably helped guests get around the bus safely. But given the lighting and the alcohol, it looked like a stripper pole.

We plopped into our seats for the short ride.

Minutes later, we hopped out of the shuttle and ducked inside my favorite honky-tonk, Tootsie's Orchid Lounge. Like all good spots downtown, it had become a little touristy, but it was still the real deal. It had been in business long enough for Patsy Cline and Willie Nelson to have played early shows. The old purple-brick building backed up to the Ryman, and in its heyday, the bar served as a between-sets hangout for Opry legends like Hank Williams, Mel Tillis, and Johnny Cash. These days, photos of those legends were peppered in with Taylor Swift, Kenny Chesney, and Trisha Yearwood, but the place felt like history, good times, and the comfort of home.

We slid into a corner booth and looked at the drink menu.

A house band, talented as they all must be in this town, crooned classic country songs.

After we ordered, I got up to find the bathroom. As the waiter pointed past the bar, I saw a familiar pair of broad shoulders leaning against the worn wood ledge. He was talking to another man, but we locked eyes and he nodded his head. He'd evidently sighted me the moment before.

Half perched on his stool, he watched me approach. "Hey there, little lady."

"Howdy, cowboy." I had to admit Dom looked cute in a Stetson, even if it was on backward.

"Am I doing it right?" he asked.

"You'll get there. But let's talk about the fact that you're *here*. With all the bars in Nashville, what are the odds we'd both be at Tootsie's tonight?"

He ignored my question and motioned to his wingman.

"Claire, this is my buddy Mike. He's one of those Yankee friends I told you inspired me to come down here in the first place."

"Nice to meet you," Mike said, extending a large hand. "He speaks the truth."

"I'd ask how you like it here, but evidently you liked it enough to convince Dom to make the move. For that, I may never forgive you." I winked.

Dom leaned between us. "Can I buy you a drink?"

"Nah. Thank you though. I'm just here with my sister's bridal party. We've got a show later."

"Yes! Where are they?" Dom scanned the room. "I want to meet the famous Lucy."

"And I want to meet any attractive single friends she might have!" Mike quipped.

"Easy there, tigers. Most of the women are taken, out of your league, or both."

Dom clutched his chest in mock pain. I turned and headed for the bathroom, chuckling to myself.

Back at the table, Lucy gave me the third degree. "Who was that?"

"Nobody. Just Dom," I mumbled into my glass.

Her eyes sparked, and I knew I had two choices: get the flock of hens to leave immediately or prepare myself for an inevitable meeting.

"Ugh, fine. Let's just make it quick." I pulled her with me back over to the bar. "You're lucky this weekend is all about you, so we'll do what you want. Well . . . within reason," I said as we approached Dom and his friend.

"Hello, Dom." Lucy extended a hand and showed off her thousand-watt smile.

"It's so nice to meet you in person," said Dom, shaking her hand, then introducing her to Mike.

"Nice to finally meet you too!" Lucy said enthusiastically. "Glad you could make it."

"Wait, excuse me?" I looked from one to the other. "What are you talking about?"

"Your sister invited us. We thought we might be able to pick up some bachelorettes making use of the bars on Broadway." Dom gave us both a wink.

"How? Why?" I sputtered.

"I follow him. You work with him. We're celebrating my wedding, and he's practically a wedding celebrity. I had to meet the Brides' Man," Lucy said patiently, as if the logic tracked. "So I DMed him, Claire. Like a normal human person this millennium. Not everyone is afraid of the internet."

"And I was delighted at the chance to check out the bachelorette scene. For research, of course."

I threw up my hands. "Oh, you both are the absolute worst. Why didn't you mention it?"

"I didn't think you'd go for it and would act pretty much like you are now." Lucy gave one of her classic grins.

I shook my head at her. "Well, now you two have officially met. I, for one, need a drink. Or three."

"I can help with that. What can I get for the bride-to-be and her maid of dishonor?" Dom asked as the bartender arrived in front of us. He had no idea how spot-on his joke hit.

"She'll have another Ranch Water with Patrón, Dom," said Lucy. "Make that two."

"Yes, ma'am," said Dom.

"Here we go again with that *ma'am* bit," I interjected.

Mike finished off his glass of brown liquid. "What's your plan for the night?"

"I'm just following Claire's orders," replied Lucy.

"Yeah, right. This is the *one* time in my life you've let me be the elder sister and take charge of things," I said. "Speaking of which, where is your friend Collins?"

"Did your fiancé come on the trip?" Dom passed us both our drinks.

"No, hold on," Lucy hollered as she ran back over to her gaggle of friends still huddled around the nearby table.

She returned seconds later with blow-up Collins in one hand and her drink already half gone in another.

"I totally forgot to bring this guy with me . . . I'm so sorry, honey," she said to the doll. "I will never leave you or forsake you. Except when it's time to dance! Actually . . . why don't you hold him for a minute?" Lucy said as she thrust the four-foot blow-up into Dom's arm.

I tried not to keel over laughing at the sight of Dom holding the inflatable. He looked less than amused and immediately sat Collins, or rather leaned him, into one of the empty barstools.

"Come on, sis. I love this song. Let's head to the floor and you can show me some of the line dancing skills you've been talking about."

"Oh my gosh, I promise I've never talked about or actually line danced here," I said, looking at Dom as she started pulling me away.

"I don't believe that for a second." He laughed and adjusted Collins's visor. "Let's see what you've got!" he yelled in my direction as I was enveloped by the growing crowd of people.

No turning back now.

Groups of cowboy boot–clad men and women on the prowl were interspersed with the dancing bachelorettes. This was their natural habitat; they were made for honky-tonks, and honky-tonks for them.

Brightly colored disco lights traced jagged paths across faces. Heels thumped on the worn wooden floor, and I noted the difference in Tennessee and Texas boots. A lot more fringe and sparkle among the Nashville club crowd; a lot more scuffs and custom-stamped leather in Dallas–Fort Worth.

My Miron Crosby low-cut booties slid across the worn wood as the band's lead singer called everyone out for a line dance. My gran would argue that line dances were not "authentic" country-and-western dancing, but the idea sure got everybody on the floor.

Lucy and her eager bridesmaids danced to my left. Not one of us looked composed while stomping and spinning and trying to remember the moves. I noticed Dom and Mike trying to dance out of the corner of my eye, Dom's head conveniently several inches above those around him. Blow-up Collins was nowhere in sight.

He laughed, turning the wrong direction yet again. Green eyes crinkled at the corners when he smiled. He tossed his head back at his haplessness with the steps.

But once he got the hang of it, Dom had some moves. Our respective groups gradually ended up on the same side of the floor. As we all turned around, I averted my eyes once I realized I was staring at his denim-clad backside conveniently swaying right in front of me. I looked around quickly, praying no one noticed. Everyone was too focused on their own footwork.

As we turned, I missed a couple more steps. "You gotta

relax." Dom's baritone came over my shoulder, a little too close for comfort. "Just follow the person in front of you."

"I tried that a couple turns ago, but what if the person in front of you is a moron from Brooklyn?"

"Touché. Got any tips, then, if you're such a pro?"

"Not a one. I told you, I only learned to waltz."

"Well, little princess, *my* trick is to find the person who aggressively thinks they know all the moves and stand a couple people behind them. Try it . . . That lady in the red should do."

We both imitated the motions of a woman in her forties who was clearly a regular. She had the confidence—and the worn-in boots—of someone who spent Saturday nights line dancing.

Eventually, the song changed. As every wedding planner knew, nothing cleared the dance floor faster than the wrong slow song. But a good classic filled it. In the right bar in the right city. The crowd started to disperse, and Lucy and the rest of our group had disappeared. Dom and I found ourselves next to each other, feet shuffling.

He extended a hand. "Want to dance?"

I took his left hand in my right, and he pulled me close with the other, adding, "Okey dokey, how do we do this, Tex?"

"Love how you asked me to dance without actually knowing what to do."

"I am nothing if not consistently overconfident," he quipped. *And not without reason*, I thought while looking into his boyishly charming face.

"This is a two-step, which should be pretty easy. First, your hand goes *here*." I adjusted his right hand from precariously close to my backside to the middle of my back. "We can pretend you're leading."

I showed him the footwork, quietly counting under my breath so he could hear. At one point, we both looked down at our feet and bumped heads. "Ow!" I jerked upward to find my face inches from his.

A lengthy pause later, he said, "Sorry . . . Two left feet."

"Must be," I squeaked. "Try not to let it happen again." The way I was desperately trying not to repeat our moment on the *Tennessee Belle*.

Finally tearing my eyes away, I focused on the older couple next to us. They had the gentle cadence of a pair long accustomed to dancing together. Their rhythms and turns were effortless, smooth. *Do they have that sort of synchronicity off the dance floor? Is such a thing even possible?* It certainly didn't seem possible with the man softly counting to three over and over again in my ear. His level of effort was adorable.

His hand was warm in mine. I was probably sweating all over his palm again, I realized with horror. Hopefully he wouldn't notice.

All I could notice was the firmness of his shoulder under my hand and the faint smell of cedar every time I got near his shirt. It fought valiantly through the smells of sweat and old beer overpowering the room. I briefly wished I could bury my head in that plaid and inhale deeply. Then I was appalled. *He's saying something, Claire. Pay attention!*

"Do you go dancing much?"

Aw. A middle school dance question if there ever was one. I grinned, defenseless. "Not exactly. I had a couple friends who liked to salsa, but I don't have the rhythm or grace for that. And I don't have the stamina for whatever grinding, jumping, bumping situation happens in clubs these days. I'm more of a slide up to the bar and people-watch type."

"I know what you mean. And in the city, you don't even go to clubs until midnight, which is getting to be too late for me."

He had that understandable and annoying habit of people from metropolitan areas to refer to their home as "the city" and assume everyone knew which one they meant. I'd heard Londoners, Parisians, and Angelenos all use it too. Even so . . .

He lost count and kicked the toe of my boot. I stumbled.

"Sorry!"

"It's okay. That's why you wear boots." We instinctively stopped two-stepping as the notes faded and another song began. We stood facing each other. I started to let go of his hand, but he held mine firm. The slow strains of "The Dance" started playing.

"One more?" He arched an eyebrow. A dare.

"Sure," I breathed. Slowly.

He seamlessly pulled me closer, and I found my arms encircling his neck. We gave up on the two-step entirely. Trying to keep some distance between us—I was a professional, after all—I was acutely aware of his legs brushing mine. I attempted to keep my chin from resting on his shoulder. I allowed myself the pleasure of the smell of cedar. There was nothing wrong with occasionally enjoying proximity to a man.

We didn't speak during the song. It didn't seem necessary. Only one dance. Well, two. Then we'd go back to being coworkers.

Actually, I'd go back to being maid of honor! I completely forgot the entire reason I was there until I saw Allison gesturing to me from the edge of the dance floor. It was eleven o'clock, and we still had one more stop to go. I was officially the worst maid of honor in history. Fiancé-stealers aside, of course.

"I'm so sorry, I've got to go." I pulled away abruptly.

"Really? What? Why?" He looked as startled as I felt.

"I didn't look at the time, and I've got to take Lucy to the next stop."

"At this hour?"

"Yes, it's a long story, but girl stuff, you know?" I turned to go. "I'll tell you about it Monday. Um, thanks for the dance. Have a great night!"

I dashed to where Lucy already had her jacket on.

"You done?" She looked more pleased than pissed.

"Don't start with me. I'm in charge of this bachelorette party and therefore hold your future—and possibly your marriage—in my hands. I plan to have photo evidence of some sort or another by the time the night is over." I took her arm in mine as we walked out the door.

We clambered into the waiting party bus, which I'd timed perfectly with our scheduled departure. We grabbed the glitter railing and hoisted ourselves inside.

"Wait," said Lucy. "Where's blow-up Collins?"

"That's on you, sis," I replied. "Before you dragged me onto the dance floor, you gave your poor inflatable fiancé to Dom."

"If I didn't know better, I'd think you might have a thing for him," she said. "Dom, I mean. Not the inflatable."

"Please don't make me kill you before your wedding," I replied. "Want me to run back in and grab it?"

"No. Don't worry about it. I'm sure we'd have popped him eventually anyway. Probably for the best to let him go."

I wasn't sure whether that had double meaning or not, but I smiled thinking about Dom stuck in the bar with a large blow-up doll in between him and Mike. That image would stick with me for days.

We pulled up to a slick, modern building, one of the newest hotels downtown. The ladies danced their way out of the van, doing one turn at the pole.

Our final stop for the night was one of Nashville's many "cowboylesque" shows. As we walked inside, Lucy turned to me, shock on her face.

"*Claire!* You didn't!"

"Oh, I did. And you'll enjoy this." Truth be told, I wasn't sure *I* would—sweaty strangers touching me or taking their clothes off was never my jam, but sometimes you just had to "lean in" on a bach weekend. I'd read as much in the internet's guide to being the world's best maid of honor. And after the dance, or rather dances, with Dom, I needed to get back on track a bit.

This particular place billed itself as a "male revue" and had a strict no touching rule, so it felt safe for my relatively buttoned-up sister. I was, not for the first time, grateful Evelyn couldn't attend. This would have sent her into early labor for sure.

We plopped into our seats at the table, and the emcee took the stage. The most spectacular drag queen I'd seen since last season of *RuPaul's Drag Race*, she wore a silver rhinestone vest that barely covered her large chest and an extremely tight pair of blue jean shorts. I wondered if they were actually painted on. Her silver bedazzled knee-high boots reflected like a disco ball onstage. Magical. There was no universe where I wouldn't topple in those heels, so I sat back, abundantly impressed.

"Y'all ready to get this rodeo started?" she boomed over her glittering microphone. "I said—are you ladies ready to get this rodeo started?"

And this time the room, full of bachelorette parties, yelled back, "Hell yes!"

Then the men took the stage. All ten of them wore nothing but denim chaps, boxer briefs, and tiny shirts or vests. They were tan, fit, and ready to entertain. I pretty much blacked out after that moment. But from what I do remember, it involved lots of Backstreet Boys and NSYNC music and many, many body rolls.

Lucy pretended to be appalled, though her massive grin and frequent bursts of "Woo-hoo!" gave her away. The men stayed on the stage and didn't touch a soul, but pretty much danced their chaps off. A man in a mesh croptop sat on the front of the stage at one point and sang directly to my sister.

It was all a huge hit. As we clambered into bed later that night at the hotel, I congratulated myself on being maid-of-honor goals.

🌵 🌵 🌵

The next day started off a bit foggy. We moved slowly that morning, and I was thankful our room included a fridge and that we'd chilled our gel masks overnight. I needed all the help I could get depuffing after the copious amounts of tequila. Lucy decided she wanted to wear the $350 Sleeper pajama set she'd just slept in to brunch, which resulted in all of us wearing them. We looked like a bunch of hungover flamingos stumbling into Ubers from the hotel.

After a much-needed meal of fried chicken and waffles, we spent the rest of the day lounging by the pool at the Graduate. It was a crisp but otherwise perfect scene for relaxation (and recovery) after a fun but tiring night. We finished off the weekend with a "panty party" for Lucy, which just about sent her into cardiac arrest. We all knew Collins would enjoy our gifts even though she claimed she "died from embarrassment."

"Thank you so much for everything, Claire." Lucy gave me a massive hug across the console of my car. I drove her to the airport that evening, which gave us a little more one-on-one time ogether before she headed back to Dallas. "You didn't have to go all out like that."

"Are you kidding me? We're Sommers girls. *All out* is what we do," I replied.

She looked at me. "You know you didn't have to, right? I mean it. I would have been fine with a weekend at the cabin in Aspen watching movies and sitting in the hot tub."

"No, I wanted to do more. You deserve it, Lucy," I said. "I miss seeing you, and it was a blast for me to be with you and experience the city. I hope it was everything you hoped for."

"Are you kidding? It was a dream. I just hope you know that I meant what I said when I asked you to be my maid of honor.

You're my hero, big sis, and I love you, no matter what . . . Even if you had decorated the room with *penises*." She whispered the last word.

I cracked up before pulling her into a hug. "I love you too. Thanks for always believing in me. No matter what I do."

"You can't beat yourself up forever, Claire. You've made mistakes, but *you're* not a mistake."

"Sounds like someone paid attention in therapy," I said.

"Well, I *am* a big fan of therapy, but I'm also dead serious," she said. "You're a different person these days. Nashville looks good on you. I'm really happy that you seem to be doing great and thriving."

"I don't know about thriving," I said.

"You know what I mean," she replied. "You set out on your own path. It was brave. I've just done what was expected of me— always have."

"Well, I've tried to. I didn't really have a choice."

"That was years ago now, and we all screw up."

"Maybe," I said. "Just not as often or to the extent that I did."

"The pressure to succeed in this family is almost crippling, and you just let it get to you. That's all. You've got to stop letting that define you now." She reached across the console and squeezed my shoulder. "But speaking of therapy, when was the last time you talked to somebody? I know it must be a lot to unpack everything from the last few years. Just be kind to yourself."

"I promise I'll look into it . . . How in the world did you get so wise?" I asked, a little choked up. "You're the baby. I'm supposed to be passing along words of wisdom to you, not the other way around."

"Yeah, yeah." She waved a hand and smiled. "I'm sorry we ran out of time to look at the final designs for my wedding, but I'm happy to email them to you."

"Good thing I like being surprised. And like I've said before, I have no doubt it will be nothing less than spectacular."

"Thanks, Claire Bear. Whenever you're ready to come back to Dallas, you're welcome to stay with me, or rather us. Collins wants us to start looking for a house in the Park Cities, and I can't wait to host guests in a new place."

"Let's just get through your big day and then go from there," I said. "But we can't talk about it anymore or I'll start getting emotional and short-circuit. I already can't handle the thought of my baby sister in a veil. So go on. Scoot. Get back home to that sexy fiancé of yours!"

Lucy squeezed me one last time, then bounced out of the car and into the terminal. And just like that, I was one step closer to her wedding date and what felt like my reckoning day with all the things I'd run from the last several years.

CHAPTER 14

"Do you think the fiftieth time you watch the same footage, Ginny will pull a runaway bride?"

"That'd be pretty tough with a toddler in tow," Dom replied without turning from his computer screen. I'd tried to razz him and failed. We had a little over a month left to go, and he was laser focused.

I crossed my feet on the desk in the dark editing bay. "True."

I was hobbling through the week, still recovering from Lucy's bachelorette party. It didn't help that I had to grudgingly shadow Dom as he edited footage from Ginny's Cheekwood wedding. Countless hours of B-roll were my new sleep aid. It took everything I had not to doze off. I was decidedly unsharklike these days. Thankfully I had something to look forward to on the horizon, which made all the tedious work more tolerable.

This upcoming weekend held the promise of mixing both work and play. One of my very dear and very English friends from college, Daphne, was getting married. A month ago, I'd managed to talk my way into covering it as one of our Real Weddings examples. The wedding was no doubt going to be quite the event, and I was over the moon that Michelle liked the idea. As part of the deal to get her to cover it, Dom was, of course, tagging along, which threw a slight wrench in my plan to find an English aristocrat at the wedding to marry.

After my third ill-concealed yawn, Dom threw me a bone without turning from his screen. "Tell me about the wedding this weekend. All I really know is to bring my nicest suit."

"That is an ideal place to start. I wouldn't usually tell you to turn it on, but I need Charming Dom out in full force. Please don't embarrass me. I actually know these people."

Daphne and I met junior year when she studied abroad for a year at Vanderbilt. Why anyone would choose Tennessee for their time abroad was beyond me, but I was thankful it brought her and me together. We weren't best friends by any means but could always share a good laugh. I showed her the best brands of cowboy boots and let her borrow my car, and she regaled me with stories of skiing in the Alps and taught me how to sit like a duchess.

I explained to Dom what little I knew about Daphne's background—mainly that she was from some posh London-based family. They owned a town house in Chelsea and a "cottage" in the English countryside. On one occasion I asked to see a picture of it since she'd mentioned it a few times. It was a castle, not a cottage, and it was just their second home. Not that I had room to talk, but Americans were also infinitely more googleable than

British aristocracy. This kind of casual reference from her made me wonder if her "quiet country wedding" might turn out to be the wedding of the century.

"Just before summer break," I told Dom, "Daphne met a cattle ranch heir, Whitcomb, and they dated for several years before deciding to tie the knot."

"Whitcomb, eh? That's quite a mouthful."

"He goes by Whitt, thankfully. Anyway, she and I did a decent job keeping up after college, which was enough for me to live vicariously through her international romance. I don't know how the two of them did it, but they survived the transcontinental courtship. Then one lovely winter evening, in front of the twinkling lights of the Eiffel Tower, Whitt popped the question to Daphne with a three-carat pear-shaped diamond."

"Just a regular ol' international love story between an ordinary Joe and his English rose." Dom certainly had a snarky side when he got tired too. Not that I disagreed: Daphne loved America and wanted to stay here permanently, so though Whitt seemed wonderful, I always wondered if she fancied her green card as much as she did him.

Either way, a wedding was happening this weekend. Daphne's temporary residency had run out, so she was stuck in the United States until all the required immigration paperwork came through. I wasn't certain why they hadn't just gone to the courthouse, but I presumed it was to go in the correct order— and throw an appropriately massive to-do. Otherwise, why forgo a wedding at an English castle and opt instead for Maryville, Tennessee?

❦ ❦ ❦

I had a feeling that attending a wedding as even something close to an actual guest would feel strange. Would I easily enjoy myself, or would I end up interviewing the guests or questioning the kitchen staff about delayed coffee service like a psychopath? Regardless, Dom and I would be making our way to East Tennessee.

Though Daphne's wedding wouldn't be in England, her family did insist that the English wedding planner and florist come over to run the event—eliminating any risk of bumping into Lottie again or any of my former colleagues. The closest thing to an English countryside wedding this side of the Atlantic would be a wedding at one of the top rural luxury destinations in the country, Blackberry Farm.

I'd never visited Blackberry Farm in person, but I knew all about it. Mom and Dad often spent time there before or after visiting me at Vanderbilt, given that it's only a three-hour drive from Nashville. I'd never had the pleasure of joining them there—not that they didn't ask, I just never wanted to give up a college weekend socializing with friends to hang out at a farm with my parents. Even if it was considered the bougiest five-star farm in the entire country.

My invitation included one guest. Proper etiquette for a single female in her late twenties, and Daphne was basically an English version of Emily Post plus a bawdy sense of humor. I originally decided against bringing a guest with the hope of finding a sophisticated gentleman to sweep me off my feet and take me home with him to Kensington. But now that we were covering the wedding for work, Dom was tagging along as my "and guest." I may not have been distraught over losing the opportunity to find love, but Dom was thrilled for the opportunity to enjoy free gourmet food and luxury lodging.

Dom picked me up at an unholy hour on Friday morning, and I was grateful not to put the miles on my aging car as well as not endure more live social media broadcasts while I was trying to navigate the Smokies.

He'd gotten out to open the door. "Hi, Tex!"

"Oh, that's what we're doing now, I see."

"Unless you're secretly from Des Moines?" He was so smug.

"Sure, sure. Then I can call you Yank or something."

"Hey, I'll take that over some pejorative about Italians."

"Ha, I wouldn't know one of those if you threw it at me. You're safe here." Maybe we were becoming friends after all.

His car was very clean, and I said as much.

"Surprised? It's the first time I've owned a car," he said proudly. "Well, it's a six-month lease, but still."

"It still counts as a milestone. Cheers to adulting!"

As Dom merged onto the interstate, I had the distinct feeling I was being watched. I looked over my shoulder and just about had a heart attack when I saw blow-up Collins buckled in behind me in the back seat.

"What in the living hell?" I exclaimed. "Where—how—did you find that?"

"Oh, you mean my buddy Collins?" Dom sarcastically asked.

"I thought by now he'd be living his best life in a hot-tub tour bus with another bachelorette group," I said.

"Well, thankfully Mike took care of him while we danced," he said. "But you bolted right after that, and I didn't have time to give him back. So he's been hanging with me for a while."

"That's so weird, Dom. Not to mention I can only imagine what people who pull up next to you think when they see that thing in your back seat." I couldn't help giggling.

"Well, he's all yours now," Dom replied. "In fact, I think you should take him as your date to the wedding this weekend."

"Great! You can drop us off and then skedaddle," I said. "I mean, he dresses well, doesn't talk back, and if I find myself stranded in the lake, he'll even come to my rescue as a flotation device."

Dom's laugh was like most things about him—big, loud, and more than anticipated. He tossed his head back. There was that crinkle at the corners of his eyes again.

"I take it back," Dom squeaked out. "Now I'm getting jealous."

"No, I think you should keep him now," I said once I caught my breath. "It would be cruel to separate the two of you after all the time you've spent together."

"I'm sure we can work out joint custody." He snickered again. "But enough about Collins. Tell me more about this wedding."

While we drove, I outlined what I knew of the small bridal party and various family members. "Daphne's dad passed away when she was a teenager. And her mom never remarried." This baffled me, as her mother was a slightly older-looking version of Daphne (meaning a total knockout) who was a bit quirky and eccentric but in the best kind of way.

I remembered one late-night study session in the Vandy library when Daphne confided that her mother would probably never marry again. "Dad was the love of her life, and she says she's perfectly content to live alone in their flat as long as she keeps up a steady flow of dates. I think that's bonkers, and she's actually pretty lonely. But she won't listen to me."

"Maybe it's just going to take meeting the right man," I said.

"That's what I keep saying," Daphne replied. "But she's pretty stubborn, and she might actually like playing the widow card. Mum loves the attention it gets her. I'd be worried about it, but it's been ages since Dad died, and she's managed to stay single this long, so I let her keep on with it."

"Well, she sounds fabulous, and I hope I'll get to meet her one day," I said.

"You have to come to England after graduation, so you'll meet her then," Daphne said a little too loudly.

"Shh," hissed someone across the nearby shelf of books.

"Oh, bugger off!" Daphne yelled back.

I died laughing, which added to the number of glares aimed in our direction. Her humor made me love her even more. Eventually we decided to pack our bags and give up studying in exchange for tacos and margaritas at Las Palmas around the corner. That was the kind of friend she was, but I struggled to convey that to Dom.

"She's warm and funny, fiercely loyal, and very down-to-earth considering the kind of family she comes from. I haven't fact-checked anything, but I'm pretty sure she's a distant relative to the royals."

"Sounds kind of like someone else I know."

It took me a solid minute to grasp what he was saying. "That feels like a very generous characterization, but I'll take it. Thank you."

"If this is sort of the British version of your world, tell me more about it," Dom asked after a moment. "We're going to a wedding showcasing extreme wealth, right? How did they get so rich—or really, how did *you* get so rich?"

"Wow, that's an extremely frank and rude thing to ask. Didn't your parents teach you not to ask people things like that? I know you're a northerner, but geez." I slipped off my shoes for the rest of the long drive.

"I just figured we could cut through all the niceties by this point," he replied. "So much of what we do involves getting personal with other people, so we might as well get comfortable— and personal—with each other. I do have your blow-up doll in the back seat of my car, after all."

"Well, let's be clear, that's technically Lucy's blow-up doll, and be careful opening up Pandora's box there, Yankee. If I answer your questions, that means you have to answer mine."

"Bring it," he replied.

I paused, then decided, *What the heck?*

"Ugh. Okay, fine. I guess I'm not telling you anything you won't google about me anyway," I said, smiling despite my best efforts not to. "What started as a moderate gravel quarry in West Texas, started by my grandparents, expanded into an asphalt empire. You should see the highways in the Dallas–Fort Worth metroplex alone. They keep building tollways, and the existing ones need to be resurfaced as soon as they finish. And they keep having to add new off-ramps and new highways to service all the new suburbs that continue to pop up as the city sprawls over North Texas."

"So . . . you're loaded?"

"No, haven't you been listening? My *parents* are. I'm just a simple girl trying to make an honest living at a wage that frankly should be criminal to offer to a grown adult."

"I'm not following," he replied.

I took a deep breath. "I don't get any of the money," I said softly. My professional subterfuge at Cedric's more than qualified for Gran's morality clause. But again, he didn't need to know that part.

"Like, not ever?"

"Not now. Not for a long time. Maybe not ever."

"Is that normal for, like, an inheritance thingy, or did you do something to get cut off?" He laughed, not realizing how close he was to the truth.

"Nothing criminal. But you have to be at trust-circle level zero for that convo and all devices off. And we're still not there yet."

He stared at the road for a moment. "Okay, I can respect that," he said. "Trust is a big deal to me too. But we *will* get there."

"Oh, will we?" I asked, blushing once again despite my best efforts.

"I'm holding your blow-up doll hostage, and I've pretended to be your fiancé. It's just a matter of time."

Was Dom flirting with me right now? His charm was always

so thick and suffocating it was hard to know, but this felt different. It was probably the breathtaking landscapes now reaching out in front of us. And the fake kiss that I couldn't forget.

The Southern Appalachian Mountains were absolutely stunning. Especially this time of year. Every tree was turning a vibrant shade of green, and anything and everything that could bloom did. The dogwoods were my personal favorite. Dom rolled down the windows so we could enjoy the breeze and the smell of ferns covering the forest floor. It was absolutely intoxicating.

I mused about what awaited us while I watched the scenery out my window. Although we weren't in England as I'd imagined, I was finally going to meet Daphne's mother. Prior to the wedding, Mrs. Middlebrook (her name even sounded like it was etched into the front of some massive stone estate in Sussex) reached out with questions that required my limited wedding knowledge. Polished, polite, and very sassy, Mrs. M.—what she insisted Daphne's friends call her—was everything I'd hoped she'd be and more from our first email. I tried explaining that I was basically blacklisted in the event industry now, but it didn't seem to matter to Mrs. M. She most likely just wanted a second opinion, especially from someone who had "been on the ground in America." After all, while I'd never been to Blackberry, her planner had never stepped foot in the entire state prior to the wedding itself.

We became friendlier when she started asking about more than just wedding details. She asked about me and how I was doing not only professionally but personally, and since I was barely speaking to my own mom these days, it was nice to have her check in on me. In return, I continually assured Mrs. M. that the wedding weekend would be wonderful given it was all to take place at Blackberry Farm. They were masterful at hosting events.

From the way Mrs. M. described the details, Daphne's wedding was going to be very nice but not over-the-top, which helped limit the risk of something going wrong. And after how kind Mrs. M. had been to me the past few weeks, I'd never let anything go wrong, even if I had to step in myself.

Dom had made a pretty fantastic playlist for us to listen to on the way, and we passed the remainder of the drive making small talk. It was also easy for both of us to sit in silence together, which definitely gave me reason to pause. In a rare sentimental moment, Mom once told me to look out for people whom you felt comfortable around even when no one had anything to say. She said some make great friends and some make great lovers— which triggered a gag but stuck in my mind. I bit my lower lip and wondered what that meant about Dom.

The smaller hills turned into bigger hills, and before I knew it, we'd arrived at one of the stunning white farmhouses on the Blackberry property. Dom valeted the car, and we headed inside to check in. Daphne's family had rented out the entire forty-two-hundred-acre estate for the weekend, with plenty of guesthouses and cottages for people to stay in. Mrs. M. was thrilled we were covering the wedding for *POC* and offered to put us up at the farm for the weekend. Michelle was thrilled she didn't have to dip into the magazine's dwindling expense account for our travel. A few more brownie points for me courtesy of Daphne's mom. Even with our "press discount," the rooms at the farm averaged twelve hundred dollars per night. Mrs. M. generously took care of our two.

Dom and I were both in historic rooms in the Main House, which was decorated to perfection from top to bottom. No amenity was spared, which reminded me of my old life in Dallas and admittedly stung a bit. As much as I'd started to appreciate standing on my own two feet, I still didn't hate sleeping in between six-hundred-thread-count sateen sheets.

After settling into my new haute-country-chic abode, I took a quick nap. Then I went for a blowout at the spa before dressing for the rehearsal dinner. If there was ever a national award for friend gestures, Daphne would be receiving one today after I discovered she'd made me multiple spa appointments. Things were looking up for this weekend. I'd worn my favorite Miron Crosby boots again along with a sleek little black Chloe dress for the party at Bramble Hall. At least for tonight, "Dallas Claire" was coming out in Tennessee.

Dom and I weren't technically covering the rehearsal dinner, but we planned to use the night as research to make our coverage of the big day even better. And hopefully have a bit of fun while doing it. This whole guest-as-journalist thing might be harder to balance than I'd first thought when I pitched the wedding to Michelle. Especially after I walked into the lobby to see Dom leaning against a lit fireplace and sipping a glass of bourbon.

"Drinking on the job already?" I asked. "You look like you're about to have your portrait painted."

"Maybe I was," he replied. "I think they offer that service here."

"It *is* fabulous," I said as a server greeted me with a tray of cocktails. I happily plucked a glass of champagne from its perch.

"It's totally cliché to say, but you clean up real nice," Dom said.

"I see you found some proper boots, Yank," I replied. His black boots were scuffed, thick-soled, and surprisingly sexy on him. He played the urban cowboy well.

"I've actually had these for years. Got 'em at a thrift store in the East Village. I asked my mom to mail them to me."

"That's . . . adorable. They look nice. Like you belong here."

"I'm trying." We stared at each other across the fire. This place was warm and welcoming, and sipping cocktails by a fire with a not-ugly guy wasn't too bad either. I was precariously balancing my professional ambition with the desire to just have a nice time for once. After a beat, Dom extended a hand for me to lead the way down the hall.

We were shuttled by golf cart over to a beautiful wooden structure that managed to look laid-back and luxurious at the same time. Upon entry, we were greeted by another tray of champagne and a stunning wall of moss and wildflowers. I found, or rather "picked," my bluebell from the wall to discover that Dom and I were seated at the head table for dinner. I wasn't sure whether that was good or bad, but we definitely wouldn't miss out on anything sitting down the table from the bride.

"There you are, darling!" Daphne basically shouted across the room in her chic accent.

Daphne looked like a model who'd walked straight out of Sloane Square. She shimmied over to us in the most glamorous white fringe Dior dress I'd ever seen.

"Well, aren't you a vision," I said, embracing her carefully so as not to spill her cocktail on a dress worth more than my car. "A little bit country, a little bit bridal."

"That was the goal! I'm so delighted you're here." She squeezed me harder. "It's been positively *ages*."

We continued fawning over one another as girls do, no matter what country they're from. Once we'd finished all the compliments, I turned to introduce her to Dom.

"This is Dom, my colleague who will be covering the wedding with me."

"Oh, it's just lovely to meet you! Claire has raved about working with you." She visibly looked him over head to toe and then winked at me. Never one for subtlety, that girl.

"Um, not exactly—" I tried to break in.

"I can only imagine what she's said." Dom chuckled good-naturedly. "We didn't start out too strong, but she's been graciously showing me the ropes. I'll try to stay out of the way this weekend."

"You'll be brilliant. And my mum is thrilled the event is getting some American press."

Daphne dragged us over to say hello to Whitt. He looked pretty much the same as I remembered from college—tall, handsome, a Tennessee cowboy in a suit. But the way the two of them looked at and embraced each other made me regret ever thinking Daphne was just in the relationship for a green card. She was clearly a woman in love, and I was truly happy for her.

"Now come say hi to Mum," she said, pulling me away. I

grabbed Dom's arm so he couldn't go sleuthing about, but nearly knocked over his drink.

"Whoa there, girl." He shook the sloshed-out bourbon off his hands.

"Just come along." I dragged him behind me and Daphne.

"I need you to help keep Mum busy. She seems a bit out of sorts, almost manic. At first I thought it was because Dad isn't here, but that's not it. All week, she's just been so sentimental and maudlin one moment and then almost psychotically excited the next. I keep telling her it's just a wedding, but she's treating it like the Platinum Jubilee."

"Well, you *are* her only daughter," I said as we headed outside to an extensive patio area. "And from my experience, weddings can turn just about everyone involved into a puddle of mush, even without the reminders of grief and other complexity. People tend to get emotional and even a bit irrational. But speaking of your dad, how do you feel this weekend? Are you doing okay?"

By that point, Daphne had finally stopped dragging me around, so I released Dom too. He gave me the stink eye before walking over to the bar area.

"You're a dear to ask," she replied. "I miss him, and I wish he could be here for the wedding. But it's been ages since he passed, and I know he would absolutely worship Whitt, which helps a ton. It's Mum who has me worried. She's either talking about how soon Whitt and I will have a baby or what she wants at her funeral one day. She's all over the place, and it's driving me bonkers."

"From all the weddings I've been to," I said, "this tracks."

"Just yesterday, we were finalizing the seating chart for the reception, and she told me that when she dies, she wants to be buried in one of those woven caskets like Lee Radziwill. You know, the American socialite? Jackie Kennedy's sister?" she said.

"You're kidding." I tried to keep from spitting out my drink while laughing.

"Oh, I wish I was just having a laugh," she said. "I made the mistake of indulging her and asked, 'So you want to be buried in a picnic basket, Mum?' To which she replied: 'Yes, darling. But a chic one. Just like Lee's. Life is one eternal picnic, after all.'"

"Stop!" I said. We both laughed until I had tears streaming down my face. I was so glad I'd decided to come. I'd needed a good laugh (or five). "I'll do what I can," I told her. Then I dabbed the tears with my cocktail napkin. "Just let me grab one of those martinis like yours and put me to work."

I went over to the bar to order said martini and check on Dom, who was watching my approach. He gave me a wolfish smirk, and my pathetic knees started feeling wobbly. What was it with this guy? I understood why so many women liked following him on TikTok or whatever, but I never thought he'd have that effect on me. It had to be the wedding. It was enough to turn just about any single person into a bundle of hormones.

"You done dragging me around like I'm blow-up Collins?" He patted the bar counter next to him.

"Sorry, but I don't know many other people here after all, and I didn't want you to bail on me tonight already." I signaled to the bartender.

"I'd never do that," he said. "That's not my style. Plus, I'm having a good time. Well, I was until you spilled half my drink and I had to lick it off my arm."

"Good to know." I shook off the image of him licking things and attempted to smile. "And here, let me get you another one."

Fresh cocktails in hand, Dom and I soon found Daphne's "mum" cheerfully chatting it up with a group of Daphne's friends from overseas. Maybe I'd meet a charming duke and could reinvent myself in England after all. If a man ever told me he "burned for me" like the duke in *Bridgerton* did, they'd be sending in the fire department for me.

"Claire, darling!" Mrs. M. kissed me on the cheek and then gave me a massive hug. "I'm thrilled you could make it, and don't you just look fabulous." She snatched the martini out of my hand and took a gulp.

Dom looked at me with a broad smile plastered on. His poker face was improving.

"Cheers." I looked back at him wide-eyed. Clearly Mrs. M. needed my drink more than I did, so I just smiled as Daphne rolled her big brown eyes at her mom.

"Thank you so much for including me and for hosting us this weekend," I continued. "Is there anything I can do to help?"

"Well, you can keep the martinis coming, dear," Mrs. M. said.

"Mum, take it easy," said Daphne. "At least through the toasts, for heaven's sake."

"Oh, Daphne." Mrs. M. gave me another side hug. "Don't you worry about me. I'll be just fine. Tell her, Claire."

"Yes, Daphne," I replied. "You go mingle with your other

guests, and I'll, I mean, *we* will hang out with your mom. Don't worry about a thing." I grinned at Dom.

With that, Daphne mouthed the words *thank you* and walked off to greet another group of elegant attendees. Not sure what help Dom would be, but at least he'd be there should I need an extra set of hands.

"Now, Claire," said Mrs. M., "tell me all about your new job and that precious farm you live on."

Apparently to some people, Nashville still maintained its reputation as a country town where we all rode around on horses, played guitars, and lived on farms.

"Honestly, this is the first real farm I've been to since moving back to Tennessee." I laughed and then told Mrs. M. about the magazine and what I'd been up to in Nashville—sans farm life. Needless to say, it was a pretty short conversation. Dom added in a few stories of his own, which charmed the Gucci heels off Mrs. M.

However, we didn't need to "entertain" her for long. Soon the waitstaff started ringing bells and asking everyone to move back inside for dinner.

"Cheers to you, Claire," Mrs. M. said. "We are all so thrilled you could be here, and I'm sure you will find at least one or two of Daphne's male friends to dance with tomorrow. I know I have my eye on a few."

"Well, aren't you Mrs. Robinson," I replied.

"Coo-coo-ca-choo, darling." She downed the last of the martini and handed me the empty glass. Then she leaned toward

Dom. "Why don't you please go get us both one more of those so we can get this party started?" Then she sauntered off to her seat. Presuming she could find it.

"Wow." Dom had that wide smile on his face again. "I don't know whether I'm more offended your conversation didn't include me as a potential suitor for you—or for *her*."

"She does seem to enjoy younger men." I laughed. "Shall we, Benjamin?" I motioned to the tables.

"Very, very funny." He gently placed his hand on my lower back, guiding me inside.

My knees were doing that stupid wobble again. *I should wear sturdier shoes tomorrow*, I told myself. I tried not to over-think things and chalked it up to the fact that I hadn't been in a legitimately romantic situation in eons. Well, except for the love boat and Lucy's bachelorette, neither of which counted. Oh, and the hot chicken place, which *definitely* didn't count. Dom needed to stop touching me or I was going to lose my mind.

"Gosh, I love that woman," I said to Dom as we secured my second—well, my first full martini. "She's a bit of a mess tonight, but she's been so wonderful to me over the past few weeks. I've really enjoyed getting to know her."

"Yeah, she seems like a lot of fun, but maybe we should cut her off after this next round," Dom replied. "She might need to dry out a bit before tomorrow."

"Fair enough," I said.

As we headed toward our seats, I took a moment to soak

up the room. The space was breathtaking, and this intimate rehearsal dinner looked like a wedding reception itself. The groom's family was clearly interested in making their own mark on the wedding weekend, and to their credit, they did.

Long wooden farm tables with turned legs that looked like they'd been collected over a hundred years were placed end to end and ran the entire length of the space. Tapered candles in glass sleeves were mixed among birch-wrapped vases overflowing with colorful wildflowers and maidenhair ferns. Vintage china and silverware adorned every place setting, and our place cards were perched perfectly in their own little beds of green moss. It felt like we'd stepped into the Shire from a Tolkien novel. It was the perfect creation of rustic elegance.

"Wow, this is incredible," said Dom, pulling back my chair.

"Yes, yes, it is. And look at you and your manners. I never thought I'd see the day a Yankee would pull out my chair for me."

"I'm not an animal," he said, taking his seat next to me.

"Well, you're certainly calling into question my perception of guys from up there," I said.

"And you're calling into question mine about girls born with silver spoons in their mouths."

Once again, there was too much to unpack, so I simply sipped my martini and avoided eye contact.

I still couldn't believe we were seated at the head table. Daphne was in between Whitt and her mom, who had somehow already found herself another martini.

"Well, did you at least bring one for me?" Daphne asked as she watched her mother pop the olive into her mouth.

"No, dear," replied Mrs. M. "You don't want to look all puffy on your wedding day, do you?" She took a big sip.

Daphne rolled her eyes and then asked me for my martini, which I pretended not to hear while pulling it in closer to me. I'd already lost one drink to this family, and I wasn't about to give away another.

"Oh, for heaven's sake," said Daphne. "You're both positively the worst."

I laughed and shrugged my shoulders before taking another gulp.

The dinner could be described as nothing short of culinary perfection, and everyone seemed to be thoroughly enjoying the evening. Decadent farm-to-table Southern dishes, course upon course of roasted meats and vegetables straight from the property, comforting pies, and other regional desserts. Despite needing to roll myself back to the room later, I felt more relaxed than I had in weeks.

Dom and I talked about the next day's schedule and then somehow ended up discussing how much we both loved Italian food. He was the expert given his legitimate Italian descent, and I loved listening to him rave about the elaborate dishes his mom and grandma made for him growing up.

Memories of Dallas and family meals at home came flooding back, and a wave of sadness rushed over me. I wondered how long it'd be before I'd sit around a dining table (that wasn't set for a wedding) with my whole family again.

Thankfully, I was jarred back to the present moment by an elbow to my side. Before I could yell at him, Dom aggressively nodded his head for me to look in Daphne's direction. She was deep in conversation with her mother, and both looked a bit agitated. I tried to clear my head and home in on their words.

"*Dahling*, your father *is* with us," I heard Mrs. M. say. She shook her head insistently.

"Oh, I know. I believe he's looking down and is so happy for us." Daphne put a hand on her mother's arm in an attempt to placate her. "It's why I have his pocket watch to carry with me tomorrow, so a part of him can go down the aisle with me."

"No, no, dear. He *is* actually with us right now." Mrs. M. blotted her eye with a napkin.

"Mum, don't cry. I feel him too."

"No, I'm serious—look." As she said this, Mrs. M. opened up her evening bag and gently pulled out a small plastic baggie full of grey ashes.

CHAPTER 15

Daphne's jaw about dropped to the floor. So did mine.

"Mum. Please. Tell me those are *not* Dad's ashes in your Chanel purse."

Now Whitt was staring speechless too. Fortunately, most of the table hadn't noticed the discussion yet.

"Don't be silly," replied Mrs. M. "They're only half of him. The whole amount wouldn't fit in my evening bag." She lowered the Ziploc back into her purse.

Daphne couldn't speak. I had no clue what to do, so without missing another beat, I simply stood up and placed the remainder of my prized martini across the table directly in front of Daphne.

Thankfully, this broke her from her trance, and she downed the rest in one gulp. Daphne then looked toward her mom, who had resumed eating her entrée, and said quietly, "Please keep Father in your handbag for the rest of tonight, and we will discuss this later."

And while Daphne looked horrified, it took everything I had not to spill out of my chair laughing. Dom simply mouthed, *Wow*, to me and then continued eating as well.

It was nice to be reminded I was not the only one with family drama. Weddings could be great for that.

The rest of the evening was seamless, and not a dry eye remained in the room after Whitt gave a moving toast about his love for Daphne and how he wished he'd had the chance to meet her wonderful father. It was a beautiful speech, and I hoped that one day someone would say such loving things about me. Dom handed me a handkerchief pulled from inside his blazer, and I let myself think for just one second that he might be the kind of person to do that one day. Not the actual person, of course. But only for a second. Then I dried my eyes and shook it off.

"I don't know how she does it, but that woman can certainly hold her gin," Dom said as we both watched Mrs. M. stand gracefully and saunter around the room to thank everyone for coming.

"Daphne once told me she has martinis with breakfast," I replied. "It all sounded very British. I want to be like her someday. Fabulous and without a care in the world. Minus the ashes, of course."

"I don't know. She might have some of you fooled, but my guess is that she's pretty lonely. If you lose the love of your life early on, it's got to take a toll on you. I don't know that you'd ever recover," he said.

"Oh, so you're a romantic too."

"Of course I am," he replied. "I'm in the wedding business, after all."

"That's just it," I said. "It's all business to you."

"Are you saying you're any different, Ms. Sommers?" He had me there.

"Most of the time, yes, it's business," he continued after a beat. "But certainly not all the time. Sure, I can turn the charm on for the camera, but when I really like someone, they'll know."

"Oh, will they?" I stood and smoothed out my dress so we could join the other guests heading back to their lodgings for the night.

"For sure," he said. "Maybe not at first, but that's because I like to develop a friendship with someone I'm interested in. Gives you time to build trust. It worked for my grandparents, and if it's good enough for them after fifty years of marriage, then it's good enough for me."

"It was that way for my parents too," I said. Dom once again helped me with my chair and then followed behind me. He needed to stop the lower back touching for both our sakes.

"Maybe that's the secret," he said in almost a whisper, a little too close to my ear. My entire body broke out in chills. I rubbed my arms, trying to get the sensation to fade.

"You cold?" he asked as we stepped outside and waited for one of the golf carts to take us back to the Main House. "Here. Take my jacket." He draped it over my shoulders.

"If you get any more chivalrous with me, I just might faint," I replied to lighten the sexual tension.

"You don't strike me as the fainting type, but if you do, don't worry. I'll be sure to catch you," he said with that beyond charming grin on his face.

"You just can't help yourself, can you?" I shook my head in mock dismay.

Thankfully, it was our turn to load up into one of the golf carts. A moment later, and I might have actually swooned. It wasn't chilly, per se, but the night air felt good on my face and acted like the cold shower I needed at the moment.

"We've got a big day ahead of us tomorrow," I said, changing the subject. "What time do you want to meet up?"

"Well, if breakfast is anything like dinner, then we don't want to miss that. How does nine o'clock sound? In the dining room?"

"Sounds like a plan." I tried to act casual as we headed into the Main House. We walked together silently through the lobby and down the hall to our rooms. I felt almost painfully aware of how close his shoulder was to mine, despite not touching. I resisted the urge to bury my nose in the lapel of his jacket, but I caught whiffs of his cologne with each step. The tension was back, and it was palpable.

We reached our hallway, and I realized we were staying diagonally across from each other. A little too close for comfort.

"Well, good night, Yank, and thank you," I said as I took off his jacket and held it out to him. I pulled out my key with the other hand and put it into the door, trying to act normal.

He silently took the jacket from me, then stepped over to his door and unlocked it. "Good night, friend," he replied, giving me a grin just before he stepped inside and shut his door.

I stood there for far too long, staring at the closed door. *Did he just call me his friend?*

I awoke to a loud knocking. When I cracked open the door, Dom stood outside, and I was glad to have thrown on the hotel robe. "You're up earlier than we agreed to last night," I said, trying to keep the door closed as much as possible so he couldn't see how tired I must have looked.

"I don't need much sleep." The cocky man winked at me again. "There's so much to do here. Let's not waste the day."

"What are you talking about? We have to work!"

"I spoke with one of the photographers this morning, and they agreed to share their B-roll with us. Daphne has an army of people to help her, and you're not in the official wedding party. How much time do you need to get ready for tonight?"

"An hour or so?" I guesstimated my hair and makeup.

"That means we have, like, three or four hours until then. I promise to feed you and have you back by your midday curfew."

"Well, I guess we could do some research on the property by trying out a few things. But bring your camera with you so we can capture anything we need to while we're out," I said, pulling my robe in tighter.

"You got it, boss," he said with way too much energy for eight in the morning.

I told him I'd meet him in the lobby in half an hour, which would give me enough time to throw on some yoga pants, pull my hair back into a messy bun, splash some cold water on my face, and generally pull myself together.

I hadn't slept much last night. I knew I had no good reason, but I overanalyzed everything Dom had said and done during and after dinner. I was making a big deal out of nothing, which made me feel ridiculous.

Allowing myself to go down that path with him felt like another way to wreck what I'd been building at work. Not to mention opening myself up to emotional risk. I'd worked too hard to build something here to ruin it over one potential fling. I looked at myself in the mirror for a moment. Dom and I were coworkers. Maybe friends, I'd allow. But that was it. He was a walking, talking version of a *Bachelor* contestant, and the last thing I needed was to make my life more awkward than it already felt most of the time by reading into things. *He is a professional charmer. And he's leaving this summer. Come on, Claire, you know better than that.* I took a deep breath, rolled my shoulders back, and finished applying my mascara.

We met up in the casual dining area just off the main lobby where Dom had requested our breakfast to-go. The staff boxed up two of the most delicious-looking breakfast sandwiches I'd ever seen along with fruit and fresh pastries. This place was heaven on earth, and I silently chastised myself for never taking my parents up on their offers to come with them when I was in college. Maybe once enough time had passed, and I'd worked my way back into the fold, we would all come back together.

The activities coordinator for the property suggested a short hike that would take us through the beautiful forests and to an overlook that was not to be missed. Dom put our to-go boxes in his backpack, and we headed out on our little adventure.

"Does this count as a company retreat?" I asked, walking a few steps behind Dom.

"For sure," he replied. "Team building."

We were silent for most of the hike, which was fine as the sounds of nature were loud enough for us to listen and enjoy. Leaves and sticks crackled beneath our feet; birds twittered overhead. It felt great to get outside and walk off everything that had been swirling around in my head just hours ago. The mood started to feel normal between us, and I was thankful. We both had a lot to prove with our jobs, and neither of us could do it without the other. I hoped he felt the same way.

We reached our destination just as I was starting to get hungry. Perfect timing. We found a few large boulders to sit on while we devoured our meals and took in views of the lake. The sunlight glistened across the still water, and the landscape looked so perfect it almost didn't seem real.

Dom moved over to a grassy area and lay down on his back to look up at the sky.

"I can't believe how accessible all of this is to people who live in Tennessee," he said. "Maybe not Blackberry, but this scenery. From Brooklyn, you can get to the Catskills or Adirondacks pretty easily—if you have a car, that is. We just rarely ever did. I'm not necessarily a 'nature guy,' but I do love being outside, and this is about as good as it gets in my book."

"Yeah, it's pretty breathtaking." I watched him move his arms and legs in the grass like he was making a snow angel. "You're like a giddy schoolboy." I laughed. "It's like you've never seen nature before."

"Definitely not like this, I haven't," he replied.

"You know, the Warner Parks are literally twenty minutes from our office. They're not exactly like this, but they're amazing public areas with wooded hills, open meadows, streams, and tons of hiking trails. You could do this every day if you wanted to."

"As if I thought I couldn't love Nashville any more." He sat up. "Looks like you'll have to be my trail guide when we get back to town."

"Only if you pay me in tacos and margaritas afterward," I replied.

"Deal," he said. "Shoot, I guess we've gotta get back and work now."

I looked at the clock on my phone. "Yep, but it's not the worst place in the world to work, is it now?" I asked, standing up myself.

"No, not at all. I'm really enjoying the view these days." He looked right at me.

Not again. I didn't know what this smooth operator was up to, but he was throwing off my game plan, that was for sure.

"I do love the hills of Tennessee." I ignored his stare and looked off into the distance. "I actually think I might jog back, if that's cool with you."

"Oh, sure," replied Dom, finally breaking his stare and reaching for his bag.

"Why don't you stay behind since you won't take as long to get ready?" I added. "You can even get some B-roll of all this to use as extra ambience for the episode."

Before he could say anything else, I took off down the trail and didn't look back. Clearly, I needed to create some space between us both mentally and physically. I could overanalyze things at a later date—just not right now. Work came first. Period. And I wouldn't let Dom get to me.

I was focused on the pounding of my feet and the pounding of my heart when my foot snagged on a tree root. I fell head over feet and lay there in the middle of the path, panting.

My ankle hurt like fire. I tried to pull myself up on a nearby tree, but the pain was too much. I was considering calling the resort for help when I heard Dom's footsteps thud on the path behind me.

"Claire! What happened?" He ran to close the rest of the distance.

"I think I've just rolled my ankle. I have an old tennis injury." I looked up at him. "And you can shut it—I know that's very waspy of me, but learning tennis wasn't by choice."

"Duly noted," he said, smiling and assessing my situation. "Here, let me see." He bent down and felt along the bone, then rolled my foot back and forth. "I think you're right, but can you put any weight on it?"

"I can try again."

He helped me stand, but this time there was no romance in his touch. I was sweaty, covered in dirt and leaves, and now swollen. *Real power move, Claire.* He released me for a moment, but I couldn't stand without his help.

"Here, let me carry you."

"You are absolutely not carrying me. Please have someone send a helicopter or a park ranger." My mother's daughter still had some dignity left after all.

"Just try to stop me," he said. And with that, he grabbed a leg and an arm and pulled me onto his back before I could say two more words about it.

"Are you serious with this?" I said into the back of his head.

"Do you have any better ideas?" he wheezed as he started to walk.

I sighed. "Why, yes, my good steed, you could trot, please. That will make the journey go more quickly." He barked out a laugh. It always felt good to bring one out of him.

As he deftly navigated the trail, I held on tightly. "Could you not choke me so much, please?" he gasped. *Oh gosh, where do I put my hands?* I accidentally ran them down his pectorals—very firm—and was trying to find a subtle spot. "Easy there, frisky," he quipped.

After that, all bets were off.

I ran my hands down his chest and he shuddered. "Oh, so sorry!" I said innocently. I inched closer to his (also firm) abs. I relished the way they tightened subtly under my hands. This could be fun.

"Claire," he said through what sounded like gritted teeth. "I gotta focus."

"You wish," I replied.

"Maybe I do."

At that, I had to rescue us both from the tension. I gave his backside a gentle but firm kick with my good foot and said, "Let's go, cowboy!"

Dom laughed so hard he almost dropped me, but the spell was broken at least.

After we both stabilized, I said, "I've been to quite a few rodeos in my day, and you're not too bad for a city horse."

"Really? Good to know. Remind me how that country song goes? The one about saving a horse?"

"You mean the one about riding cowboys?" I blushed. Thankfully, he couldn't see how red my face was turning or how big my smile was.

The rest of the way down, he serenaded me with the most botched-up version of Big & Rich's classic bar ballad. It was both the funniest and sexiest thing I'd ever heard.

❦ ❦ ❦

The rest of the day was spent getting ready for the wedding, icing my ankle, and then interviewing the main characters for the day—i.e., Daphne, Whitt, Mrs. M., and the bridal party. Thankfully, Dom went into "work mode," and the two of us checked everything off our list that we wanted to collect as far as detail shots were concerned. I'd allotted more time than usual to interview Daphne prior to the ceremony, which was done for totally selfish reasons. I wanted to spend extra time with her before she went overseas. An English vacation wasn't happening anytime in my near future, but I had only myself to blame for that.

Thankfully, Whitt played his role of charming Southern groom to perfection, and he gave us lovely sound bites to use alongside his thousand-watt smile and frat-tastic hair. I'd been told years ago that the trick to securing the perfect male bang "swoop" was for a guy to put on a baseball cap after a shower and quick towel-dry. This left the hair looking gently tousled, and if the hat was placed just right, it also created the perfect wave just above his brow. Who knew if it actually worked, but whatever Whitt did to his hair was magical. He made for dashing screen time.

However, upon arrival at Daphne's suite, I could tell there was panic in the air. I'd come to believe that if you worked on weddings enough, you'd get a sixth sense about something not-quite-right. That, and the room was a disheveled mess.

"Oh, Claire, thank heavens you're here. Something dreadful has happened," Daphne said while rummaging through pillows on the sofa.

"What's wrong? Are you looking for something?" I asked, stepping over piles of blankets that had been discarded on the floor.

Dom followed behind and moved gingerly over clothes and random items. Thankfully he hadn't pulled out his camera. I'd never have allowed him to film Daphne in her robe and in distress, no matter what was going on or what TV drama it could create.

"I can't find Dad's pocket watch anywhere, and I've literally torn apart the room looking for it."

"I can see that." I motioned to Dom with a nod to wait back outside. He took his cue and gave us some privacy.

"I was planning to pin it to my bouquet so that Dad would be with me in spirit when I walked down the aisle," she said, tears welling.

"Did you ask your mom and the wedding planners if they had it?"

"Mum was already worried I'd misplace it when she gave it to me, and I didn't want to make matters worse, so she doesn't know yet. But I told the wedding planners. They went to check a few places it could be, but they haven't had any luck. I'm starting to think I left it back home, which would be just awful. I've actually kept it together and haven't been too emotional about Dad until this happened. I don't think I can walk down the aisle without it and not sob the whole time. This is supposed to be the happiest day of my life, but I do so wish he was here—and now I can't stop crying all because of that bloody pocket watch."

Tears were now rolling down her cheeks. I made my way across the disheveled room, took the pillows out of her hand, and gave her a hug.

"Listen, we will make this right together. There's always a solution to a problem like this, and I'm going to help you figure it out," I said.

I reached down to the tissue box that had been knocked onto the floor and grabbed one to blot her tears.

"We've still got a couple hours before the ceremony, so let's get you to hair and makeup, and then I'll see what we can sort out with the pocket watch. Okay?"

She sniffled and continued blotting her eyes as she nodded her head in agreement.

"Okay, that's my girl. I'll also call room service and get this place cleaned up. Dom will take you over to the spa in our golf cart, and I'll meet you in just a bit," I said, leading her to the door.

Dom of course agreed to help, and I made sure they were well on their way to the spa before I ditched my shoes and hobbled back up to the main inn.

"Come on, I know you're in here," I said aloud to no one as I rummaged through my travel jewelry case.

"Aha! There you are!" I pulled out a heart-shaped gold locket from among the other jewels I'd been gifted over the years for various birthdays and holidays from my parents. With few special occasions happening in my life these days, I hadn't worn much of my fine jewelry in years. Nevertheless, I still treasured the pieces, which served as reminders of happier times with my family, and had brought them for the occasion. I couldn't think of a better moment for my large, gold Tiffany heart-shaped locket to make another appearance.

♥ ♥ ♥

"Knock knock," I said as I opened the cracked door to Mrs. M.'s suite.

Mrs. M.'s cottage was near the Main House just like Daphne's, but thankfully I found her in a much different state. I could hear the Rolling Stones blaring through speakers as I approached her door. Upon entry I saw a large cheese and charcuterie board and two open bottles of champagne chilling on ice on her coffee table. She greeted me in a silk robe with fur trim and an almost-empty glass of champagne. Mrs. M. was positively beaming, having a party for one, and I was thrilled to see it.

"Claire, *dahling*, it's so good to see you again today!" she said as she air-kissed my cheeks. Have you seen Daphne in a while? I was supposed to ride over to the spa with her, but she's abandoned me, and now I have to go all by my lonesome. What a dreadful way to treat your mum on your wedding day," she said, pretending to be annoyed.

"Don't worry, Mrs. M.," I said. "I'm more than happy to escort you over to the spa, but first I need a little help with something."

"Of course, Claire dear. What can I do for you?"

"Well, do you happen to still have Mr. Middlebrook's ashes in that fabulous clutch of yours?"

❦ ❦ ❦

I arrived at the spa with Mrs. M. just five minutes past her scheduled hair and makeup appointment. We were both feeling very proud of ourselves. Before she headed to the back, I gave her a hug and asked if we could interview her once she was dressed and ready for the ceremony. She agreed and then gave me the slyest of winks as she headed to the back.

"Do I even want to know what you two have been doing together until now?" Dom asked as he stood up from one of the chairs in the chic reception area.

"To be honest, I surprised myself a bit today with some quick thinking," I said. *This might have even made someone like Evelyn proud*, I thought with a smile.

"Well, now I must know what you've been up to."

"Come with me," I said.

I made sure all the ladies in the wedding party were decent

before allowing Dom to accompany me to the dressing area of
the spa that had been reserved for Daphne and her bridesmaids
to get ready in.

Daphne had just finished putting on her wedding dress and
veil. She looked positively stunning.

"You look like a dream," I said, admiring my dear friend.
"And I've got something that I hope will make you feel a little
better about your dad today."

I handed Daphne my locket. The gold glinted in her palm.

"I know it's not your dad's pocket watch," I said in a hushed
voice to give us a bit of privacy. "But this is my locket, and with
your mother's help and a little, um, well . . . 'dust' from her handbag last night, I think it just might help the situation."

She looked at me with a puzzled expression.

"We can pin it onto the ribbon of your bouquet just like you
originally planned. Just keep it closed until after the wedding,
when we can transfer its contents back to your mother's handbag.
Hopefully this will help you feel close to him today," I finished.

Daphne didn't say a word for a minute, and I worried I'd
actually done more harm than good. Then she started beaming
from ear to ear and gave me the biggest hug.

"You're the best mate a girl could ask for," she said, hugging
me harder. "Thank you so, so much, Claire."

"It's my pleasure, Daph. Oh, and it can count as your 'something borrowed'!" I added.

"You are positively brilliant! I promise to have it thoroughly
cleaned and polished before sending it back to you," she said with
a chuckle.

"Don't you worry about that right now," I replied. "Since you're happy with it, I'll take it up to the florist and have them attach it to your bouquet. Crisis averted."

She gave me one last squeeze and then I headed out.

"Color me impressed," said Dom as we rode over to the florist's prep tent.

"Thank you. It took a bit of physics to get a small amount of those ashes from Mrs. M.'s baggie into the locket, but we did it. There *may* be some smidgen of him left behind here at Blackberry, but I'm just going to think of it as leaving a mark on a place that's now part of their family story," I said.

He gave me a look.

"What?" I said with a smirk.

"I can't decide if you have a dark and twisted or utterly brilliant soul."

"Can it be both?" I grinned. "I honestly don't want to think too much about the details, but at least Daphne is happy and has her father with her."

"Well, you're a great friend, and she's lucky to have you in her life," he replied.

It was hard for me to accept a compliment. It had been that way for me since I was exiled from Dallas. But today was a good day, and I would hold on to the positive feelings as long as possible. At least, my positive feelings about Daphne and her family. Dom, however, was another story. Those feelings were starting to get very complicated.

Before I knew it, it was the end of the night, and only happy tears were shed throughout the rest of the wedding. Dom and I wrapped up all our interviews for our piece well before the reception started, and I even had time to enjoy a very careful dance or two with Daphne and her friends. I sent Dom off to capture some clips of guests dancing during the first hint of a slow song, and the band kept it pretty fast-moving most of the time. We didn't need to cross any lines again. I'd had my hands on him enough for one weekend—maybe one lifetime.

It was a magical day for a fabulous friend, and it was painful to say goodbye to her at the end of the party.

"Please promise to come visit me in Nashville when you get back from your honeymoon," I said to Daphne, wrapping my arms around her before her send-off.

"Of course, love." She squeezed me back. "And then you're coming with me to see Mum in London for a proper catch-up. I'll hold your locket hostage until you do."

"I'm not sure when that will be, but I'll make it happen," I said, reluctantly letting my incredibly kind and generous friend go.

Daphne and Whitt rode off in their horse-drawn carriage, decorated with vintage ribbons and a beautiful hand-carved "Just Married" sign on the back. As we stood on the gravel path, watching them disappear around the bend, my phone and Dom's pinged simultaneously.

Michelle. Her typically perfect timing.

"Dang." Dom whistled as he read.

"My thoughts exactly."

Michelle's email was succinct. We had planned to cover country music playboy Dixon Jackson's latest wedding, this time to Betsy Beauville, the twenty-six-year-old opening act for his tour. It had promised to be the most glamorous *and* most dramatic event of the social calendar. But alas, Betsy had found Dixon in a compromising situation with his children's nanny, and the blessed festivities had been called off. Now Lucy's wedding was looking like an even more likely contender for that slot, and we needed to up our game.

"Well, it's official," Dom said, his voice dripping with annoyance. "Dixon is a cliché, and we are incredibly screwed."

"I know. That wedding was going to be perfect for us. What an uncreative way to bomb your marriage, buddy. Not to mention the pressure this puts on my sister's wedding as we don't have any option now but to cover it." The anxiety seemed to creep up into my chest.

"We'll just have to knock it out of the park then, won't we, Tex?" He gave me a wink.

I knew Dom was trying to be nice and comfort me, but he had no idea that Lucy's wedding could be more of a disaster for us than a saving grace. Thankfully, I had one last night on six-hundred-thread-count sheets at the farm to comfort me as well. I was going to take full advantage of a good night's sleep and a king's breakfast before heading back to face the even more precarious future of the magazine.

CHAPTER 16

The fried catfish had been a bad idea. A very bad one.

On Fridays when we closed an issue, it was tradition for everyone in the office to order dinner together. We'd hustled to include the shots from Daphne's wedding last weekend in the August issue, which was going to press at the end of May.

To celebrate another print issue, knowing each one might be our last, this time we tried out a mom-and-pop meat-and-three nearby. I knew my order tasted, well, fishy. But I wasn't paying attention when the orders were placed, so I went with the evening special. It ended up being not special but spoiled.

My stomach roiled. It grumbled audibly.

"You okay over there?" Dom asked without turning from the screen. A few feet away, he was making cuts in Daphne's footage.

I was grateful for the darkness of the editing bay so he couldn't see my embarrassed flush. "Yep!" I squeaked out.

This was not the image I wanted to project at the office.

Sommers women typically aimed for more professional and less projectile.

Within five minutes, I dashed to my desk, grabbed my purse, and bolted for the parking lot.

I made it to my apartment in the nick of time and was beyond grateful that I didn't get sick in the car. My Range Rover never would have recovered. I would have needed to burn her or sell her for parts at that point—both moves I couldn't afford.

I fumbled with my keys and barely made it inside my door. I dropped my bag, stumbled out of my shoes, and raced to the bathroom.

Catfish was never happening again.

My phone pinged: You okay? You ran out of here like a bat out of hell.

Been better but I'll survive.
You didn't look so good.
Thanks.
I know it's awful when people say that. But what I mean is that you're always beautiful—you're just not always green.

I laughed despite myself. It did *not* help the stomach cramping.

He pinged again: Need anything? How can I help?

No, it's okay. I'm fine. Just threw up and should feel better.
Seems to be just a case of good ol' food poisoning.
Catfished by the catfish, you know how it goes.

He texted back: Be there in ten.

I laid my forehead on the toilet bowl, too exhausted to move. Several delirious minutes must have passed.

"Claire?" A deep voice came from the bathroom doorway. "The door was unlocked." I opened my eyes to see Dom looking sheepish and concerned.

I must have forgotten to lock my door in my sprint to the bowl.

"Ugghhhhhh . . ."

"Good thing it was just me."

"You're not a serial killer, are you?" I managed to lift my head to give him my best stern look but probably just landed on deranged.

"If I was, I would have murdered you way before now at one of the weddings in the middle of nowhere. You're safe for the moment."

"Lots more spots to hide a body in the woods." I nodded weakly. I really needed to lay off those true crime podcasts.

"Lots less barf."

"That was mean," I started to say, but was overcome with a dry heave. Before I knew what was happening, he was squatting behind me, hands pulling my hair back.

When the feeling passed, I sat down again and he sat on the floor against the opposite wall. The tile felt nice and cool.

"You didn't have to come here. I could have called someone. I don't know who, but I could have . . ."

"No college friends here?" He arched one of those irritating brows.

"I have, like, two friends left in town," I admitted. "With everybody else, it feels weird to be like, 'Hey, haven't heard from you in eight years and have no idea what your life is like since I deleted Facebook, but would you want to come over and catch up?'"

"And it's been like eight minutes since you've seen me . . . I'm happy to be here, really."

I started to feel warm inside and less shaky.

"I, um, think you have vomit in your hair, Claire." He pointed to a strand near my chin.

Never mind, I wanted to die. "Don't look at me! I take it all back. Go away, Dominic."

"That is basic stuff. It's rule number one. You need someone to hold your hair back. Can't be blamed for what happens if you don't." He shrugged.

"Why, are you some sort of sicko expert?"

"I have a sister who gets squeamish easily."

"That's revolting."

"It's also true. Here, you need to shower. Think you can stand if I get you over there?"

"This is all so mortifying," I said as I leaned heavily on his arm.

"Don't worry, I've done this before. Just think of me as the kid brother you never had."

He had no idea how impossible that was, but a girl could try.

When I got out of the shower, I found a T-shirt, sweatpants, and pair of clean underwear neatly folded on the toilet. The thought of him rifling through my drawer made my inner

Sommers girl throw a hissy fit, but it was also a bit sweet. I could think so only now that the vomit was all washed off, and I was pretty sure there was nothing left in my stomach.

I came out to the living room. He was sitting on the pink sofa, looking at his phone. He glanced up and those green eyes struck me with their brightness. I was in a weakened state for sure.

"Want to watch something?" I asked. "I think that's just about all I could do right now."

"Be thrilled to. What do you want to watch?"

In my one-room studio, the options were "sit on my bed" or "sit on the couch." Bed seemed super risky. I plopped down next to him.

We turned on reruns of *The Office*. A safe choice, as I didn't really feel like discussing all the other options, but I knew that a straight-up romance was totally out of the question.

He brought me my pillow and the quilt from the foot of my bed. By the second episode, my pillow was on the arm of the sofa, my head was buried in it, and my feet and legs were stretched across Dom's lap.

I woke with a jolt and rolled over. His head had lolled back on the sofa, and his hand was wrapped around my ankle. I woke him with my movements.

"How are you feeling?" he asked gently.

"Much better, I think." My stomach had settled, fortunately.

"You hungry?"

"Seems dicey."

"Can I get you anything else then? Need me to stick around?

I'll stay on the couch," he added quickly before I could pro-test—or get any ideas.

"Really, you don't need to. I'll be fine. Just help me up and then you can go."

He pulled me up from the couch, and I stood facing him, very aware that our bodies were inches apart. In a deft maneuver, he slipped an arm around my side and helped me walk the few steps to the bed.

"Are you sure you're fine by yourself? You're beautiful as ever, but you still look pretty sickly."

"Really, Dom, I'll be okay. You're already too kind to come over here and check on me the way you have. It means a lot. I bet the worst has passed."

"Just to be safe, I'll hang at least until you fall asleep again."

I lacked the energy to talk him out of it or even consider the notion that he was just trying to find a way to stay, so I tossed him my spare pillow and left him the quilt. "Won't you get bored just sitting here watching me sleep?" I asked in the most pathetic tone.

"Don't worry about me. I've got books on my phone and some reels to edit. Try to get some rest."

At least half an hour passed, but I couldn't sleep.

In my tiny studio apartment, my headboard and the sofa shared the same wall, my nightstand doubling as an end table. I could hear his soft breathing just feet away and his body shifting on the couch cushions. I glanced over. His face was barely visible in the dim light of his phone, lips pressed together in concentra-tion. I was suddenly not sleepy. Hyperaware of our proximity.

Finally, I spoke.

"Dom?"

"Yeah?" he replied in a gravelly whisper. "You okay? Can I bring you something?"

"No, no, I'm okay," I said softly. "I just can't sleep yet. My mind likes to race at night these days."

"That I understand. Adulting is hard."

"You're telling me," I said, fully rolling over on my side to face him. "And to think on top of everything else we're responsible for in life, we have to take care of ourselves when we're sick too. That is, unless you have a heroic coworker who's willing to help out."

"Nurse Dominic reporting for duty," he said. "Want to talk about what's keeping you up? My listening skills are almost on par with my nursing."

"Thanks," I said. "It's just work pressure and family drama. Lucy's wedding on the horizon is bringing up a bunch of junk from the past, and it's a lot to deal with. Just the usual Sommers family expectations that can be crippling. You know, the fun stuff."

"Let me ask you this: Why do you try so hard?"

"What do you mean?"

"You can be so buttoned-up sometimes, like your hair and your life and your everything have to be put together. You want to do everything on your own, even when you can barely stand up in the bathroom." He chuckled in the darkness. "But that doesn't seem to be the real you. You seem most yourself when you let loose, act goofy and ridiculous with me. You have a quirky sense of humor. You're not formal. You work hard, but you don't seem like a cutthroat competitor either."

If only you knew. "I think I've spent my life believing that's what I needed to be, what I was supposed to be. I didn't know of another way to be part of the family or make my parents proud."

"You know they must love you, right? That's classic parent stuff."

"Sure, but do they love me as much . . . as my sisters? Would they love me if I wasn't falling in line as the middle Sommers girl? I always feel like I'm disappointing them, and I have done that my whole life." I took a ragged breath.

"Can you give me an example?" His deep voice was gentle. "I feel like, were I in their place, I always would have been so proud of you."

"You really care to know?"

"I wouldn't ask if I didn't. I wouldn't *be* here tonight if I didn't."

I found myself strangely comforted by his words, his steady presence.

"You should know that, as a kid, I was in the same activities as Evelyn, who was always just better. No matter how hard I tried, I was never as good—never the team captain or the one with the solo performance. And I've never quite been able to find my own thing to be the best at. Instead I've just bounced around between activities and hobbies, jobs and cities."

"Maybe you just haven't found the right one yet?" His optimism was adorable, albeit naïve.

"Or maybe I'm just not meant to be the best. Full stop . . . Take sophomore year when I was on the steering committee for the junior symphony ball. Most kids secretly drink at the ball, and I was driving a bunch of tipsy friends home and got into a fender bender. I was sober, but my back seat was some sort of bacchanalia for teenagers with prominent last names. Someone snapped a picture—all of us lined up in cocktail dresses and cowboy boots. It ran on the society gossip sites and was an abysmal embarrassment to my parents. And it solidly confirmed my spot as the screwup."

I could see him shaking his head in the dim light. "That's awful and so embarrassing. But most kids wouldn't have been put in the spotlight like that. It's not fair."

"Maybe not, but it was the Sommers family reality." My head was starting to hurt.

"I can't pretend to know exactly what that's like," he said. "It's not the kind of pressure you're feeling, I'm sure, but I've got my own family baggage piled up, so you're not alone there."

Gone was the charmer, the ham, the performer. Even the goofball I had so much fun with seemed to fade away into the darkness.

"You've just listened to my whole poor-little-rich-girl sob story. I'm all ears," I said. "But only if you want to share."

"Well, I'm a classic single-parent kid." He moved the pillow to the end of the couch nearest me and flipped onto his stomach to face me. I got the faintest whiff of his woodsy scent as he shifted. "My parents split when I was little, but Dad came around just enough to constantly disappoint me. I learned to have low expectations of him or else I'd always be set up for heartbreak. That's tough to learn as a kid."

"I'm so sorry, Dom," I replied. "I hate that for you."

"Like I said, it was hard as a kid, but I think it's made me an easy person to get along with. Lots of acquaintances, few real friends, right?"

"Some of us are too closed off for many of either," I said.

"Nah, cut yourself some slack, Tex. If I'm honest, I guess I don't get very close to many people, but I don't get let down either. Then only a few people have to earn or keep my trust."

He was right. Once trust in someone was gone, it was really hard to build it back up.

In the dark, we covered it all. My overbearing parents. His uninvolved parent. Sibling rivalries. Other embarrassing moments. I couldn't quite bring myself to tell him the full story of why I left Dallas, but I got closer. It was a step.

I don't know why I kept telling him personal things. I wished I could retract them. And yet I didn't. There was something about Dom—an utter lack of judgment that made me want to open up the ickiest parts of me, the ones my mother tried to train out. The ones I knew no one would like.

In the morning, I sat up with a jolt. Bad idea. My head was still achy, but I did not feel like puking all over the sheets. A good sign.

Dom was still asleep. One arm thrown over his head, his shirt pulled up and exposing a very firm abdomen. I certainly didn't mind that view first thing in the morning.

I allowed myself a solid thirty seconds of admiring—for purely aesthetic purposes, mind you—before I got up and padded to the bathroom to wash my face. I reached for my makeup bag, hearing my mom's mantra about a full face. I pulled my hand back. This man had cleaned up my literal vomit. This man had also told me about his childhood wounds and adult insecurities. We were past a point, for better or worse.

When I opened the door, he was sitting up. Shirt pulled down, I noted sadly.

"Can I make you some breakfast?" I was back in Southern hostess mode. Another good sign.

"You sure you're hungry?"

"Actually, yes. I think I could keep something basic down. It's the least I could do."

"No, you sit, and I'll cook. I've been crashing at Mike's, and his kitchen lacks basic cutlery, let alone pots or pans. This would be a treat."

He rifled through the contents of my fridge and pulled out the eggs, some veggies, and cheese.

"Wait, that's the good cheese." I reached for the truffled gouda with a sniff.

"You saving it for a charcuterie board, Sommers?"

"Well, maybe. I just like to keep supplies. It's one of my few culinary specialties."

"You not much of a cook?"

"Not at all. It wasn't included in the *Sommers Girls' Guide to Success in Business*. The home-ec chapter was replaced with regular economics, obviously."

He laughed, dimple flashing. "Then here, I'll use the not-so-fancy cheddar and you can save the truffle stuff. I imagine that would be too tough for your stomach today anyway. But I'm coming back sometime for that specialty meat and cheese board."

"Deal."

He pulled together toast and one heck of an omelet, simple but perfect.

It was surprisingly intimate, him making me breakfast while I was in my pajamas. I could imagine a not-terrible version of life where the days started this way.

"I've been thinking about what you said last night," Dom said as he flipped the omelet onto my plate and plopped onto the other counter stool. "In my family, it's less about success and more about provision. I feel like I'll never do or be enough to make up for my dad leaving. Like, I know intellectually that it's not my job and that my mom doesn't actually want that from me. But for so many years of my childhood, I felt that pressure. Even through college I was always running back home to be around in case anyone needed help. I had to leave to give us all a little space. It's been good for me . . . You ever wonder what it would be like to just let go—to stop worrying what they think and stop trying to earn some nebulous approval?"

I sighed. "I don't know if I could do that. My life has been an endless cycle of trying to be better than everyone else. You know, coming in second in my family is practically failure."

"What if you just . . . stopped? Just think about it." He put a hand on mine for a moment. My skin burned long after the contact.

"I will, thanks."

We ate in silence for a moment, then he pushed his stool away from the counter and put our plates in the dishwasher. "Well, I've got to go. I told Mike I'd meet him for Ultimate Frisbee."

"What are you, fourteen?"

"Can I come by again later to check on you?"

"It's okay, I'll manage. And I'll let you know if I get caught in the bathroom again and need Life Alert."

"Please do, Tex." He opened his arms, and without thinking, I walked into a big hug. I guessed we were doing that now. I buried my face in the soft fabric of his shirt and breathed him in none too subtly. His arms squeezed my back, but he let go after a moment. I instantly regretted the loss of contact.

He stepped away with a last glance at my face and then gently opened and closed the front door.

That evening, I woke from a nap to my phone vibrating.

Thought I'd replenish your supplies. Look outside.
Warning label should say "Do not consume in one sitting."

I opened the door and found a paper bag on the porch. He was so thoughtfully sneaky.

I set the bag on the kitchen counter. He'd brought me crackers, fancy meat and cheese, and a two-liter of ginger ale. Maybe I didn't always have to muscle on alone. It was nice being taken care of sometimes. Just a little bit nice.

CHAPTER 17

The following Saturday morning, I was en route to pick up Dom and drive to Franklin for our next wedding. Downtown, a dreaded bachelorette backup happened again. A flatbed-trailer-turned-party-wagon was being pulled up the hill of Korean Veterans Boulevard by a bright-red tractor. On its front, a giant sign read, "I Got Plowed!" Despite the early morning hour, a crew of bachelorettes in matching T-shirts and cutoff denim shorts was already dancing about the flatbed, sloshing red Solo cups as they went.

As the tractor chugged slowly up the hill, traffic slowed to a crawl. Suddenly, my trusty Range Rover's steering wheel started vibrating. The engine light went on. I heard an audible *pop* and then saw a puff of smoke drift from under my hood. The car stopped. I had just enough momentum to pull quickly over to the right curb and throw on the parking brake before drifting back downhill.

No. No, no, no. Absolutely not.

This was not good.

The country music blaring from the tractor grew fainter as the bachelorettes continued on their way, oblivious to the disaster they'd caused. I laid my head back and closed my eyes, attempting to breathe deeply and stave off a panic attack.

My bank account had barely four figures in it and could not withstand a major repair bill. And I wasn't about to ask for money from my parents or sisters.

But more immediately, I needed to get to this wedding, stat. I couldn't make it there without Dom's help.

He picked up on the second ring. "Hey! Where are you?"

I outlined what had happened and where I was.

"Oh my gosh, I'm so sorry. That's such a headache." The note of genuine concern in his voice warmed my insides and calmed my racing pulse, slightly. "I'll come pick you up in ten."

"I owe you one. Bye."

While I waited, I called AAA, grateful my parents had maintained our family membership. Small coverings, but I'd take them. The friendly tow truck driver agreed to pick up the car, even when I told him I wouldn't be waiting at the site. I tried not to think about the inevitable bills coming my way.

Dom soon picked me up and I helped him navigate thirty minutes outside the city to one very famous country music singer's private estate in Franklin. It wasn't his wedding we were attending but that of his only daughter, Hope.

"Please tell me this is a prank," Dom said as he unfolded himself from behind the wheel of his sedan.

"See, this is why I refused to tell you anything about this one ahead of time," I said, laughing. "I've been waiting all week to see the look on your face when we do the walk-through."

With Daphne's episode wrapped and edited, we were turning our lens to our next target. It was getting closer to our deadline, and I had pinned much of my hope on this outside-the-box wedding.

Hope's family acquired the equestrian farm we now stood on about ten years ago. It boasted sixty acres of rolling green hills, open fields, a small lake, a quite large and beautiful white clapboard house, and the loveliest rustic barn—if you could call it that—I'd ever seen. The barn and open pasture beside it would serve as the ceremony and reception site, and the view in every direction was spectacular.

"Claire, is that a unicorn?" Dom asked, slowly pulling the camera out of his bag.

I giggled. "Sure looks like one to me." A white horse with a silver spiral horn protruding from its forehead was grazing in the pasture before us.

After our Blackberry Farm weekend and my bout of food poisoning, Dom and I had resumed business as usual for the past week. It felt like we'd blurred the lines, but I was fighting to maintain my professional distance. That was how it had to be. No time for distractions, dalliances, or anything else that could take my eye off the game.

Thankfully, neither of us had much time to marinate in feelings, as we went straight from covering Daphne's wedding to prepping for Hope's massive affair. And this one was definitely going to be something to write—or video—home about.

I'd introduced myself to the bride, Hope, a few months before when I did my prenuptial interview with her. We'd discussed the overall "vibe" of her upcoming wedding as well as gone over details of how she and her fiancé, Mark, had met. Hope's father was famous in his own right, but I tried to keep the focus on Hope and the event as I was sure she spent the rest of her life in her father's shadow. (I, for one, knew what that was like.) After all, these preparatory interviews were a way for us to get a head start on our piece and a taste of what we might be walking into come wedding day. It also helped clients feel more comfortable opening up to me on their actual wedding day if we'd spoken beforehand. Hope had given me a detailed description of what her team of vendors was planning to create, and I knew it was something I'd have to see to believe. We were going to have quite the magical event to cover with more than enough detail to highlight in the magazine.

Starting with a unicorn.

"This is ridiculous," Dom said upon closer inspection. "As if that fake unicorn horn wasn't bad enough, they even braided the poor horse's hair and dyed it pink. Is this a six-year-old's birthday party or a wedding?"

"It just so happens that Hope grew up obsessed with unicorns and all kinds of magical creatures, so she wanted to incorporate them into the theme," I said.

"You mean there's going to be more than this one?" His green eyes were huge.

"You'll just have to find out, won't you?" I motioned for him to follow me into the barn. "The girl loves a fantasy novel, so the possibilities are endless. Now, let's get a sneak peek before heading up to the main house for the interviews."

We walked around the other side of the whitewashed barn structure, where the massive antique doors had been opened and adorned with large wreaths made entirely of baby's breath. Inside, every wooden beam in the ceiling was wrapped in lush greenery and dripping in white wisteria blooms. The floor of the barn was covered in faux moss, and benches carved to look like bent tree branches served as seating for the guests. The benches flanked an aisle covered in white rose petals, and at the end of the aisle was an arch made entirely of white dogwood blooms. It was breathtaking and looked exactly like the wedding scene from the *Twilight* series. In our phone interview, Hope told me those books and movies were her favorites and served as inspiration for her ceremony décor. The florist, who was based in Nashville, had perfectly re-created just about every single detail.

"Wow," said Dom, taking it all in with his camera. "This is quite spectacular."

"Totally agree." I marveled at it all. "When Hope told me this was all based around a fantasy series about vampires, I didn't know what to expect. But this is actually gorgeous."

"Wait. You haven't seen *Twilight*? Or any of its sequels?" Dom asked.

"No, and you have?" I replied, laughing.

"No, of course not," he blurted out a little too quickly. "I mean, yeah. I have sisters! And I assumed every girl in America had seen them. They're cult classics for women. My audience is going to eat this *up*."

I crossed my arms and scanned the room for any details I might have missed. "Yeah, I was never interested in any of that vampire stuff. Though I might have to check it out now, having seen all this."

"I'm down for a movie marathon," he replied, still filming.

I didn't answer him and wondered whether he was suggesting a date night or just a casual movie night as friends. Either way, I had enough context to know that watching *Twilight* together was a no-go. He'd have to choose something else.

"Let's head over to the tent and get some footage there too," I said, moving on.

"You know what we should do?" Dom said, walking beside me now. "We should go to the Belcourt Theatre one night and check out one of the classic films they show there every now and then."

"You're into old movies?" I asked, now interested despite knowing better.

"Remember, I was a film major," he said. "I'm clearly not using my degree to its full potential, but I plan to one day."

"Fine arts feels very New York of you."

"I know, I know. Totally cliché for a kid from Brooklyn to study film in New York, but I can't help what I like, so I just lean in and own the stereotype."

I laughed. "Oh, who cares about that," I said. "Your video skills are coming in very handy with our project. Even if it's not what you want to do forever, your talent is extremely useful in this industry."

"To be honest, I've thought lately about quitting the whole

Instagram thing. Same with consulting. Maybe I could try to find a job in the film industry, but it's hard to walk away from the regular consulting paychecks and the extra freedom I get from social media stuff," he said. "I never thought my Brides' Man gig would take off, and the more I grow in that space, the harder and harder it is to give it up."

"I get that," I said as we walked into an enchanted wonderland of a tent.

"Holy moly," said Dom, prepping his camera. "What was the inspiration for all this? Snow White's forest?"

"Close, kind of," I replied. "This one's actually *FernGully*."

"You're kidding," he said.

"Nope. She wanted her very own enchanted rain forest, and it looks like that's exactly what she got," I said.

"She sure did," he replied. "I can't believe we're in Tennessee."

The clear-top tent was anchored by fourteen-foot faux weeping willow trees. Candles in glass orbs hung from every branch. The elevated dance floor floated in the center of the space and could be described only as an enormous Lucite shadow box filled with thousands of faux flowers in a rainbow of colors. The bars were covered in green moss and adorned with hundreds of colorful butterflies. The clear ceiling was almost entirely covered in twinkling fairy lights that would look just like a sky full of stars once the sun set.

But the real showstopper was the centerpiece on every dining table. Atop every amethyst silk tablecloth was an antique birdcage that housed two real-life lovebirds. The rosy-faced little birds were hopping around and singing, and the space looked, sounded, and felt exactly like an enchanted forest from the movie. I wasn't precisely sure how authentic they were to the rain forest setting, but their chirping certainly added to the wild vibe.

"This tent deserves an award," I said. "I'm in complete awe, and I've seen a lot of fabulous reception décor in my day."

"Hope's ideas could've really gone sideways and looked cheesy, but this is so cool. Still not sure about the fake unicorn, but I can dig this." Dom laughed.

"Me too," I said. "Plus, you can only talk a bride out of so much, and if she was willing to compromise on some of the design elements but still wanted a unicorn, then that's what the planner made happen. Planners pick and choose their battles to meet their clients' wishes without jeopardizing their reputations for taste."

"That makes sense," Dom said. "But why the heck is it so cold in here? Seems like more of a *Frozen* vibe than a rain forest vibe, don't you think?"

I hadn't realized it until then, but Dom was right. It was pretty frigid in the tent.

"I'm sure it's to keep the flowers cool," I replied. "They will probably turn down the AC once it's closer to the start of the reception. After all, it's May in Tennessee, and with a clear-top tent, if you don't keep it cold in here during the day, it could turn into a greenhouse."

"But my hands are freezing and my nose is starting to run, so let's get out of here for now."

"Hmm. Lovely, Dominic."

"Tell me yours isn't."

I couldn't, as he could clearly see.

He finished shooting details, and then we hopped back in his car to drive up to the main house. We found the bridal party together in one of the suites. They were all wearing matching silk robes and were busy with the hair and makeup team. Hope filled me in on her day so far and how her dad had written a special song to sing for her first dance with Mark at the reception. If one's dad was a CMA and Grammy Award–winning country music artist, was it even ethical to host a reception where that didn't happen?

We managed to get a few sound bites from Mark, too, who was playing darts and sipping bourbon in the rec room with his groomsmen, his dad, and Hope's father. The walls were covered in album covers and platinum records, and a recording studio at the far end could've rivaled any studio on Music Row. Hope's dad, Clint, looked as cool as a cucumber in his Stetson hat and with a cigar in hand. He brought the "star power" to this wedding, and I'd be lying if I said I wasn't a bit intimidated to speak with him. However, he couldn't have been any nicer.

"Hope's mama and I have looked forward to this day for a while now, but it's going to be bittersweet," Clint said in his deep country accent. "She's my only little girl, and as much as I love Mark, I'll have to kill him if he breaks her heart."

Mark looked over from his seat nearby, and Clint gave him a wink. I couldn't imagine how it must feel to have Clint as your father-in-law-to-be. Probably very cool but also a little scary knowing he could snap his fingers and make life miserable in an instant. It was fun to watch Mark smile back but squirm a little too.

We finished up our interviews and then took a quick break

back at the barn before the festivities really got going. Dom leaned up against the side of the barn as he ate a sandwich.

"All these wide-open spaces look pretty good on you," I said, taking a bite out of my chicken salad.

"Thank you very much, little lady," he said, laughing and mock-brushing dirt off his shoulder. "Isn't that a line from a country song?"

"I'm impressed you know that," I said. "It's from the Dixie Chicks, or they're the Chicks now, actually. One of my favorites too. So now we've established that you know at least two country songs. One about riding a cowboy and one about wide-open spaces."

"Clearly all the classics," he said with a laugh. "Okay, so I'm not as versed in country music as I should be living in Nashville, but I do know that song. Did you need some room to make big mistakes, or were you looking for new faces when you decided to move to Nashville?"

Dang, he was good. Cheesy, but good.

"Something like that," I said. "But you make it sound so cliché."

"Don't forget I'm a film student from New York. Cliché is my middle name."

But before we could continue our conversation, we were interrupted by shrieks coming from inside the tent. Simultaneously, we both put down our food and ran inside. Standing underneath one of the trees was one of the wedding planners, holding up a birdcage, a look of horror on her face.

"Those poor little birds!" she practically yelled. "They're *all* dead."

CHAPTER 18

"What do you mean 'they're all dead'?" Dom asked.

"I—I don't know what happened," the wedding planner said in total panic. "They had food, water, and were totally fine an hour ago."

Just then, a member of the waitstaff came over to inspect what was happening.

"Has it been this cold in here all day?" she asked.

"Yes," replied the planner. "We had to keep the AC running on high since last night to keep the flowers from wilting in the heat."

"Well, I don't have that exact species of bird, but my parakeet back home can't stand temperatures below seventy degrees," the server said. "I think they might have frozen to death."

"What?!" the planner cried. "That's absolutely horrible."

"I doubt it was painful for them," the server added.

"Oh, dear God." The planner was almost in tears.

I decided to step in and try to help if I could.

"Hi, I'm Claire." I moved closer to the planner and the deceased décor. "I'm one of the journalists here to cover the day—"

"*Please* don't write about this," she interrupted.

"Oh no, no, we won't." I looked over at Dom and he nodded. "I just wanted to offer to help. I know this is bad, but at least it happened before any of the guests came in."

"Yes, that's true," she said, setting the cage on the ground. She seemed to be calming down.

"We can help you gather up all the cages so that someone can remove the birds," I said. I wanted to help but wasn't about to suggest that Dom or I dispose of the birds ourselves. "Then why don't we see whether the florist can add a small arrangement inside each birdcage. No one will ever know the birds were there."

"The clients will." The planner sighed. "But you're right. It's better than the alternative, and I appreciate the help. The rest of our team is getting the wedding party ready for the ceremony. If you can help me reset the tables, that would be amazing."

And with that, Dom and I carefully removed the cages while the server with the parakeet was kind enough to remove the birds and take them home with her for a "proper burial." Apparently, she lived on a farm, and when the planner offered her a massive tip, she was more than happy to take care of the fowl problem.

"Just when you think you've seen everything," Dom said later as we placed the final cage back on its table, now with a lovely floral arrangement inside.

"I keep telling you that nothing surprises me anymore," I said.

The botched bird situation had eaten up most of our free time, so we washed our hands about ten times and then headed back to the barn for the main event.

The ceremony was beautiful, and as Hope and Mark stood beneath the towering floral arch, I couldn't help but think this scene truly looked like something out of a fairy-tale wedding. I even started feeling a little emotional—until they started to recite their vows.

Hope had told me earlier that she and Mark had written their own vows but failed to say more about them. At first, I thought my hearing had failed or I was having some kind of stroke.

"What language is that?" I whispered to Dom from our perch in the back.

"I . . . I actually think it's a pretend language," he replied.

"What are you talking about?" I asked. "What do you mean *pretend* language?"

"Do you have one of the programs with you?" he asked. "I bet there's a note in there about it."

"No, but let me grab one."

I didn't have to go far before I found the table at the back of the aisle and a basket full of programs. Each program was iridescent, in the shape of a flower with a beautiful lilac ribbon tied at the bottom. Under the order of service, a small line read: "The bride and groom have chosen to recite their own vows to one another in their favorite mythical tongue: Sindarin, one of the Elvish languages of Tolkien." My eyes were wide as saucers.

Both the Elvish and English translations were printed below for everyone to follow along. Dom was going to lose it for sure.

I quietly moved back to my seat next to Dom, who was still filming. "You're not going to believe what I'm about to tell you," I whispered as I casually fanned myself with the floral program.

"What is it?" he asked.

"It's Elvish," I said, holding back a laugh.

"What?" he replied a little too loud.

"Keep your voice down," I said, now pointing to the line in the program as proof.

"Like, from *The Lord of the Rings*?"

"I can't believe she didn't mention this to me earlier," I said. "But yes, I think so. This wedding is just full of surprises."

"For once, I'm at a loss for words," Dom said. "They are clearly perfect for each other if this was something they both enjoyed. I bet they go to all those conferences for people who like fantasy stuff."

"Maybe that's what they're doing for their honeymoon," I added. "I haven't asked them about it yet. If it is, I'm going to die."

We were both holding back giggles at this point, but thankfully the couple finished reciting whatever it was they were saying to each other. I wondered whether we'd need to add subtitles to our video if we showed this part of the ceremony.

As soon as the officiant pronounced them man and wife, the ceremony musicians played a set of chimes and the officiant asked for every guest to open the small box that was placed at the base of every bench. Inside each box was a butterfly that flew into the air and fluttered around the entire area above all the guests. I supposed that since real fairies weren't available, butterflies were the next best option. It was actually the perfect ending to this mythical ceremony, and everyone cheered in delight.

"Thank goodness it wasn't as cold in here as it was in the reception tent," Dom said. "I don't think I could've helped clean up dead butterflies too."

"Oh geez," I said. "I hadn't thought of that. Nothing would kill the vibe like a boxes full of dead insects."

We followed Hope and Mark into the field with the wedding photographer to grab video of the two of them after the service. They wanted to take their postceremony pictures at sunset in the field with the unicorn before joining guests at the reception. We managed to remain professional and act like everything was totally normal as Hope sat atop the unicorn and Mark led them both around and posed.

"This is epic footage," Dom said under his breath. "Do you think Mark wants to be a minotaur, a vampire, or an elf in his next life?"

"I legit don't want to know," I said. "This fantasy is walking a very fine line as it is, and any role-playing they're both into is not something I need to know anything about."

"That's fair." He laughed. "Still, if this doesn't make it onto TV, I don't know what will."

"Fingers crossed they let us run it once they see our cut. It could be a contender for the season finale," I said. "Either way, it will certainly work as clickbait."

"I think we've got what we need here," Dom said. "And unless you want to grab any more interviews right now, we can take a break."

We headed over to the back side of the barn and sat down next to each other on the grass. The sun had just set, revealing a bluish-purple glow in the sky.

"You could watch the sunset over Manhattan a few blocks from where I grew up, but this . . ." Dom trailed off, his gaze extending over the open pasture as it slowly disappeared into the night sky.

"It's sure something else," I added, taking in the view myself.

"Tell me," Dom said. "What do you miss most about Dallas?"

"Besides the margaritas and Tex-Mex?"

"Well, that's a given," he replied. "You do have a soul."

"I miss my family the most," I said. "I've told you how we aren't in the best place right now—at least not all of us—but I miss how things used to be when we were growing up. So when you ask if I miss Dallas, I do, but I don't miss the bubble we lived in. I've never cherished anonymity so much as I do now."

"I can understand that," he said, running his fingers through the grass. "A fresh start is a gift. And to be fair, so is anonymity."

"What's that supposed to mean, Mr. Influencer?" I asked.

"I don't know. It sounds so egotistical or ungrateful when I say it out loud."

"Has that ever stopped you before?"

He let out a feeble chuckle. "Listen, I'm a single guy doing bridal stuff. But I went to film school. I wanted to be a director. I'd rather be telling people's stories, making something challenging or artful.

"But I know what audiences want. I'm a long way off from being the next Scorsese or Burns. I'm wearing a custom-tailored jacket because I could get it for free. I'm smiling into a camera because I know that brides who are concerned about demonstrating good taste would trust me. They might even wish their grooms were a little bit more like me. But in reality, they shouldn't, because I'm actually just a guy who acts like a small dream is a big one."

"What's keeping you from the big dream?"

"I didn't have a lot of connections, but also . . . Do you know how many twenty-two, or now twenty-eight-year-old white guys with cameras say they want to be directors? I was a walking cliché. So I found something that could be a niche. Not my passion. Not my dream. But it's worked out, I suppose."

"I should say so," I said without thinking. *Strong work, Claire. Way to sound unsympathetic after he's revealed his deepest hopes and ambitions.*

"Now I feel like a jerk. Plenty of people would kill to have the kind of audience I have, the kind of freedom."

"You're not a jerk. I just meant you've done a great job of making it work." Far better than I ever had with a fallback option. "Have you thought about a pivot?"

I wished I had more to offer him. But I was surprised by his words too. Gone was the cocksure, quippy face for the camera.

"Honestly, that was part of why I took this job. The docuseries seemed a step in the right direction," he said. "My mom, as you can imagine, has a lot of thoughts about how I'm using my degree. She can barely navigate social media as it is, so forget about believing it's a viable career path."

"I get it," I said. "They're still our parents even if we're solidly adults. But it can be hard not to feel like we have to live in their shadows or their expectations forever. Clearly we both needed the space Nashville's provided."

Everybody at work and online saw charismatic, entertaining Dom. I felt like I was getting a glimpse of serious, vulnerable Dom. The one who actually cared so much and dreamed so big it scared him.

"Thanks for listening," Dom said.

"Thanks for telling me." I smiled and looked over at him. I companionably nudged him with my shoulder, then stilled.

Our faces were dangerously close now, and the air around us smelled like honeysuckle and fresh-cut grass. Over Dom's shoulder I could see that a few fireflies had begun to light.

"Have you ever caught fireflies?" I asked, trying to break the tension.

"Like, as a kid?" he asked, his smile a little crooked.

"Yes, as a kid," I said.

He laughed. "Sure I did. I think it's a childhood rite of passage."

"Just checking," I said. "If not, I'd have made you do it right now."

"Well, I appreciate you looking out for me," he said, winking. "Looks like we've come a long way from that cold welcome you gave me when we first met at the office."

"Do you blame me?" I asked. "I thought you were being groomed as my replacement."

"No chance," said Dom. "I would never do that to you."

He didn't realize, of course, how I'd tried to do that very thing to Lottie. I felt a rare wave of shame roll over me.

"Speaking of not missing key moments in life, we'd better get over to the reception so we don't miss anything," I said quickly, then shifted my legs to stand.

I could tell he wasn't quite ready to break up our chat, but we needed to get back to work, and I needed to shake off all the feelings. He slowly stood and extended a hand to me. I grudgingly took it, trying to ignore the feel of his hand engulfing mine. I let go to brush grass off my dress.

We arrived at the reception just in time to catch Hope and Mark's first dance. There was barely a dry eye in sight as Clint sang the love song he'd written for them. The couple beamed as they swayed together across the sea of flowers beneath them. Dom captured every moment, and I tried my best to avoid eye contact with him for the rest of the event. The night was oozing with love and a hint of magic, and I didn't trust myself.

The evening ended with a bang. Literally. The newlyweds were sent off in a vintage convertible under an open sky of fireworks. Another happily married couple in the books and another late-night drive home with Dom.

Just as we were packing up our gear to walk to Dom's car, Clint sauntered over to us.

"Congratulations, sir. What a beautiful wedding. You must be so proud."

It was still extremely intimidating talking to a man whose music was a staple of my adolescence and early adulthood.

"I am, I am." He shuffled his boots in the gravel. "But I

wanted to talk to y'all. We're real grateful you came out and recorded so much of our Hope's big day for the magazine."

"We're so grateful for the opportunity," Dom said quickly.

"All that said, her mother and I are a little uncertain about it being shown to the whole world. Some pictures in the pages of our local little magazine is one thing, but we've worked to keep so much of our lives private. It feels a little . . ." He shrugged his shoulders, at a loss for words. As if he knew no words would make us feel better about the news he was delivering.

"Just so I understand, are you saying we can't use the footage we took today?" I croaked out.

"I'm not sayin' that just yet. Just that I think we need a minute to simmer on it before we make any final decisions, if that's okay with y'all."

He clearly wasn't asking for our permission, but we really didn't have a choice in the matter. Yes, he signed papers agreeing to allow us to cover the event, but we'd never run anything if a client changed their mind. Especially a country music star equipped with all the resources to slap us with a lovely little bit of litigation.

Dom and I tried to mumble something understanding as he turned to rejoin his family.

We got in the car in silence. My brain spun. We had just weeks now until Lucy's wedding and a little over a month until the next board meeting. Michelle was hoping to have a series deal in place by then. Not to mention, I was banking on the fact that we could use this wedding as a substitute for Lucy's. I started sweating just thinking about all the potential drama involved with me and Cedric's firm for everyone to see if Dom shot it.

"What in the world are we going to do?" I muttered to myself, a tension headache already building behind my eyes. Gone were the fireflies and magic; instead, reality had slapped me in the face.

"Hey." Dom shot me a quick look from the other side of the dark car. "This isn't the end of the road, partner." His deep voice stumbled over what I could only assume was supposed to be a cowboy drawl.

It is not cute, I told myself. *I will not find this charming in the face of a crisis.*

Still, I could feel a reluctant smile starting to form. Apparently, my face didn't get the memo. "You got an ace wedding tucked up your sleeve or something, cowboy?"

"No, but even without the elves, this show has potential." Before we pulled out, Dom handed me his phone. "I know you're like a technology hermit or something, so I know you haven't seen this yet, but look."

He had his direct messages pulled up to a group message. My Instagram account was also included, but I checked it so seldom I'd missed this completely. Technology hermit wasn't that far off from the truth, to be honest.

I read in silence. A producer out of LA wanted to talk to us about buying our series. They had been following the stories we'd run in the magazine and on the website, and those, combined with Dom's stories and reels, had given them a pretty solid sense of the narrative and content.

"Wait, have they seen any of the content? This sounds

serious. *Serious* as in more than just LA 'would love to have a conversation.' *Serious* as in a real offer to come."

"Sure." Dom shrugged. "A few weeks ago, they reached out just to me, and I sent them our first episode as a sample. Not that I expected anything. It's Hollywood, but a foot in the door is a foot in the door."

Wait. What?

Dom didn't seem to notice he'd just knocked me off my feet. "It's a pretty sweet deal. They'd buy the rights to this project from us, pay *POC* for their expenses but not much more, and would even like to set up a pitch meeting for future ideas with their entire team."

"Is this for real? I didn't realize you were . . . shopping the project."

This seemed to get his attention. He shot me a long look. "I sent it to demonstrate what I could do, like a résumé—not so they would buy that exact one! I figured if they didn't want the show, I could at least talk to them about jobs after my contract ended. It's certainly more along the lines of what I'd like to be doing."

"But why didn't you tell me about this sooner?" I asked. *This could be huge.* My mind whirled; this could be a chance for me to be more than the failure my family saw me as. This could be real TV money, a TV future.

"Honestly, I didn't think it was relevant. And I mean it's not like I hid it from you. You just don't read your DMs. But now that things seem to be falling apart a bit, I wanted to see what you thought. We might need this kind of backup plan."

A backup plan. But just for us. Not for *Piece of Cake*.

Suddenly, the whole thing seemed a little sour. Because what Dom was suggesting toed that line of underhanded. Yes, it would be great for me, but what about the people who had helped me get to where I was, the team that was counting on me?

He had a point, but I also couldn't help feeling a little blindsided. *And* a little disloyal, which surprised me even more.

"Thanks for showing me, but I don't think I could do this while we still have a shot at making this work with *Piece of Cake*. I know you just got here, but these people have given me a lot over the last few years. I couldn't pull the rug out from under them."

"That's fair," he mused. "And I really respect the loyalty. But it's good to know we have a backup plan at least, right?"

"I guess." But even as I said it, I knew I didn't mean it.

CHAPTER 19

With the deadline weeks away, and knowing we'd be crunched after Lucy's wedding, we needed to get the other episodes into a final-cut version. Dom's film degree and editing experience were really coming in handy, as there was no way the magazine would approve an additional freelancer budget on top of everything else we'd expensed. All for a Hail Mary.

I thought of Kevin's family situation, Nancy's mortgages, even Amaya's massive student loans. And now my car repairs, which had come in at a painful, nearly impossible estimate. We all had so much riding on this working out. Selling the project to save my own skin and Dom's seemed unthinkable. We had to make this work.

Dom was working round the clock in the studio. I hadn't seen him much since Hope's wedding. I smiled, remembering him staring at the purple sunset over the field—a bright spot in an otherwise crappy day. I wrapped up writing a beach-honeymoon packing list for the thirty-sixth time. Then I submitted my draft to Kevin, who wouldn't send his comments back until the afternoon.

I ducked out for coffee at Barista Parlor before our staff meeting. Without even asking Dom, I automatically grabbed his Americano along with my iced oat latte. I'd need all the caffeine I could get given that I was leaving for Dallas the next morning. I'd procrastinated all week, and now I'd need to work in overdrive to finish up work and have time to pack before catching my flight.

When I came back, Michelle had gathered the team in the conference room. I slipped into my seat and slid Dom his coffee. He gave me a grateful look that warmed my traitorous insides. I noticed that Nancy, the copy editor, was notably absent. I hoped she was sick and not out for good. How could they expect us to put together a magazine that wasn't proofread?

"Thank you all for coming today. I won't keep you long." Michelle tossed her impeccable bob.

"First, Claire and Dom, I'll get right to it: Hope and Mark's unicorn fantasy wedding is officially out. It's not a huge surprise, but it sets us back. You two will really need to knock this Dallas wedding out of the park."

Despite the family's initial excitement, it sounded like Clint had succumbed to his publicist's advice to keep a lower profile with the media coverage of his daughter's *Lord of the Rings*–meets–*FernGully* wedding. And to be honest, I couldn't really blame him. The couple *did* speak in Elvish. Clint was merely protecting his family, but unfortunately it screwed us by taking out our best coverage thus far.

Instead of griping, I channeled Evelyn and squared my shoulders: "You can count on us."

"What a waste of time and energy," Dom said under his breath to me.

"Second, Nancy has chosen to accept her early retirement package."

"You mean she got laid off," Kevin interrupted, disdain evident in his typically affable voice.

"No, she was presented with several options and *chose* to take her retirement early—and save the company some significant expenses. It was a true team player move." She held up a hand to quiet any possible responses. Nancy had been here longer than almost anyone, and I could imagine that her salary was one of the few remaining that would have even made a dent in our shortfall.

"I don't have to remind everyone that times are challenging." Michelle stood up at one end of the table. "The publisher is considering further ways to cut costs and gain revenue, but honestly, if anyone has ideas, we're open. *Piece of Cake* has a hundred-year legacy. We've survived all sorts of changes in this country and in this industry. But people just aren't buying magazines the way they used to."

Janice raised her hand. Maternal, she was always looking out for the team. "We've heard a lot of this before, Michelle. What are you saying, exactly?"

"I'm saying that even with staff and budget cuts, we'll probably have another couple of issues before we have to cease publication. Hopefully this video project will find a partner. That might save our necks and allow what's left of us to pivot."

Everyone not too subtly turned their attention to Dom and me. No pressure, as ever.

Michelle continued. "But otherwise, I imagine the publisher will sell to another larger national company. Most of us would be let go because they usually just buy the brand name and a few key staff."

Amaya looked like she was about to throw up. Kevin looked pissed off. Janice had a look of exhausted resignation. Everyone else had a combination of panic, disbelief, and hope on their faces.

I mustered what I hoped was a confident smile but probably looked young and inadequate more than anything else.

As everyone began to file out of the room, I felt glued to my seat. I wanted to shrivel up and crawl under the table. I needed a quiet moment to clear my head. How was work supposed to carry on as normal after a meeting like that?

I was starting to sweat and having trouble focusing on the rest of my to-do list for the day.

Pressure doesn't always have to be a bad thing, I reminded myself. *After all, pressure creates diamonds, right?* I was a Sommers. I could do this. I had to. I finally stood.

I had to grab some samples for the fall trends spread, so I walked to the fashion closet, grateful for the chance to steal a moment alone. I put my hand on the closet door and saw Dom walking down the hall toward me. "Hey, wait up."

I motioned for him to follow me in. "Sorry," I said once I closed the door behind us. "I have to pull some fall bridal samples. What's up?"

"What do you mean, 'What's up?' I want to talk about that meeting. We all knew it was bad, but you looked ready to cry in there. Are you okay?"

"Yes, yes. I'm fine . . . It's just sinking in more that, like, people's jobs are riding on this project. And we're getting so close to the deadline. It seemed like an ambitious idea and a way to help, but I never really considered that we might actually fail—or what that could mean."

In truth, I'd mostly been focused on what it would all mean for me. Success and security and my parents' approval, or yet another failed attempt at greatness. I hadn't processed fully how it would tangibly impact other people's lives.

"It's not truly all on us. You know that, right? This is a big company, and they have other ways of figuring it out. And if they don't, a century of business decisions doesn't rest solely on your shoulders." A crease formed between his eyebrows, and he pursed his lips in concern.

"I know that, but I'm just stressed about everything. Our project, the idea of having to look for another new job, and then there's Lucy's wedding . . . Everybody I know will be there, and I don't know how to act around them all after everything that happened. It's so weird and everybody is judging me all the time and I'm never going to live up to their expectations and my old boss is coming and it's just *a lot*." It was too much. I felt uncharacteristically wobbly. I was going to fall apart here in the musty fashion closet. In front of Dom, no less.

"Hey!" He grabbed me by the shoulders, jolting me out of my ravings. His green eyes bored straight into mine, and I stopped. "It's going to be okay. You'll figure it out. You're a brilliant, capable woman. And I'm here to help however I can. We're a team."

I nodded. Unable to speak and very aware of his warm grip on my shoulders.

Finally, he dropped his hands. "So what is this place?" He looked around the room.

"It's the fashion closet. We keep all the samples for photo shoots in here."

He walked over to the rack of wedding dresses. "I cannot *believe* I've never been in here. What a missed opportunity for my channel." He pulled out a hideous specimen from the fall runway shows, a particularly poufed skirt littered with sequined butterflies. It looked like the couture version of the dELiA*s catalog.

"Truly a tragedy, I agree." I giggled.

"Who on earth is wearing these?!"

"Someone with an overactive imagination and a lifetime of princess fantasies?"

"Do you wear it with a tiara?"

"My old boss always said, 'Only true princesses should wear tiaras. And even then, make sure it's a real one.'" I thought of Cedric with a wince. Shook it off. Did not need that kind of self-loathing energy right now.

I went over and pulled out a slinky slip dress in blush pink. "Very nineties. I kind of love the move toward nonwhite dresses. It's fun and also less about the implied perfection of white."

"I still can't believe we're not filming this. Here, slip it over your head." He helped me slide the hanger around my neck so the dress hung in front of me. I grabbed the sides in my hands and mock curtsied, sashaying in it. He took a couple of pictures.

"Yes! You're killing it," he said in a goofy imitation of a photographer while I posed. "Nice. Nice. Now give me your best Blue Steel."

"Oh, so now I'm a male model from *Zoolander*? How flattering." I laughed while trying to exaggerate and purse my lips for the camera.

"Listen, even as a film major, my movie model references are limited." He snatched a veil off the central worktable that was scattered with various accessories. "Here, put this on."

I pinned it haphazardly in my blonde hair. I caught a glimpse of myself in the full-length mirror. All askew but smiling. It felt good to forget about everything for a moment, to let loose.

He moved forward and backward like a crazed paparazzo and almost knocked me over as he tripped over a rogue pair of shoes.

He grabbed my arm to help me balance and pulled me in closer. We stood there, breathing heavily for a few seconds, before he set his phone down on the table. He then slowly adjusted my veil and his hand stopped, gently fingering a strand of my hair.

As he got even closer, I inhaled the now-familiar scent of cedar. I looked up into those twinkling green eyes. He paused, his hand still in my hair. Slowly, he slid it down the side of my head, cupping my cheek. I found myself involuntarily leaning into his hand while tilting my head up to his.

His lips met mine, gently. Soft and full, they tasted like the cherry ChapStick he always wore. It was gentle at first, and then his other arm wrapped around me, pulling me close.

The wooden hanger of the dress jabbed between us and we were jolted, briefly, out of the moment. He yanked it over my head and immediately kissed me again, hungrily. I couldn't pull him close enough. We were standing on paper shopping bags and a wedding dress or two, but I didn't care. He was all that mattered in this moment. I ran my hands up and down the firm planes of his back, desperate.

This was not a fake kiss for the love boat. This was just us. Only us.

I nibbled his bottom lip as he pushed me against the side of the clothing rack. Nothing else existed. I didn't feel the need to try or do or be anything more than *me* in this moment.

The bright light from the hallway burst onto us, and we jumped apart.

"Oh. My. Um . . ." The new intern stood at the door, unsure whether to flee or stay. "I just needed . . . I'll come back . . . I'm so sorry."

"No, it's okay, Hannah. We're done in here." I tamped down a giggle as I tried to play it off. I looked sheepishly at Dom, who was grinning from ear to ear.

"Don't worry about it," he said to her, picking his phone up from the table, giving me a wink, and then slipping past her out the door.

I stayed to grab the samples I still hadn't pulled, while he made his way back to the editing room.

I didn't see him the rest of the day, and I had to leave early to finish packing. We'd be able to talk more on the flight to Dallas tomorrow. The pit in my stomach returned.

That night, packing at my apartment, I waited to hear from him. I composed but never sent two or three texts. Too much to do, though, before our early morning. Finally, my phone pinged.

> **Dom:** Well, today was interesting . . .
> **Me:** It certainly wasn't what I was looking for
> when I went into the fashion closet.
> **Dom:** I can't wait to see you tomorrow. Lots to
> talk about.

I wasn't quite sure what he meant, but he certainly had my full attention.

> **Me:** Agreed. Looking forward to it.

I focused on pairing shoes with outfits fit to impress (or at least not embarrass myself) in front of everyone I'd ever known. And Dom.

CHAPTER 20

No city in the history of air travel has built a perfect airport. You're either too far from the gate off the bat (see: JFK), have to travel too far between connections (I'm looking at you, Atlanta), or you get dropped off near your gate but navigating anywhere else is a particular level of hell (DFW wins this one by a literal mile).

Our fair city of Nashville's airport features live music from talented, aspiring musicians, but it's also been under construction for what feels like a decade in an attempt to keep up with the growing pace of visitors. I navigated my Away suitcase through the tarp-covered tunnels the next morning, my mind in a muddle.

Dom and I booked our flight reservations separately, and since we came from different directions, we had no practical reason to share an Uber to the airport. I'd woken up stressed about seeing my family and with a stomach full of butterflies about seeing Dom again. If I was looking to complicate things even more before Lucy's wedding, I'd certainly managed to do so.

Things with Dom could go two ways. First way: Because we'd become way more than just friends and coworkers, this could lead to something great—pending whatever came next for him after his contract ran out. I wasn't sure how I felt about that.

Or second, this could be just like the *Tennessee Belle*. Just a blip. A mistake. A moment that didn't mean anything. Something had shifted either way. I decided it was best to play it cool and let him do the talking until I really knew what was going on in his head.

I didn't see Dom at security or even at our gate. I'd taken my window seat and was getting my book and phone charger out. Still no Dom. I was admittedly beginning to get anxious when he appeared at the front of the plane. He ran a hand through his tousled brown hair, the other hand holding a carry-on handle. We locked eyes over the seat backs, and he gave me a wry grin.

Too late to look out the window and act cool. Nevertheless, I tried.

But he stopped at my row and slid in. "I was hoping we'd be together," he said.

"Oh, really?" I tried to focus on my *Southern Living* but couldn't help the slightest of smiles.

We sat in silence during takeoff. As the plane leveled off, Dom cleared his throat and turned slightly toward me. "Listen, about yesterday, we were both wound up and feeling the pressure. It was an intense moment. I don't want you to . . ."

So this is how he's going to play it, I thought as he continued to talk. My heart was about to explode, but I kept it together. No way would I let him think I was super invested in this now. I cut him off. "It's okay, I get it. Neither of us was in our right mind. Too many emotions. We need to focus on getting through these next couple weeks. Never should have crossed that line."

"It's not just that. It's also that . . . I have an offer back in New York . . . I meant to tell you." He had the grace to look ashamed.

"When would you have informed me, Dominic? And what was all *that*"—I gestured out the window, as if he could see the fashion closet in my mind—"if you're just trying to leave?"

"Claire, I've always been leaving. Nashville was never the plan. I just didn't know the next gig would come up so quickly."

"How delightful for you. Well done, congrats." I tried to raise my magazine again but he put a hand on it.

"Hear me out. I'd like to stay. But if the magazine goes under, I need a backup. I don't have the savings or the safety net to make it otherwise. So I put out feelers, and I have an offer to run socials for a film production company. It's not the dream, but it feels like I'm finally in the ballpark. I've been meaning to tell you, but I honestly didn't think you'd care."

"How could you *not* think I'd care? We're . . . friends, right?" Before he could answer, I went on. "And what was all that about being able to stand on your own two feet if you didn't believe it for yourself?"

"I do, but I also needed a backup. Not all of us have a trust fund waiting."

"That was a low blow." I sniffed. Struck.

"I'm sorry."

"No, it's fine. I understand that's how you see me. Better for us to just get through this weekend and do what we set out to do. We have a lot riding on this project. Too many other people's futures—not to mention my sister's actual wedding. And it sounds like you need to do well enough to move on to the next shiny thing, regardless."

"That's not fair. But sure, yes, let's just get through. We knew this was always going to be temporary."

I couldn't believe he actually said it aloud. We both knew it, but his words and actions had led me to believe he might consider sticking around. I'd tried to convince myself otherwise, but who was I kidding? I'd let my heart do the thinking and not my head. And it had ended up exactly where I thought it would: in a mess of my own making.

Fortunately, it was a short flight, and we were able to read and bury ourselves in work. My dad picked me up at the airport to take me home, and I left Dom waiting at baggage claim to find his own way to his hotel.

I climbed into my dad's immaculate Cadillac. The leather was comfortable and smelled like him. We'd hardly spoken when I was here for Claire's engagement party, but I was happy for him to pick me up this time.

"How's it going, sweetheart?"

I updated him on the latest with the magazine and our project, omitting the crippling fear that I'd fail and everyone would be jobless.

"And are you doing okay, staying afloat?" My dad was always

concerned about safety nets, for me now more than ever. "You'd let us know if you were in trouble, right?"

"Yes, Dad, I would. I'm doing pretty well. Things are tight, but I'm slowly saving some each month and covering my bills."

"Well, I hate that for you, hon, but it was how it had to be. I've been impressed and, to tell the truth, a little surprised you've made it on your own this long."

"Honestly, I think it's been good for me. Don't get me wrong, it's hard. But I'm learning a lot about finance and responsibility that I think I never would have otherwise. I'm almost grateful to you and Mom for cutting me off."

He looked away from the road and at me for a moment. "Claire, you know that wasn't our intention, right?"

"Sure, no, I mean . . ."

Dad cleared his throat. "Your grandmother's trust had a morality clause. It was triggered when you were fired for cause and everything came out."

"I knew about that part, yes."

"We never wanted you to think we didn't support or love you. But we *did* hope this would be a lesson to you. I thought we'd explained that to you better."

"I think all I heard was 'You're cut off and will never get any more money,' and then everything else became noise and details," I admitted.

"Well, we should have worked through it more with you. And you're not cut off from your trust forever—just until you're forty. If all goes well between now and then, of course."

For the first time, this fact felt a little freeing, I realized. Age forty was too long to just wait around for an influx of cash, but not forever. I'd already had to figure it out, build my own life. I was proving to myself that I could make it. And the process was starting to feel pretty good. I certainly had developed a new appreciation for money and hard work these past few years that might never have come if I'd always had access to my inheritance.

"Honey, I don't say it enough, but I'm so proud of how hard you're working. Starting over is never easy, but you've got that Sommers spirit, now more than ever. You're blazing your own trail. Keep your chin up."

I took a deep breath and blinked rapidly to pull myself together. I was a puddle of emotions from the past twenty-four hours. Dad was always gentler than Mom, but this was uncharacteristically supportive. He must have felt my energy as he reached across the console and gently squeezed my hand. I gave him a weak smile.

We arrived at the house, and I'd managed to compose myself once again. Lucy had moved back home for the last two weeks after classes ended to prep for the wedding. Most of the clients we worked with while I was at Cedric Montclair Celebrations either quit their jobs months before their big days or weren't even working in the first place. Wedding planning was their "job." I used to think that was normal. Not anymore.

I found Lucy in the kitchen, leaning against the counter. Absently scrolling on her phone while eating a yogurt.

I hugged her from behind. "Whatcha doing?"

"Not much. Look." She held up her phone, open to Dom's profile. "Is this you?"

A heavy filter distorted the shoulders-down image, but I recognized the pink dress that hung around my neck in the closet yesterday. The caption read: "Sometimes, the best days are unexpected. You can't script them. So when planning your wedding, or your life, allow yourself to be surprised. You might end up with a moment that's beautiful in its imperfections."

I mean, he was good. Too bad none of that was true. I shrugged and ignored Lucy's probing eyes.

"He decapitated me. Cute."

"What happened with him, Claire?"

"Nothing, he's fine. He's at his hotel. I'm sure you'll see him later today."

"No, why are you being so weird? Did y'all fight? Did you *kiss*?" I avoided her eyes. "You *did*! Tell me everything!"

"There's not much to tell." I described what happened in the fashion closet and then his abrupt departure. She snickered at the poor intern who discovered us. "But you know he's never really been my type. And most important, we always knew it wasn't going to last. He's already got an offer back home in New York, so he'll probably leave soon."

"You know that things can change. Especially if y'all sell this project, right?"

"Right, sure. But it would never work. I don't want to hold him back or try to do long-distance. Not to mention, I'd want him to *want* to stay regardless of this project panning out or not. Who wants to be second place to a job?"

Lucy gave my arm a sisterly squeeze. "I understand. But it sounds like he's into you. And you like him, don't you?"

I took a breath. I could admit that to myself and to my baby sister. "Sure. I mean, yes. I do." There it was. "But we're too different. And he's just not from this world. It's too complicated. I mean, look what just happened between us, and things were just starting. I need to let him go." I waved a hand at the kitchen, then laid my forehead on the counter.

"Well, that's dumb. I'm rooting for him. But in the meantime, you've got bigger fish to fry. Let's go get me married and get your documentary series sold! Save the world!"

I loved her for her genuine, unflagging optimism.

CHAPTER 21

Everyone drove fast in Texas, a state where the speed limit could be seventy-five miles per hour. But also, *everyone* just drove in Texas, which meant I was stuck in bumper-to-bumper traffic yet again.

I'd spent the better part of Friday running last-minute errands for Lucy—in her beautiful new Mercedes SUV. I was enjoying a car with both a functioning accelerator and AC. It gave me a sense of fulfilling my maid-of-honor duties, got me out of the house, and kept me too busy to dwell on Dom. Okay, that wasn't true—Dallas traffic provided ample opportunity for contemplation while trapped behind the wheel. But a girl could sing along to the radio and pretend, at least.

Did I like him? I'd admitted as much to Lucy. But that still didn't change the facts: We were so different. He was leaving. I wanted to be the reason he stayed, but I also didn't want that kind of pressure. It was guaranteed to lead to disappointment. Better to have a clean break now than to watch whatever spark we had flicker and die.

And I was so close to succeeding, to proving my worth through the magazine. I'd failed at so many things, not measured up. This felt like my final chance. The stakes were high. Everybody I'd failed in the past would be here in Dallas. I needed to focus. No distractions. No Dominic.

I switched lanes and turned up the volume.

ᘒ ᘒ ᘒ

That night, I admired my new silk Givenchy dress in the floor-length mirror in my room. The soft green contrasted nicely with my skin tone, I noted, as I tucked a blonde strand behind one ear. I bemoaned my freckles for the zillionth time.

Evelyn had generously taken me to the NorthPark Neiman's to try on dresses to wear at the rehearsal dinner and Sunday brunch. She said it was her sisterly duty since I'd picked up so much maid-of-honor slack. The unheard-of level of kindness almost gave me whiplash, but even if it was just pregnancy hormones making her soft, I'd take it. And this dress.

Collins's family had rented out the Marie Gabrielle space for the night. As I walked inside, I noted Cedric's team had outdone themselves again. I steeled myself for seeing them this time, and sure enough, I spotted a familiar salt-and-pepper mane across the room.

It was always impressive to watch Cedric in his element, zhuzhing florals, angling candles, adjusting place settings, perfecting ambience. He was a design pro at the height of his craft. In the past four years, his event empire had continued to expand across the South, the country, and even the world, despite the pandemic. *Vogue* had featured one of his events in Tuscany in their last issue. He was a veritable wedding god.

I waited for him to notice me. My face flushed, and I prayed I wasn't sweating on the silk. No use delaying the inevitable. I gave a tiny nod of my head in acknowledgment, expecting him to turn and walk away. Instead, he beelined.

"Hello, Cedric."

"Hello." He was curt, but at least he hadn't pretended not to see me.

"You've done such a beautiful job, as always. I know Lucy will be delighted."

He waved a hand dismissively. "Thank you. Now, Lottie has informed me of your current employer, as well as the project you're working on."

"Yes, it's all—"

He cut me off. "This was not part of what your mother and I discussed when it came to your involvement. I don't have to tell you what a big day this is for her and your sister and this whole city, frankly."

"Yes, indeed, I know that." I felt a little defensive. I wasn't a total imbecile.

"Well, I've informed your mother that you cannot film this for your little blog or whatever it is." Cedric squared his shoulders. He ran a hand through his full hair. "I won't sign the release, and neither will anyone on my staff."

"Wait, why not? I thought you spoke with Michelle, my editor. It's great press for everyone involved. We're really good at staying out of the way too."

"That's awfully ironic, coming from you of all people." He pursed his lips. "And no, that was Mary Ellen." I remembered his regional director well. Like a razor blade hidden inside a candy bar. "When she asked me if I was okay with 'the whole Claire thing,' I simply thought she meant you being a part of this wedding. I appreciate your mother, so I agreed to it despite our complicated history. I'm sorry that wires got crossed and you understood I was okay with *you* making a documentary. I believe in forgiveness, I'm not heartless, but that doesn't mean I want you inserting yourself into every area of this wedding or profiting from it. If I catch you so much as filming one moment, I will walk out. It'd be you or me, and we can guess which one of us your mother will choose tomorrow."

My heart was in my throat. "But . . . that seems extremely harsh. Can you please at least let me explain?" But he was already walking away.

This was a disaster.

I thought about Michelle's final words to us and the faces of my colleagues in that tragic meeting. This wedding was our last chance at finishing the series, which meant our last chance at saving the magazine. Our world, my world, in Nashville was about to implode.

And it was all my fault. I had, on some level, told myself that my actions at Cedric's were poor sportsmanship but part of playing the game, trying to get ahead, especially because his company ultimately came out on top with all the positive press I unleashed. But deep down, I knew that wasn't true. My selfish, competitive past mistake had cost me that job and a lot more—and was about to cost an entire team of people their livelihoods. Michelle never would have given me a chance on this project if she'd known it would end up like this. I'd have to let my whole world know about my skeletons—and the past four years and all the good work I'd done would go up in smoke. Had I learned nothing?

I closed my eyes and took deep breaths as a weight settled on my chest. I had two options. Give up, survive the weekend, and then deal with the fallout. Or figure out how to change Cedric's mind. We were out of time for other alternatives. And in the meantime, I had to put on a brave face to not ruin Lucy's rehearsal dinner. I trudged to our table.

Since Dom was technically my plus-one, Lucy seated him next to me, I noted with annoyance.

I took my seat, determined to be cordial but nothing more. He didn't need to know I was barely holding it together. Where he was concerned, I was fine. Perfectly *fine*. "Hiya, Tex." He pulled out the chair next to mine and plopped down.

"Hello, Dominic. Glad to see you made it." I noted his crisp navy slacks and polished leather shoes, then found my eyes drifting up his torso to admire the well-cut blazer and shirt before I caught myself. The man could wear clothes well, I'd give him that. By now, I knew that some of it was the influencer pay-for-play, that he'd wear certain brands in his stories and mention their names. But not all influencers looked quite that way in said clothes, I also knew.

My traitorous mind started to wander back to the feel of those arms.

"I need to tell you something." I exhaled. No use delaying this part. "The planner I used to work for, Cedric?"

"Yeah, have you seen him yet?"

"Yes, and he doesn't want to give us approval to film tomorrow." I put a hand on his arm before I could catch myself. "I'm going to handle it, so don't worry. But just a heads-up that they're being pretty prickly."

"That's going to ruin everything, Claire. I can't believe they would do something like that. Does he understand how much we have riding on this? What reason did he give?" Poor Dom looked genuinely perplexed.

"Well, I told you we didn't end on the best terms, and I guess he finally connected the dots between me and *Piece of Cake* and the project."

"This is unbelievable. I can't believe someone would do this, especially so last-minute. I'm going to talk to him tonight." Dom was preparing to go all caveman, but I didn't need anyone fighting Cedric for me and creating a bigger mess.

"No! Please don't do that." I panicked. Fortunately, we were interrupted by other guests getting to our table.

As our closest friends and family took their seats, I scanned the room, searching for distraction. Dom had met Allison and a couple of the other bridesmaids at Lucy's bachelorette. But I was in no way psychologically prepared for him to meet Evelyn, who sat directly across from us.

Fortunately, she was too pregnant to focus on interrogating

him. The few boyfriends I'd brought around always received the third degree—and a failing grade—from my elder sister. Not that Dom was a boyfriend, but she could typically sniff out (and crush) any romantic possibilities I had.

"Hello, you must be Evelyn," he said, standing to shake her hand across the table once they made eye contact.

"And you must be Dominic. I've heard so much about you."

"Oh really?" He turned to grin smugly at me.

I mouthed back, *From Lucy.*

"I hear you're Claire's coworker on this little project she's working on for the magazine," she said, sipping her water and rubbing her belly, which she managed to make look deranged.

"You've heard correctly," replied Dom. "But it's kind of a big deal. They brought me down from New York to help since I've got some decent videography skills, but this is really all Claire's brainchild. And if we can pull it off, she might just be responsible for saving the entire magazine and a lot of people's jobs."

"Oh really," replied Evelyn, who'd mercifully stopped rubbing her belly. "That's a lot to put on just two people."

"Yeah, but Claire can handle it. I've seen her thrive under pressure at work, helping with things that aren't even her responsibility at times. She's a real force of nature."

"That doesn't really sound like the Claire I've watched for the past twenty-nine years," Evelyn started.

"Well, I imagine she learned a lot of that from watching you. I hear you're quite the business shark," he said smoothly.

I looked over at him in amazement. He really was a skilled charmer.

Evelyn grinned now. "Well, I don't know about that, but I certainly like to think I've got a knack for running businesses. I'm not sure how a baby will fit into it all, but I plan to keep working even after she arrives."

"I watched my single mom work every day of her life and still manage to show me unfailing love and support. I think I respect her even more for it. I imagine you'll do the same."

"Thank you, Dom. That's very kind of you to say. And I'm impressed with your mom's ability to 'do it all.' Obviously, I'm not experienced as a mother yet, but I can't imagine it's easy. Totally worth it, but not easy. I'm ready for the challenge though." She smiled and raised her glass of water to Dom.

He smiled back, and just like that, I knew Dom had won over both my sisters now. Perfect. Just in time for him to leave.

Out of the corner of my eye, I could see a range of expressions flitting across my mother's face as she watched our interactions. She was always so attuned to how her girls were behaving themselves. It was like she had a built-in radar.

The surf and turf—Collins's favorite—was brought out, and I focused on cutting my steak.

"You don't have to murder it, Tex. He's already dead," Dom whispered a little too close for comfort.

"Shut. Up. Or. You're. Next," I muttered back while hacking at the meat. I hated a pink steak, but ordering well-done was also not a wise choice.

"Easy there, don't wave it that close. I don't have insurance on this face."

"I might accidentally improve it. You never know. And everybody loves a good social media transformation story."

"What are you two plotting over there?" My mom was louder than her typically poised self. In fact, I'd never seen her have more than two glasses, but tonight she was already a couple of signature cocktails deep.

"Nothing, Mom." I gave her the smile that Sober Mom would have known was a lie.

"Well, I'm so glad you could make it. Even if y'all can't cover it for your little website, it's nice to see Claire bringing a date." Mom grinned haphazardly.

Dom attempted to change the subject. "This is such a gorgeous party."

"It is, right?" Mom was well on her way to drunk. This was not good. "We're still shocked that Cedric agreed to plan it after Claire made such a disaster for him. It's a miracle—and a testament to my own relationships with people—that I can still show my face in this town, to be perfectly blunt."

"I find all that hard to believe." Dom was clearly trying to divert her, unsuccessfully.

"No, you don't understand. Oh. Don't you know? Claire, dear, tell him. Surely he needs to know."

I felt all eyes at our table suddenly on me. I couldn't take it any longer. "That's enough, Mom." I motioned for Evelyn to take her glass and distract her. "Please."

"No, what's she talking about?" Dom said.

"We can talk about this later," I muttered to him under my

breath. A moment later, he got up and left the table. I took that as my cue to follow him out.

As soon as I came close to where he was standing by the empty bar in the lobby, he started in on me. "So what happened? What's the full story? It sounds like I need to know. Especially if it's messing with our final event and getting this project finished in time."

I took a deep breath.

"In short, I was gunning for a promotion as Cedric's company expanded. I sold the news of a big, top-secret celebrity wedding to a tabloid and attempted to get Lottie and some others blamed for it. It was an awful, psychotic thing. I had to leave Dallas to start over."

"What? I didn't realize that you were fired because you basically sabotaged your own company." He shook his head in disgust. "I thought you just goofed up some flowers or something, kept coming to the office late. That kind of screwup. And you wouldn't talk about it. But, like, what kind of person does that? I don't know that woman. I certainly couldn't ever trust her."

"It's not that simple," I sputtered.

"Enlighten me." He folded his arms across his chest.

"I got the job at Cedric's because he's a friend of my mom's. He plans all the society events in town."

"Yes, I gathered that."

"Well, after college I was the only one of my siblings who didn't have something else lined up. Grad school, a company, a relationship, a real estate deal, *anything*—I was just preparing to move home and apply for jobs. And having trouble finding one that fit the bill as acceptable. I felt like I was living in a pressure cooker."

I took a deep breath and continued. "Mom got me a position at Cedric's. And you know what? I was pretty good at event planning. I liked being a part of the team, I liked the creative work, I liked problem-solving. I did a great job there too. Could have made a successful career of it. But it was never going to be good enough for my parents. I think they thought it would just give me something to do while I found the next 'big' thing in my life. They didn't anticipate I'd actually want to become one of the help, and they told me as much at the time. My mom kept dropping hints that if I was going to work there for much longer, I should run something—not just be an assistant. So I did the only thing I knew to do."

"Which was? I'm listening." It was hard to read his expression.

"Whatever was necessary to get ahead. To win at all costs or go down trying. And I blew it."

"That's twisted. Why didn't you tell me this yourself? The whole truth? We talked about almost everything." Dom shook his head. His eyes looked so hurt. "And now this really screws things up for me too."

"I knew you'd see me differently. I'm not that person anymore, I don't think. I barely even recognize that girl. And I really didn't want to let you down."

"Well, you hadn't until now. If you'd told me, we could have tried to figure this out together, find another solution. I thought we were partners. I trusted you," he said, shoulders sagging. "I told you really personal stuff. All you've done is keep me at arm's length. And now the whole project is in jeopardy." My heart squeezed.

"That's valid, sure," I managed to get out. "But what I did was so awful, I can barely talk about it with family and people who already know me. Let alone someone I was starting to have feelings for."

"This, this is just a lot. I need some time to think and figure out how to fix this. The doc, I mean. I don't know if there's any way to fix . . . us."

"There is no 'us.' You made that clear on the plane, so why do you care?" I found myself getting defensive again, throwing up walls of self-protection. I didn't need his approval. We could just make this about saving *Piece of Cake*. "Let's just stick to work and get through the weekend the best we can. It's not like we were ever going anywhere."

He just stood there for a minute, looking at me, taken aback. Those full eyebrows drooped, and I fought the insane impulse to run a finger along one.

I deflated. "Maybe you're right. Maybe Lottie was right. Maybe something is wrong with me. I swore I would never go back to that place or be that person again. But . . . here we are."

"I'll see you tomorrow, Claire." He walked to the elevator without another word, and I felt the remaining pieces of my heart drop and shatter on the floor.

I pulled my composure together, for Lucy's sake if not my own. I had to go inside and smile and say his stomach hurt. I invented some severe gastric symptoms as payback. But the truth was, it cut deeply that he was right about not telling him the whole truth sooner—but also that he didn't see the real me. His whole view of me from the last few months was now tarnished by this one really bad mistake. That was no way to build a relationship anyway. Dom merely reaffirmed my instincts to call this one DOA.

CHAPTER 22

I awoke in my childhood bedroom and stared up at the coffered ceiling. A few neon stars that Lucy and I had covertly stuck to the plaster still glowed all these years later. Mom had been appalled, I remembered, at the potential damage. But even after we were instructed to peel them off, a few stragglers remained. Lucy and I were always injecting some chaos and disorder and imperfection into our home. Yet Lucy somehow managed to play a calming and centering role too. Unlike *moi*.

I had a little time before hair and makeup were set to arrive, so I strapped on my sneakers, grabbed a granola bar from the kitchen, and snuck outside. The caterers were already bustling in there, and I was barely noticed sneaking out.

The Bachman Branch of the Trinity River flowed behind our house, and a few running trails wound alongside it. I took off, hoping to sweat out some of my anxiety and angst.

The sun reflected off the still water. Birds chirped. A cool breeze barely wafted over me.

Dom filled my thoughts. He slipped into this community so easily, in a way, frankly, *I* never had despite growing up in it. For a tough guy from Brooklyn, he sure fit into the Dallas socialite set. But I could grudgingly admit it was more than that. He had a warmth and an ease with people. His natural curiosity and kindness came out. He was goofy but could also be so sincere. People felt like he was genuinely interested. Too bad it extended only so far.

A restless night had done nothing to soften the pain of knowing that his whole perception of me had changed. Even if we weren't meant to date, I respected him as a person. I thought he respected me. It stung.

I ran along the river and decided to enter our house through the back. I opened the wrought-iron gate with my key, grateful we'd never changed the locks. The rose garden was in the rear of the property, rows of white and pink blooms giving off the most abundant perfume. I strolled through the central path and tied my shoe on a stone bench. This was by far my favorite place in the world. In June, the blooms were still pretty lush, kept that way by a fortune in sprinklers, I realized.

I walked past the smaller swimming pool and tennis court before stopping dead in my tracks. Last night I hadn't gotten a proper look at the setup. Cedric's team had worked their singular magic.

The main rectangular swimming pool ran perpendicular to the house, which you wouldn't know because it was almost completely covered in a cloud of white. I walked closer, stunned at the beautiful lotus and water lily blooms floating beneath my feet. A glass aisle was laid across the center. You felt like you were walking—or sitting—in a Monet painting. Complementary flowers lined the sides of the aisles, with chairs extending on either side of the now-concealed pool deck. I had no idea what wizardry kept the central flowers from floating freely, but my sister would walk down the aisle above a lush bed of white blossoms.

Beside it, the ornamental gardens had been tented for the reception. Cedric had managed to integrate the existing stone sculptures (French, Greek, and Italian antiques, of course) into the design. Tables dotted the scene, covered in custom cream linens with Italian lace overlays. Cut crystal stemware and antique silverware donned each place setting and would sparkle later that evening from the glow cast down from the crystal chandeliers overhead. And the flowers. The all-white flowers also created a table-runner effect that filled the entire length of each table and spilled over and down the sides.

A backdrop and stage had been erected at the end opposite the house, then covered in a cascade of white peonies and roses and mirrored by florals draped around the doorframes and windows of the back of our house.

It was an enchanted garden, rivaling that of a royal wedding. Lucy was royalty in our family, and in my opinion, she deserved nothing less. I felt grateful to Cedric for bringing that to life for her. Then again, I resented him for crushing my own dream. I sighed and headed upstairs to shower and get ready.

❧ ❧ ❧

After attending so many weddings for work, I found it odd to be trapped in the bridal suite instead of roaming the grounds. I texted with Dom. He was curt but communicating. He was casually and quietly taking some photos and videos on his phone for his own personal channel, on the chance *that* got approved. Perhaps Cedric wouldn't sniff at all publicity, just publicity that involved me.

Evelyn was lounging in an upholstered chair. Mom had magnanimously offered her palatial dressing room for us instead of Lucille's childhood suite. Evelyn absently patted her bump while firing off emails on her phone. With so many businesses to run, I supposed she couldn't completely go offline.

Our mother's longtime hairdresser, Donna, came to do the bridal party. Donna had done my hair for every big moment: high school dances, debutante balls, charity galas, Evie's wedding, all of it. There was a beautiful consistency to knowing we were in her capable hands.

I stood in the mirror and slipped on my dress. Lucille, in true fashion, had worked to select bridesmaid gowns that we'd actually like. The silvery blue played off my eyes, I had to admit. The night would be tones of silvers and blues and greens and whites, all a heavenly garden, and we fit right in.

I found myself with extra time before pre-ceremony pictures started, so I decided to head downstairs and see how the setup was progressing. Despite everything from the past twenty-four hours, I still wanted to know all the details of the wedding. I couldn't take off my wedding reporter hat just yet. Evie and Mom were giving the seating chart a final once-over, with an assistant planner who could've been me back in the day. In true Mom-fashion, she acted like nothing happened between us the night before. I was still licking my wounds after her tipsy teeing me up in front of Dom. But our relationship needed time to mend, and today wasn't the day to force that process. I sincerely hoped that day was in our near future though. These past few years had created a distance between us that was based on more than just our respective locations. Admittedly, it was partly my fault that we weren't as close anymore.

I was lost in thought about, well, *everything* when I nearly ran headfirst into Lottie coming out of the formal living room.

"Oh, hiya, Lottie," I said, startled.

"Afternoon, Claire," she said in a surprisingly neutral tone.

"So far the weekend's been nothing short of spectacular, and I'm sure today will be the same," I said, hoping that flattery would disarm her a bit. I was also trying to tread as lightly as possible but was clearly nervous.

"Thank you. Your mom and Lucy are dream clients," she replied.

"Lucy's an amazing person. I'm lucky to be her sister," I said. "And I know this isn't the ideal time, but I've really wanted to talk to you about what happened at—"

"You're right," she interrupted curtly. "It's not the time for you to get anything off your chest, so let's just try to get through today without any issues, okay?"

"Oh, okay," I replied, but she'd already started walking toward the kitchen.

I thought about following after her, but instead gave up and went to find Dom. I couldn't help but wonder how he was doing, even if he still thought of me as a dumpster fire. Yet he seemed to have vanished. Not in the kitchen or the den, where my father was cloistered. Not in the billiard room with Collins, Ford, and the rest of the groomsmen. Where could he be? I went out back, studiously staying out of Cedric's minions' way.

I recognized a few florists and caterers and waved, but no one smiled back. Memories were long, I supposed.

I turned a corner around a hedge and heard his deep voice. As I peeked my head around, I quickly pulled it back. He was talking to Cedric. *After* I told him not to. Did he want to get me completely removed from this wedding? Was he trying to ruin everything in my life?

"Like I said, I know you don't know me or have any reason to trust me," Dom was saying.

"You're right, I don't." Cedric was curt.

"But you've got it all wrong."

"How so, pray tell?" I could envision Cedric folding his arms the way he used to when he was projecting strength or disinterest.

"About Claire . . . Hear me out. I know she screwed up big-time with you."

"That's putting it mildly."

"I get that. But I've heard her talk about it, about who she was back then. And I can tell you with certainty she's changed. The woman I know is hardworking and cares, deeply, about her responsibilities to people. The whole reason we're doing this video project in the first place is because she cared enough to imagine a way to save the magazine and a bunch of people's jobs.

You can look where we're standing and know she didn't need to bother that much. There's a lot riding on this—for other people even more than for her."

"Go on," Cedric said after a beat. He didn't sound totally pissed, which I took as a good sign.

"The Claire I know is loyal. She learned a lot from you. She's used that to help other people, not just herself . . . You've known the Sommers family a lot longer than I have, but I can only imagine what it was like growing up with that kind of pressure to be perfect, to live up to this dynasty. Most days, that's just what she does—pushes herself and everybody around her to be the best. I'd probably subconsciously screw it up myself sometimes too." He paused, and I could imagine the compelling expression on his handsome face. "I don't know where you're from, but I'm not from this world."

"Neither am I," Cedric interjected. "Couldn't be further from it."

"Well, people like you and I start from the bottom. We've got nowhere to go but up. We have nothing to prove, to lose; she had everything. It's tough both ways."

Cedric *mm-hmm*ed.

"So you have to understand that it would be a lot to deal with. All I'm asking is that you give us a chance. If you find we're interfering in how things go, we will stop filming. You can review the footage before we make the final cut, whatever it is. We'll play ball. But give Claire the chance to show you she's changed. I promise you won't regret it."

"I'll consider it," Cedric mused. "Now I must go check on

my team, if you'll excuse me." I could hear him shuffling, so I fled behind some adjacent shrubbery. I looked from underneath and saw Dom's shiny tux shoes heading the opposite way down the path.

What in the world was that? I was stunned. I didn't know Dom thought all that about me, especially given his reaction last night. And I was shocked that Cedric didn't immediately send him packing. Maybe they had some guy-from-the-wrong-side-of-town sort of understanding. Either way, I'd run out of time and needed to head back to the bridesmaids and get a move on. Fingers crossed his valiant speech had worked.

❦ ❦ ❦

The hour had come. I looked out the rear window at family and friends filling the neat rows of Chiavari chairs.

"Lucy said she needed to grab something in her room," Evie told me.

"Ah, I'll go see if she needs help going pee." Wouldn't be the first bride I'd had to assist that way.

"Gosh, that is utterly revolting." Evie scrunched up her nose in distaste. I waved a dismissive hand at her over my shoulder as I went up the rear stairs.

I went into Lucy's bedroom. The en suite bathroom was empty. I heard a creak and slowly walked toward her closet. I opened the door to find my baby sister, her gorgeous Lela Rose gown spread around her, sitting on the floor in her walk-in closet. Tears streamed down her face.

CHAPTER 23

Oh, Luce . . . What's wrong? I'm here." I plopped down beside her on the closet floor, undoubtedly crumpling my gown.

She couldn't catch her breath. I held both her hands in one of mine and rubbed her back with the other. "Here, take a deep breath, in and out. There you go." I coached her until she stopped hiccupping.

"I. Just. Can't. Do it," she eked out.

"Why?"

"I'm scared."

"Of what, hon?"

"What if this is a mistake? What if it doesn't work out? What if one day Collins realizes I'm not as great as he thinks and goes off and finds someone else? What if I get old and gross after we have kids and he doesn't want to have sex with me? What if I don't want to be a lawyer after all and I'm just a wife and a mom—will he still see me the same? Or what if we got divorced, which would just let *everybody* down? What if—"

I cut her off to slow the death spiral. "Easy there, tiger. Where is this coming from? I think you're just having a lot of feelings about today, but it's all going to be okay."

I dabbed her eyes with a tissue. "Listen, I certainly don't have the answers to everything, but I can tell you this: Collins knows you—the real you—and loves you. And you are enough. Just you. He doesn't love this family or your law degree or any of it. He loves you. It's not like I've been married, but I have to believe that love like that would carry you guys through anything that came your way."

My baby sister gave me a small smile. "You really believe that?"

"I do, more than anything. You are brilliant and beautiful and kind. Stronger than anyone I know. Plus, you embody the best of all our Sommers qualities. And you're the one with the great therapist. I imagine you've got some decent tools to handle hard stuff."

"True," she mused, looking down at a stray shoe. *There, she's back.*

I sat there holding her hand for a moment, then I grabbed another tissue and started pathetically trying to blot her makeup without smearing it down her face. We'd have to summon the professionals back before she walked down the aisle. I guess if she made it to the aisle, that would be the least of our concerns.

I heard a creak and spun around. Lottie stood at the open

closet door, a strange look on her face. "I'm so s-sorry," she stammered. "Didn't mean to interrupt."

"No, I think we're okay. Right, Lucy?"

My sister nodded. I held her hand and helped her get to her feet. As she walked back into the bedroom, Lottie and I simultaneously jumped in to smooth and resettle the bustles of her skirt. It felt like old times.

"Well done. Didn't think you had that in you." Lottie turned to face me as Lucy walked out the door.

"I'm not a monster," I said. Before she could reply, I took a deep breath. "But I'd understand why you might think so . . . I realize it's been years, but I still owe you an apology for what I did in Mexico. It was shady and competitive and really put all your hard work and your job at risk. I'm sorry."

"I appreciate that. It was a pretty horrific thing to do, and it really hurt me at the time too."

"And I'm also sorry for never replying to your email. It was generous of you to reach out, and I wish you knew how much it gave me to think about. You really nailed it. I didn't know who I was. Not sure I do now either, if I'm honest."

"Well, I'm glad it was somewhat helpful . . . Anyway, it's all in the past." She paused and cocked her head to the side. "You know, when Dom said you'd changed, I didn't want to believe him. Even if he is very convincing."

My jaw dropped. "Wait, he talked to you too?"

She had the grace to look embarrassed. "He tracked me down this morning. Said a lot of stuff. And it's not just coming from anyone. That guy is basically a social media wedding icon and doesn't seem like the type of person to embellish. He insisted that the person you are today, that he's known in Nashville, is wildly different from the person who tried to ruin my career and Harriet and Brody's wedding. I had to admit that the person he described sounded a lot more like the person I remember than that person too." She half smiled, reluctantly. "So despite my misgivings, I'm willing to give you a chance. Cedric is tentatively onboard too. Watching you with Lucy just reinforced that decision. We've still got six hours left, though, so don't let me down. I've got my eye on you." She laughed as if she wasn't 100 percent serious.

"I won't, I promise."

"Good. We all have a lot riding on this wedding."

"Amen to that." I allowed myself to cautiously hope.

☙ ☙ ☙

By some miracle, I managed to make it to the front of the tent without tripping. Behind me, a string rendition of Wagner's "Bridal Chorus" began to play as Lucy and our dad took their places at the back of the aisle.

She was breathtaking. Smiling widely, genuinely, with eyes only for Collins as she carefully strode, holding Dad's arm. Her custom Lela Rose gown was magnificent, but it paled next to my sister's radiance. Screw it, I finally allowed myself a few happy tears.

It was nearly impossible to pull my eyes away from Lucy during the ceremony. At one point, Evie reached forward and grabbed my hand. I squeezed it, united in our happiness for our little sister.

Evelyn was really throwing me for a loop these past few months. Her pregnancy was bringing out a softer side that I was absolutely relishing. It was a day for hope.

At one point, I caught Dom's eye. He was staring straight at me, without wavering. I turned my attention back to the ceremony, but every time I glanced his way, his eyes were on me.

After the ceremony, we made our way to the rose garden for portraits. Dom trailed behind, filming. He had to move quickly to make up for lost moments now that he had Cedric's permission.

After the extended Sommers crew took our photos, I loitered nearby while Collins's family got organized. Dom had methodically interviewed both families and the wedding party while they waited for portraits. Now he had a pause in filming for the moment, so I slid next to him. "Want to take a walk?"

"Don't they need you here?"

"Our side and the bridal party are done, so now we'll all have to chill at cocktail hour while Lucy and Collins do their thing. I've got time."

"Well, okay then."

I motioned toward the tennis court. It was easier to say what I needed to while walking because I didn't have to meet his eyes. "I heard you put in a good word with Cedric and Lottie. Everybody back in Nashville will be very grateful if we can pull this off. You didn't have to do it, but I really appreciate it."

"Don't mention it."

"I have to ask, why did you talk to them? You could just take the job in New York and be fine. You don't owe me or us anything."

"That may be true, but I thought a lot last night about what you said." I could feel his head swivel my direction. "I was hurt you didn't tell me everything and let me think it was just some small accident or misunderstanding. Everybody has jobs that aren't a good fit. But you did what you did on purpose. And then basically lied to me about it."

"That's all true," I admitted. "I knew you'd see me differently. You're the one person I felt knew me, the real me, or at least the one I wanted to be. I was terrified to tell you."

"I trusted you," he said. "I told you some of my biggest struggles, my deepest dreams. I thought you were doing the same."

"I was. I just didn't think I could really tell you the whole story. It's been a hard few years, to put it mildly. I wanted you to see successful, top-of-her-game Claire. Not the one who's consumed by competition and bases her identity on things that don't matter."

"But you told me about all that," he protested. "It would have been easy to let me in on the rest."

"You didn't know me or my family," I continued. "It wasn't your world, and you didn't have any expectations. And I didn't really care what you thought. At least at first. That was freeing. Then we got close . . . and I started to care. Too much."

"I did too."

We stood there in the dusky light. The scent of roses filled the air. The big-band music from cocktail hour was soft and romantic at this distance.

I gave him a half smile and sighed. "And I do care. But some things simply aren't meant to be, are they?"

He shook his head, a wistful smile mirroring mine. "I guess not. But maybe—"

"It's okay, Dom." I took his hand without thinking. "You have a life to get back to in New York, and I have one to build in Nashville. Even if we save *Piece of Cake*, this was always supposed to be temporary."

"Temporary," he echoed, squeezing my hand. Then I pulled mine away as if it were on fire. "It was," he said. "You're right."

I took a small step back. "We can just let it be what it's been. We've both done good work, had a good time together, hopefully created something that will help our futures and a lot of other people's. We've got that."

"Yes, Claire." He sighed. "But for tonight, can I . . . Will you still dance with me?"

"Of course." My heart felt as crumpled as my hemline.

"I promise to pretend you're letting me lead."

Before I could reply, a soft cough came from where Lottie stood on the path. "It's time for the bridal party entrance, Claire."

Dom and I followed her to the reception. He went to film our entrance, and I lined up with the bridal party.

The reception was a beautiful blur. I wiped more rare tears as Lucy and our dad danced. I noticed my mother and Evelyn subtly wiping their own. Perhaps Sommers women *could* cry. The cake, the bouquet toss, all picture-perfect.

As the music shifted from fast to slow, I was walking off the dance floor with a few bridesmaids when I felt a tap on my shoulder.

I flushed. "Oh, Dom! How's the filming going? Do you need me?"

"Actually, I do." He held out a hand. "You promised . . ."

I slipped my hand in his, and he pulled me close. Gone were the awkwardness and hilarity of Tootsie's. In their place were a wistfulness and melancholy. Some things just weren't meant to be.

"I mean it," I said softly, grazing his shoulder with my chin. "I can't wait to see what happens for you, what you do next up there. I might even stay on social media to find out."

"Wow, that sets the bar pretty high for me. And as they say, 'I'm only two hoots and a holler away.'"

I giggled despite the ache in my chest.

Too soon, it was time for Collins and Lucy's send-off. We walked together around the house to the driveway. The path had been lined with beautiful antique lanterns and potted topiaries. It felt like an enchanted forest and not my parents' side yard.

As we lined up, I stood across from Evelyn. Immediately, I could tell something was off. She looked like more than simply pregnant. More like she was strolling the seventh level of hell. Her jaw clenched, teeth gritted.

I knew Evelyn better than most, and in that moment, I could tell. It was time.

I reached her in two steps. "Are you okay? It's the baby, isn't it?"

"Shut up, Claire. We're so close. Almost done here." She blew out through tight lips.

"Did your water break?" All I knew was that in the movies, that meant you had to run or the baby would be born in a taxicab.

"No, silly. I'm just having contractions. They started during portraits. But they're still spaced out enough to give us time." Leave it to Evelyn to be timing her delivery with the patience of a CEO. "My app says I don't need to go to the hospital until they're like three minutes apart, and I'm still at four or five."

"You are unbelievable. Were you going to tell anyone?"

"No! And don't you dare say a word until our baby sister is— *oooh!*" She grabbed my hand and squeezed it hard. I plastered on the biggest smile possible and reached for sparklers for us both.

Dom finally came over and stood next to me. I leaned over to whisper in his ear, "Find Ford *now*. Please."

"Roger that!"

I was going to miss his airplane jargon.

After about thirty seconds, Evelyn released a breath and the pressure on my hand. She stood up straighter. "Now I've got a few minutes, so let's get our girl going. Where the heck is she?"

"You are a freaking machine, Evie."

"Why, thank you. But do you really think I'm some kind of robot or that it's always so easy for me?"

"Well, none of this looks easy at the moment. But I mean it—you have always been such a trouper. A hero. I probably never told you enough because I've been more than a little jealous, but I admire you more than you know." I tried to slip an arm around her back in case she needed support.

"I'm good at acting, and I've worked hard. But that doesn't mean I don't also make mistakes. Or that I don't have weaknesses or doubts. I have no idea what I'm going to do when the baby comes. I run three businesses. *Three*." She visibly gritted her teeth again. "I have zero clue how motherhood is going to fit into all that. I don't even know how I'm going to manage maternity leave." She blew out through pursed lips.

"You'll manage it with the same grace and poise and terrifying skill that you've used for everything else. And we'll be here to help you."

"Thanks, Claire. That means a lot." She was getting misty again. "I hope you know, even if I'm hard on you, I really admire how you've gone to Nashville and started over. It takes guts to go out on your own, especially without all of this to back you up, to catch you. I never had the courage to do that."

Before I could reply, her eyes got big and she grabbed my hand again. No way had it been more than two minutes since the last one. I spotted Dom and Ford approaching us from behind the rows of guests and motioned to him to hurry.

"Guys, we've gotta go."

I channeled every bit of my training from Cedric in that moment. Our family cars had been moved off-site along with the guests'. There was no time to send one of the men down the street to retrieve it from the country club parking lot.

I spotted Lottie helping Lucy and Collins line up and get ready to run toward their getaway vehicle, a vintage 1950s Rolls-Royce Phantom. With any luck, it would be big enough to hold all six of us.

I told Dom and Ford to walk Evelyn around to the other side of the car, staying out of the send-off portraits. I watched as they opened the door, then quickly plastered on a smile as I hustled to Lottie.

"Lottie," I started, "Evelyn's gone into labor and we're jumping in with Lucy and Collins to get her to the hospital. I'll tell Luce, not that she has much choice since it was their car or wait for an ambulance. But could you please find and inform my parents?"

"My goodness, yes," Lottie said, eyes wide. I felt a momentary flash of pleasure that even she could still be surprised by something at a wedding. "Please let me know if there's anything else we can do. We'll handle everything here at the house tonight."

"I know, y'all are a well-oiled machine. I think we're good otherwise." I started to walk away and turned back. "And, Lottie, if I don't get another chance to say it, thank you for everything today. It's meant more than you know."

"You're welcome. It's been a good lesson for me too. Good luck at the hospital. Now go!" She smiled and shooed me with her hands.

I dashed behind the guests, almost parallel to where Lucy and Collins made their way to the car. I had time to bolt around the back, throw open the front passenger door, and hop in.

Inside, Evelyn was seated on the back row between Dom and Ford. Poor Lucy and Collins had flipped down the jump seats and were perched there in their finery.

"All right," I told the driver. "To Presbyterian Hospital, please!"

CHAPTER 24

Waiting rooms are impossibly uncomfortable places.

My sister sat in her wedding dress in a dingy plastic chair. Her poufed skirt was hilariously out of place in the waiting room of Presbyterian Hospital, and I almost laughed maniacally at the sight.

"You guys really should go enjoy what's left of your wedding night," I chided.

"We have the rest of our lives together. Right, honey?" Lucy patted his leg.

Collins's tux was unbuttoned and slightly askew. He looked a little less convinced than my sister, but he nodded. Whether out of exhaustion or obedience, who was to say?

Dom sat next to me, absently rubbing my back. Confusing as it was, I appreciated the contact. He'd stayed this entire time, despite a 9:00 A.M. flight to Nashville in a few hours. He'd brought us all snacks from the hospital food court and had even been texting with Lottie and Cedric's team to coordinate the loose ends we'd left in our haste. Collins and Lucy were experiencing the postwedding letdown and were practically toast over in their seats. My mom was back in delivery with Evelyn and Ford, and my dad was napping in a chair. That man could always sleep anywhere.

After what felt like an eternity, the doctor came to tell us the news.

"It's a baby girl, and both mom and daughter are doing well. You'll be able to go back in about thirty minutes, once they've finished cleaning everything up and done the final checks on the baby."

My dad, Lucy, and Collins got up to see Evelyn and the baby first so the newlyweds could head to their hotel and salvage some of their wedding night. (Good luck, y'all!)

I turned to Dom. "Thank you for sticking around. I know you've got an early morning."

"You know I wouldn't have missed the chance to see you in emergency mode and try to be helpful in any way possible." He smiled, the one where his eyes crinkled, and my heart melted. So much was unspoken.

I smiled back, sadly. "Thank you for everything this weekend. You didn't have to do, well, any of it. But it's meant more than you know."

"Turns out, I'd do just about anything for you, Claire."

I didn't have proper words, so I did what I do and brushed past it after a moment. "Well, I know you need to go by the hotel before your flight. But I'll see you back in Nashville. We'll have a few days to wrap this up before the deadline and you leave for good. We'll talk more then."

We stood, and he pulled me into a comforting hug. He muttered into my hair, "As they say, 'We'll always have Dallas.'"

Then I watched him walk through the glass double doors, carrying part of my heart into the night.

◁ ◁ ◁

I knocked on the delivery room door gently. "Can I come in?"

"Of course," Ford said.

Mom was sitting in the lounge chair in the corner, awake but eyes closed. Evelyn lay back on propped-up pillows, exhausted but smiling. "Wow, Mama, you continue to amaze me," I told my sister.

She barely lifted a hand to wave off the compliment, but she smiled wider.

Ford laid my niece in my arms. I appreciated that he didn't ask if I knew how to first.

"Oh. Wow. She's perfect," I whispered, touching her golden, downy fuzz with a finger. I felt a welling of love like nothing I'd ever known. *Especially* for anything related to Evelyn.

I looked up and locked eyes with my big sister, who just nodded at me, as if she understood the complicated jumble of emotions I was feeling.

Her tiny fingers were so small, and they curled involuntarily around mine as I rubbed them.

"Her name is Caroline Grace," Evelyn's tired voice scratched out.

Out of nowhere, my eyes became faucets. This level of water-works was unacceptable. I blinked rapidly, to no avail. I was going to make a scene.

I handed her to Evelyn, kissed baby and mother (wetly) on the foreheads, and dashed to the hallway without a word.

I needed air. I needed to control whatever was happening. I'd been so tightly wound, so anxious, so sad, so happy, and it was all too much. This was not me.

I turned a few corners and found a dead-end hallway near what looked like a janitor's closet. I slid to the floor against the door. My rumpled gown pooled around me in a puddle of pale-blue fabric.

I wasn't sure what was happening. Everything I'd tamped down came burbling to the surface. The pressure to save the magazine and my coworkers' livelihoods. The anxiety to stand on my own and prove myself to my family. The pain of feeling outside their good graces. The self-loathing at what I'd proven capable of in the past. The complicated, overlapping stresses of being a part of Lucy's wedding and confronting Cedric and his team. The ache I felt that Dom was leaving. The terrifying reality that maybe, just maybe, I didn't know who I was or what I really wanted, on any level.

Minutes passed. My breathing slowed.

"Claire?" a voice said, soft and hesitant. I looked up at the last person I expected to see, my mother, still perfectly coiffed but more uncertain than I'd ever seen her.

Sommers women weren't good at emotion. I understood.

"Mind if I join you?" Without waiting for my reply, she slid down beside me.

"Mother. You realize you're on the floor?" This was a night for it, apparently.

"I do, dear. I have sat on the floor before."

"But—but you're in *Chanel*."

"I am aware. Do you have more questions?"

"Probably. How much time do you have?"

She barked a laugh. And then, much to my surprise, draped her elegant, Chanel-clad arm around me and pulled me close to her side. My mom had never been a hugger.

"What's going on, honey? I've never seen you like that."

I subtly wiped my nose with the back of my hand like a street urchin and hoped she didn't notice. "I've just never felt that way, holding Caroline. She's so little, and it's so scary. I've never loved anything so . . . instantly. It's terrifying. How do parents *do* it?" I felt childish and overwhelmed.

"Oh, my dear Claire," she said, this time the words a benediction and not a condescension. She sighed. "I worried, you know, after Evelyn, that my heart would not have room for another child."

"I do believe I internalized that fear in utero, by the way. It's where I trace all my neuroses."

She released a rare, genuine chuckle. "Be that as it may, from the moment you were born, that's how we've felt about you. They put you in my arms, all bloody and bruised and kind of ugly—"

"Thanks a lot, Mom."

"But to me, you were the most beautiful baby I'd ever seen. We loved you instantly. And always. You never had to *do* or be anything else." She gave me a squeeze before continuing. "I know we've been hard on you sometimes." At my expression, she winced.

"But, Mom, that's always how it's felt—that no matter how good or successful I was, it wasn't quite enough. I would never measure up to Evelyn or be as beloved as Lucy. Sometimes it was easier to just not try than to find out that my best efforts weren't enough . . . that *I* wasn't enough."

"Honey, I didn't realize you felt like that. We just wanted you to be proud of yourself and your accomplishments. I'm sorry for putting pressure on you, especially over the new opportunities with Cedric Montclair. I was just excited it seemed like you'd finally found a path for yourself. And, Claire, after everything that happened, I admit I was disappointed and very, very embarrassed. We tried so hard to protect you, to keep what happened quiet. Cedric never would have said anything, out of loyalty to us and because the press was very helpful to him. But when that one blind item ran, people talked, and I probably overreacted by telling you to go offline."

"It felt like I needed to hide. Like you were so ashamed of me."

She gave me a squeeze. "Oh, honey, that dumb trust fund morality clause was all something your grandmother had set up years ago. We never meant for you to feel like we were cutting you off from our relationship or from our support. Then you left so fast, though, and we tried to give you some space. But perhaps we didn't know exactly what we were doing either."

"I thought I was in exile . . . but you're right, I didn't exactly stick around long enough to see where we stood."

"We would have helped you in an instant if we thought you

really needed it. But we also thought it might just be time to stop picking up the pieces and let you sort it out for yourself. Stand on your own, once and for all."

I nodded into her shoulder.

"And"—my mom had the grace to look regretful—"I am very sorry about causing a scene at Lucy's rehearsal dinner. I was feeling all the emotions of marrying off our baby, but that's no excuse for putting you in that position. Please forgive me."

"I do."

"But you, my daughter, have always been enough. Know that, please. We love you. We push you because we believe in you—and because we frankly can't help ourselves. I'm sorry if that's made you feel like you had to compete with everyone or achieve certain things for us to love you or be proud of you."

She pulled me in for another one of those rare hugs. I smelled her perfume, which never failed to make me feel both small and safe.

We pulled apart, and I stood up, nearly ripping the hem of my dress. I held out a hand to assist my mother. She still managed to move with such grace, even when sitting on linoleum tile.

Maybe I had projected a lot on them and internalized my own feelings of disappointment. Receiving not just my mother's approval but her unconditional acceptance and love was a balm and tonic I didn't know I needed. Maybe we never outgrow our desire to please our parents, to feel their love. I still didn't feel like we were "fixed," but we had taken a big step.

Today had been lifetimes. I'd woken up a jumble of nerves and emotions and with bags under my eyes the size of a Birkin.

Dom intervened with Cedric and Lottie. My baby sister got married. My big sister became a mother. My gorgeous little niece stole my heart in the purest and most unmerited way possible. And my mother made me feel more loved in five minutes on a dirty hospital floor than in a lifetime of formal celebrations.

Mom adjusted my strap, then looped her arm through mine. "Now let's go back and see that grandbaby of mine. I don't think you had time to get a really good look. And Lord knows, I don't think I'll *ever* get enough."

I laughed, and we walked down the hall arm in arm.

CHAPTER 25

The following Wednesday, Michelle rapped on the conference room table in an attempt to get our attention.

Over the past couple of days, Dom and I had pulled together the footage from Lucy's wedding and created the final episode in our series pitch. Hopefully it would sell to a streaming service or other partner with a big platform, but even if that didn't happen, we'd created something that could live on our website and hopefully find a new audience for *Piece of Cake*. The rest was out of our hands.

We didn't talk about anything personal that final week. I knew when his last day was. And it felt like we'd said it all in Dallas.

"Thank you for your time today," Michelle began. "As you know, we've been working hard to put out the physical issues of the magazine as well as ramp up our website content and other initiatives. But hopefully your hard work has paid off.

"I wanted to update you all that we have put together a compelling, beautiful, *dramatic*"—she paused for emphasis—"package to pitch this real-weddings series. Dominic and Claire have been working diligently on it and have made a great team these last few months." Then she motioned for us to stand.

I hated moments like this, all eyes on me. But Dom grabbed my hand and pulled me up next to him. We stood there, smiling at everyone, still holding hands. I let go the instant I realized it, and I felt him tense.

But we had done what we set out to do. Fingers crossed it was enough.

◁ ◁ ◁

We muddled through the next couple of days. On the day of his departure, Dom came by my desk with his meager canvas tote bag of desk items and a camera case slung over his broad shoulder. "Walk me out?"

He waited while I gathered my things. We both knew what came next.

We got to the sidewalk outside our offices. Friday night traffic had already started on Broadway. "Well, this is it." He stood watching the cars pass. "Look me up if you're ever in New York on one of your mom's Fifth Avenue shopping trips, Tex. I can show you some great vintage shops."

"I'd like that. And I'm sure I'll stay up on what you're doing online thanks to the algorithm, but let me know if you come down this way again."

"I'll have to—gotta keep up my new line-dancing skills." He shimmied his hips in a way likely meant to be funny, but it landed closer to provocative. I chuckled to cover up the pang in my gut.

A car honked. The neon lights from the bar next door flashed on as twilight arrived, casting his face in a purple glow.

"Before I go, I wanted to tell you why I really talked to Cedric and Lottie."

"Good. I still don't really get it. I'm grateful, but just . . . confused."

"Because I know you, Claire. I know the Claire that cares about people. Who can somehow fix anything with a couple of safety pins." He smiled at me and that pang in my gut turned into a tornado. "I know the Claire that talks about her sisters all the time but doesn't seem to realize that she's just as amazing and smart and hot."

I felt tears gathering in my eyes, fighting with a laugh. I tried to deflect. "You've seen me be a *hot* mess."

But Dom wouldn't let me. "No, I've seen you bend over backward to earn your family's approval. And here's the thing: You shouldn't have had to earn it or compete for it. You are worth it. Just being you. Not in comparison to anyone else. Not because you've checked off certain boxes. No one ever should have told you, out loud or implied, that you were inadequate."

"Dom . . ." I stopped. Words didn't seem like enough. He was leaving Nashville, leaving me, but leaving me a better Claire than he'd found me. "Thank you. I'm still not sure I know how to live in a world where I'm not constantly fighting for my spot. But thank you. For, well, everything."

"Claire, you're a wealthy white girl from a stable family. I'd say your spot was always pretty secure?" He gave me a gentle half smile.

I chuckled at the truth of his insight before sobering again. "That's just it—none of those things were enough to guarantee . . . that I . . ."

"That you what?"

I opened my mouth to speak, and he put a hand on my shoulder, the weight warm and comforting. "That I had a place. That I was loved. That I was enough."

Dom's eyes met mine. The moment seemed to stretch out and fade away. "You've always been enough. And I think you'd be pretty easy to love."

"What are you saying?" This was *not* the moment for whatever he was trying to say.

"I want to be with you, Claire. Just the way you are, cheesy as that is. There's no secret flaw that could scare me off. No hidden mistake. Because I know you pretty well. I'd say I even know your heart. And it's beautiful, perfect, messy, and trying so hard. You're not the person you were, and you're certainly not defined by your worst moment."

"I'm confused." I shook my head. "What, why . . . why now?"

He took a deep breath. "I'd stay right now. I wouldn't go if you asked me. We could figure it out."

My heart leapt, but I tamped down the feeling. After spending most of my life not really knowing what I wanted, I felt like it was finally right before me. He was right there. But I still couldn't bring myself to accept it.

"Oh, Dom, I just . . . I know you won't be happy. And that's too much pressure on me." I let out a shaky breath, resolve wobbling along with my lower lip. "I appreciate what you've done and what you're saying, but you don't have to do this. Go live your dream."

"You're still doin' the thing." He shook his head sadly. "The one where you try to get ahead of it."

"Maybe, but what I'm saying is also true." I felt myself leaning toward him. I fought my hands' impulse to reach toward him and keep him close, in direct contradiction to what my mouth was saying. His green eyes bored into mine. I had to look away first because I would cave if he stood there much longer.

He was silent a moment. Sighed. He wasn't going to beg. He bent down and, before I knew it, gave me the gentlest kiss on the forehead before straightening and turning away.

CHAPTER 26

I'd thought it would be impossible for our offices to feel emptier. But in two months, my cubicle area—and my life, really—had gone from a ghost town to positively haunted. I heard Dom's laugh every time someone got coffee. I smelled his cedar and soap scent in everything from Uber drivers to air freshener. I spotted his broad shoulders at every bar or restaurant I entered. My heart lurched in disappointment each time I walked into work and he wasn't sitting at his desk, poring over B-roll.

There were silver linings though. True to her word, Michelle took the series Dom and I had built and pitched it hard. She called in every contact she had on both coasts.

It *did* pay off.

Our little show, also called *Piece of Cake*, was going to be released on one of the biggest streaming services starting next week. The staff was throwing a party to celebrate. And the publisher had held off on the magazine's sale to see the impact of the new revenue streams.

We were optimistic. Janice was trying to buy a condo near Nancy's off 30A, and Kevin was hoping to afford residential care for his mother-in-law. Amaya was paying down her loans and trying to move out of her parents' house, a fact I'd learned by actually attending our last company happy hour.

And I'd taken Lucy's advice and started seeing a therapist again. It helped to have someone other than my mom, which *had* helped a great deal, too, to talk through my feelings of inadequacy. I'd spent most of my life looking around at my competition, my siblings, my peers. But Lottie and Dom and even Lucy had held up a mirror, forcing me to look at myself for the first time. Dead-on, eyes open, no flinching. To ask who I was, stripped down, just me, not in relation to anyone or anything else. It was terrifying, but ultimately freeing.

I was learning, slowly, to stop measuring my value against the success of others, to stop expecting love to be tied to achievement. Lifelong habits were hard to break, but I was trying.

I not only had to learn not to try to earn love—I also had to learn to accept it when it was offered freely.

That second part was proving the most difficult, but I was trying. I'd spent so long feeling like I didn't deserve love without action or merit, that when it was right in front of me, I didn't always receive it. It's why I pushed my family away at the first sign of disapproval and why I was so quick to believe that my feelings of inadequacy translated to them not loving me enough. It's why although I still believed pushing Dom to pursue his dream was the right decision long-term, I knew I'd done it from fear and insecurity, not strength. I was determined that would change. No true Sommers woman lacked an understanding of her own worth.

At the end of the day, I came from an influential, successful family—but I also came from a caring, supportive one. My mom and I spoke, not every day, but at least once or twice a week. I was less afraid to tell her how my life was going—good and bad. And my sisters and I had reactivated our sister text thread. Exchanging jokes, baby pictures, mortifying moments with Dad at work, gorgeous wedding details, and bad online dates (me).

We were getting there. I might always worry about embarrassing my dad or disappointing my mom, but I could choose to stop chasing the commodities of our social circle—approval, achievement, pride, wealth—in my relationships. Those things weren't love anyway. I needed to find my own passions and pursuits, to find what brought me joy, even. And I was starting to be okay with letting my family members each speed ahead in their own lane. And with staying in mine. They didn't have to be the yardstick by which I measured my own life. That could be my own health, happiness, satisfaction.

I did what I did, my worst moment, in a desperate and misguided attempt not to succeed but to carve out my identity. That moment didn't need to define me.

Lottie had been right. I didn't know who I was. But I felt I'd finally figured out what version of Claire Sommers I wanted to be.

More than anything, I accepted that even if I never attained certain levels of success or standing, it wouldn't affect whether I am loved enough by my family or by myself.

Maybe the next time romantic love, or even the possibility of it, was right in front of me, I'd be ready. I'd be able to accept it and not feel I had to earn it. All a girl could do was try.

CHAPTER 27

OCTOBER

In addition to the series finale, Lucy's wedding had run on our big September issue cover. But I clutched a copy of *Piece of Cake* to give to another bride I was about to see. Lucy's whole weekend was what it was, in large part, because of this woman's work. And because of her grace, if I were honest.

I walked up the ornate white stone steps to Atlanta's City Hall Tower.

We were covering it for the website—that one of the South's top young planners was getting married made for a delicious metaheadline—but I was also here for personal reasons.

Lottie Jones was marrying her photographer boyfriend of nearly four years, Griffin Flores. True to form, Lottie had eschewed a big event and was getting married at the City Hall

Tower—beautiful in its own right—but the intimate rooftop reception still promised to be dazzling, albeit simple.

Cedric Montclair was, in an unheard-of move for his employees, planning it pro bono. I couldn't wait to see what over-the-top detail he snuck in over Lottie's protestations.

We'd stayed in touch after Lucy's wedding, even grabbed coffee in Nashville this summer after she worked another wedding that *POC* covered. Small steps, but helpful ones.

I was still shocked Lottie and Griffin agreed to let us cover their wedding. But it was a sign of renewed trust in me, and I'd do my best to keep it.

I slipped into a seat near the back, just in time for the pre-ceremony music to begin. Her fiancé, Griffin, entered with his best man, the only attendant. His dark hair gleamed, and underneath a neatly trimmed beard was the widest grin imaginable. Even I could tell he was a kid about to get his Christmas wish.

I didn't know many details, but from what Lottie had said, their road hadn't always been easy. They'd done long-distance, felt things out, really worked hard. And four years later, here they were.

"Canon in D" began to play. Lottie walked the aisle on her father's arm, eyes ahead and only for Griffin.

My heart winced a bit in jealousy. But part of my new outlook was choosing to believe that I deserved love—and would find it. Even if it sometimes felt I'd let it slip through my fingers.

I was happy for them, really.

A white vintage A-line dress brushed just below her knees. Soft tendrils escaped her honey-colored bun, a grandmother's antique brooch the only accent. She clasped a loose pink bouquet in one hand, his hand in the other as they stood solemnly before the judge.

Lush, wild clusters of pink peonies and white hydrangeas interspersed with soft dusty miller lined the aisle of simple white folding chairs. Two larger arrangements in antique silver urns flanked the couple. A single cellist sat in the corner of the room. All simple, but stunningly elegant.

She couldn't stop smiling, and I realized I'd never seen her so at ease.

They quietly said vows they wrote themselves. Our small crowd watched in happy silence.

I tried not to shift too loudly, every movement echoing on the cold marble tiles. Someone sniffled. The sound reverberated in the cavernous space. The groom's mother caught me staring and winked at me across the room.

This bride had sent me on quite a journey, forcing me to finally reckon with my past and my future. With my identity, even. It hadn't been easy, but I was grateful.

I had no right to be here, but here I was. How I ended up here remained a bit of a mystery to me. Her forgiveness was simply a gift, one of the type I was gradually learning to receive.

Maybe, just maybe, that could be me someday.

A squeak of rubber on marble echoed. I sensed him before I heard him. A low voice rumbled in my ear. "Hey, Tex, this seat taken?"

He smelled like cedar and sunshine. "It is now," I replied, afraid to turn my head. "What are you doing here?" I whispered.

"Shh, don't disturb the happy couple. I'm here for a wedding, obviously."

As the ceremony came to an end, I was on pins and needles.

"You came back? Or, I guess, came to Atlanta?" I said, finally looking him in the face as the few guests began to file out.

"I did." He laughed, and I realized I'd missed those dimples more than I thought. His hair was cut shorter, in a way that aged him nicely, I noted. A crisp navy blazer pulled across his shoulders.

"How? Why?" I became really articulate when nervous.

"How is easy. We used a lot of Griffin's photos and videos of your sister's wedding because, well, I got a little distracted that day, couldn't keep my eyes off the maid of honor. He and I stayed in touch. He's flown up for a couple projects with us in NYC. He told me where you'd be," he said. "But that's not why I'm here, as much as I like Lottie and Griffin."

I just arched an eyebrow at him and waited. "It's not?"

"You gonna make me beg this time?"

"No, so listen, I'm the one who should be begging. About what you said—"

"Here's the thing," he said, cutting me off and grabbing my hand. "If you truly don't want me, I'll go back north and stop bothering you. But I think you do. I think you want me the way I want you." He took a breath and flashed me his most charming smile. "And you should know that I was pretty miserable up there without you. That's my way of saying that if you make me turn around and head right back, I will be, well, pretty miserable."

"I don't think I could live with myself if that's the case." I tried to match his lighter tone despite my racing pulse. "But what about your job, the dream one?"

"It's not the only job out there. Sure, New York has some great opportunities for film stuff. But it occurs to me that I might be slightly idiotic, just a tad shortsighted, for thinking the only way to chase my dream is to not be with you."

"Well, I didn't really help you with that either . . . I'm sorry this summer I wasn't at a place where I could let you in when you asked me to. After a long time of not knowing myself or what I want, I finally feel like maybe I do. You were a huge part of that. I'd love for us to give this a shot.

"And," I continued before he could interject, "I was pretty pathetic without you too."

"Oh really? Because I find that hard to envision."

"A total mess. I banned Lucy from DMing you about what a sad, mopey disaster I was, but she threatened."

"Who's to say she didn't?"

I let go of his hand and playfully hit him on the shoulder. It felt good to resume our banter.

His eyes sparkled. "Now, I know it'd be a lot of pressure if I moved back to Nashville just for you. So I won't. But I just *happened* to take a job I'm really excited about at a production company. They do music videos and are branching into TV and film."

"Really? Congrats! For how long?" I was already calculating how much time we'd have.

"Maybe for a while? It's full-time with actual grown-up benefits and everything. I'm thinking about shutting down the

Brides' Man for good and focusing on something I'm really passionate about. I already signed a two-year lease on an apartment in East Nashville. As any good Brooklyn transplant would."

"So you're staying? For good? For . . . me?"

"Like I said, I just happened to take a job in a city I like near the woman I've got this thing for. Sounds pretty not miserable, right?"

I swallowed. "Yes, it does," I squeaked out.

As the room emptied, we were still in our seats, knees crammed together as we turned to each other on uncomfortable courthouse chairs. Dom's arm was across the back of my chair, and his hand gently took my shoulder and pulled me to face him. I could see the flecks in his green eyes and the little corner crinkles as he gave me a hesitant grin. The dimple flashed, and there was no going back.

Almost without thinking, my hand encircled his neck and pulled him down to me. Our lips met this time without hesitation. Soft, full, and sweet—I couldn't taste enough of his mouth and that ChapStick he was always wearing. He was intoxicating and, apparently, mine. My hand ran through his thick hair, and I felt him give the slightest shudder. This was going to be fun.

As he ran his hand along my lower back and hip bone, I got goose bumps of my own. I wanted to climb onto his lap in the middle of the courthouse but still (barely) had the presence of mind to realize that probably wouldn't be appropriate. My mother would have been appalled at our lack of decorum already, but then again, I'd disappointed her worse and lived to tell the tale.

It wasn't a movie kiss in the rain or even something worthy of Alcott or Austen. But it was us, again. For real this time. And I knew we'd have more. That was all that mattered.

"So remind me again how long you're staying?" I said after we finally came apart.

"Maybe forever?" He smiled that dimpled grin I adored.

"I mean, that sounds good to me, but let's start with the two-year lease."

"Roger that, Tex."

A NOTE FROM THE AUTHORS

Over the last twenty years (!!), the two of us have walked through much of life together. Including seasons when we've witnessed each other at our best and, frankly, at our worst. We've learned a lot about grace and redemption through the ins and outs of our friendship. It's an unexpected gift.

We are grateful that many of our low points existed before the proliferation of social media. (Even lighthearted study-abroad shenanigans and terrible early-aughts ensembles don't need to live forever online.) But the same can't be said for our children, who exist in a much more connected world—in good and bad ways—than that of us analog '80s kids. In addition to wanting to create a funny, romantic, optimistic read, we hope to in some small way address the more sober topics of identity and redemption. Our kids will come of age in a world that judges quickly and forgets slowly, if ever. Our prayer is that they will learn and grow from their mistakes instead of allowing them to define them forever. We are all works-in-progress, and this book illustrates that it's never too late to try to better ourselves and the world around us.

What you hold in your hands is a work of fiction. While it's peppered with real places and loosely inspired by some real events in both of our careers, it's purely a novel. We're thrilled to have another chance to create stories together, and we hope it brings you joy, laughter, and a bit of fantasy.

XOXO

Asher + Mary

ACKNOWLEDGMENTS

A second novel is a lot like a second child: a wonderful experience that feels a bit easier because you know what to expect. Well, kind of. That being said, the sequel to *Without a Hitch* never would have been born without the same village of friends, family, and coworkers who supported us the first time around.

Thank you to Ali Kominsky and the team at Dupree Miller for always advocating for us. Thank you to our amazing team of editors, publishers, and marketing gurus at HarperMuse. Amanda Bostic, Becky Monds, Jocelyn Bailey, Lizzie Poteet, Kerri Potts, and Margaret Kercher—we've been honored to work with such brilliant and kind women. Thank you for trusting us to write another story based around wild wedding shenanigans, and for allowing us the space and time we needed to do so. Especially for the extra time.

I (Mary) will be eternally grateful to my inner circle of friends—Amy, Jen, and Ceesun—and to my parents, Nita and

John, for helping with childcare and offering ongoing support while I worked. Your help and constant words of encouragement allowed me not only to survive but to thrive during what was probably the busiest year of my life. You were there for all the events, answered all my calls, and even let me dictate our Halloween costumes. Thank you for loving me even though you know I'm crazy.

To Georgia and John Albert: I love you so very much. I hope that one day you will look back at this time and remember that when I was away from you, I was pursuing my dreams. I'm excited to watch you pursue your own dreams one day. And I hope that in your future, your family will be as loving and supportive to you, their parents, as you both were to me.

To Asher: Once again, you took my crazy stories (and many of your own) and turned them into a piece of fiction worth reading. You're a brilliant writer, but more importantly, you're a great friend, and I'm so thankful these novels brought us back together. We will always have *The Firm*.

There are two people left to thank, and I was basically married to both the year I wrote this book. To Alex, my "work spouse": We will always remember this year, and that it never would have been possible without you. You took MSS to a new level and kept everything together when I was busy writing. Thank you for your honest feedback when I shared stories and ideas with you. You supported me in every way possible, and I'm so thankful to you for helping make all my dreams come true for my career. You are a wonderful person, and it was an honor to be your "work wife."

Okay, now to my real spouse, Paul. Thank you for once again clearing space in our insanely busy life for me to write this book. You know all the good and all the bad, and you love me anyway. How can I ever properly thank someone for that? You've known me as a wedding planner and as a writer and have supported all my careers over the years. You understand me better than anyone else, and it's an honor to be married to you. In a way, this book is a lot about you/us. We bounce back. Maybe not as far as Claire, but we've overcome so much despite the odds. We didn't let our past define our future. That, my love, will always make you my hero. Thank you for being my hero.

After writing a book about a regional magazine, I (Asher) remain thankful for so many of the talented journalists and incredible people I worked with (many of whom have left the industry we all loved). I also remain indebted to the book community. The authors, journalists, bookstagrammers, book clubbers, and friends who have supported us and celebrated our work make all of this possible. Emily Giffin, Jodi Picoult, Lauren Denton, Susan Coll, Lisa Patton, and Debbie Macomber—it means the world to be championed by such heroes of mine.

Mary, thank you for sticking with me and pushing me along on this road. I'm so grateful we've embarked on it together. And, books aside, our adult friendship has been the best thing we've created together. Jeanette, Suzy, Jill, Sheri, Meredith, Maggie, Erin, and the rest of my circle—thank you for cheering me on even when I wanted to throw my laptop out the window or couldn't stay awake because I was writing-while-pregnant.

To my siblings, for better or worse, we'll never be the

Sommers crew, but I'm so grateful you're my people. As the eldest, I feel like I have spent more than half my life waiting for y'all to grow up. And you have. And you're intelligent, kind, hilarious, beautiful, and compassionate people. I'm so thankful to be your sister and friend.

This partnership would not have been possible if not for the many people who pitched in with our children while we stole moments to write. Thank you to Sarah Williams for moving to London and partnering with my family on that adventure. Thank you to the rockstar parents in our UWS community who offered to host playdates on deadline days. And thank you to my in-laws, Rhonda and David, for all the ways you helped us navigate this crazy season as a family.

Thank you to my extended family, especially my mom, Kristi. Every word I write has somehow filtered through the stories you introduced me to. I love that my children are now getting their imaginations sparked and horizons broadened by Marmee as well.

And finally, Emerson, Sullivan, Montgomery and Osborne—I have loved you from the first moment I knew of you, and nothing could change that. You are, and always will be, perfect to me. There is much in this world that seeks to dampen your spirit, but I pray y'all never lose your sense of magic and wonder. Define yourself by what you know to be good and true. The rest is noise.

Justin, every year, it seems, we imagine the next will be less chaotic. They never are. But I couldn't have survived this epic season (or this decade) without your steady presence, dark humor, abundant grace, and unconditional love. Thank you for this crew of little ones, this life we're building, all of it. Someday, we'll slow down enough to watch TV shows. And in the meantime, there's no one else with whom I'd rather savor every moment we're able to snatch in our hands.

DISCUSSION QUESTIONS

1. If you read *Without a Hitch*, how did you feel about Claire when *Piece of Cake* opened? How had your thoughts changed by the end?

2. Claire goes from being a wedding planner to writing for a bridal magazine reporting on wedding trends. What's one trend you love? What's one trend you could do without?

3. Do you think Claire's anger toward Dom at the beginning of the novel is justified? Why or why not?

4. What's the most bizarre thing you've personally seen happen at a wedding? Can you relate to any of Claire's experiences?

5. Do you think it's true that opposites attract? How have you seen that work—or not work—in your own life?

6. Families can be complicated. Have you ever been in a situation where you felt like the black sheep of your

family? How did you relate to how Claire handled it?
Are there ways you see that she could have handled it
better?

7. There's a lot of humor in this book. Did you have any
laugh-out-loud moments? If so, when?

8. In Dallas, Claire comes clean about her past. Do you
think Dom's reaction was justified? How would you
have reacted to your partner confessing past mistakes?

9. Toward the end of the book, Dom offers to stay in
Nashville for Claire. Did she make the right decision
having him get on his flight instead? What would have
changed if she'd said yes?

10. If you were Claire's best friend, what advice would you
have given to her at the beginning of the novel? How
would that have changed over the course of the story?

ABOUT THE AUTHORS

Mary Hollis Huddleston

Photo by Abigail Volkmann @
abigailvolkmannphotography

Mary Hollis Huddleston is the Co-Founder and Creative Director of Please Be Seated, the premier event rental company in Nashville. She started her career as an event coordinator in Dallas, initially at Diamond Affairs Weddings & Special Events, and later helped launch the wedding division of nationally recognized Todd Events. Mary's career inspired *Without a Hitch*, her debut novel about the high-stakes world of luxury Southern weddings. She also has a lifestyle platform, Mrs.

Southern Social, focused on modern, at-home entertaining and is developing two curated collections with the Southern Living Collection at Dillard's. Her work has been featured in *Southern Living*, *Southern Lady*, *StyleBlueprint* and *NFocus Magazine*. She resides in Nashville with her husband and two young children.

Visit her online at mrssouthernsocial.com
Instagram: @mrssouthernsocial

Asher Fogle Paul

Photo by Jenny Anderson

Asher Fogle Paul is an author and a human interest and entertainment journalist. Most recently she served as digital features editor at *Good Housekeeping*. She's also held posts at *Us Weekly*, *People*, and *Reader's Digest*, and her work has been published in *Marie Claire*, *Cosmopolitan*, *Esquire*, *House Beautiful*, *Elle*, and *W*, among others. Asher has an MS in magazine journalism from Columbia University and a BA in English from Texas Christian University. She lives in New York City with her husband and four young children.

Visit her online at asherfoglepaul.com
Instagram: @asherpaul
Twitter: @asherfogle

From the Publisher

GREAT BOOKS

ARE EVEN BETTER WHEN THEY'RE SHARED!

Help other readers find this one:

- Post a review at your favorite online bookseller

- Post a picture on a social media account and share why you enjoyed it

- Send a note to a friend who would also love it—or better yet, give them a copy

Thanks for reading!

Sweet Home Alabama
meets *Emily in Paris*
in this hilarious romp through
the world of extravagant
southern weddings.